Praise for DARK LADY OF HOLLYWOOD

"A finalist in the William Faulkner Creative Writing Competition, Haithman's hilariously funny novel gives readers a bird's–eye view of the Hollywood machine and its players. With witty, fast-paced dialogue and characters readers will cheer for, this debut is a deeply satisfying story of love, loss, and acceptance."

—Carol Gladstein, *Booklist*

"It takes a special kind of talent to simultaneously skewer Hollywood and Shakespeare while writing a thought-provoking novel, and Dark Lady of Hollywood proves Diane Haithman has this genius."

— Jill Allen, *ForeWord Reviews*

"A sly, cynical, sublimely entertaining showbiz tale crafted with irreverent flair and an insider's self-assurance. A dazzling first novel. I couldn't turn the pages fast enough."

—Ray Richmond, *This is Jeopardy! Celebrating America's Favorite Quiz Show, The Simpsons: A Complete Guide to Our Favorite Family*

"An accurate, wonderful, striking look behind the scenes of show business."

—Sandy Fries, staff writer, *Star Trek: The Next Generation*

"Delves into the world of Hollywood the way only an insider can."

—Cari Lynn, *The Whistleblower, Madam: A Novel of New Orleans*

"Makes a delicious meal of the entertainment business—one biting line at a time. I found my summer read!"
—Susan McMartin, staff writer *Two and a Half Men*

"One of those rare books about Hollywood that gets it right."
—Loraine *Despres, The Scandalous Summer of Sissy LeBlanc, Dallas* "Who Shot J.R.?" episode

"A truly enjoyable, darkly humorous look at the TV industry. Should be required reading for anyone even remotely interested in 'the biz'."
—Jeffrey Peter Bates, Writer/Director, Onyx Productions Direct

"I am not exaggerating when I tell you that I feel like I have met many of these characters."
—Dave Fulton, feature film publicist

"Diane Haithman has a unique comic voice. Her writing sparkles like diamonds and cuts like them, too."
—Mitchell Levin, senior story analyst, Dreamworks SKG

"Eccentric characters, sly observations on media culture and wry humor woven with darker themes of mortality and loss."
—Henriette Lazaridis Power, *The Clover House*

"Brings a surprising flair for sharp-paced comedy and piercing Shakespearean insight."
—Ben Donenberg, Artistic Director, Los Angeles Shakespeare Center

Dark Lady
of
Hollywood

Diane Haithman

New York

Harvard Square Editions
www.HarvardSquareEditions.org
2014

Cover design: by Peter Chua Design

Published in the United States by Harvard Square Editions

ISBN 978-0-9895960-1-5

www.harvardsquareeditions.org

Printed in the United States of America

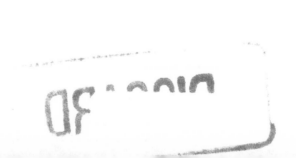

For Alan, Sasha, Darrow, Heidi

and

William Shakespeare

*Heartfelt thanks to those who have helped to
shape this tale and send it on its way…*

Jeffrey Peter Bates
Paula Brancato
Charles Degelman
Loraine Despres
Alan Feldstein
Sandy Fries
Dave Fulton
Nancy Hersage
Laura Hitchcock
Jeffrey M. Kleinman
Mitchell Levin
Cari Lynn
Athena MacFarland
Susan Rubin
George Stelzner
Tracy Wood

CHAPTER ONE

**Since nor the exterior nor th' inward man
Resembles that it was.**

— King Claudius, *Hamlet*

"See, here's the *thing*, Kenny . . ."

I'd forgotten how my immediate supervisor, Danny Gordon, never really shook hands. He'd just put his in yours and leave it there, like a small, limp package waiting for UPS. We'd been holding hands like this ever since he walked into my office to welcome me back. Sweet.

"The thing?"

"The . . . *thing*." Dan nodded then fell silent. I decided it was up to me to end the non-handshake and gentlly disengaged myself from it. Dan still said nothing. The pause was clammier than his hand. "Say whatever the fuck it is you have to say, Dan," I suggested pleasantly.

Danny winced; he tended to take profanity very personally. His small brown eyes had been fixed on the floor. Now, as he looked up, they darted every which way behind the narrow glasses — furtive weasel eyes trying to escape from his desperately hip green rectangular frames, from his head, from my office. From me.

"The thing is, Kenny, I've been in communication with the writers, and they don't think they can work with you anymore, Kenny. Kenny, they say they just can't . . . *sing* under these conditions. I mean, *your* condition. Trust me, if we had time to find comedy writers who can function when they're depressed, I would. I just don't know what to *say*, Kenny."

That was three too many Kennys. I willed myself to stay calm but my heart began to rocket around inside my ribcage like the metal pellet in a pinball machine. I pressed one hand against my chest in the guise of straightening my tie. It probably wanted to get away from me too, my heart — even my heart wanted to leave me now, and you know what, I couldn't blame it.

"They . . . *know*, Ken," Dan said.

"Know?" I asked, keeping my heart in my chest with my hand.

Dan's thin fingers played over the nascent bald spot in his dark hair. Swear to God he had less hair than when he came in. "This isn't me talking, Kenny. It's the network." The apologetic whimper had come crawling back into Dan's nasal voice. *That bottled spider, that foul bunchback'd toad.* "Do me a solid, Kenny. *Patty's Going Out* and *He's on the Force* both got canceled, and it's only October."

"Yeah, saw it on *Deadline*. At least *they* sent me an update." I found myself absently tracing "He's off the Air" with one finger in the dust on my formerly gleaming glass desk. Not original — some mouth-breathing TV blogger had posted that smug headline on his website. After saying it over and over, week after week, meeting after meeting, I'd honestly begun to believe that *He's on the Force* would be the perfect comeback vehicle for former child star Donny — *Don* — Calder after two years in a minimum-security prison.

"I had . . . concerns about Don," I said. "But I figured *Patty* would at least make it to November. I thought she had what we were looking for. People loved her on *America's Got Talent*."

"Yeah, well, fat is fine for competition, where there's crying. We don't need it at 9 p.m. when everybody else has thin people."

Dan was right about that. *Patty's Going Out*, our series launch announcement read, would be "the ongoing lament of a young woman's dating problems in New York City." It was only ongoing for three episodes. We quickly discovered that people wanted to see an incredibly beautiful, sexy young woman having dating problems in New York City, not a woman who might actually *have* dating problems having dating problems in New York City.

Now, our only hit was a sophisticated nine-thirty comedy starring white-hot *Saturday Night Live* veteran Bert DeMarco, another Harvard dropout. Following in the footsteps of his father, Bert's character had become a veterinarian. Problem was, he didn't like animals, and animals didn't like him. It was called *Bite Me*.

In more recent episodes, developed during my absence, the focus had moved from Bert's antics in his veterinary practice to his life as an incredibly handsome, sexy young man having dating problems in New York City.

It was my idea to bring Bert DeMarco on board in the first place. Messengers bearing flowers, or spectacular baskets of fruit and cheese, marched for three months between Burbank and CBD Productions in Beverly Hills. The C stood for Bert's own dog, Coco, who had a small but pivotal role in the pilot episode. The comedy department went ballistic about the bills, but we got DeMarco. We call this process "development."

"I think that we both know there's only one thing standing

between us and Number Four," Dan said.

"*Bite Me*," I replied.

"Correct. The anchor of our Wednesday night comedy block. Perfect demographics: men 18 to 49. Women love him too because he won't let the dog sleep on the bed during sex. Kenny, we've finally stopped *skewing old*."

"I know. I launched that show, Dan."

"Reality programming, Kenny. We're up against *reality programming*. No freaking writers to go on strike every time someone takes away their sock monkey," Dan fretted. "And you don't have to pay real idiots 1.5 mil an episode like we're paying DeMarco. I'm *depleted*, Kenny."

Reality, Danny — I'm up against *reality*. "If they want reality, they should turn it off," I grumbled. I lifted the shiny gold nameplate on my dusty desk — Kenneth C. Harrison, Vice President, Comedy Development — and weighed it in my hand. Heavy. You could hurt somebody with this. "Look, *Bite Me* is crap without my creative input," I said. "*I'm* the reason we can say 'It's Cable TV for a Network Audience' on those mugs we give out at the summer press tour. We were the Number Four network for four years. Now we're barely hanging onto Number Three. You want to go back to picking up the *Los Angeles* fucking *Times* and reading 'mired in fourth place' every time the goddamned Calendar section mentions our name?"

"I'm not trying to be difficult, Ken, but this is my call, not yours." Dan squared his stooped shoulders to the extent that they were capable of forming an angle. Then he grinned. "I didn't like the mugs that much, but I *loved* the *Bite Me* candy rectal thermometers."

Dan was easily distracted. I tried to bring him back into the room. "And without me, you don't have DeMarco," I reminded him. Arrogant prick wasn't working for me nearly as well as it used to, but the door seemed to have opened a crack. My tone turned coaxing. "I'm the one who *massaged* him. I sent him flowers. I sent flowers to his fucking *dog*. Bert called me as soon as they arrived to tell me that Coco loved them."

"Yeah, well, he didn't call you an hour later to tell you Coco loved them so much, he ate them. Let's put it this way: *you* are the main reason the CBD office in Beverly Hills had to order new Berber carpet for the main lobby." Dan shook his head in lieu of further detail. "Besides . . . this is hard to say, but it's not just the writers who say they can't work with you anymore. It's . . . well, it's DeMarco.

"*Bert?*" Okay, that was a slap in the face. "But Bert and I . . . we have a *relationship*."

"I'm sorry, Ken. I wasn't going to tell you, but you had to push." Dan was now actively pulling out strands of his own hair. "You need to learn when to stop pushing, Kenny. Your baby is now our franchise. We own it. We love you, but . . . we don't *need* you."

We love you, but we don't need you. The opposite of what Alice had told me some eight months ago: "I'll stay with you as long as you need me." Her pale, sharp features glowed with the pride of self-sacrifice as she said it. Those were her words, but here's what she meant: "I'll stay with you even though I don't love you — because *you* need *me*." That's something I couldn't live with, especially because it was true.

I moved out the next day.

Packing *is such sweet sorrow*.

I am alone now, I guess you could say. A Nielsen household of one.

The only thing I had left was my job, and I couldn't afford to lose it. So instead of arguing, I decided to massage Danny. "So . . . I guess I need a new franchise," I said, my voice on a tightrope. "Your thoughts, Daniel?"

Dan brightened. "I think I've got a win-win for you, Kenny. There's a slot for a development director over in Movies and Minis." ("Minis" was short for mini-series, which was short for TV that was going to go on way longer than it should.) "We think you'd be perfect for this exciting new opportunity. Writing the press release in my head. In fact, we were just saying the other day that you'd really be a great help to movies, you know, when they do cancer."

When they do cancer. "Okay" was all I could think of to say.

"It's the best way to protect our slogan: 'Prime Time Is Your Time.'" Dan stopped speaking for an uncomfortable moment, then erupted into inappropriate giggles that contorted his thin frame into what looked like a hip hop pose, one karate heel kicking out and splayed fingers crossed in the vicinity of his groin. "Kenny, one of the writers has come up with *such* a great story line for the next *Bite Me*. The working title is 'Taming of the Shrew.' Do you love it? It's from Shakespeare."

"Really?"

"How cool is that?" Dan returned to his usual round-shouldered posture as the giggle exorcised itself from his body. "I had to take Shakespeare at Palisades High, but the only thing I remember is the kid next to me having to memorize the line 'Alas, poor York, I knew him well.'"

"It's not 'York.' It's Yorick. And it's not 'I knew him well.' It's '*I knew him, Horatio!*' Hamlet's talking to Horatio. He's standing next to an open grave with Yorick's goddamned dried-up skull in his hand, and he's talking to fucking *Horatio*."

Dan stared at me in shock. "Whatever," he offered warily. I forced a smile and put extra emphasis on his name, hoping it might be helpful in some random way. "*Dan*. I know, we have our . . . words, sometimes. We push each other hard. We *bounce off* each other. But in the end I can always count on you to come up with something excellent." That's right, just keep on talking. Doesn't have to make any sense. "That's why we've always had such a sweet collabo going, you and I. Creative tension has always been our franchise."

Dan responded to this unexpected and illogical praise like a fresh bowl of weasel food. "It is? I mean, it is," he stammered. "You're right about our creative partnership, Kenny. Tension is what it's all about. In fact, in all of our years working together, I don't ever recall feeling quite this . . . uh . . . tense."

I nodded enthusiastically. "Could things *get* any more tense?"

"It's all good, Ken." Dan let out a long, shuddering sigh. "Listen, I've got to get to the ten o'clock . . ."

"And I don't . . . kidding."

"I know, right?" The sigh again. "Anyway, I'll send someone to the office to move your stuff over to movies. Do you know where it is? In the Hacienda. Right across the way from us."

"I've been with the network for five years, Dan. I know what's on the other side of the fucking parking lot." The aging, Spanish-style Hacienda Building stood across from the contemporary, three-story glass box where we were standing now. I'd often heard our building referred to as the "Entitlement Complex," which seemed a lot funnier before I was asked to move out of it.

Movies and Minis was the only legitimate department in the Hacienda, bounced over there from their suite over here because the network hadn't had a movie or miniseries hit for fifteen solid years. VOD, need I say more? I was being banished to the land of the dinosaurs, a window office in Jurassic Park, a development hell that still existed but from which nothing ever emerged alive. The rest of the Hacienda was an ant farm of failed, high-level network executives who now had lucrative production deals — "boy deals," they called them, since the old boys gave them to each other after their short careers crumbled. I always figured I'd have an office there someday, and frankly I was okay with that. Just not today.

"We'll re-assign you to a parking space in front of the Hacienda."

"Cool." I knew this was not so I could park closer to my new office, but because the spaces over there were smaller. I could already see the dings in the shiny silver paint on my Mercedes. "Do I . . . get to keep the plant?" The plant was a gift from Standards, grateful because I'd agreed to cut the word "balls" out of an early *Bite Me* script. Little did I know how quickly the network would return the favor.

"It's . . . a little hot and dry over there for a bromeliad, Ken. But do what you think best."

I nodded.

"It's going to take them awhile to get you moved. Maybe you want to take the rest of the day off, and we'll have everything ready for you tomorrow morning?"

"Sure, I'll take the rest of the day off," I said. "See, I'd hate to have any of your sensitive comedy writers believe that his latest script is a substantial piece of shit just because he happened to take a piss next to me in the executive men's room." I cocked my finger at Dan and used my thumb to fire off a fictional bullet. "Kidding again. Hey, after five years, you know me . . ."

"Hah." Dan didn't laugh it, just said it. "Hah. Sure, take the rest of the day off. And if don't see you on Monday — or, you know, again, ever . . . well, take care, Kenny. I mean, that was stupid. *Duh*, of course I'll see you. Oh yeah, and leave your men's room key with my assistant, okay?" He backed out of my office so fast he ran smack into a passing mail cart.

And whether we shall meet again I know not. / Therefore our everlasting farewell take.

"Later," I said.

I left my former office and headed for the parking lot. I paused for a second to switch from my regular glasses to sunglasses in front of the corner drugstore, located beside the soda fountain on a street of eerily regular faux cobblestones. A Wright Brothers-style bicycle shop and a peppermint-striped barber pole added to the illusion of some indefinite but comforting period in American history. All it takes is a careful camera angle to keep the shaggy sunburned palm trees, the studio commissary and gift shop, and the Bank of America ATM out of the shot. These plywood storefronts have stood in for the good old days in more TV shows and movies than I can name.

The good old days. A studio tram loaded with visitors rattled by over the cobblestones. I waved. They waved back, in case I *was* somebody. I took it as a good sign. It was only a matter of time before I returned to my slot as vice president of comedy development, just as soon as everyone here at the network realized what I already knew: I was fine.

I was a straight white male, thirty-six years old, right in the middle of TV's most desirable demographic: men 18 to 49. *I'm* our target audience. I'd been in network television long enough to know that the demos don't lie. But demographics did not explain why the dark gray lenses of my cool new Oakley sunglasses suddenly fogged and blurred with tears.

Since nor th' exterior nor the inward man / Resembles that it was.

CHAPTER TWO

**The forms of things unknown, the poet's pen
Turns them to shapes, and gives to airy nothing
A local habitation and a name.**

— Theseus, *A Midsummer Night's Dream*

How could I hate Alice for offering to stay with me, despite the minor complication of not loving me anymore? She was planning to put all formerly outlined plans to leave me on indefinite hold. In fact, she would devote as much unswerving energy to not leaving me as she did to defending her guilty clients downtown. Young, attractive public defender Alice Anderson, often interviewed on camera by KTLA News, so bright that I often wondered if her hair was red from the heat coming off her brain. She'd be "likeable" on the audience research card. She always followed the impartial path of justice, and even the no longer loved have a right to legal representation. How could I hate Alice for that?

I didn't know, but I was sure as hell going to try.

Because of the excellent benefits provided to management at the executive level, I took Dan Gordon's advice to stay away from the office temporarily. It would be easier for him to negotiate the best deal for me, he said, if I just stayed away. Temporarily. As long as I needed.

He had this look of panic in his eyes as he said it. I think I understood. Here was a thirty-five-year-old hypochondriac, still pulling the needles out of his scalp from his morning acupuncture session, raw inside from his noontime high colonic, no carbs for more than two years, and I was thirty-six. I tried to reassure him. Like I said, excellent benefits, all the perks, desirable demographics.

I also agreed with Alice's infallible logic that if I was going to move out — though I was welcome to stay — I should do it *before*. Before I got too . . . tired or whatever was going to happen, let's not talk about that now, okay? There was some time pressure from my standpoint, so Alice helped me locate a small condo-for-rent near the Beverly Center, in that vast amorphous zone known as "Beverly Hills-adjacent" in the real estate ads. It only took her three days — She's good.

Okay, here's what happened, how everything changed. One night, about a month after leaving our leased beach house on Pacific Coast Highway near Temescal Canyon, I awoke — Beverly Hills-adjacent — jolting out of foggy dream in which I sat in my former living room wearing nothing but my Oakley sunglasses, desperately trying to coax a ring of silent men in white lab coats to explain what insidious cosmic force had randomly chosen to fuck with my desirable demographic. I was thirty-six years old. I didn't drink; I wasn't fat; I didn't smoke. No toxic dump in my back yard, no asbestos under my fingernails, no burnt bacon on my plate. No family history. I *worked out*.

They didn't answer me, simply turned in unison, raised one hand, and silently pointed at the TV. All except the sexy young surgeon on the end. I think I love her.

My eyes flew open at the shock of this exquisitely twisted

concept. Ten years in network television, and now four out of five dream-doctors were telling me . . . this? I would have just stayed there, cowering under my sweat-soaked sheet, but terror had triggered in me an urgent need to urinate. But I couldn't stand up. The bedroom was spinning way too fast. I was going to have to slide off my bed like a crab, then crawl to the kitchen on my knees. No problem. I was getting used to this method of travel. I'd already ruined the knees of two pairs of brand new, pre-washed Lucky Brand jeans.

But it was dark, and I was dizzy. Instead of rounding the corner with my usual expertise, I whacked my head hard against the corner of the metal bookcase that came with my new, furnished, single-guy rental condominium. I'd left all the furniture with Alice.

Lightning shot through my cranium. I reached a hand up to my forehead to check for the sticky blood I was sure would soon be dripping into my eyes. No blood. My hand wandered over to the edge of the bookcase to see if that's where the blood was. Still no blood. Groping a little farther in search of pieces of my head, my fingers met the cracked spine of a large, heavy book.

I'd had some stuff moved here from our house, including the random assortment of boxes I'd carted around with me every time I'd moved since college. Never unpacked 'em, just kept moving 'em. I always figured I'd unpack them when I got married. It seemed wrong to open them up in a rented beach house. Sometimes I wonder if we'd still be together if I'd opened up my boxes then. Sometimes, I don't care.

A couple of these boxes were full of books. I'd taken the volumes out and put them on the bookshelf, to make the place look — hah — homey. As I unpacked, I paid no attention to what the books actually were.

I don't know why I lifted the big volume that touched my

hand and tucked it under one arm. I don't know why I hauled it along with me as I made my way back to the bedroom, still on my knees, Jesus, head splitting right down the middle of my brain. I don't really know why I clung to it and held it tight; I just did.

When I reached my room, I grabbed the doorframe with my right hand and pulled myself to my feet. I switched on the light; it hurt my eyes. When I could open them again — squinty, tearing, one at a time — I finally looked at the book tucked under my left arm, a thick, worn out, pea-green volume, embossed in gold with the words *The Complete Works of William Shakespeare.*

The book wasn't worn out because *I* read it. I bought it at a used bookstore on campus. I'd had it since UCLA, where, as a freshman English Lit major, I had managed to score an "A" in Introduction to Shakespeare without actually reading any of his plays. Hey, I was eighteen, and I had the notes. You can get by on the notes.

I sat down on the bed to avoid passing out. And I had to laugh, even if the motion caused my cerebral hemispheres to separate for good. Here I was, eighteen years later, finally getting my introduction to Shakespeare.

During the next eight long, solitary months, I read all the plays. Seriously. Every word. Eight months; twelve comedies; ten histories named after kings, most of them Henrys; five romances; eleven tragedies; sixteen hundred pages of tiny, tiny type. I really never planned to keep reading the stuff, but it made *sense*, it made sense to me in a way that nothing else did, or ever had.

I've always been in comedy. But for Shakespeare, my feeling is that tragedy is the better franchise. I like to think I know a little bit about humor after executive positions in comedy development at two different networks for more than ten years and, frankly, most jokes written in the late 1500s just aren't funny anymore. No, not even "quirky," which is cable's term for not funny but the critics are afraid to say so. Plus, do not tell me you can't tell when it's a woman dressed up in men's clothing, you *can*, with or without the fake mustache.

This may explain why tragedy helped me more than comedy. When you're inside of a Shakespearean tragedy, it's impossible to think of anything else. Everyone in them always winds up dead at the end — and I'm talking bodies everywhere — but there was something so clean, so pure, so just, so . . . *fair* — I guess that's the word I'm looking for — so fair, that kept me hanging on. Blood was never spilled without a reason. People died for a reason. Murder always had a reason.

Comedy ends in marriage; tragedy ends in death. That's the way it was. I got that right on the exam.

I have to admit it, though — my introduction to Shakespeare also scared the shit out of me. I was used to getting by on the notes. Sometimes I had to put down the heavy, pea-green volume for an hour or two and go back to watching re-runs of *Bite Me* or whatever show I'd recorded most recently. With TV, I wasn't sure I liked where I was standing, but at least I knew where I stood. I was on dry land. As much they drew me, Shakespeare's tragedies were . . . water, deep, black water with no bottom that I could see. I'm a swimmer, and no one but a fool would dive without knowing how deep the water is.

The water was so very, very, black; so very, very deep. And it was not until I reached bottom that I discovered her: the Dark Lady of the Sonnets.

I'd finished all of the plays. I'd even plowed through the section called "The Non-Dramatic Poetry" — got to be the worst chapter heading ever created, nobody's ever Googling *that*. But I'd read it, all the non-dramatic poetry: *Venus and*

Adonis, The Rape of Lucrece. I'm no critic, but this rocked.

But now I was done, and I didn't know what to do. I just knew I had to do something. On that particular day, that bitch of a day when it wasn't Danny Gordon but one Dr. Hugh Goldberg of Beverly Hills's Cedars-Sinai Hospital saying, "Here's the *thing*, Kenny," I had to read more, I had to. But there wasn't any more. Sixteen hundred pages of tiny, tiny type, and I'd already read every word.

But then, as I turned all the pages I'd already read, faster and faster, agitated, wired, I found something at the back of the book. Behind the plays and the "non-dramatic poetry" were the sonnets. Shakespeare's sonnets. One hundred and fifty-four of them. I started laughing like a live studio audience as I discovered there was more to *The Complete Works of William Shakespeare.*

I thought I liked — loved — the tragedies, and I do. But sonnets — whoa. Here was instant gratification, everything I ever needed in fourteen lines. No characters, no story, no plot points — just feeling, pure and simple. And the final couplets were, as we say in the business, truly high-concept — the whole thing in two sentences, no need for further explanation. I could pitch these.

Don't worry. I had no plan to turn myself into one of those pretentious Hollywood dicks who quote poetry all the time. There's a guy down the hall from my office who sometimes quotes Yeats while swaggering down the hallway and gnawing a pipe, very slowly to make sure nobody misses seeing him. He's the same guy who created *Topless Cops* for CineView. Sometimes, just to raise his blood pressure, I'd drop by his office and ask him to revisit his original press statement that the defunct action series was really all about "female empowerment."

The only thing I cared about as I turned pages with

shaking hands, with numb, tingling fingers, was the Dark Lady of the Sonnets.

"Who was the Dark Lady — perhaps we'll never know," said the introduction to The Complete Works. "All we know is that Sonnets 127 through 154 deal in either an abstract or literal way with a mysterious woman with a dark complexion and perhaps dark hair, who was the mistress and Muse of the poet. The tortured tone of these sonnets also suggests the Lady may have betrayed him by entering into a love affair with another. The poetry suggests that Shakespeare was tormented by the fact that he loved a woman who would not have been considered beautiful by Elizabethan standards." Probably not beautiful by Hollywood standards either, judging by the amount of blond hair with black roots being tossed around in this town.

The Dark Lady might have been married, a lady-in-waiting in Queen Elizabeth's court. Or she could have been a winemaker's daughter, stomping grapes and pleasuring the field hands in the moonlight. Some believed she was one of London's most notorious harlots. No one knew for sure if she was a lady or a whore. Not only did this woman bedevil Shakespeare's mind as he wrote the sonnets, but some of the women in his plays might be modeled after her as well. Maybe Hermia, Rosalind, Cressida, Cleopatra, or Hamlet's nervous gal pal Ophelia.

I was happy to see that Lady Macbeth was not on the list, confirming my original theory that she was just a bitch.

"We will probably never know the true identity of the Dark Lady," continued the introduction. "And we will never know what shape the poet's body of work might have taken had she never cast her spell." I flashed on a vision of Shakespeare before he met the Dark Lady, sitting around the table picking at takeout sushi with the writing staff of *Bite Me*.

Shakespeare had his Dark Lady; he was not alone. I would not be alone either, not any more, not so terribly alone adjacent to Beverly Hills. No, Alice; no, Danny Gordon; no, Dr. Hugh Goldberg of Cedars-Sinai Hospital — I would not be alone. Never had anything felt so right as this.

No scholar had ever been able to discover the true identity of the Dark Lady of the Sonnets, not for four hundred years. The love of his life, his inspiration to write plays too astonishing to have sprung from one human mind. But to hell with the scholars, I had an even tougher job ahead of me. Christ — I had to find her in *Hollywood*.

CHAPTER THREE

**The fairest hand I ever touch'd! O beauty,
Till now I never knew thee!**

— King Henry, *King Henry the Eighth*

The next morning, I had a change of heart. I stopped by my old office on the way to my new office, shook hands with the twenty-four-year-old who had replaced me in that many hours, and picked up the plant.

If I was going down, so was the bromeliad.

As I walked into the Hacienda, I could hear a young secretary — excuse me, *assistant*, there's no such thing as a secretary in this business — on the phone in some distant office, chattering away about how work was going. "It's *crazed*, I'm like so *crazed*, I'm like, *dying!*" she gasped. "With this new job, I don't even have *time* to be bisexual!"

I was beginning to notice how often young entertainment industry types said they were just *dying* when, as far as I could see, nothing whatsoever was happening to them. With the big bromeliad blocking my vision, I almost smacked into a guy I did not know coming the other way. He was somewhere in his mid-thirties, an exasperated frown on his owlish face. "Sorry,"

I said. "Big plant. How ya doin'?"

He peered at me through round, wire-rimmed glasses. "I'm a gay, Jewish guy from West L.A., and I'm about to sit down under a palm tree to write a heartwarming MOW about a snowy family Christmas in Pittsburgh. For Jaleel White."

I wanted to tell him don't worry, this Movie of the Week (MOW) would never see the light of day. "Good luck to you, man," I said instead.

"I wrote a play once," I heard him murmur sadly as I walked away. "It ran for three weekends at the Blank Theatre . . ."

The rest of my stuff had already been moved into my tiny new office, dominated by a low, white ceiling fan that threatened to decapitate me. Apparently, the executive who had this office before me was much shorter — at least, he was *now*. I was going to have to make some calls, pull some strings. Then I remembered: I can't pull strings, not anymore. I know I shouldn't say this, but God, sometimes it was better than sex.

I'd already met the head of Movies and Minis because, at one point earlier in our careers at another network, I had fired her. Blair Smith was about fifty now, with threads of gray in her thin, straight blond hair. She was one of those tall, big-boned women who look like men in drag. "Good to see you again, Kenny," she said, her tone making very clear that it was not. "I'm very sorry to hear about your, ah, situation, but we're all excited to have you on board."

"Thanks." I grinned at Blair. That really was a nice thing for her to say, so nice that I was willing to get past the insincerity. Blair was the only one around here who seemed to get it, although given her age she'd probably be gone by next week. But for now, it felt good. Hey, that's all I had — a *situation*. "And, Blair, I want this to be business as usual."

"Agreed," she said. "And that's why I've got your first

project right here in my hand. It's a Peters/Brown movie about a woman who's got . . ." her voice trailed off into nothing.

"I know. I read the press announcement. Amazing that this department still has files from 1979."

"Good." Blair cleared her throat as if to make sure the word she'd been about to say hadn't gotten stuck in there and screwed up her cells or anything. "Tyne Daly. But they've got no script, just a star. I mean this is the script, but it's no script." She placed a huge stack of white paper in my arms, way more paper than ordinarily required for a two-hour story. "Tyne doesn't like it either, but she's had two MOWs in her contract with us since before she did *Cagney and Lacey* for CBS. And by now we've got so many people attached to this project it's cheaper to actually produce it than to pay them off."

"I'll do what I can with it."

"At least this assignment is geographically desirable." Peters/Brown Productions had their offices on our lot due to an exclusive production deal with the network. The entertainment industry is very incestuous, as well as short on studio space. "The writers would like to talk to you this morning, if you're ready. They're very anxious."

Of course they were anxious. They were writers. "Tell them to give me fifteen," I said. I needed a few minutes to swallow my latest assortment of ineffectual prescriptions from Dr. Hugh Goldberg. Blair nodded and walked out of my office, ducking the fan.

I left the Hacienda, headed for the walkway to Peters/Brown in the blazing October sunshine. What might be "climate change" elsewhere is just a normal taste of fall in Burbank. Despite the heat, there was no smog or haze. You could see the tops of the San Gabriel Mountains, sharp and clear behind a large shopping complex and a multiplex movie theater boasting twenty-four screens. The whole world, or at least that part in my immediate view, was framed in shiny green palm fronds and sweet-smelling white hibiscus flowers tinged with peach. Sometimes I was struck by how ugly this town was — on days like today, by how beautiful.

I was already on the Peters/Brown area of the lot when it became clear to me it is a bad idea to swallow a handful of new prescription drugs on an empty stomach. I stopped walking as my world slipped sideways. I shook my head, trying to get back my equilibrium. At the same time, I lost control of the Tyne Daly script. Random sheets of paper fell from my grasp. Even in this alarming moment of vertigo, I couldn't help thinking this script was probably no worse with the pages missing.

Luckily, I was near the open door of one of the sound stages on the lot. I could go inside, get out of the sun. I stumbled up the four small steps up to the narrow side door that led into the cavernous sound stage.

"Hey, the line starts back here, asshole!" I heard an angry voice say, just behind me. I turned to see who had spoken. It was then that I noticed a long, restless line of people waiting to enter this particular studio. Pale, overweight people in shorts and sneakers, with tote bags and tiny cameras, itchy fingers poised to tweet should their favorite sitcom star stroll by on the way to the set. These people were shooting pictures of celebrity parking spaces. That said it all. The unruly crowd waiting here in the heat today could be none other than a live studio audience.

Confused, I looked back at the sign beside the entrance to the building: Peters/Brown Studio 7. Studio 7. Shit — of all places. Everybody in the country, probably the world, knew what show taped here in Studio 7. TV's most outrageously popular daytime talk show, *Really, Girlfriend?* — hosted by the reigning queen of American pop psychology, Jazzminn Jenks.

I'd never watched *Really, Girlfriend?* (RGF in the trades) but

I knew its advertising rates were the highest in its daypart, higher than any other talk show, game show, or soap. And I knew Jazzminn Jenks from the giant billboard, strategically placed near a busy intersection, on one of the outside walls of the lot. The big, bright sign featured tiny Jazzminn sitting right in the middle of her overstuffed pink sofa, clapping her small hands with delight in response to some unknown stimulus and wearing an oversized pair of pink bunny slippers. On the billboard, there were more pairs of slippers, four or five all in a row, in front of the sofa.

There were two things everybody in America knew about *Really, Girlfriend?*: all the guests were women, and each guest was required to take off her shoes and put on slippers before she joined Jazzminn Jenks on the pink sofa. Like a big pajama party. Jazzminn would always smile and pat the seat cushion next to her: come, sit next to *me*, girlfriend. Then, she and the guest would curl their big-slippered feet up under their skirts and gab.

Actually, now that I thought of it, I remembered I had seen a few minutes of the show once. Even though my memory is now so tragically short, Sarah Palin with a rifle and pink bunny slippers is something you don't forget.

"Hey, you — asshole!" Same message, different voice.

"Sorry — I'm not cutting in front of you — I'm from the network," I gasped out. The militant rustle of cameras and tote bags indicated that no one believed me. I gave a feeble grin. "Really. Hey, why else would I be wearing a suit in this weather?" Without waiting for a response, I yanked the door open and staggered inside.

"I'm sorry sir, I know it's hot, but be patient. We're not letting people in yet!" A perky, college-aged page in a bright blue blazer, her shiny black hair pulled back into tight ponytail, rushed over very importantly to block my entrance —

obviously not the first time she'd done this today. She was swinging her glossy tail of hair on purpose, and her little gold nametag said she was Peggy Chen.

"It's all right, Peggy, I'm with the network — development." I gave perky Peggy Chen a wink, which she of course just ate up. "I'm sitting in today — just wanted to grab a seat in the back before the crowd comes in. That okay?" Smiling, Peggy Chen waved me in and pointed to an empty seat in the top tier. She immediately returned her focus to defending the door against any tourist who might break from the pack, crazed by heat.

I slipped past her — then, instead of climbing up to my seat, ducked into the tiny men's room behind the stands and, as quietly as possible, threw up everything I'd eaten since *Friends* went off the air.

I splashed some cold water on my face before making my unsteady exit. But I knew I wasn't ready to deal with either the bad attitude of the crowd outside or the climbing temperature. I was obviously going to miss my writer's meeting. Besides, I'd lost most of the script. So, clinging tight to the railing, I half-walked, half-crawled up to my seat in the back row, and then waited in the dark, alone in the empty stands. I'm pretty sure no one could see me up there.

I looked down at the empty set — a fake living room with a gas fire roaring away like it was Christmas in Vermont and a bright pink sofa in the center. And then, suddenly, there she was: Jazzminn Jenks, striding out onto the stage, surrounded by an entourage of very thin, worried-looking female assistants dressed in various shades of black. She was five feet tall and no more than ninety pounds, most of it cleavage. She looked about thirty-five years old, which meant she had to be over forty. She had a gleaming, shoulder-length pile of that Hollywood hair, bright blond, its roots a black starfish washed up on a sandy beach.

But right now, Jazzminn Jenks wasn't smiling her delighted, billboard smile. She was screaming. From betwixt her pink-frosted rosebud lips came these words, in a shriek *like mandrakes torn out of the earth*: "These are the wrong fucking slippers!!! Get me the right ones, Goddamnit!!! NOW!!!"

I was stunned. This loud harpy was "America's girlfriend"? Really? I hate to argue with Shakespeare, but when it comes to what goes on behind the scenes in the entertainment industry, sometimes the fault *is* in our stars.

And then, out from behind the back wall of the set, clutching a pair of pink bunny slippers exactly like the one that had caused Jazzminn's sudden meltdown, emerged the loveliest creature in the world.

Most radiant, exquisite, and unmatchable beauty!

Even though the bright stage lights made my head ache like a son-of-a-bitch, I just had to look at her. A cascade of warm, brown curls that glinted with golden lights, as unruly as Jazzminn's straight, blond hair was clipped and coifed, flowed down the back of her soft white dress, almost to her tiny waist. Her flawless skin was the color of sweet honey dripping from a spoon. Her slightly slanted eyes were a shade I'm not even sure I can describe — green, I guess, but alive and sparkling with bright particles of amber and silver and gold, picked up by the hot lights. Her slender feet were bare. It seemed strange and wonderful that she had no shoes. From whence could a person who looked like this possibly have come? What country, what century, what planet?

She also had these really great tits. I could tell through the white fabric. I look at tits. I'm not fussy about size or anything. I just like them all, as a category.

Without saying a word, the creature took away one pair of Jazzminn's size-four pink bunnies and replaced them with the other. Then, carrying one of the wrong fucking slippers in each hand, she disappeared.

Jazzminn's billboard smile returned as she poked her little feet into the new ones, just as the lights came up and the studio audience began to flow into Studio 7. I could see the red light beginning to flash above the door, meaning it would soon be locked tight. There was no escaping now. But I did not want to escape. I had seen her.

"Hi, everybody, I love you!" Jazzminn called out, running to the front of the stage in her enormous pink slippers to blow big handfuls of kisses, left and right. The absurd footwear gave her movements a charming, girlish awkwardness, at strange odds with that porn star chest. From somewhere in the wings, streams of little pink soap bubbles wafted into the air. "Maybe your mother doesn't love you, or your father doesn't love you, or your therapist doesn't love you — but *I* love you," she crooned. "Because — who am I?" With an exaggerated gesture, she lifted one small hand to cup her ear. "Come on, gang. You know the answer. Who am I?"

"Our *girlfriend!*" the audience shouted back in happy unison, their long, sweaty hours in the heat instantly forgotten. They were already laughing and clapping as the warm-up comedian whooped it up in front of them.

I don't remember who Jazzminn's guests were that day or what inappropriate behavior they confessed to on the air. I did not see them slide into their bunny slippers or curl up on the couch. My ears were deaf to what they had to say. I could think of nothing but the barefoot, honey woman in the flowing white dress, and whether I would ever see her again.

Before I knew it, the show was over. Jazzminn Jenks had worked her talk-show magic on the audience. They appeared excited and happy as they grabbed their tote bags and cameras, scuffling out of their seats to head for, I don't know, Universal

Studios or Knott's Berry Farm or something.

They had to step over me on the way out, though. I had, by now, pulled out of my dreamy trance, only to realize I felt not a whole lot better than I had when I came in. I closed my eyes, leaned my forehead against my hand and drew in a few shuddering gasps, hanging ten on a wave of nausea. With the other hand, I motioned my fellow audience members to go past me, which they seemed only too happy to do. Yeah, definitely going to Universal Studios.

"Excuse me, sir, are you all right?" I sensed a hand on my shoulder. Not a particularly light touch — a firm, warm hand. It had been at least eight months since anyone had touched my arm who wasn't poking around for an available vein. I opened my eyes to behold the woman with the unruly brown hair and the green-gold-silver-amber eyes, staring down at me with an expression of deep concern. She was here.

I lifted my head and stared back. No, not at her breasts — into her eyes. I also checked to see whether she was wearing any shoes yet. She was, some kind of little gold sandals — no bunny slippers, thank God. "Yeah, thanks," I finally said, my voice raspy and soft. Definitely not the sound I was going for. I tried clearing my throat. "I . . . came here right from a workout at the gym, and I forgot to eat anything, like a fool. I've just gotta sit here for a second. I'll be fine."

"You are probably suffering from dehydration due to the unseasonable heat. Maybe you should have some fruit juice. We have all kinds of juice backstage. Want some?"

I shook my head. I shouldn't have — it hurt. "I'm fine. Terrific. Really."

She did not look convinced. "Well, okay. But if you need anything at all, just let me know. I'm Jazzminn's personal assistant. I've got to get backstage. I don't know what Jazzminn wants yet, but there will be *something*." She wrinkled her cute nose for a split-second, but very quickly her smile returned. "Just call down for me. I'm Ophelia."

Her name was *Ophelia*? Ophelia, as in wacky virgin from *Hamlet*? *Chaste treasure, maiden presence* — sweet Ophelia? Hello, it didn't take a scholar to figure this one out. Fate had stepped in, a heavenly plot point just in time. This wonderful, not-at-all-blond person, whose roots miraculously matched the rest of her hair, was the Dark Lady, the Dark Lady of the Sonnets, the Dark Lady of Studio 7, the Dark Lady of television's most popular daytime talk show, *Really, Girlfriend?* My Dark Lady.

I had not even had to look for her. She had found me. She had touched me.

"You take care, then," she said, turned, and began to skip down the stairs toward the stage.

"Wait . . . I think . . . maybe some juice might help after all," I called after her. Actually, I was suddenly feeling a great deal better. Not bad at all, in fact. But I figured a pathetic request for aid would bring her back. It was much too soon to let her go.

"Sure." She seemed pleased to be able to do something. "I'll get you some. Back in a sec."

"Ophelia! Where the fuck are you?" It was the voice of Jazzminn, howling from somewhere backstage.

"Coming!" Ophelia trilled back in a voice like spun sugar — but with such an expression of supreme distaste coming over her face that I almost burst out laughing. In a few moments, I could hear Ophelia murmuring something backstage to Jazzminn. "Well, *God*. He's not gonna puke up there or anything, is he?" Jazzminn shouted.

I don't know what Ophelia told her, but soon a whole bunch of those thin young women in black, led by Ophelia in her flowing white dress, began appearing at my side. They were bearing bottles of juice of all kinds and colors, their faces contorted with anxiety.

"Thank you all, but this one will be just fine," I said, motioning at whatever it was Ophelia held in her incredibly soft hand. Her hand *had* to be soft, didn't it? "The rest of you can go." Relieved, the anxious little women quickly dispersed.

I gave Ophelia a calculatedly weak smile as she placed in my hand a frosted plastic bottle containing, Jesus, what was this, a banana-coconut smoothie. I cracked it open and took a sip. It was thick, slippery, and sweet. Not a beverage, not solid food, but something wretchedly in-between.

"This is wonderful, thanks," I murmured. "Could I *be* any more embarrassed? And, I'm sorry — I didn't even introduce myself." I shook her hand. Very soft indeed. "I'm with the network — development. Ken Harrison."

"You're a network executive?" She seemed to like that. In fact, she sat down next to me, so very close, smoothing her thin, white skirt over obviously amazing legs. "I'm very interested in development, where everything is still fresh and open to change, you know? I've been working for Jazzminn Jenks for the past four years, but actually I'm an actress. I'm studying drama at Lana Bishop in Hollywood."

An actress? Oh, great. No matter what kind of encounter I tried to have with an actress, it always turned into an audition. But, at this moment, her acting aspirations just might be something I could work with. I needed something to capture her interest, something to hold her before she disappeared, melted away into nothing like everything else. In the past eight months, I'd had just about as much nothing as I could take.

"Really?" I managed to sound surprised that I had met an actress in Los Angeles. "That's fascinating. I'm involved in a lot of casting for the network shows. Right now, I'm in movies and mini-series."

I had said the word "casting" in front of an actress. I

waited for the Pavlovian response. Her eyes began to sparkle again. My God, what marvelous eyes. I decided to push forward. "Ophelia, I'd really like to thank you for helping me out today. Let me take you to lunch this week. We could talk about your career. I certainly don't have all the answers, but I have been in network television for more than ten years."

"Ophelia, I need you. Is that guy dead yet or what?" bellowed Jazzminn Jenks.

Ophelia jumped from her seat and made a face — not at me. "Um . . . when were you thinking?" she asked, hesitantly.

"Tomorrow?" I said quickly — then forced a chuckle. "I didn't mean to sound pushy, it's just that I'm booked with lunch meetings for the rest of the week, and I had a cancellation for tomorrow. I'm not sure that's going to happen again for a while. Things have been just *crazed*."

"Oh, yes, here too! I'm just *dying*!" Ophelia nodded happily.

"Ophelia!"

"All right — tomorrow," Ophelia said. "We usually break right around noon, so if you come by here then, I can meet you. Not in here — just outside. Right now, I have to go. Good-bye . . . Ken?"

I nodded. "Ken. And . . . Ophelia." I wanted to say her name. Lovely — although it did cross my mind that's a hell of a lot of syllables for a man in my condition.

"Noon, then. I'll drop by." I gave her an enigmatic half-smile, the kind that usually worked with women and always worked with actresses. I haven't forgotten everything, you know.

CHAPTER FOUR

Enter Ophelia.

I don't care where you're going, or how late you are. You just don't climb over another human being like he's not even there. Shame on all those people — their mommas didn't raise them right, as my grandma on my mother's side always says.

At first I was just going to leave him alone, because that story about the gym — well, I'm not saying I didn't believe him, but there are a lot of people with serious drug problems out here in Hollywood. It's a sad state of affairs really, and I didn't see any reason to embarrass him by calling attention to it. For all I knew he was in a twelve-step-program, one of the nicer ones on the Westside, and had already successfully completed Step Eight. You've got to give a person encouragement for making progress toward a goal.

Now, if I were to go back home and tell my Grandma Nettie Mae — on my mother's side — how many very wealthy, successful, powerful Hollywood executives, men with everything in the world, still have a taste for illegal substances, she would probably say something along the lines of: "White folks is a mess." In fact, that's exactly what she'd say. She's a bigot, my grandma, but one with an innate sense of fairness, I think. No, that's not true. She's really an awful, awful woman. But at eighty-nine, she still bakes the most extraordinary chocolate chip brownies, knits me cable-stitch sweaters, and I love her dearly.

But those people just made me angry. I had to do something. Besides, he looked so fragile, sitting there with his head in his hands, his skin as pale as the stars in the Hollywood Wax Museum, swimming in that gorgeous, slate-gray Armani suit. His sandy hair was short, like a military buzz cut that's grown out about half an inch. We invite a lot of military personnel to join our studio audience. They usually seat them right next to the Make-A-Wish kids and pan the cameras there for a moment before every commercial break. One might see this as manipulative, but I've always thought the chance to be part of a live studio audience has to make a person feel better about being shipped out to Iraq. There's still something very magical about live TV, there really is.

Then I realized I had to be wrong — no military man could possibly afford this suit. This was a network executive suit. This was exactly the kind of suit they mean when they call someone a "suit" in Hollywood. Personally I never much cared for that expression, it sounds like there's no one inside. And I truly believe there's always someone inside, someone very special, whether the suit is Armani, or Men's Wearhouse.

I also had to be practical. The ghost-pale man in the Armani suit, though perhaps bravely on his way to conquering his addiction, did look as if he were going to be sick, right then, right there — and I had no desire to face Jazzminn's reaction should such a thing occur in her newly-remodeled, white-maple, state-of-the-art studio, complete with an Italian marble test kitchen with sub-zero freezer for our cooking segments, and ten new overhead video screens to project her bleached — I mean, blond hair all the way up to the back tier.

You can't really thank a person for not vomiting, but in the end I was grateful to Ken for making the right choice. I think it was the banana-coconut smoothie. You just can't feel bad with one of those in your hand. It's like your own private tropical vacation. If there is joy to be found in a small thing, I love to share it if I can.

And I was so flattered that he asked me out to lunch! Although, it does happen to me a lot here in Hollywood. Almost every day, now that I'm thinking about it. In fact, I get taken out to lunch so much I don't even really know how much lunch costs anymore — at least, not at any of the city's finer restaurants.

Still, I really am surprised each time I'm asked — I'm not kidding — that feeling just never goes away. It's what it must be like to win an Emmy for production design for the third year in a row. Or like getting fresh flowers, and who ever gets tired of orchids, birds of paradise, blue irises, and tiger lilies? Plus, with my estimated yearly lunch savings, I am able to make a substantial annual donation to the Meals On Wheels program. I can do lunch and do good, all at the same time.

Because I work on a studio lot, the people — not people, men, they're all men — I do lunch with do tend to be somewhat . . . similar. Caucasian males from twenty-five to maybe fifty-five at the oldest, bright, aggressive, cutting-edge. They all have lengthy titles, but frankly I don't know what they do all day. They're in the entertainment industry, but they can't write, or act, or direct, or operate a camera. I don't mean to be critical. No one is perfect. But they call themselves creative executives, and I've as yet seen no evidence at all that they create anything —although, to their credit, they seem extremely skilled at changing what others have put on paper.

I was going to have to cancel a lunch to have lunch with Ken. Canceling at the last minute is a favorite game in Hollywood. It means someone with more power has asked you out, and you want that person to know it. I don't like to play games. It's bad manners. But in this case, I was canceling a lunch with someone powerful to do lunch with someone less powerful. My scheduled date was in feature film development. Ken was television — which means no matter how expensive the suit, he'll always be sitting at Hollywood's B-table. I never really understood that since more people watch TV than go to the movies. But that's the way it is. Oscar trumps Emmy. And that fact made me feel much less guilty about undoing lunch, just this once.

I do lunch even when I'm not hungry. Although I usually am — I have a very healthy appetite, probably because my grandma on my mother's side always told me as a child: "Clean your plate or I'll go upside yo' head." Besides, I never seem to put on an ounce, no matter what I eat — something I'd never dare tell Jazzminn for fear she'd jump out the nearest window with a dried seaweed snack clutched in each tiny hand. I don't blame her, really I don't. She has food issues stemming from her childhood.

Doing lunch is my calling here in Hollywood. I do it for my budding acting career — of course one must network — but I also do it because I feel sorry for men like Ken Harrison, mid-level creative executives charged with the overwhelming psychological burden of making a great deal of money while having no particular skills. I think that's what power means in this town.

I don't want power. I am an artist, thank you very much. I could never be a power player in the entertainment industry, not even at mid-level — in fact, the whole idea of even being a man for any length of time makes me feel completely exhausted. Maybe for just long enough to install Word for Mac and open a few jars, but I could never keep it up all day.

No one sends men flowers. Sometimes I want to send them back, just so they'll know how it feels to pull a glossy pink ribbon off a shiny white box full of orchids, birds of paradise, blue irises, and tiger lilies, but I can't because they'd take it the wrong way. So instead, I do lunch. I order all the courses: Soup, salad, entrée, and dessert. I do it for them. I do it for the suits, so they'll know that at least one person in Hollywood believes there's someone inside.

I don't want power. I prefer flowers. But that doesn't mean that I'm not curious, every once in awhile. I wonder what it would be like to be Ken Harrison — or, if I'm going to expend the energy to wonder, I might as well go ahead and wonder what it would be like to be Ken Harrison's boss, or *his* boss, or — just hypothetically — the head of the network entertainment division.

One day my acting career will blossom like a bower of bougainvillea, all bright magenta blooms, I just know it, but it's been ten years and . . . well, every once in a while I wonder what it would be like to be a suit, what it would be like to have the power to run Hollywood, to have so much of everything given to you that narcotic drugs are the only thing that's still left to take.

What I feel is not envy, and certainly not penis envy — sorry, I don't want one, no matter what's implied by the psychological literature. As with condominiums in today's soft economic climate, I see no advantage to ownership. No, when

I wonder what it would feel like to have all that power right there in my hands, within my grasp, to touch it, taste it, smell it — I really just see myself as an actress doing research into character.

Sometimes, when I'm driving up here on Mulholland Drive, on the cusp between Beverly Hills and the Valley, the Southern California sky a big blue blank, winding around the curves past big houses with decks cantilevered out over the hillside on tall stilts, pools, lounge chairs, and umbrella tables just hanging out there over nothing — I wonder what would it would be like if, one day, at the end of the day, all the maids, gardeners, nannies, and pool men locked the gates and wouldn't let the owners of the houses back in. Just took the castles, the way armies stormed the gates and took the kingdoms in days of yore, before there was a Hollywood. I don't wonder it every day, but some days I do, especially on those sunny days when there's not a cloud in the sky. I don't know why it happens that way. It just does.

I never tell anyone about my daydream, and certainly not the suits. After doing lunch for ten years, I understand them well enough to know they wouldn't understand. But this time there was something in his eyes, mournful gray eyes the color of a Midwestern thunderstorm, looking up at me with dazed wonder when I put my hand on the shoulder of his gorgeous Armani suit, that made me think that maybe this suit, Ken Harrison, would.

CHAPTER FIVE

**I have unclasped
To thee the book even of my secret soul.**

— Duke, *Twelfth Night*

"No!"

Ophelia looked startled; so did the waiter. He'd just asked if we'd like to hear today's specials.

I had not been in a restaurant in eight months, and knew there was no way I could deal with what I was about to hear courtesy of Spago Beverly Hills: An endless litany of crimes committed in the name of California cuisine. Unnatural pairings between Cobb salad and chunks of lobster; sordid threesomes involving squab, foie gras, and kumquat chutney; ravioli stuffed with things that just didn't belong in there. I used to like this kind of food; now I was cursing the LAPD for not hauling Wolfgang Puck off to chef prison for even thinking of putting smoked salmon on a pizza. "We're sort of pressed for time," I apologized.

Ophelia was not, however, listening to me any more. She was offering a wide-eyed, friendly smile in response to the suggestive stare of our waiter, a very young, tall, toned, ambiguously Asian man with jutting cheekbones and a flowing pony-tail of dark, silky hair. He wore a loose-fitting black suit with a filmy white T-shirt underneath, stretched across his prominent pectorals — the kind of shirt you wear because it's too tight.

"No, never mind the specials," she said, ignoring my little outburst. "Just pick out something delicious for me, and a glass of wine to match, would you, I'm sorry, I'm afraid I didn't get your name?"

"Call me Maro."

"Maro," she repeated.

"Maaah-ro," he corrected, although that's exactly what she'd said.

"Maaah-ro. That's nice."

Personally, I thought Maro sounded like a vegetable, but maybe that's just because I had not been invited to call him it. "And I'd like a plain grilled chicken breast with some white rice on the side. Skip the pasta with the black truffles," I said. I wouldn't like it, but I could probably eat it. Maro did not come right out and say "whatever," but I felt it as he walked away, still casting a longing eye over his shoulder at Ophelia. He wasn't the only one looking at her, either. Men young and old shot admiring looks at our table across Spago's brick-floored, open-air garden. Women stared at her, too.

Our table was just in front of the sculpted granite fountain that stood at the far end of the garden patio, dribbling water down its stony face into a garden of orchids and bromeliads. I'd read somewhere that this fountain had the word "passion" in twenty languages etched into the stone. The fountain was shaded by two one-hundred-year-old olive trees, yanked from the earth somewhere and transplanted to the middle of Beverly Hills, like much of the noontime clientele. The age-old branches framed Ophelia like a painting as men stared at her.

Like a painting, she didn't seem to care.

Once again, as it had been in the car on the way over, her attention was focused completely on me. Her gaze felt like the warm sun that had bathed us as we drove here, top down, in the Mercedes, like the breeze that had ruffled my short hair. Her brown curls flew everywhere. She was the first woman ever to ride beside me in that car with the top down who didn't seem to care what happened to her hair.

I didn't know how she could be in such good mood. When I picked her up at noon outside the stage entrance to Studio 7, you'd have had to be a block away not to hear Jazzminn Jenks shrieking. From what I could deduce, she was dissatisfied with what Ophelia had ordered her for lunch from the commissary. Something about the mayonnaise.

"You can't text my order, Ophelia, or they don't get it right. You have to get off your ass and walk over there and tell them what I want and that it's for *me*," she was shouting. "Do I have to tell you how to do everything? You should talk to Julio in the kitchen. Just go right in the back. He knows me."

"I'm sure he does. You had him fired a couple of weeks ago. He moved back to El Salvador."

"Oh, yeah. Well, call El Salvador, get him back. And don't tell me they had a flood in his village — that was yesterday. He knows the way I like mayonnaise. He adds that spicy stuff I like, what is it, chipotle, I think?"

"I'll get right on it. I think all their phone lines are down, but I'll try the cell. Now, I'm going to take my lunch break, if that's all right, and on the way back, I'll pick up your gold Capri pants at the tailor's."

"Too late, Ophelia. My personal shopper found the same ones in a size zero at Barney's this weekend, so we don't have to take in the twos. How great is that? She bought me six pairs."

Well, I learned something, standing there. I didn't know women's clothes came in a size zero. Seems to me that's the size you'd wear if you did not exist. But what do I know about Capri pants? What *are* Capri pants?

"It must be, like, so great not to have problems finding clothes, Ophelia. Like you, you must wear, like, a *six* or something," continued the voice of Jazzminn.

"It is wonderful. Not a day goes by that I don't thank God that I'm so huge," I heard her say. "But we still have to pay the gentleman. He already did the work."

"Okay, pay him. Just don't bring those enormous pants back in here, ever. I can't look at them. They make me puke."

"Over my dead body — size six," Ophelia vowed. She slipped out the door and closed it behind her. "Hi, Ken!" she said brightly. "I hope I'm not late. Jazzminn was having some . . . mayonnaise issues."

"Mayonnaise issues," I repeated, matching her brisk gait. It felt good to walk fast. For the record, it feels good to walk, period. "So, I'm going to laugh now, okay?"

"Never mind, I'll do it for you," Ophelia said, laughing more loudly than I expected. The girl was a reported size six, but the laugh was at least a ten. "And now I'm going to stop laughing, because it's really very sad," she added, trying to discourage the merry bubbles in her voice and doing a lousy job. "Jazzminn isn't a bad person. I mean, she is a bad person — but there's a good reason. She is the victim of a Hollywood epidemic called bulimarexia. She's got both eating disorders, can you imagine? Either she's cutting the food into a hundred little squares that she won't ever eat, or she eats it and then. . ."

"Moving into too-much-information territory . . ." I interjected hastily.

"Sorry." Ophelia laughed again, even bigger. We kept walking at the same energetic pace down the walkway that connected Peters/Brown to the network lot. "More than I ever needed to know, too, believe me. How are you feeling today, Ken? Better, I hope."

"I feel great, thanks for asking." I hate it when people ask. "That's my car over there," I said, pointing, not without pride, to my freshly washed silver Mercedes wedged into its inadequate parking space in front of the Hacienda. "I thought we'd take a little ride over the hill. I just need to get off this lot, for a change. Have you been to Spago Beverly Hills?"

She said she had not, and now here we were. Maro was just arriving with my order, the Bland Plate, balanced up high on one arm. He had hers balanced on the same hand, a spectacular arrangement of grilled fish and vegetables in a bright red sauce with a big frizz of deep-fried beets on the side. Maro set down the plates, and then presented Ophelia's wine. "For you," he said huskily, leaning in close. "I asked the chef to combine my two favorite specials into one. That's the way it should be, the two of them, together. I hope you like it. Let me know . . . later."

Hi, I'm over here on the other side of the table, I'll just start in on my chicken, I said to myself.

"How old are you, Maro?" Ophelia asked.

"Twenty-one."

"And do you do anything besides wait tables?"

He frowned — might take him awhile to come up with an answer to a question as hard as this one. "No," he finally said.

"Well, Maro, I'm not qualified to give career advice, but you seem very intelligent and personable. I think you may be underestimating your potential." Ophelia's voice was filled with a surprising yet genuine concern for the immediate future of Mr. Pecs. "I think, instead of flirting like a high school boy when you can see that I'm entertaining a companion, your time might be better spent taking some night courses at East Valley

College. Here — I just happen to have an introductory brochure." She dived into her capacious red Coach bag and emerged with a shiny leaflet for Maro. I was wondering the same thing he was, probably — why the hell was she toting promotional materials for East Valley College around in her purse? But we were both too dumbfounded to ask.

"What a nice young man," Ophelia said as he walked away. "I'm sorry I had to be so harsh with him, but higher education is very important even though I'm sure his big break will come. I just knew picking up that brochure at my bank was going to come in handy some day. Twenty-one is such a hopeful age."

"How old are you, Ophelia?" I asked playfully, not expecting to get a straight answer out of an actress.

"I'm thirty-two," she replied, without hesitating. She tasted the fish. "Delicious. Cooked just the way we used to prepare it on . . . the island."

"The . . . island?"

"The island where I was born, where I grew up." She kept her eyes focused on her plate. "I'm from the Caribbean, a very tiny island called Sadilla. I grew up on nothing but fresh seafood, right from the net."

"Sadilla," I repeated. The unfamiliar name felt good in my mouth. "Sah-dee-ah. Never heard of it. What's it near?"

"It's not near anything. It's . . . remote. But very, very beautiful. It's noted for its spectacular sunsets. Boats come from miles around. Where are you from, Ken?"

"I'm a North Hollywood kid, the Valley." I replied. "But let's not talk about any place you can get to off the 101. Please — tell me about Sadilla."

"Not much to tell. It was a happy childhood." Her voice assumed a dreamy singsong I figured must be some kind of an island thing. "My father was a fisherman, who first came to the island on a voyage from Scotland. My mother was a native

Sadillan, a dancer, entertaining visitors to the island until she fell in love with him. They were married in a traditional ceremony by the local holy man, who to this day has never been off the island. The air there is always sweet with the scent of coconut and flowers. You can tell the people of my island from the others nearby by their eyes. They have eyes like mine, eyes of many colors. My people have a word for it: *catua* eyes. My mother had those eyes too. They drowned at sea when I was in my teens, my parents — in a fishing accident. Squid, actually. Sometimes I miss Sadilla so much, I cry."

Her eyes of many colors misted over. Hell, I was beginning to miss the place myself. "That's rough. I'm sorry . . . and how did you end up in Hollywood?" I asked gently.

"Well, ever since I was a little girl, I always wanted to come to the United States. So I studied very hard in school, and I won a scholarship to Yale University and studied drama there. At first, I thought I'd go to New York to do theater, but I missed the sun of Sadilla so much, I came to Los Angeles instead. I can't survive under dark skies."

"Do you like it out here?"

"I love Los Angeles!" Ophelia replied quickly. "I've always wanted to be an actress. Always."

I considered eating a bite of chicken. "So . . . how's that been working out for you?"

She wrinkled her nose, then smiled. "Well, as you know, it's extremely difficult to break into the business."

"Tell me about it. What have you done? Are you mainly movies or TV?"

"Of course, I'm open to both."

"But which one have you done?"

"Well . . . neither, actually.

I laid down my fork, surprised. "Neither?"

"No."

"Seriously?"

"Yes."

"How about commercials?"

"No."

"Voice-overs?"

"No. When I first got here, everybody told me I should be a model. And I did do a little, but I'm too short to be a *super*model and mediocrity has never appealed to me. Besides, it wasn't really what I wanted to do. I'm a serious actress, and that has nothing at all to do with lingerie. So I gave it up. It was taking too much time away from my acting studies."

"Who are you with?'

"With?"

"Your agent. Who's your agent? ICM? CAA? Paradigm?" I couldn't help the impatience creeping into my voice. I was rehashing dialogue I'd been through a dozen times before with countless wide-eyed starlets. But I sternly banished the feeling. This wasn't just another wannabe with a nice ass. This was the Dark Lady of the Sonnets.

"I don't have an agent. I mean, I did — until recently. But he never called, so . . . how was I supposed to know he really *was* dead?" That last part came out in a wail. Then she mustered a weak smile. "But certainly I'm more concerned for his family than for myself."

"I can't imagine you not getting hired, with or without an agent," I said — not flattery, the truth. "If you don't mind my saying so, you are lovely, Ophelia."

She did not protest, just uttered a long, theatrical sigh. "This is Hollywood, Ken. There just never seems to be a part for a half-Scottish, half-Sadillan Woman with Cat*ua* eyes."

I looked at her for a long minute. True, Ophelia Lomond was not exactly the girl next door as envisioned by Central Casting — although come to think of it, in my current place of residence, the girl next door is a transsexual from Salt Lake City who calls herself Glinda. I've heard plenty of casting agents whisper to each other about how this or that minority actor "can't open a movie" — that is, do big box office in the first weekend before anybody finds out what a dog the movie really is. There was nothing racist about it, they always assured each other quickly. The only color they were thinking about was *green.*

Still, someone this extraordinarily beautiful, with enough talent and brains to walk away with a theater degree from Yale, never getting even a bit part, a walk-on, a TV commercial for expensive sports cars or some over-the-counter product to be used only as directed by the outrageously gorgeous? Look, everybody and his brother is in those Target commercials, even gay couples. I was having a hard time swallowing it.

"I mean, unless the story calls for some sort of 'island girl' or an 'exotic,' I'm out of a job," Ophelia continued, building steam. "We all studied Mendel's peas in junior high school. I don't see why I'm so difficult for people to understand. Do you know how sick I am of being described as 'cafe au lait'? If I hear it one more time, I'll jump out a window. In Hollywood, I think that's French for 'unemployed.'"

"I took Spanish," I offered, by way of changing the subject.

"Why else do you think I'd work for a lunatic like Jazzminn Jenks for four years?" Ophelia fretted. "I mean — don't tell anyone I said that about her, okay? I just figure that, maybe, if I'm on the lot long enough, working for the most famous woman in American daytime television, something will break for me. Or maybe I'll meet someone who can help me, right there on the studio lot. It's better than an audition. I'm the one who rides with her guests in the limos from the airport, the one who calls to make sure they have everything they want in their hotel suites and dressing rooms, who orders vegetarian biscuits shaped like carrots for their little dogs. Maybe someday one of her guests will take an interest in me and open some doors. Oh, gosh — excuse me."

Then Ophelia sneezed, a dainty, kitten sneeze. And, afterward, her momentary lapse into frustrated-starlet bitterness disappeared as if she'd somehow sneezed it away. She dabbed at her nose with her napkin. "But I'm not worried," she continued, eyes shining with the dew of anticipation. "Things always work out for the best, even in Hollywood. Don't you think so, Ken? I do."

I wanted to ask her to try coughing — hell, maybe she could achieve peace in the Middle East. "Bless you," I said instead. "And . . . of course they do. Things do that — work out, I mean. I'll take a look at our current development slate." I tried as hard as I could to sound as though there were something on it besides the Tyne Daly project. "I have a hard time remembering all the treatments, but I'm flashing on one or two that would be perfect for you."

"Really?" Her face glowed.

"Oh, yeah, absolutely. I think what most talented people in this town need is to meet the right person. It's all about who you know."

She received this tired cliché like no one had ever said it before. *Actors.* "Maybe that's what it takes," she nodded happily. "I hope I can survive Jazzminn Jenks long enough to find out."

"Why don't you come by my office tomorrow? We'll . . . talk."

To my surprise, disappointment suddenly clouded her face and turned her pouting lips downward at the corners. "Oh. Come by your office. To . . . talk. Late at night, I suppose. Wearing something see-through, correct? I see what you're saying, Ken."

I was puzzled. "What do you mean, Ophelia?"

She jumped up from her chair and threw her linen napkin to the floor. "Oh, please. Look at me. If I were sleeping my way to the top, honey, I'd be there." Her *catua* eyes flashed anger.

"Hey, wait a second!" I was shocked by her outburst — where was the sweet, modest Ophelia who'd been sitting across from me only moments before? This Ophelia was angry, and beautiful, and she knew it. But I was furious, too. I really did want to help her, if I could. I was prepared to take on Hollywood for her, even though she didn't know it. And believe me, after what I'd been through these last few months, the last thing I was thinking about was exchanging body fluids on the office furniture.

I leapt from my chair, too. "Sit down, Ophelia, we're in the middle of fucking *Spago*," I hissed, grabbing her arm. "Sit." Reluctantly, she sank into her chair. "Look, if I say I'm going to do something, I'm going to do it. You've been in the business for ten years, so I know you've probably been promised a lot of things just because some producer or director wants to get you into bed. But you've got to trust me. I'm not going to offer you a bit part for a blow job. I'm not that kind of guy — well, maybe I am, but I know you're not that kind of woman. I don't want sleep with you; I want to help you."

"Oh, please. Of course you want to sleep with me," she hissed back.

"Let me re-phrase that. I have no intention of asking you to sleep with me, how's that?" My voice remained low enough that I hoped no one around us could hear. "I said I'll help you, and that's what I meant. And, news flash — people who are fighting cancer with every ounce of strength they've got don't waste precious time on aspiring actors unless they mean business."

Uh oh. That just slipped out. I was so busy thinking about her thing that I had let my thing slither out of its hole, and now the three of us were doing lunch together at Spago Beverly Hills.

Suddenly I could hear the nasal voice of Danny Gordon, dripping pity: "She *knows*, Kenny . . ."

Ophelia lifted surprised, beautiful eyes to meet mine.

"Cancer?"

"Yes." I told the truth because I couldn't think of anything else to say. "I'm sorry, Ophelia, I didn't mean to blurt it out like that. In fact, I didn't mean to tell you at all. I shouldn't have told you. You were just . . . well, you were pissing me off, that's all. It's nothing for you to worry about. I'm completing my treatment. I'm handling it. I'm fine." Annoyed with myself, I stabbed my chicken in the breast.

"Cancer," she repeated. "Oh, Ken, I'm sorry. Is it . . . serious? I sincerely hope not. I mean, of course it's serious, it's cancer, but there have been remarkable medical advances. We all know someone who's just fine after treatment, don't we?"

I hesitated before answering. "Well, my oncologist, Dr. Asshole, and I have differing opinions on my prognosis. But he happens to be wrong. I know my body better than he does. I'm doing just fine. I'll be back at the gym in no time."

"What does he say, exactly?"

"Can't tell you, because I've stopped listening," I replied cheerfully. "Would you listen to an oncologist who once tried to pitch you a sitcom about an oncologist? I'd have told him what I thought of that idea if he wasn't also in the middle of shoving a tube into my chest."

"Oh, sweetheart," Ophelia murmured. "I mean, I'm sorry, I shouldn't have called you sweetheart. I barely know you —

but, oh, sweetheart . . ."

Hey, wait a second, what was this? Here I was, mentally kicking myself for having told her, horrified because my secret was now lying on the table like something I'd tried to spit into my napkin but missed. As I was walking from my old office to my new office, alone except for my bromeliad from my friends at Standards, I'd vowed never to tell anyone else about the thing until I had it licked. But the way she was looking at me now, the way she called me sweetheart . . .

"I can't believe I'm so stupid," Ophelia's voice remained filled with shocked wonder. "When I first met you, the way you looked, like you were carved out of wax . . . I'm sorry, but I thought you were on drugs."

"Drugs?" I couldn't help a snort of laughter, given the complete pharmacy assembled in my medicine cabinet. "Ophelia, you have no idea."

"What . . . what kind of cancer do you have? Never mind, I'm sorry. It's really none of my business, sweetheart . . ."

I cleared my throat. "Lymphoma." I studied her face for that expression of embarrassed distaste I'd recently seen in Danny's weasel eyes, just before he presented me with his fucking win-win. I waited for the look and steeled myself to take it when she looked away, because even that look was better than no look at all. But she didn't look away. "Aggressive, large cell, non-Hodgkin's lymphoma, if you want to be specific," I added, testing the waters.

"Ken . . . my God, you're so young . . ."

Did I really look like wax? "Yes. That's why it's aggressive. Sometimes it's more aggressive when you're younger," I replied. "But then, so am I."

"It was wrong of me to ask," Ophelia whispered. "I'm sorry, so sorry . . ."

"No, no, please. Caring is never wrong." That line came

from just before the first act break in the Tyne Daly script. I was thrilled that I had Ophelia's attention, but frankly I didn't have the energy to write my own dialogue just now. I smiled sadly, lifting my head and, once again, looking deep into those *catua* eyes. I could see tears forming there; bingo. The emotions of an actress lie so conveniently close to the surface. "Let's enjoy the rest of our meal, shall we?" I raised my glass of mineral water in a somber toast. All the world's an MOW. And so far, I was a player.

"How . . . how much time do you have?"

"Oh, God. You, too? Don't worry. I think it's safe to order dessert."

A tear tumbled down her cheek when I said it. She quickly brushed the tear away. It fell into her brown curls and sparkled there for a moment before it dissolved. "I'm not hungry anymore." Her voice shook. "Would you mind if we go now? I should be getting back. I'm sorry. This is just . . . something I wasn't prepared for. I need to get out of here."

"Sure, I understand," I nodded. "Listen, I'm the one who should be sorry. I shouldn't have told you. I curse myself for burdening you with this." Yes, that's what I said. I'm not a writer; I'm a suit. "But somehow . . . there's something about you, Ophelia. I just couldn't lie to you. I just couldn't."

"No, I'm glad you told me," she said. "But please — we have to go."

Now, tears were coursing freely down her lovely face. I didn't know what to do. People were starting to stare — most of them men, obviously more than willing to knee me in the nuts for making her so unhappy. "Shhh," I murmured. "Please, please don't. I only thought you should know because . . . you'll be seeing me again. I still want to help you with your career, if I can. I'd like to see you get everything you deserve. You're special, Ophelia. I can feel it. You'll let me, won't you?

Say you will."

"How can I?" she whispered. "How can I take anything from you when . . ."

"Please." I put my hand on her slender wrist and held it, hoping she couldn't feel the shudder of pleasure and fear that ran through my body at the touch. "Please. You aren't taking. You're . . . allowing me to give. It's the one thing you *can* do for me."

She nodded slowly, at the same time withdrawing her wrist to fold her hands in her lap. "If that's what you really want," she choked out. The woman was sad, but not stupid.

"Good. Just leave everything to me, okay?" I said, relieved. "Now, are we going to pick up the gold Capri pants on the way back, or not?"

"Oh, you heard that."

"Ophelia, Wisconsin heard that."

She laughed merrily, the tears now blessedly disappeared. "You are funny, Ken. I can see why the comedy department wants to keep you. No, we're not getting the Capri pants. I'll just send the tailor a check — twice what Jazzminn thinks she's going to pay him. I think it's only fair since no one will ever see his painstaking workmanship."

"And I will die a hundred thousand deaths / Ere break the smallest parcel of this vow," I murmured. I wasn't thinking about Capri pants anymore. This was it. This was how I would secure my bond with Ophelia forever. It was Fate. Somehow, I would find just the right part for the Dark Lady of the Sitcoms, the Dark Lady of Hollywood, for a half-Scottish, half-Sadillan beauty with *catua* eyes.

"I'm sorry, Ken. I didn't quite hear you?"

"Never mind, just talking to myself, a bad habit of mine," I smiled. My appetite was returning. I reached for one of her curly red French fried beets, dark as blood against my pale hand. I popped it into my mouth and crunched. "What I meant to say is don't worry. We'll throw your career into high gear, together. I may not have much going for me in the health department, but I have great contacts."

CHAPTER SIX

People live out there got to be crazy.

— Nettie Mae Easley

That evening as I drove along the curves of Mulholland Drive, I didn't think about gardeners, nannies, and pool men storming multi-million-dollar mansions and making kingdoms out of prime Southern California real estate. Instead, I was thinking about floods on Pacific Coast Highway and mudslides in Malibu, of raging brush fires in the San Gabriel Mountains, of hot Santa Ana winds and blinding fog rolling in off the polluted surf, of El Niño and El Niña and huge tectonic plates that heave and shift along the San Andreas Fault.

Scientists at Pasadena's California Institute of Technology spend their lives studying the earth's crust to predict the exact location of the next earthquake — and whether it's going to measure 2.0 or 4.2 or 6.7 on the Richter Scale, whether it's horizontal or vertical, or whether this time it's The Big One, so big that no one will be left at Caltech to try to figure out what hit us. All the while knowing, way down deep beneath their PhDs, that you can no more read the future in the fault lines than you can in the lines on the palm of your hand.

I thought I'd met every kind of man Los Angeles had to offer, the whole Whitman's Sampler. White men, black men, Latino men, Asian men; rich men and poor men; young men, middle-aged men, old men, old men pretending to be young; actors, models, doctors, lawyers; executives, *creative* executives, producers, writers; surfers, computer systems analysts; men from the Westside, the Valley, Orange County, Crenshaw, Hollywood; film editors, animators, gaffers and key grips; gay men, straight men, and every sort of man in between.

But never a man who was . . . *dying*. That's new. The idea was as amazing to me as Ken Harrison believing that I'd never done lunch at Spago Beverly Hills. I didn't want to hurt his feelings.

So this is the thunderstorm in his gray eyes. He says he doesn't believe it, but that's only because he doesn't want to. I can see it. I don't think I'd have cried if he'd told me he was dying. I cried because he told me that he wasn't. Because his thunderstorm eyes looked straight at me, smiled, and told me to order dessert.

I didn't mean to start sobbing, I just couldn't help it, and the more I tried to stop, the more I couldn't. And then to see all those people putting down their slices of smoked salmon pizza to stare at us, stare at *me* — none of their sympathy for the dying man, all of it for me, because he made a beautiful woman cry. People say I'm beautiful — that's how I know — I must take that into account at all times when assessing life's situations. He's dying, but they're ready to murder him for ruining my mascara. Well, right then I just felt like killing *them*, even though my thoughts are usually the opposite of homicidal.

They should have paid no attention to my tears. They were the wrong kind of tears — tears without cancer, a beautiful woman's tears dripping into a thirty-five dollar entrée created especially for her at Spago Beverly Hills, luxury tears. The fact that I'm used to all this doesn't mean that I believe it's normal. I didn't have a choice of what kind of tears to cry any more than I could stop them from falling. And Ken never cried at all. A thunderstorm in his eyes, but no rain.

Thirty-six. I'd only have four years left to become an actress if I died at thirty-six. It's the same age that Princess Diana was when she lost her life in that high-speed car crash in Paris, dogged by the paparazzi even in the moment of her death. Her wedding was so beautiful — a crystal coach, a diamond tiara; twenty-five feet of silk, taffeta and lace trailing behind her down the aisle at St. Paul's Cathedral. I loved the way he kissed her, the way the glad morning church bells pealed through London. I know things didn't work out for them. I know that from NPR though I never watched any of the TV movies. But it's the wedding that I remember, not what happened after.

So terribly, unspeakably sad. One minute I'm eating French fried beets with another creative executive; the next, I'm witness to a tragedy. A real tragedy, right here in Hollywood. The real thing. I'm in awe.

I don't know what makes me feel this way. Awed, shivery, horrified, and . . . moderately aroused. I wouldn't say that out loud, but it's a factor in this equation. It's not attractive in the same way as a handsome face or a strong, masculine hand — but it draws me in. There's something here that makes Ken Harrison seem to me to be something more than just another suit.

Ken says he loves Shakespeare's tragedies. That's weird, isn't it? A sitcom exec who loves tragedy. Personally, I prefer the comedies. I wish I knew how to be funny, but I'm not. I just love comedy. I love how everything always comes out right in the end no matter how complicated the story is. It's always just a case of misinformation, mistaken identity. People aren't who other people think they are, but by the end, everything is clear. But I can't make this into a comedy no matter how hard I try. Right now all I can do is cry and cry.

"That's excellent, Ophelia. For the first time since we started rehearsing, you were in touch with your motivation. You've obviously been doing your homework."

Through a blur of the wrong kind of tears, I looked up at my acting coach at the Lana Bishop Theatre in Hollywood and stammered out a thank you.

CHAPTER SEVEN

**The actors are at hand: and, by their show,
You shall know all, that you are like to know.**

— Quince, *A Midsummer Night's Dream*

When I arrived at the office at 8:30 the next morning I found a message on my desk, jotted down by the assistant I shared with a couple of other development people in Movies and Minis. Donald, a recent graduate of Harvard Law School, was uniquely overqualified to pen this Post-It note: "Please call Ophelia Lomond at *Really, Girlfriend?*"

Well, that was enterprising. She'd tracked me down — and so early in the morning, too. So that was her last name, Lomond. I dialed the number. "Ophelia Lomond, please."

"May I say who's calling?" asked a young-sounding female voice.

"Ken Harrison, returning."

"Oh! Mr. Harrison. We were expecting your call. Ophelia can't come to the phone right now. Ms. Jenks is having some . . . breakfast issues, but she asked me — *hi*, I'm Sasha! — to thank you again for the lovely lunch, and tell you that she will be performing major roles in several scenes in an open workshop this evening at the Lana Bishop Academy of Acting in Hollywood. Would you like her to hold a pair of tickets for you at the door?"

Aha. Audition time. In the course of my career, I can't even count how many workshops, showcases, open mics, bad performances of good plays, and good performances of bad plays I've been to, all in the name of finding the next fresh new face for a situation comedy. I think I've left a permanent ass print in a seat in the back row of every theater with fewer than ninety-nine seats within a fifty-mile radius of Burbank. I prefer the ones with parking.

"Of course. Of course I'll be there. But one ticket will do."

I was half-an-hour early — the first one in the audience at the Lana Bishop Theatre, situated on a seedy stretch of Hollywood Boulevard about a block east of the Hollywood Wax Museum. On the sidewalk outside, between the stars of Ray Charles and Vivien Leigh, lay a foil condom wrapper and a big glob of spit.

I'd brought along the sonnets so I'd have something to do to fill the time before the show. Not the big, heavy green volume. I'd recently invested in the paperback version.

I picked up my ticket, then entered the theater, choosing a seat as far in the back as possible. I sat down, took off my suit coat, polished my glasses on the cuff of my crisp white cotton shirt, and tried to read. I gave that up in a hurry. Things got too distracting as the crowd — most of them actors — began to congregate. These people were always *on*, hugging friends they saw an hour ago as if they'd just returned from the moon, flipping hair, twisting scarves, making faces, playing with their own clothes, playing with each other's clothes, laughing loudly at not much, assuming odd, painful-looking dance-class poses for reasons I could not fathom. And, most importantly, never, ever placing themselves directly in a seat, but making a major comic bit out of balancing on the arm, or draping themselves across the back, or this one — my favorite — suddenly deciding, with an elaborate flourish, to fall into someone else's lap. They all seemed to be going through the rites of some deeply irritating non-Equity religion.

I frowned, closed my book, and scrunched as far back in my seat as possible to get out of the way of two giggling young women — dressed in low-rise miniskirts and high-rise tops with a pound of not particularly attractive flesh in between — as they pushed past me. They had on clunky sheepskin boots with their tiny skirts — made them look like Clydesdales. I prayed for the lights to go down quickly as I fished in my pocket for a couple of antacid tablets. This had less to do with the unfortunate side effects of chemo than with what I knew about amateur theater in Los Angeles.

A few minutes later, a sweet-faced, middle-aged man with spiked, white-blond hair, sporting one dangling garnet earring in the shape of a cross, came by to hand me a program, a makeshift affair typed on a sheet of orange paper. When I saw what was on it, I jammed my hand back into my pocket and gulped down the last three antacids in the roll: "Advanced Script Analysis Workshop II: Scenes From Shakespeare's Comedies." The comedies. I *hate* comedy.

And, contrary to what I'd been told, Ophelia was not "playing major roles in several scenes." She was only in the very last one: from *The Taming of the Shrew*, with Ophelia as the shrew herself, Kate.

I endured a sampler of *A Midsummer Night's Dream*, *The Comedy of Errors*, *The Merchant of Venice*, and *All's Well That Ends Well* (it did not). I figured all this depressing good humor was worth it, though, for the chance to see Ophelia on the stage. It was time for her entrance.

In a medieval gown the color of wine, she really could

have been Shakespeare's Dark Lady, wild hair cascading over bare shoulders. She was a bonny Kate, the prettiest Kate in Christendom, a super-dainty Kate, the babe of Padua. *Straight and slender and as brown in hue/ As hazel nuts and sweeter than the kernels.*

She was also a Kate who couldn't act her way out of a paper bag. Oh, *God.*

So this explained why the beautiful Ophelia Lomond hadn't managed to land a part in ten and a half years — that, and not being willing to sleep her way to the top despite her amazing potential for success in that area. It didn't have anything to do with her racially ambiguous appearance or her freaky Scottish-Sadillan heritage, plaid kilts and coconuts. I don't even like Shakespeare's comedies, but part of me wanted to leap onstage to keep her from murdering them.

Why had no one, in ten and half years, sat this woman down and told her she couldn't act? Well . . . for the same reason that I wasn't going to: Fear that she wouldn't be able to take it, fear that she would simply leave and go find someone who would tell her what she wanted to hear. It wouldn't be hard to find that guy. No one would ever tell her, including me. There will never be such a thing as reality for a babe this hot.

I was clean out of antacids, and almost out of time. The scene she and her Petruchio were doing — he was good, I think I'd seen him on *CSI: Miami* — was nearly over. I decided to head backstage. The door to the communal dressing room was wide open. Makeshift curtains provided the only privacy for actors changing out of costume. It appeared that most of them had already done so and had returned to observing the annoying rites of the First Church of Notice Me.

I did not see Ophelia among them. Then, the full, wine-colored skirt of the Kate costume came flying over the top of one of the curtains followed by a starched white petticoat, then the embroidered bodice. Ophelia appeared from behind the curtain, wearing a white T-shirt, hopping from leg to leg as she struggled to zip up her skinny jeans. She was barefoot and bra-less. "Ken!" she said, surprised, as she caught sight of me. "You made it. Thanks for coming. How . . . how are you?"

"I'm perfectly fine. Hey, congratulations on your performance."

"Thanks!" she grinned. "Hang on for a second while I find my shoes." Gracefully, Ophelia dropped to her knees among the discarded costumes, looking as though she'd just tumbled out of some gondola into a sea of Elizabethan laundry. She located her shoes, a pair of little white sneakers, then slipped them on without bothering to untie them first. "Okay, ready to go! What have you got there, a copy of the plays? That's real dedication."

I'd forgotten I was still holding the sonnets. "It's . . . a little Shakespeare, yes. But not *Shrew*. As you know, I tend to prefer the tragedies – unless, of course, you are performing. Uh . . . a drink? Frozen yogurt?" I immediately regretted this. Like you can tell a woman she's your Dark Lady over *frozen yogurt*.

"Sure, either," she said. "Let's just walk, and we'll see. Bye, Alan, you were great, as always!" She gave a quick hug to her Petruchio — at that moment caught between centuries in tights, doublet, and a CSI baseball cap — and we headed out the stage door.

As we strolled down desolate Hollywood Boulevard, it quickly became clear that we could get a tattoo, a big pink wig, or a hooker of either sex — but there was no frozen yogurt to be found. And we'd have had to walk at least a mile west before we could find a place I could buy Ophelia a drink that didn't also offer Live Nude Girls.

"I'm sorry, maybe this was a bad idea," I apologized.

"Don't worry about it," she replied gaily. "I'm not really hungry. I haven't wound down from the performance yet. Thanks again for coming. I mean, I know this wasn't very polished. We didn't have much time to rehearse, but I thought it might give you some idea of what I can do."

"It . . . did."

"Well, since every place is closed, maybe we could do one of my favorite things," she offered shyly. "We could walk a few more blocks to Grauman's Chinese Theatre, and stand in the footprints. You know, to see which stars have our same size feet."

"Uh . . . okay." This activity was going to mean more to her than it was to me. These days, those stars are for sale. But if that's what she wanted, we'd play tourist on Hollywood Boulevard. "Yeah, sure, why not? Let's do it."

We were now standing in the dark, just outside the over-the-top, Oriental-neon facade of Grauman's Chinese, just down the block from the Hollywood and Highland complex, home to the Academy Awards and some Cirque du Soleil thing that had died prematurely. "I want to apologize for thinking that   you   were   just   trying to . . . well, you know what I'm saying. The casting couch scenario. I'm really, truly, thoroughly sorry," Ophelia said. "I try to give all men the chance to be different, but it's happened to me one too many times."

"Don't give me too much credit. I love the casting couch scenario," I admitted. "But it's like you said — if you were sleeping the way to the top, you'd be there. Come on. Let's see who's got your feet."

Ophelia laughed as she stepped forward. Her white sneaks completely covered the deep, square holes, one smaller and one bigger, left by tiny platform shoes once worn by Carmen Miranda. "I think the only person who still has feet as small as these old movie stars is Jazzminn Jenks."

I laughed, too. "Unless she's wearing those damn giant bunny slippers. It's enough to give you nightmares, to think about a pink rabbit that big."

"I know. But that's how I got my job. I went to the interview in bunny slippers. Jazzminn thought it was funny. I really don't have a very good sense of humor, but for once it worked. Aren't you going to try this? Everybody tries it."

"Not into it," I said. "I've never really been star-struck. Maybe it's because I was raised here. Never had the acting bug in high school, either, even though everybody else in my class was always waiting to be discovered. I was captain of the swim team instead. I love the water. Oceans, lakes, rivers, drinking fountains, I don't care. I was a lifeguard at Zuma Beach for three summers in a row."

"Well, I had the acting bug since elementary school — pre-school, even. I spent every minute I could onstage. I don't know why, really. Maybe it's because I can't swim."

"How can you not be able to swim? You grew up on a tropical island."

"I just can't, that's all," she said sharply. Abruptly, she changed the subject. "Come on. Try John Wayne."

"No. Let's keep walking. I don't like standing in a dead guy's footprints."

She put her hand on my shoulder. "Of course, honey. I understand."

My stomach started to hurt again, worse than it did during Ophelia's performance of *Shrew*. I turned my back on her so she wouldn't see me bite down hard inside my lower lip. "It's got nothing to do with my . . . rapidly improving health situation," I said. "I'd just rather watch his movies than see empty holes in cement."

"Of course. Me too. John Wayne is much better than his

footprints. He . . . always looked so comfortable on a horse." She was vainly attempting to soothe. She walked around so she was standing in front of me again. "Um . . . so . . . where do you live, Ken? What part of town? Are you . . . married or anything? I don't see a ring."

"I rent a condo near the Beverly Center. And . . . no, I'm not married. Or anything. I was living with someone until recently but . . . it didn't work out. We had . . . different goals. How about you?"

"I'm not married either. I'm divorced. I was . . . married to another actor, when I was very young. A wonderful, wonderful actor."

Ophelia probably wondered why this news suddenly made me groan and drop to my knees, right there in John Wayne's footprints. The sonnets fell from my hand onto the grimy sidewalk as I covered my face with my hands. Usually I was good at taking it, pain — but this time it just hurt too damned much. Not surprisingly for Hollywood Boulevard, no one turned to look, too busy watching the break-dancers and the unemployed actors dressed as the characters from *Star Wars*.

"Oh, my gosh, are you all right? Let me help you," Ophelia fluttered around me like an agitated hummingbird. "Should I call an ambulance to take you to emergency? Oh, no, I left my phone at the theater . . ."

"Just hand me the book," I said through gritted teeth.

"What?"

"Shakespeare. Give me Shakespeare."

"Oh. Gosh. That's odd. Okay." Ophelia crouched beside me and picked up the sonnets. Still on my knees, I took my hands away from my face and held them out to her. "Now open it, and put it in my hands."

"All right . . . oh my gosh. What page?"

"I don't care. Just do it. Please."

Her own hands shaking, Ophelia handed me the little paperback, open to Sonnet 29.

"When in disgrace with Fortune and men's eyes, / I alone beweep my outcast state, / and trouble deaf heaven with my bootless cries," I read aloud, my voice pinched with pain.

"What??"

"Shut up, Ophelia. 'And look upon myself, and curse my fate, / Wishing me like to one more rich in hope, / Featur'd like him, like him with friends possess'd'" . . .

"Give me your phone. I'm dialing 911."

"No! *'Desiring this man's art, and that man's scope, / With what I most enjoy content least;* ' . . ." I was beginning to breathe easier, although I'm pretty sure by now Ophelia wasn't breathing at all.

"It's not the plays. It's the sonnets," she murmured.

Yes, it was the sonnets. Ah, Shakespeare, *thy medicine on my lips.* I lifted my tear-filled eyes and said the next lines of Sonnet 29 directly to Ophelia. *"Yet in these thoughts myself almost despising, / Haply I think on thee, and then in my state, / Like to the lark at break of day arising / From sullen earth, sings hymns at heaven's gate."*

There was still pain, but now I was able to stand, to rise from sullen earth. By chance — Fate? — She'd opened to one of my favorite sonnets. No way was I going to say that final golden couplet on my knees in John Wayne's footprints.

"For thy sweet love remember'd such wealth brings / That I scorn to change my state with kings."

I don't know if I said the couplet aloud or just heard it in my mind, but it worked. Everything was going to be okay — although I realized, looking at Ophelia's panicked face, that I'd have to wait for a more opportune time to pitch the Dark Lady concept. "I'm all right, Ophelia," I said calmly. "It was just a cramp or something. It's gone. But maybe we should call it a night."

"You read a sonnet," she said, wonderingly.

"Yeah. Weird, huh?" I felt my face flush red. "It was just something to concentrate on. Like a mantra. Could have been a grocery list. Could have been anything. Biofeedback technique."

"Do you always carry sonnets around with you?"

"Just a coincidence, although I may have told you I'm very fond of Shakespeare," I said. "Come on. Let's go. I'll walk you to your car."

"I'll drive you home. I can't let you drive tonight."

"It's over. I'm fine." Christ, how often do people with cancer have to tell other people that they're fine? I'd said it more in the past few months than ever in my whole life before. "I'm fine. Let's go."

We walked back to the Lana Bishop Theatre in silence, she carefully averting her eyes, me concentrating on the business of remaining upright. I wasn't entirely successful. The Dark Lady of the Sonnets, strolling bra-less down the Hollywood Walk of Fame with the hunchbacked King Richard the Third.

We reached the tiny parking lot behind the Lana Bishop Theatre. The only car left in it was my Mercedes. "Hey, where's your car?" I asked.

"I . . . parked it someplace else," she said vaguely. "Close by. Anyway, Ken, I have to go inside before I go home, to get the Kate costume so I can take it to the cleaners. And I have to look for my bra. The dressing room was such a mess I couldn't find it after the show."

"Really? Didn't notice."

Ophelia folded her arms across her chest, hunching her shoulders. "I don't want to sleep with you. I want to *help* you," she teased. She had butchered Shakespeare, but she did a pretty good imitation of me, I thought. "But I guess this is a sign that you are feeling a little better, I hope? Go on home, Ken.

You're exhausted."

"I'll walk you to your car first." As bad as I felt, I wasn't about to let the most beautiful woman in the world stroll down Hollywood Boulevard alone at night without a bra.

"No," she returned quickly. "There's still a night watchman in the building, he always walks me. I'd feel better if you just get on the road. And promise me you won't drive too fast. You drive way too fast, Ken. That day we drove to Spago you almost got us both killed."

"I won't," I lied. Actually, my plan was to drive so fast that I'd get home before I had time to get into an accident. "And I'm sorry I almost killed you. Well, if you're sure somebody's here, I'll take off. And I'll touch base with the comedy people tomorrow about your career options. I've got a good vibe about this. I really do."

"Don't worry about my career. Just take care of yourself." Ophelia unfolded her arms, which made me very happy for a couple of seconds there. "Good night, Ken. Thanks again for coming to my play."

CHAPTER EIGHT

Ain't been to a movie since 1965. Don't like them things, except *The Sound of Music.*

—Nettie Mae Easley

I'm not moderately aroused anymore. I'm moderately terrified.

I came to Teru Sushi on Ventura Boulevard for lunch with a suit — I mean, a creative executive — today. His name is Todd, he's thirty-five, his left eyebrow is pierced, he's lost four pounds in three days on the Raw Diet, and he tells me that he does something very important for HBO. I'm sure that's true — but I confess I didn't come here because I wanted to hear about his upward trajectory in the cable world. Instead I was here eating sushi — a food I don't really get, it's just too small — in a frantic attempt to return to normal, to try to make things feel the same as they had before, even though I'm sure they never will again, not ever.

At first it was . . . interesting to feel sorry for Ken. A few tears, a twinge of heartache. Not painful, just a sensation. A 3.2, not a 6.7. It was a tragedy, but not really . . . *tragic*, if that makes any sense. But I wasn't ready for this, not this restless, relentless monster that my sympathy has turned into. Now, it feels like I'm the only one in the room with someone who's choking on something, someone who is depending on me to reach my hand down his throat, through phlegm and tonsils, and pull it out — because I'm the only one who knows it's in there.

I'm not brave enough for this. I'm beautiful — not brave. I wish he hadn't told me. I wish I didn't know there was a Ken Harrison, creative executive, dying of cancer in Hollywood. I just realized something: I've never lost my appetite before.

I wanted to be brave though, I really did. I just didn't know how. So I had to tell someone, even if it was Todd of HBO. Luckily, men on the Raw Diet are a little easier to handle than the others; they just don't seem to have the same urges. So I was able to distract Todd from my breasts for long enough to talk about it. I decided to pretend that Ken's sad story was an idea for a script. I don't like lying, but it just didn't seem right for me to tell Todd something that Ken couldn't even admit to himself.

Todd wrinkled his nose as he twiddled his chopsticks in the wasabi. "You want my input? Don't have the guy die. It's a downer," he said. "Besides, you're a woman. Don't try to do men. Do a chick flick. Hey, ever see *Bridget Jones's Diary*? Maybe you could do that, except black, I mean, you're, like, black or something, right? Two of her friends should be white, though. I'll bet you could write something like that. "

"I can't change the story. He *is* dying." My voice caught as I said it.

"Not if you want to sell your script he's not."

"That doesn't make sense — people die in movies all the time. Isn't it always about murder?"

Todd perked up instantly. "Oh yeah, murder's okay." He nodded happily. "Murder's good. People love murder. Yeah —

put in a murder. That's different than *death*. Nobody wants to go there."

"Why?"

"Not why: who," Todd nodded sagely. "I mean, you could do a why, but then it gets too complicated. You'll lose people. It'll be a lot easier if you do a who. Make the why something real easy. Sex, or money, or both. Then you can do a who committed the murder, not a why."

Now it was my turn to wrinkle my nose, although I stopped almost immediately because it was giving Todd an erection. After awhile you can tell without looking. There's a miniscule change in facial expression, a glazed look in the eye, a sudden fidgety and disproportionate concern for the placement of the napkin.

"That wasn't what I meant. What I meant was, why do people love murder?" I demanded. "It's still death, isn't it?"

"Yeah, but murder's not about dying. It's about killing. Killing works — not dying."

"But why?"

For Todd's inability to explain this I suppose can only blame my own nose, so thoughtlessly, carelessly wrinkled. "Just trust me — you'll never sell your project if the dude dies," he said, staring with studied interest into his own lap. "Have somebody kill him. Or have him kill somebody. Doesn't matter. Bring in some CSI's and let them solve the case. Do murder."

Do murder. Let's do lunch, let's do murder. I felt weak and cold, hearing it. Todd continued to nod and fiddle with his napkin until his smart phone buzzed and slithered on the table. Just before he grabbed it, he licked his thin lips and whispered, "Oh yeah — and make that girl you mentioned, his friend, really, really hot."

CHAPTER NINE

Methinks it is like a weasel.

— Hamlet, *Hamlet*

"Hi, Ken!" Dan said, his voice a blend of good cheer and sheer panic. "Glad you could make it. How's it going over in Movies and Minis?"

It was probably some warped sense of guilt that led Danny Gordon to invite me to tonight's little party, celebrating the arbitrary milestone of *Bite Me* winning its time slot for ten weeks in a row. Also arbitrary was the theme: The whole place was decorated with brightly-colored piñatas, sombreros, serapes, maracas; portable steam tables stood laden with tacos, enchiladas, frijoles, guacamole. Everything needed for a Mexican fiesta — except, insofar as I could tell, Mexicans.

Then again, maybe I was only here because Danny hadn't bothered to check to see who was still on the A-list. There were people here who got fired from the show way before I did.

I sipped a non-alcoholic margarita from a disposable plastic glass shaped like a cactus. I desperately wanted a real drink, but was afraid mixing tequila with my awesome daily pharmaceutical intake might cause a nuclear meltdown somewhere in Eastern Europe. Dan was standing alone in a corner, trying to pick the cheese off a taco. "I'm doing great. Feeling great. On a movie with Tyne Daly," I said. "In fact, I can only stay a minute. I'm meeting her for dinner at the Ivy."

"I heard about the movie. See, I knew you'd be great for them when they do — well, you know."

I took another sip of my fangless margarita. "Say, I've got a question for you, Dan."

"Go."

"Well, I happened to meet a terrific young talent the other day — an actress. I really believe she's going to be major. I was thinking she might be great for a guest role on *Bite Me*."

"Yeah? What's her name?"

"Ophelia."

"Tell her to change that. What's she been in?"

"I . . . think most of her work has been in the theater. I saw her in a Shakespeare play in Hollywood the other night. Comedy."

"Hmm." Danny considered this. "That sounds like something DeMarco would go for. He likes to work with unknowns." This I knew. DeMarco's ego couldn't handle *knowns*. "And he also likes to think he appreciates theater, and Shakespeare is definitely A-list . . ." Danny continued to ponder. "We are starting to run out of new women for his character to date. What does she look like?"

"I think she's . . . oh, mid-twenties," I said. "And beyond that, gorgeous is all you need to know."

"Well, tell me more anyway. We don't want to use a girl who looks just like someone he's already dated on the show."

"Trust me — she doesn't."

"Tell me," Dan insisted." Well, I guess she's about five-five, slim, great figure, long, curly brown hair, amazing eyes.

She's sort of . . . exotic. She's from a small, Caribbean island."
Caribbean? That means . . . black, right?" I shrugged. "Yeah, I
guess so. I think she said she's half-Scottish. I guess she's sort
of . . . I don't know. And her eyes are . . . I don't know what
color they are, either. She's hard to categorize. I still think
gorgeous is the best description."

"Well, *Ken*," Dan fretted. "I mean, sure, I guess we could
have DeMarco go out with somebody who's, you know . . . not
white or whatever, but we couldn't just *do* it, we'd have to do
something, you know, *about* it. Not that I have a problem with
doing something *about* it, it's not like we don't do shows *about*
things, it's just that this is the Wednesday night comedy block.
I mean if he went out with her once, that's fine, but more is
really kind of too *cable* for us right now, do you know what I'm
saying? *Distracting*. If this was drama it would easy, we could
just kill her, but our Wednesday comedy lineup is too
important. We can't *risk*. Besides, if we were going to do
something *about* something, I don't think we'd do it with
someone who's, you know, *half* anything because then . . . how
do you know what it's *about*?"

Hello, my name is Ken Harrison, and I work in an industry
where we actually have conversations like this. Although, let's
be fair to Dan, I can't promise you that somewhere during my
years in TV I have not presented an equally absurd argument.
They call it "chemo brain;" my memory has been chemically
Swiss cheesed. Maybe I played the cello. Maybe I was good.

As usual, Danny was continuing when there was no further
need to speak. "We have to make sure our viewers know what
we're trying to *say*. Remember way back in the late '80s, when
they all tried those 'dramedies,' but viewers couldn't figure out
why a half-hour show didn't have a laugh track? How else do
you know when to laugh? And was it comedy, or drama?
People wanted to *know*. Learn from *history*, Ken. I'm just

saying, we don't want to confuse people, particularly not after ten weeks of winning our time slot."

"Just like you don't want your comedy writers to feel bad, right, Danny?" I asked, my voice as frosty as my non-margarita. "Well, you listen to me. I've got to say there's something that feels real actionable about the fact that you pushed me out of the comedy department, where I was a vice president, to Movies and Minis, where my title has dropped to development director, just because I have a . . . situation. Now, if you can't get Ophelia on the show as Bert DeMarco's latest squeeze, then you'd better get those sensitive writers of yours to sit down in a hurry and write a script where an astonishing Caribbean beauty comes into the veterinary office carrying a goddamned ferret with diabetes or you'll be talking to my attorney. Do I make myself clear?"

"I thought we had the whole transfer thing all settled, Kenny," Dan said, wounded. "We *talked*. Everything is *fine*. You're having dinner with *Tyne*. At the *Ivy*. Who *is* this woman, anyway?"

I gulped down the rest of my margarita. Margarita: lime Gatorade with Kosher salt around the edge. "Just make it happen, Dan," I said — then, turning my back on Dan and his cheeseless taco, I walked out.

CHAPTER TEN

Words, words, words.

— Hamlet, *Hamlet*

STEWART

Tell me, how are you feeling after your stem cell transplant, Janice?

JANICE

Oh, a little tired, I guess. But the doctors just gave me the good news – Stewart, I'm . . . I'm going to live!

STEWART

Thank God! I thought I was going to lose you. Hey, don't ever let me talk about divorce again, do you promise?

JANICE

I promise. You know, Stewart, I think I can walk if you help me. For once in our lives, shall we do this thing . . . together?

Tyne Daly stars as Janice in the very special TV film *A*

Matter of Months.

I read the script over the pale dinner of turkey breast and ginger ale I'd purchased at a Ralphs supermarket on my way home from the network lot. I always went to the Ralphs in West Hollywood, the nearest one to my new apartment, only a couple of miles away. It's known as "the gay Ralphs," since it's on Santa Monica Boulevard, right in the middle of the gay bar scene, in the heart of Boys Town. Nobody means anything by it; it's just so you'll know which Ralphs.

By the way, just because I work in TV doesn't mean I don't know my punctuation. There *is* no apostrophe in Ralphs. Maybe there's two gay guys named Ralph in charge, the Ralphs. I don't know what the deal is. Anyway, it's convenient, and they've got a good selection of soups.

I visited the gay Ralphs a lot — partly for something to do, partly because these days, I can only carry one bag of groceries at a time. I also didn't want to stay in the store for too long at a stretch, because walking through the frozen foods section made my teeth chatter. And there's only so long you can warm up around the hot barbecued foods before you have to move out of the way, so someone can get a chicken.

Pre-cooked turkey breast, popsicles, white bread, canned noodle soup, ginger ale, Jell-O. Maybe a new shape of plain pasta for a thrill. No food that held an opinion.

According to the script, two days after her stem cell transplant, the weak but smiling Tyne Daly, her head wrapped in colorful silk scarf, was going to get up — get up — and walk — walk!!! — with her completely trashed immune system, down a germ-filled hospital corridor, arm in arm with her husband, to face a new, divorce-free, cancer-free day. By the next morning, they'd probably be roller-blading on the Venice boardwalk. The scene would definitely be included in the sizzle reel.

I grabbed a pen and started scribbling a new scenario for the writers. Just a few suggestions and notes.

> Two days following her stem-cell transplant, Janice lays mumbling and delirious, teeth chattering, IV tubes pumping fluids and antibiotics into a body wracked with fever. She feels that she is drowning in the phlegm that rattles up from wasted lungs. Medical personnel, wearing sterile surgical suits and masks for fear that everyday bacteria might touch off some rampant infection, think nothing of wandering in to discuss her prognosis, assuming she cannot hear.
>
> She will lie in this critical state for more than three weeks, allowing no one to take it out of her swollen hands: The Complete Works of William Shakespeare.
>
> He is particularly humiliated by a visit from his sixty-five-year-old mother, who drove up from her home in Leisure World — a retirement community for active seniors near San Diego — after reading his e-mail detailing the perils of an autologous stem cell transplant, a last-ditch effort to save his life. She wanted to make sure, if the worst transpired, she would have no regrets about failing to say good-bye.
>
> But Mom does not come into the room alone. With her is her new husband, Douglas, quite a few years younger. Mom married Douglas shortly after Dad, a longtime employee in the Disney Studios marketing department, died suddenly of a heart attack while walking to his retirement party on the studio lot. Dropped dead, right there at the intersection of Mickey Avenue and Dopey Drive.
>
> If he could but speak, he would have said: "Hi, Mom — and hello to you, too, Uncle Douglas, thank you and your potentially life-threatening assortment of personal bacteria for stopping by." Because Mom's new husband, Douglas, is also Dad's younger brother, Douglas.

From the horrified look above the surgical mask, I could tell that Uncle Doug remembered his nephew — stepson — as a carefree, sandy-haired Valley kid on a skateboard, cutting class and making out, not a moaning, writhing bald man in his mid-thirties, who might actually be fairly attractive if he wasn't coughing up blood.

Janice's throat is too dry to speak. But if she could get any words at all to emit from her cracked lips, she would tell Stewart, and Mom, and Uncle Douglas, in no uncertain terms, to screw themselves.

Then I threw my notes away. I was not going to risk being kicked out of another network department for making the writers feel bad. I knew what they wanted to hear. If nothing else, my visit from Mom and Uncle Douglas — "Don't worry, nobody's expecting you to call me *Dad*" — had taught me the best way to handle this story. I wrote across the top of the final page of the script: "Realistic and inspiring. I cried."

I jumped when the phone rang. It was Dan Gordon. From the tone of his voice, my guess was this was the last time he'd ever speak to me.

"Good afternoon, Kenneth," he said. "I met with Bert DeMarco and the *Bite Me* staff this morning, and there are several uncast parts in an episode we're filming in a few weeks. The story is: Bert's met this great new woman, and she's dropped by the veterinary clinic at lunchtime with a bottle of champagne and nothing on under her coat except a red lace teddy. Bert wants desperately to nail her right there in the office. But he's inundated with people who are bringing in their pets for various emergencies. The place is full of animals, but they keep trying to find someplace where they can do it without being interrupted. It's quite a funny script. We think your friend could be one of the people with a pet. They're all speaking parts. Please tell me she gets along with cats."

"Sure. Cats are definitely down with her." I figured they had to be, unless they were stupid cats. "This sounds perfect. Thanks, Dan. I really appreciate this, man. I don't want to go into it, but I owe her a favor."

"Well, she's going to have to come in before I can make any promises. She doesn't have to read — I'm going to be honest, any idiot could do this part — but Bert has approval over all casting. It's up to Bert. But he seems excited about meeting your exotic hottie. Ten minutes. Can she do that?"

"Of course, she can come in." I was thrilled. "But, Dan, I'd just as soon not get in the middle of this. It's your show now. Besides, I'm just *crazed* today with work. Do you mind having your assistant give her a call? She's right on the lot. She works for Jazzminn Jenks."

I wanted the ball back in Ophelia's court. I knew I'd made her uncomfortable the night before on Hollywood Boulevard — to put it mildly — but I figured I'd get a thank-you of some kind for this one, even if she thought I was a serial killer. *Bite Me* is, after all, the anchor of the Wednesday night comedy block.

"She works for Jazzminn Jenks? Cool. Sure, we'll touch base. Let me put Catharine on the line. She'll take down the info and get it taken care of. So, Kenny . . . I assume this means I'm not going to be hearing from any lawyers this week?"

"No lawyers," I agreed. "Thanks again, Dan. Didn't mean to be such a prick yesterday. You understand . . . things are a little hard right now."

"I understand," Dan said. "Now, I've got to run, I've got a doctor's appointment." He paused, then lowered his voice — friends again. "I've got this, I don't know, this tickle in my throat I can't get rid of, and I'm feeling a little run down, I don't know how to describe the feeling, just kind of — ugh.

Hey, Kenny . . . what were your symptoms, you know . . . before you found out you . . . had it?"

"A throat tickle? Run down?" I asked, with a sharp intake of breath. "Good God, Dan. I really don't want to say anything, but I'd suggest you hurry to this appointment, right now. Go — quickly! Fly like the wind. I'll hold for Catharine. But — don't worry. I'm sure it's nothing."

I heard a little gasp, and then Danny was gone. I know, I shouldn't have done that. *Should* I?

CHAPTER ELEVEN

**One thing you can say,
The girl's got good hair.**

— Nettie Mae Easley

I had just squeezed my eyes shut and raised the scissors to my long, curly brown hair, sweat dampening my forehead as I brought the open blades up close to my scalp — when a low level functionary from the comedy department phoned on behalf of a Mr. Gordon to inform me that I had been cast in my network television debut as Woman with Cat #2 on TV's top-rated prime time comedy, *Bite Me*. Working episode title: "The Heavy Petting Zoo."

I said thank you very much, complimented him on his excellent telephone diction, then hung my head and lowered my scissors to my lap. Why cut my hair now? I thought as my tears dripped onto the shining blades; I might as well just cut my throat.

Besides, without my hair I seriously doubt that I'd get to keep the part. And I should cut off all my hair right now for even thinking a thing like that.

I'll bet Ken lost all of his sandy hair when he went through chemotherapy, even though it's nice and thick now. The hair falls out because chemo attacks the hair follicles. I've read that, it's a scientific fact. Ken never told me that he went through chemotherapy, but I'm sure they tried everything to save him at Cedars Sinai Hospital. It's supposed to be the best, all the stars have their surgery at Cedars. But, no — I didn't plan to cut off my hair out of sympathy. I was going to chop it all off because my hair is much, much too pretty for such an ugly world. I hate my hair.

Anyway, my shorn head wouldn't have mattered one whit to him because here was the other part of my plan: Never, ever to see Ken Harrison again.

I'd thought it over — and over, and over. It was all a mistake, our meeting on the set of *Really, Girlfriend?* a twisted twist of Fate. But I'm the one who twisted it even more, tangled it into a knot. I could have, should have just given him my last banana-coconut smoothie and walked away.

I forgive myself for accepting his lunch invitation. I didn't know, and I was too upset by the end to remember to offer to pick up the check – as if that would make things better. But even after I knew, I said yes. I accepted his help. Sure, since you're dying anyway, there's no real reason why you shouldn't use your power as a white male creative executive at a Big Three network to get me a bit part on a sitcom first, is there? Yes, that's exactly what I said, although not in so many words. I only wanted to make him feel better, but I used him. The thing I hate most about Hollywood, and I did it.

I haven't been sleeping. That's unusual for me. I can sleep anywhere, even on transatlantic flights, right through the movie. Now I bounce around all night, snacking. I can eat, but I can't sleep. I don't know what's true anymore. I only know that the phone rang two seconds before I chopped off all my curly brown hair, and that now, right or wrong, I am Woman with Cat #2 on the top-rated comedy *Bite Me*, the anchor of the Wednesday night comedy block.

And I know that, at least one more time, I will see Ken Harrison again. That makes me happy. I think.

CHAPTER TWELVE

What's in a name?

— Juliet, *Romeo and Juliet*

My plan was working better than I could have hoped. I'd have to send Danny something — maybe some cheese, and a get-well card. Of course, I would have been more excited about this if I wasn't so pissed at Ophelia I couldn't see straight.

As I predicted, my role in engineering Ophelia's biggest acting coup to date was rewarded with a thank-you. And not just a phone call — that afternoon, she stopped by my office to tell me the news in person, pretty as a Disney songbird in a canary yellow dress. Our assistant, Donald, escorted her directly to my office, even though she had no appointment. He'd been bitchy lately because he was studying for the California bar but was suddenly all smiles for Ophelia, who had encouraging words about his new tie.

"The head of the comedy department called me on Monday morning, and I ran right over to meet Bert DeMarco," she bubbled as she stood, beaming, in my doorway. "I don't know what's wrong with my cat yet — I find out when I see the script. I hope it's nothing serious. I only have one line, but Bert wants to have lunch with me next week to discuss my character arc. Isn't that great? Thank you, thank you, thank you!"

"You're welcome," I said coolly, barely looking up from the script I was reading. I did not ask her to come in or sit down.

Ophelia was taken aback by my chilly response. "Anyway, Ken . . . I was hoping I could invite you out to lunch this week, you know, just to show you how grateful I am — but you look . . . very busy." She took a couple of steps backward into the hallway while tying her fingers into a knot. "It looks like I picked a bad time. Maybe I should go."

"No, actually, I'd like you to stay for a moment." This time, my voice dropped from cool to sub-zero. I set the script aside, and removed my glasses. "Please, have a seat. And, if you wouldn't mind — close the door behind you."

Hesitantly, she closed the door, then perched on the edge of one of the two chairs in front of my desk. "Yes, Ken?" She licked her lips.

"Water? You look a bit thirsty." I poured her a glass from the stainless steel pitcher that always stood on the cabinet to my left, just below the television, the DVD player and the relic VCR no one had ever removed. I always kept water on hand in case a writer started to choke, which happened often. She nodded warily as her delicate fingers closed around the glass.

"Well, Ophelia, I'm not sure if I have room in my schedule to do a lunch for the next little while — things are just *crazed* — but since, I think we would both agree, I did you a fairly sizeable favor last week, I'm wondering if I might impose on you with a small request."

"Sure, Ken!" She smiled. I did not. Her smile faded.

"I'm planning a little vacation, and as you know, I have to

move fairly quickly on this sort of thing these days. I'd like to make some reservations right away. I'm thinking of heading for the Caribbean."

"The Caribbean," she repeated, mystified. "Uh . . . nice."

"Yes. So I hear. And I've got to say, your description of Sadilla intrigued me. I'm thinking of going there. I'm very excited about it, really. What do you think?"

Ophelia looked startled — then frowned. "Sadilla? Well, it's . . . not much of a tourist destination. It's just a little fishing island. Just sand, and fish. No good restaurants, or clubs, or decent hotels. No airport — you'd have to get there by boat, unless you've got access to a private plane. And . . . since you're a swimmer, it's only fair to let you know that, since I left, they've developed a serious sea urchin problem. The beaches are covered with 'em. Poisonous, you know."

"I have sandals," I replied pleasantly. "So, I'm trying to get oriented here. Bear with me. Is Sadilla further to the east or to the west?"

"Uh . . . west."

"So, in other words, it's closer to Trinidad than to the Caymans. Am I right?"

"Absolutely! By the way . . . the weather is horrible there this time of year."

"Is it?" I asked, leaning forward intently. "Well, tell me something, Ophelia. I'm stumped. How the hell can the weather be horrible on an island that doesn't exist? Tell me that. How???"

Ophelia jumped up from her chair. "I have to go. You obviously . . . aren't feeling well." She held one hand up to look like a telephone receiver, waggled it, and offered me a weak smile. "Call me?"

"Stay right where you are." I jumped up from my seat, too. "Trinidad happens to be east of the Caymans. Southeast —

according to a world map that all any idiot has to do is *look at* to see there is no goddamned island of Sadilla anywhere in the whole fucking Caribbean Sea! No legendary sunsets, no fishing boats, no beautiful people with *catua* eyes. What kind of shit are you shoveling here, Ophelia?"

There was a long pause. Then: "You watch your language," Ophelia scolded.

"What?"

"You heard me. I don't like that kind of talk."

"Oh — sorry. I mean . . . what the fuck am I apologizing for? This is my fucking office. And — don't change the subject! I think you owe me an explanation. Why did you lie to me?"

"Fine. I'll tell you." With that, Ophelia sat back down in her chair, primly crossed her ankles, and folded her hands in her lap. She nodded in the direction of my chair, indicating that I was to have a seat as well. "May I have some more water, please?"

I sat down and poured her another glass — then one for myself. My head ached from cussing her out. "Okay, let's hear it." It came out as sort of a moan. "And fast because I've got a couple of writers coming in to pitch at three."

She sipped her water daintily, ignoring my request for haste. "Well, Ken, I don't think this should be too difficult for a smart executive like you to figure out. You know how hard it was to find a part for me on network television, even one line as Woman with Cat #2 — not that I don't appreciate it, Ken, I really do. We both know the deck is stacked against me. I just figured that deck is a little less stacked if I'm the exotic Ophelia Lomond from the tiny, beautiful island of Sadilla than . . ."

"Than . . . what?"

There was a long, long pause. "Than . . . Karen Watts, from Indianapolis, Indiana," she whispered.

"Karen Watts, from Indianapolis, Indiana," I repeated.
"Shhh!"

Well, it was shock enough to search the Internet for Sadilla
and find no references of any kind, not even on Trip Adviser.
Now, I was finding out there was no Ophelia Lomond, either.
The lilt of the Caribbean I'd loved so much in her voice was
actually . . . the twang of the urban industrial Midwest?

Without saying a word, I picked up the phone. A look of
panic crossed her face. "No, I'm not calling Bert DeMarco to
tell him you're not the island princess your resume makes you
out to be," I said. "I'm just going to ask my assistant to cancel
my pitch meeting. I get the feeling your story is going to be
way more interesting than anything those writers could come
up with." I put in a quick call to Donald. "Okay, Ophelia. I
want to hear it all. What else have you told me that isn't true?
What about Yale Drama School?"

"I graduated from Yale with a 3.9 average. Except I didn't
study drama, I majored in biology. And I wasn't on scholarship
— my parents paid the full tuition, as they are fond of
reminding me."

"I thought you said your parents were dead!"

"I also told you I lived on a tiny island called Sadilla!"
Ophelia — or whoever the hell she was — exclaimed. "My
parents are not at all dead. My dad is an ophthalmologist, and
my mother is a first-grade teacher. He's not from Scotland, and
she's not from the Caribbean. They're both from . . .
Cincinnati, originally."

"Cincinnati. I see. And . . . he's black and she's white, or
the other way around, right?"

Ophelia groaned. "The other way around. But except for
that, they're exactly the same — two Midwesterners who both
graduated from Oberlin College and then moved all the way
from Ohio to Indiana. That was the biggest adventure of their

lives. But out here, people keep saying I'm *exotic*. In fact, more than exotic — they act like I'm from another planet. I've had it. So I decided to invent my own island."

I thought about that for a moment. "Okay, you wanted an island. Wouldn't it have been easier to pick a real island?"

"I don't know. Probably. I just felt like starting from scratch. They're always talking about some superstar like Lady Gaga or Cher re-inventing herself — why shouldn't I? Frankly, I don't see that there's any difference between my island and Jazzminn Jenks's bottle-blond hair and plastic breasts. At least *I'm* real. And don't give me any shit about being ashamed of who I am, honey. Don't even start. This is strictly a career move. A-choo!"

"Hey — watch your language." There was that sneeze again. Defiance was so rare for Ophelia that she seemed to have an allergy to it. I was still pissed, but had to hide a smile at the calculating creativity of her story. And, listen, I'd be the first one in line to re-invent myself now if I could. "So, do your parents have a problem with your telling people that they were married by a Sadillan holy man and deep-sixed off a fishing boat?"

"They don't care as long as I come home for Thanksgiving. Every year I get snowed in at O'Hare Airport, waiting for my connecting flight. My parents said if it'd help me get a job, go for it. They've been dealing with this kind of crap a lot longer than I have. But I don't expect you to understand." She tossed her head, with no sneeze — beginning to enjoy her rebelliousness, or at least getting more used to it.

"Oh, believe me, I understand," I said coldly. I was angry, too. After all, I was now using the shiny gold name plate from my old office as a doorstop. "I'd give anything to go back to not understanding — but I understand. Let's just say the deck is stacked against *us*, shall we? It didn't used to be stacked against me, but now it is. And I know it's always been stacked against you, but unless you've been living under a rock since you came to Hollywood you know it's not as stacked as it would be if you weren't . . . you know . . . so . . . *stacked.*"

She was still staring at me, *catua* eyes sparkling with anger. Wait a second — *catua* eyes, my ass. Time to retire my Sadillan-English dictionary. But, I have to say, the fact that the word did not exist did not keep her eyes of many colors from being so very beautiful.

Then, slowly, her gaze softened. She furrowed her brow as she thought over what I'd said. "The only thing more incomprehensible than the statement you just made is the fact that . . . I think understand it," she said finally.

"You . . . do?"

"Yes, I do." She seemed awed by her own admission. "I understand you, Ken. I'm not sure I want to, either — but I do."

She . . . understood me? I didn't know whether to be elated or disappointed. These days, as I wandered sleepless through the small rooms of my rented condo, I realized I'd been getting a fair amount of comfort out of being misunderstood. It's one of the few things in this world you can do *better* when you have cancer, and I wasn't sure I was ready to give up the only real perk of this disease. This was getting way too complicated. God, why couldn't I just go back to staring at her tits?

She understood me.

"Let's just finish this up," I said, exhausted and vaguely nauseated by all this understanding. "You are divorced, correct?"

"Yes."

"And you told me you're thirty-two . . . how old are you, really?"

"Thirty-two. Really. I don't lie about my age."

"You don't have a problem with re-arranging the geography of the world between Jamaica and Barbados, but you don't lie about your *age*?"

"No, I don't." She seemed very proud of this.

"Well, if you want to get anywhere in this business, sweetheart, start. If you say you're thirty-two, they'll think you're thirty-seven. If you want them to think you're thirty-two, you have to say you're twenty-seven. There's an unspoken five-year rule, and I suggest you start observing it because, frankly, you are no spring chicken."

She nodded thoughtfully — unfazed by my bluntness, simply processing information. "Thanks for letting me know." Then she added, in a wail, "Don't you see, Ken? I don't know any of these rules, because I never get any parts. Now, my foot's in the door, just a little bit, thanks to you. I'm sorry I lied to you. Can you ever forgive me?"

Actually I'd forgiven her as soon as she walked in wearing that yellow dress, but I wasn't about to tell her that. "Let me think about it," I said, doing my best to sound hurt. "Ow — I definitely blame you for this headache." That was real. I put my cold glass of water against my hot forehead. "And, while I'm thinking about it, where did the name Ophelia Lomond come from?"

"Well, Lomond came from — that song about Scotland, you know, Loch Lomond."

"Oh, yeah, I forgot, your father is Sean Connery." I rolled my eyes. "And . . . Ophelia?"

"I don't really remember. It just seemed to come to me, in a dream one night. Maybe I fell asleep on my copy of *Hamlet* while I was at Yale or something. I just liked it."

"Okaaay. Slept with Hamlet." I jotted this down on a note pad, which made her laugh out loud. I laughed, too. "Anything else I should know?" No. You now have my whole story." She grinned, scanning my face anxiously at the same time. "And I sincerely apologize for lying to you. I . . . didn't really know you. You were just another Hollywood executive – until right now. Besides, I don't think of Ophelia as a lie exactly. She's more of a fantasy."

"Well, I lied to you, too — I wasn't *captain* of the swim team at North Hollywood High. My fantasy." I grinned back. "And I like the name Ophelia, too. I'm . . . fond of Shakespeare, as you know. Just the tragedies — I hate the comedies. In fact, I hate comedy in general. Ophelia is a very tragic name. I think I'll keep calling you that. You win, *Ophelia*. Your secret's safe with me — at least, for now." I paused for a long moment. "But I might have to ask you for something . . . in return."

"Sure! Name it."

"Not now. I'd like to talk about it later, if you don't mind. Some place private."

"My offer for lunch still stands."

"I was thinking . . . more private than a restaurant."

"Why don't you come to my place . . . for dinner? Is that private enough?"

That surprised me. "Sounds perfect," I replied, as coolly as I could. "Thank you, Ophelia. I'd like that very much."

"How about . . . Friday?"

"Fridays are bad for me. I'm usually *crazed* on Fridays." I have chemo on Fridays. "I could do Thursday or Sunday . . ."

"Sunday. It'll give me a chance to get the place in order. I live in Studio City. I've been working so much lately, what with the Shakespeare scenes. It's a wreck!"

I pictured the standard-issue L.A. actress apartment — small, colorful, near the 101 Freeway, north of Ventura Boulevard; exotic rugs, scented candles, in a 1962 two-story walkup with an algae-ridden pool and a dingbat name like Starlite Terrace or the Shangri-La. A lot of talk about moving out of the Valley soon, to someplace on the Westside. Perhaps a futon. "Don't worry about it. You should see where I live. My ex-girlfriend kept the beach house," I joked.

"Yes. Well . . . bye, Ken! I'll leave the address and directions with your assistant on my way out. I'll see you Sunday. Around seven. And — thanks again for everything."

"*Baloda*," I replied solemnly.

"Huh?"

"*Baloda*. That's Sadillan for 'You're welcome.'"

CHAPTER THIRTEEN

**O for a Muse of fire, that would ascend
The brightest heaven of invention**

— Chorus, *King Henry the Fifth*

Throughout the centuries, no scholar has been able to uncover the true identity of Shakespeare's Dark Lady. But, even without my Ph.D., I think it's safe to say she was not a breathtakingly bad biracial actress from Indianapolis, Indiana — a biology major with a 3.9 average, whose parents paid her Yale tuition and now planned to hold it over her head for the rest of her life. My Dark Lady got snowed in every Thanksgiving at O'Hare. This Karen Watts was about as exotic as a tuna casserole, and Sadilla was Fantasy Island. Maybe the beautiful *catua* eyes were contact lenses. After all, her Dad was an eye doctor. *Catua* contacts. I couldn't even think about it.

It had been a long, long weekend, and sleep would not come to steal me away from mine own company. Mine eyes would not shut up my thoughts. I paid for a lot of movies-on-demand.

And now, I had a new problem: I was lost. A sleepy, lost guy with cancer. I was trying to follow Ophelia's directions but had somehow made a wrong turn. I glanced over to my lamb's wool-covered passenger seat. I'd gotten her flowers, nice ones. Beside them lay the directions, scrawled by my assistant Donald. Half blind with studying for the bar, he'd probably made a mistake.

North on Laurel Canyon, taking the curves way too fast, right on Mulholland Drive, then left on Vista de la Vida, a quarter of a mile . . . well, this couldn't be right. Instead of apartments, all I saw were lavish, hillside homes with sweeping driveways and gated entrances, houses with six bedrooms and pools — and, you could guess, panoramic views of the city lights. I was up above the smog line, with clean air, coyotes, and people who threw parties with valet parking. I was right in front of 3768 Vista de la Vida, but . . . this couldn't be it, could it?

I pulled off the road, and reached into the back seat pocket for my ancient Thomas Brothers map, squinting at the page in the fading light, no GPS in this classic vehicle. This was it. No other, lower-rent end of Vista de la Vida existed anywhere else in Studio City. I turned into the long, long driveway of an enormous white house. Its stark, modern lines were softened by warm, golden oak trim. Hot-pink bougainvillea vines clambered everywhere. Frosted footlights studded the well-tended gravel path that crunched under my tires as I headed up towards the massive double doors of the front entrance.

I brought my convertible to a stop in a graveled area ringed with a semi-circle of squat, lush palms just to the left of the front door. Glittering strings of tiny lights wound around their thick trunks. Parked next to me was a shiny new red Jaguar XJ6 left at a careless, crooked angle, bearing the vanity license plate RGF123. No wonder Ophelia never left her car in the seedy lot behind the Lana Bishop Theatre.

The cool evening air carried the sharp sting of eucalyptus.

I clutched my flowers by their cellophane wrapper and stepped out of the car to find myself face to face with a large skunk. It stared at me — then, with a defiant flip of its silky, white-striped tail, lumbered off into the dark green ivy of the hills.

The wide double doors swung open and out popped Ophelia, in a slim, gray skirt and a clingy silk cardigan in the same bright color as the bougainvillea blooms. Diamond stud earrings, big ones, sparkled on her earlobes. She was barefoot — what was it with this woman and shoes?

"Hi, Ken!" she called out. "You made it. Did you have any trouble finding the place?"

"No," I croaked out. My recent short course in Shakespeare had left me no more articulate.

"Oh, good! I love living up here. This morning when I woke up, there was a deer peeking in my bedroom window." She stepped down off the porch as if to approach me, then winced after a few steps of bare feet on gravel. "Ouch, ouch, ouch," she grumbled good-naturedly, hopping back up on the porch. "You come this way instead, okay? Come on in. I think I left my shoes under the sofa."

I nodded dumbly, and followed her. By the time I got inside the two-story foyer, she'd slipped on some pretty black flats that she'd retrieved from somewhere. "For the TV star. Congratulations." I handed her the flowers, with an awkward peck on the cheek. She smiled, giving the mix of orchids, blue irises, and tiger lilies an appreciative sniff. Women always do that. "Thanks, Ken, you shouldn't have."

"How . . . how long have you lived here, Ophelia?" I asked as she led me into a sunken living room — exquisitely appointed with sofas, chairs, and oversized ottomans upholstered in soft, taupe suede. Floor-to-ceiling windows offered the predicted spectacular view beyond an inviting, steaming swimming pool — which, oddly enough, was completely round, ringed with Spanish tile. How do you know which is the shallow end in a round pool? And hell of a pool for a woman who could not swim. I couldn't take my eyes off it. "Great pool," I said, gesturing weakly.

"It is, isn't it? I picked out the tile from this wonderful big warehouse in Pasadena. They had every kind of tile you can imagine, from Mexico and Italy and Spain. I don't know how to swim, but I still love this pool. Do you . . . still swim?"

I shrugged. "I don't know. I don't know if I still swim. I haven't tried in a long time."

"Do you want to try now, before dinner? It's heated. The water is like a bathtub."

I shook my head. "I didn't bring my trunks." So what? Nobody up here but coyotes. And, of course, me. I don't have any issues with male nudity, but if that bothers you, while you swim, I could take my *Bite Me* script, go upstairs, and study my . . . line!" Ophelia burst into giggles. "Never mind the pool. Come on — I'll put these lovely things in some water and give you a quick tour. We have a few minutes. I don't think dinner is quite ready yet. Let's go see."

Apparently, Ophelia was not doing the cooking tonight. I could hear someone rattling around in the kitchen off the dining room. We walked into the airy, sky-lit space to find a lovely young woman with straight, shoulder-length black hair and bright pink cheeks, barefoot, wearing faded blue leggings and an oversized white blouse. She was fussing with a saucepan on a stove embedded in the speckled granite surface of a large center island, complete with a mesquite grill. She was almost as pretty as Ophelia, but not quite. I liked this kitchen.

"How's it coming, Lizzie?" Ophelia asked, hanging one arm lazily around the young woman's neck. "It smells yummy. Ken, this is Liz. She's in the film school at USC. One of her part-time jobs is cooking for me once in awhile, when I have guests. That is because I don't want to kill them." She laughed merrily. Liz laughed, too.

"Hey, Ken, nice to meet you." Liz gave me a penetrating look, probably interested to know what the guy with cancer looked like. Then she frowned into her saucepan. "I don't know if this is going to thicken, Ophelia."

"Hmmm." Ophelia peered over Lizzie's shoulder into the pot. "I don't know what it's supposed to look like."

I peered into the pan as well. "Just looks like it needs some time and a little more flour." They both looked at me in surprise. "I took a cooking class for single men a couple of years ago," I explained. "The last week, we did sauces."

"Single man says more flour!" Ophelia clapped her hands in mock command. She handed the flowers at Liz. "Pretty, yes? Ken is obviously a man of both culinary ability and good taste."

"I'm going to serve out by the pool — you think? I've got the heaters going, it should be nice," Liz said.

"Perfect. We'll be back."

Ophelia led me through the kitchen, then through a glass solarium with lots of delicate ficus trees and a white baby grand piano. We turned a corner into a smallish den. A big-screen television and lots of sleek, black AV equipment nestled into a wall of white oak shelving.

Along another wall were a number of professional-looking photographs, all different sizes, of a strikingly handsome black face, a face with a perfectly shaved bald head — a face that struck me as strangely familiar. I waited patiently for my memory to function. Oh, yeah, I knew who this was. "You a big Lakers fan?" I asked.

"No, I don't like basketball. I believe that too many young African American men aspire to be sports stars instead of considering careers in more practical fields. Personally I don't think there's anything better about, say, being a dentist than being a basketball star, but there are more *jobs*, right? It's not a wonderful fantasy, it's just heartbreaking. No. That's my ex-husband."

"Wade Stark is your ex-husband? *Wade Stark* of the Los Angeles Lakers?"

"No. They traded him to the Pistons last year, remember?"

I'd somehow missed this bit of sports news. But *which team* was hardly the point. "I thought you said your ex-husband was an actor."

"The actor was my second husband. His name was Carlos."

"Oh. So, you married Carlos the actor *after* Wade Stark."

"No. I married Wade after Carlos. Carlos is doing off-Broadway theater now."

I paused. "So, that would make Wade Stark . . . your *third* husband?"

"And absolutely the last, I promise! This is where I lived with Wade. I liked the house so much, he gave it to me. I think that was really nice of him, don't you? He's a great guy, despite being an unrealistic role model. We're still really good friends."

"Very nice. Very generous man, Mr. Stark." I found myself short of breath suddenly. "So . . . who was your first husband?"

"Ah. Arnie." She sighed. "He was a painter, and he was a homosexual. It only lasted four weeks before I found out. He didn't know either. I had to tell him. It was intermission at *The Lion King* at the Pantages. It was horrible."

It took me a moment to digest this. "I understand," I said finally. "You were young. How could you be expected to know he was a *painter*?"

She laughed, a silver trumpet. "On the bright side, I sold one of his early canvases to Jazzminn Jenks for $200,000 — so

I sent him the money and he wrote to say he's leased a darling new studio space in Florence. And after our marriage was over, he told me he always knew deep inside that he was gay, but I was so beautiful that he just forgot for awhile." She bit her lower lip thoughtfully. "So I suppose I can only blame myself."

"Sure . . . shame on you." I cleared my dry throat. "So . . . is that everybody? Because if there are more, I'm going to have to start taking some notes." I thought of Hamlet's bitter advice to his Ophelia: "*Get thee to a nunnery.*" *Way* too late for that line around here.

"That's everybody! I've had enough husbands that I bet the sauce is ready by now." She laughed again, and then turned sober. "But I did love them all, Ken. Each one was very different and very special." She put a hand on my shoulder, just as warm and firm as it felt the first time she touched me in Jazzminn's studio. "I'm sorry I didn't tell you all this before. I just thought that telling you might imply that you should care and why should you care about my life, when yours is . . ." She lowered her eyes, embarrassed. "I should stop talking now. Come on, let's go eat."

We re-traced our steps to the kitchen. Through the sliding door, we could see Lizzie laying plates and napkins on a redwood table by the pool. Wisteria vines hung in wisps from a wooden arbor above. Two heater trees stood on either of side the table, glowing red in the darkness.

"Ken, you were right about the flour!" Lizzie was triumphant. I took the silverware from her hands and finished off the place settings. "The sauce goes on the chicken. It's grilled, and mashed potatoes, and then I made some whipped butternut squash with nutmeg. Ophelia and I went to a Barnes & Noble today, and we looked in the health section to see if there was any book about what to feed people who've had chemotherapy and stuff, and it said you guys eat mostly soft, bland kinds of things. I just guessed that this would be okay. Is it?"

"It sounds fantastic. Thanks." I was both touched and annoyed by the idea of these two beauties discussing my diet at Barnes & Noble. "Let me help you bring it in from the kitchen."

"No, just sit down and be a guest, Ken. We'll get it." Ophelia waved her hand at the table. I would have protested, but my house tour had worn me out. Ophelia and Lizzie soon re-appeared with delicately fragrant plates and a sweating bottle of cold Pinot Grigiot. With an Elizabethan courtier's flourish, Ophelia laid my plate before me.

"Well, that's it!" Lizzie set down the other plate, then the wine and glasses. "Guys, I'm out of here, okay? I'm editing a film tonight."

Ophelia nodded. She gave Liz a hug, and a quick kiss on the lips, before she sat down. "Good luck with the film."

"Bye, Liz — thanks for the dinner," I said.

"Bye, Ken." Liz paused for a minute. Then: "Listen . . . Do you need, like, bone marrow or anything?" she blurted out. "Because I could donate. I've got, like, *so* many bones. Maybe I'm a match, like it said in the book."

"Goodbye, Liz," Ophelia said sternly. She turned back to me as Liz grabbed her backpack and fled. "I'm so sorry about that. She's very young. Would you like a glass of wine?"

"Sure, thanks."

Ophelia set to work with a corkscrew. I was going to offer to do it — I'm the guy — but, to be honest, I wasn't sure I'd be able to. Standing there with my corkscrew stuck halfway in was not a mental image I was prepared to deal with tonight. She did not seem to expect me to volunteer, however.

"Well, since our last meeting was . . . awkward, this time I want to officially thank you for *Bite Me*." Ophelia raised her glass. I raised mine to hers. "Eat!" she urged. "Food gets cold quickly out here."

I ate. The contents of my plate, as well as three glasses of the Pinot, were gone before I knew it. Ophelia ate a little, too, but mostly she watched — with doting pleasure, the way you look when you feed a ravenous stray dog. I was too hungry to care.

"Liz made a dessert, too — it's in the refrigerator," she said happily, when I was finished. "I'll go get it."

Before I could stop her, she jumped up from the table and returned with an enormous cheesecake on a crystal plate, topped with fresh blueberries. "Look at that," I murmured. "It's . . . art. But I . . . can't." Ever since I went through chemo my digestive tract has been inventing new and different ways to piss me off.

"Not even a little piece?"

"No. You have two. One for me."

"I'm not having any, either. The camera adds ten pounds, you know." She was clearly delighted to have this new problem to fret about.

"Maybe I should go on camera," I replied, keeping my eyes focused on the rich cake that no one would eat. She could eat it, she just wouldn't. If she wanted, she could have her cake and eat it, too. And mine. The whole damn cake was hers, if she wanted it.

"How do you feel, Ken?" she asked, softly.

"I'm fine, thanks. That was a joke. I'm just not a big dessert eater these days."

"I don't mean just right now. I mean . . . what does cancer feel like, all the time? Is it okay to ask that? I'd like to know. I studied biology, so I'm curious."

"Sure. It's okay to ask." Nobody ever had asked, so I had to think. "I'm tired. Weaker than I was. My appetite's shot —

usually. Getting out of bed in the morning is hard; going to sleep at night is even harder. And . . . that's it."

She seemed satisfied with my lame description of the situation. So I don't know why I kept talking, but I did. "That's why I got so angry when I found out that Sadilla doesn't exist," I continued slowly. "It's not because you lied to me. I don't give a damn if you want to make up an island. This is Hollywood. Invent any kind of foreign real estate you want. It's because Sadilla . . . Sadilla is . . . Sadilla *was*, the only place I could sleep. I'd imagine it at night, white sand and the sweet smell of coconut and flowers. The only place. Ophelia, I don't sleep. I can't sleep. I can't sleep at all."

I said this very calmly, just stating a fact. But then this awful thing happened. A huge sob shook me, then another, and another — three harsh, dry, ugly, overwhelming sobs rose from somewhere deep in my chest before I could stop them. I snatched off my glasses and covered my face with one hand, squeezing my eyes shut as I turned away from her.

She didn't say anything, or try to touch me, or comfort me — just left me alone while I struggled to get hold of myself. I really think that is the kindest thing anyone has ever done for me. After another minute passed, she said calmly, "Come on. Let's go inside. It's getting cold. You're shivering."

I nodded. Luckily, my ridiculous sobs had produced no tears, so I uncovered my face and put my glasses back on. I was cold. The heater trees were not enough to keep me warm in my thin shirtsleeves. I rose, and followed her into the living room.

"Stay right there," she said and left the room. When she returned, she carried an enormous Lakers sweatshirt that must have belonged to the six-foot-eight-inch Wade Stark. "Maybe this will help," she said, holding it out to me.

Still numb, I slipped the big sweatshirt over my head. I'm

six feet tall, but the sleeves hung down past the tips of my
fingers. This is what it would look like if the Lakers decided to
start recruiting short, skinny white guys with no hands.

"I'm cold, too," she said. "Plus I've reached my fifteen
hour limit on the contact lenses. My eyes feel like they're full of
sand. I'm going to run upstairs for a second. I'll be back. Sit
down. I'll make us some hot tea when I get back."

Uh-oh. Contacts. "Sure. You go ahead," I said. "I'll make
the tea. I'll find my way around."

By the time she returned, I had the kettle bubbling on the
stove and an assortment of teas laid out on the little glass
breakfast table beside the flowers. My back was turned,
reaching for the cups, when I heard her enter. Did I dare to
look?

I turned around, and there she was, with the *catua* eyes
flashing their many colors behind a pair of round, rimless
glasses. They were real! I've never been happier. She'd pulled
her curly hair back into a ponytail, then pinned it carelessly to
the top of her head. She still wore the diamond stud earrings,
but the form-fitting sweater and skirt had been replaced with
an Ophelia-sized Lakers sweatshirt, gray sweat pants, and
Nikes. She looked amazing.

"The real me," she said gaily, curtsying.

"You sure? Because I keep getting surprised, and I'm not
sure I can take anymore." I poured her a cup of hot water, she
could pick her own tea bag. "I'm sorry, Ophelia," I added.
"For what I said earlier, about sleeping on the island of Sadilla.
It probably didn't make a bit of sense to you. I think I'd better
stay away from wine until I'm back to normal. Maybe . . . a
month or two, tops."

"No, Ken. It made perfect sense."

"It did?" She nodded. I thought about that, and felt a little
better. Of course, it made sense to her, of course it did. She

was born on Sadilla. She knew what it was like. She knew you could sleep there, on the warm sand. "Funny how the only place we both feel at home is on an island that doesn't exist," I murmured.

"That's right," she nodded sadly. "We're both misfits, Ken. I can't get a job in Hollywood because of the color of my skin. And Hollywood can't live with you anymore because you're dying."

"Hey — whoa." My left eyelid began to twitch. "I told you I had cancer. I didn't say anything about dying."

"Ken, please. You don't have to hide it anymore. At least, not from me. We understand each other, remember?"

"I'm not hiding anything," I said it little too loudly. "Look, I grant you, this hasn't been the easiest eight months of my life. You don't go through chemo and a stem cell transplant for nothing. Jesus, *Stephen King* couldn't have dreamed that one up." I shuddered, thinking about it. "It . . . takes a lot out of you, I admit. But not everything. I'm still here. Hey, I have chemotherapy on Fridays. Why would they bother giving chemo to someone who's checking out?"

"What kind of chemotherapy?"

"Dr. Asshole calls it 'palliative.'" I think that means it's supposed to calm you down."

Those actress tears appeared again in her eyes. "That's not what it means, Ken."

"Ophelia, if I'm not going to listen to the Chief of Oncology at Cedars-Sinai Hospital, what makes you think I'm going to discuss my prognosis with an undergraduate biology major?" My voice went up another decibel. Now I sounded like the unshaven guy in the floppy coat you always see in the back of a bus, the one everyone moves away from lest he decide to shout or expose himself. "I'm not dying, if that's okay with you."

"We don't have to talk about it, Ken. I'm only saying this for your own good. Wouldn't it be easier to just say 'I'm dying,' to make peace with it, than to sleep on an invisible island?"

Now both my eyelids were going. That damn word again. "Don't pat yourself on the back too hard for telling me 'the truth,' Ophelia. Nobody tells you the truth about you because you're too beautiful. That's why you're so fucking . . . *happy.* You're the one who sleeps on an invisible island. Hell, you don't even know that the reason you haven't gotten a single goddamned part since you moved to L.A. has nothing to do with the color of your skin. Nothing to do with café au lait or caramel macchiato or chai latte anything else on the menu at the Coffee Bean. That only explains why you've got a chip on your shoulder the size of a Buick. Honey, you *can't act.*"

"Wh . . . wh . . . wh . . . wh . . . what?"

Well, I've never heard one syllable turn into quite so many. But by then I was so worked up that the look of shock and hurt on her lovely face wasn't enough to slow me down. "That's right," I shouted. "You, Ophelia, are the most beautiful woman I've ever seen — and the worst actress! And believe me, I've seen a lot of actresses. You're . . . you're worse than Kristen Stewart!"

There was a long, long silence. Then: "I think you should leave now, Ken," Ophelia said. To my surprise, she didn't sound angry at all. "You're upset, and it's my fault. You just hurt my feelings a lot — but I know that's only because you're hurting. I think maybe you just need to be alone."

Sudden tears stung my eyes when she said the word "alone." That was a worse word than "dying," much, much worse. But I realized then that only way to gain her permission to stay was to take a deep breath and put two unbearable words together. "Yes, You're right, Ophelia. I'm dying. Please, don't let me die alone," I whispered. "Be my Dark Lady."

"Your . . . Dark Lady?"

"Yes. Trust me — you'll never get another part after *Bite Me*. You can't act. You can't act! But I can offer you a terrific role, something outside of the entertainment industry — something from . . . a galaxy far, far away." Christ, how could I read sixteen hundred pages of William Shakespeare and then quote *Star Wars*? Fuck me! Well, too late to worry. I raced on. "How would you like to be . . . Shakespeare's Dark Lady? The perfect role for a girl named Ophelia."

Ophelia's eyes widened in horror. I panicked a little. "The Dark Lady . . . of the Sonnets?" she gasped. "That Dark Lady? But, Ken . . . she's so . . . so ugly!"

Unlike me, Ophelia had apparently read her Shakespeare in college. My mistress' eyes are nothing like the sun or In faith, I do not love thee with mine eyes / For they in thee a thousand errors note. But even in this awful moment filled with awful words, I had to stifle a laugh. Here I was, wondering if she was about to kick me out of her house for being a raving lunatic – worse, a raving lunatic with literary pretensions — when that look of shock in her stunning, bespectacled eyes was caused by my suggestion that the gorgeous Ophelia Lomond portray someone homely.

"We don't know that," I replied, trying to help her through this crisis. "We just know she wasn't pretty by Elizabethan standards. But hey, have you ever seen Queen Elizabeth the First? The woman had *no* eyebrows. I always thought of the Dark Lady as being beautiful, but born into the wrong century. Nobody was able to appreciate her in that time and place but the poet Shakespeare. She inspired him. He needed her to do his greatest work."

Ophelia was beginning to look less panicked but still seemed anxious. I could see her breasts rising and falling under her sweatshirt with her quick, nervous breaths.

"Ophelia, you're right. I'm . . . dying," I said, trying to fill the silence. "I'm dying all over the place. I've got cancer. It's everywhere. It's in my blood. It's in my bones. There's not a normal goddamn cell in anywhere my body. This is my last request. Be my Dark Lady. My inspiration."

There was a long, long silence during which, really, I almost died. Then: "Why do you want me to play your Dark Lady if I'm such a lousy actress?" she burst out.

"You're not. You're . . . a great actress," I lied desperately, blood slamming in my temples. "I don't know why I said that. You're right, you never get cast because you're not black or white and that's the only way Hollywood knows how to think. It's got nothing to do with your extraordinary lack of talent. Maybe I'm just jealous because . . . you can eat cake and you won't and I can't. I'm sorry. Forgive me."

"No, you're the one who's right," she said after a long pause, her voice tinged not with anger, but with wonder. "I can't act. I can't act at all. I'm . . . terrible. This is a . . . a *revelation*, Ken. Gosh. Maybe I always knew. I think maybe that's why I majored in biology at Yale. Somehow I knew, just like Arnie always knew he was gay but didn't admit it to himself." She put at hand to her heart and sighed. "You know, I've held onto that job with Jazzminn for four years even though I don't need the money because I told myself I'd make good contacts, but you know what? I think I was afraid to have all day free for auditions because it was just too painful to see that look they always get in their eye when I'm done with my scene. That *look*. I guess nobody wanted to tell me, because they could tell that I wanted to be an actress so much."

"Or because they wanted to get into your jeans," I replied, ever so gently. "But I don't care if you can act. I can't stand actresses." I used to have a rule before I moved in with Alice: never date actresses. And, being a man of my word, I didn't date them that much after I moved in with her, either. "I'm still prepared to offer you the role of a lifetime," I continued urgently. "The Dark Lady. The Dark Lady of the Sonnets — the Dark Lady of Hollywood. My inspiration. Please."

"Well . . ." Ophelia did not look convinced. "You say you want me to be your inspiration, but what is it you want me to inspire you to do, exactly?"

Hmmm. Do? Did I have to *do* something? Isn't terminal cancer enough to keep me busy? I wasn't going to be writing sonnets, that's for damn sure. But I had to think fast. "I want you to inspire me to . . . want to live, even though I'm dying," my voice said. Hey — that was pretty good, I thought, just before I put my head down on the table, buried my face in the sleeve of Wade Stark's sweatshirt, and wept brokenly, this time with tears, the whole messy, humiliating act.

It's true — God, it's true. I have terminal cancer. I'm dying and I'm thirty-six. My Dad worked for The Mouse for forty-five years and I've never been to fucking Disneyland. *I have faint, cold fear thrills through my veins, / That almost freezes up the heat of life.* Please, please don't let me die alone.

Ophelia waited until I finally raised my head. "You are dying, Ken," she said. "I'm so sorry. I can't begin to tell you how sorry I am. And I'm very, very flattered that you don't care that I can't act. That's the nicest thing anyone has ever said to me. But don't you see, that's the reason I can't be your Dark Lady of the Sonnets."

The blood now pounded so hard in my temples that I could see it in my eyes, red veins floating in my eyes. I'd been honest with her, and with myself — for the first time. Didn't I now deserve the answer I wanted to hear? Didn't Shakespeare's characters always get what they deserved, foul or fair? I deserved her, now. That was fair. "Why . . . why not?" I quavered.

"Because it would be acting, and I'm no good at it," Ophelia said, her cheeks flooding with tears that I knew were real, because she can't act. "You don't even know me. You only know that I'm from Indianapolis, Indiana, that I'm the world's worst actress, and that I'm beautiful. I can't mean as much to you as you need me to. No, Ken. It's just not true. I'm not your Dark Lady of the Sonnets. Would that I were she."

"You are, if you want to be." Who else but the Dark Lady of the Sonnets would say: *"Would that I were she?"* Who the fuck really talks that way? Fate had not yet left the building. "Please, Ophelia," I begged, dropping to one knee. "If you would be she, then do be she. Please, help me, Ophelia. Help me."

"I wish I could help you, Ken, but I can't. I can't be someone I'm not."

"Well you've been doing a damn good job so far, *Ophelia Lomond.*"

She ignored that. "Please get up, Ken. After three marriages, men on their knees make me extremely nervous."

I gave up. I rose from my knees, wrapped in shame and Wade Stark's sweatshirt. I sat back down, slumped in my chair. I didn't know where to look, what to do with my eyes, with my hands. Now I wished desperately that I hadn't confirmed my imminent death, that I hadn't cried in front of her. Why, oh why did I give up being in denial? It was working so well for me.

She poured a cup of tea and set it in front of me, with a watery smile. "Some tea . . . Mr. Shakespeare? It's Earl Grey."

Was she mocking me? I couldn't tell. I lifted the china cup, pinky extended, nodded politely, then turning it over and poured a urine stream of Earl Whatsis all over her polished wood floor.

"I'm through with this little tea party," I said, rising from my chair again. "Farewell, Ophelia. *Thus hath the candle singed the moth.* Now I know why you invited me here. It's not because you understand me. It's because you want that bit part on *Bite Me* so much you'd kill for it, if you had to." Fury felt better than shame, so I clung to it. "You're right. I should leave now. I guess you aren't the Dark Lady, after all. You are just a beautiful and extraordinary woman, to whom I wish the best of luck. I apologize for wasting your time. And I guess if you want to call up some shrink and tell him I've lost my mind and I'm a danger to myself and others, it's your choice. It's out of my control. Like everything else."

"Your life may be out of your control, but mine isn't," Ophelia said softly. A little tea splashed over the edge of her cup. "I suppose, since I'm not your Dark Lady, Jazzminn Jenks and everyone else on the studio lot will know I'm Karen Watts by tomorrow morning. And I suppose I can say goodbye to my small but pivotal role on *Bite Me*. I might as well just pack my stuff and move on back to Indianapolis, huh?"

I thought this over. Here was the last tiny bit of power I had left over her. "No," I said — and it was gone. "I got that part for you because I thought you were the Dark Lady, but now it's yours, if you still want it. You aren't the Dark Lady, and you can't act worth a damn — but you are still Woman with Cat #2, if you want to be. I want you to take the part."

Ophelia nodded. "All right." This time, she gazed at me with such pity that I had to look away. "Thank you, Ken. For *Bite Me*. And for coming to dinner. And . . . for offering me the role of a lifetime, I suppose. But I want you to know, I didn't invite you here just to make sure I'd get the chance to go on national television and say: 'Doctor, what's wrong with my cat?' It's *not* the only thing I care about. I also did it because . . . you looked so . . . I don't know how to explain it . . . so . . . *thirsty*, Ken."

"Ophelia . . . how do I look?" I should have just walked

out of there, but I'd never been able to ask anybody this since I got cancer, and I couldn't stop myself. "Do I look sick? Do I look like I'm dying? Could you tell, even before I told you? Please, tell me the truth. What do I look like?"

She eyed me up and down. "You're a little thin," she said gently. "And you could use some sun. You have dark circles under your eyes. You need sleep. And a better haircut. But no — I couldn't tell right away. You look good, Ken. Kenny . . . are you going to be okay tonight?"

I would *not* say "I'm fine." "I'll find my way out," I said instead. "And you don't need to worry about how I look, because you'll never see me again." The sleeves of Wade Stark's giant sweatshirt had slipped down over my hands again; this sort of spoiled the effect when I thrust my right hand skyward in a fist. "But I'll find my Dark Lady. I will. *Believe it.*"

"I hope you will, Ken."

"I know I will. By the way, I lied to you. I'm not dying. I mean, I was before, but now . . . lady, I wouldn't give you the satisfaction!"

"Please — don't go yet," Ophelia whispered, her face still stained with tears. "I have to ask you something. I know, I'm not much of an actress, but . . . before we never see each other again, do you really think I would have been good? As the Dark Lady of the Sonnets? Would I have been . . . good?"

I stopped walking. "You, Ophelia Lomond?" I said, turning back to face her. "As Shakespeare's Dark Lady? The mysterious Dark Lady of the Sonnets? Ophelia, I don't know who the hell the real Dark Lady was — but I know that you would have been *better.*"

CHAPTER FOURTEEN

**He never finish high school,
but he make up these poems.
For me. Real pretty, some of 'em.**

— Nettie Mae Easley

The Dark Lady of the Sonnets. *Sonnets* — even the word breaks my heart. It's such a perfect word: elegant, two syllables, so concise and sweet. I think there's something special about s's, and n's, about words that have both, like sunny and spinnaker and symphony and glisten, so many of my favorite words. Los Angeles has them, too.

And me, the Dark Lady? In spite of the mildly racist and sexist overtones, that is *so* enchanting. I would never argue political correctness with a dying man. I've been called beautiful before, so many times, twice just this morning in the elevator — but never in a way that makes me think of myself as a jewel from another century instead of what I am to Hollywood, a flawed gem. The Dark Lady of Hollywood.

He's mad, of course. I don't know if it's stress, or perhaps that alcohol is contra-indicated with his medications — either way, he's definitely gone over the edge, come unhinged, and it's all my fault. In his case, going crazy is probably the sanest thing to do. But I think my only choice was to choke back the tears and pretend it didn't matter, to pretend I wasn't moved to my very soul by the offstage drama he proposed to play. Having him hate me is the price I pay for doing the right thing. He's better off without some who is, as he says, so . . . fucking *happy*.

He's right. I'm an execrable actress, dreadful, horrible — although suggesting I'm worse than Kristen Stewart seems unnecessarily cruel. I don't feel saddened by finally getting this out in the open, I feel relieved, buoyed by it, really — even though I have to say I resent the fact that a bad actress with a white complexion still has a better chance in Hollywood than I do, especially in the vampire genre. I'm real — but in entertainment industry terms, that doesn't necessarily make me a believable character.

But was it the right thing to keep the role on *Bite Me?* I don't know, but somehow giving up the part doesn't seem to make any more sense than throwing away the gorgeous flowers that Ken brought for me, just because there are things in the world that aren't as beautiful as flowers are. Ken won't be any less miserable because I have tiger lilies in my trash. He told me to keep the role and I will. I'll live with the guilt. It's the least I can do for him.

And, honest, I kept talking about it to him just to . . . just to keep talking. Just to keep him there, so he wouldn't get into his Mercedes, drive away, and die.

Well, I couldn't just sit out there by the pool in the dark forever, sobbing and eating blueberry cheesecake by the handfuls. Quietly, so as not to wake neighbors, skunks, or coyotes, I slid open the glass door to the kitchen and wandered into the den.

The room was still filled with all of Wade's futuristic audio and video equipment, his own personal sound-mixing studio. He'd always donate the last set of sub-woofers to a youth home in South Central as soon as something bigger and louder went on sale at Best Buy. I usually ignored all of his toys, I'd rather read a book or a magazine — but tonight I knew I couldn't make my weary eyes focus on a printed page. For the first time since Wade gave me this house and all of its gadgets, I decided to watch a movie.

Let's see, where was the button . . . here, on the wall right next to the sofa. I'd kept a vase of fresh sunflowers on the table in front of it for so long I'd almost forgotten it was there. I felt for it in the semi-darkness, knowing that this would lead to a lively discussion with the housekeeper on Monday about how to remove blueberry stains from white paint. I found it and pressed. As Wade's movie screen descended from the ceiling with a low mechanical whir, I marveled that it really was silver, the silver screen, with all of its seductive s's and n's.

In my distracted state, sickened by sorrow and cream cheese, chances were poor of my being able to find the DVDs, much less of inserting one properly. I hoped there was one still left in the player. Wade was never very good at remembering to put things away, I was forever tripping over size sixteen athletic shoes. I loved him with all my heart, but there's something to be said for marrying men of a standard size.

I hit the play button on what I hoped was the correct one of the four remotes that lay before me on the coffee table. The dark room rumbled to life with the opening credits for a murder-mystery-thriller called *Overkill*, starring former body builder Stone Jones.

I jumped as a quart of red blood spurted from the middle

of the "O" at the same time as an electronic drumbeat bounced out of a speaker somewhere behind me and a low, gruff male voice intoned: "When I say kill — it's *o-vah*."

At first, I watched because I felt too queasy to move from the sofa and I couldn't figure out how to turn off the DVD player. But then, as much as I hate to admit it, after about a half-hour of murder and mayhem, of crashing cars, bullet holes and broken glass, I found myself rooting for Stone Jones. After the long ache of this evening, there was something refreshing about Stone, his gun, his glistening biceps and his one-track mind. Even as I blocked my eyes against violence so over-the-top I could still see red inside my closed eyelids, after awhile I found myself whispering along with him each time he said it, making my voice as husky as possible: "When I say kill — It's *o-vah*." I licked the last of the icing off my fingernail. You go, boy.

Stone Jones never read a Shakespearean sonnet. If he did, he wouldn't know what it meant. Lucky Stone. Ken Harrison has read them, all of them, understood them, and it hasn't made him stronger. It's only driven him out of his mind. *Him* — which one of us just ate a whole cheesecake with her bare hands? Introspection is an infection. Maybe Ken was better off being angry at what's happening to him, denying it, challenging it, flipping it the finger, than letting me make him tell the truth and then falling apart before my eyes.

What is dying, really, but murder in the passive voice? Maybe sushi Todd was right. Maybe Stone Jones is right, too. Dying doesn't work in Hollywood. Murder does.

CHAPTER FIFTEEN

**Mad call I it; for, to define true madness,
What is't but to be nothing else but mad?**

— Polonius, *Hamlet*

"So then — you follow me, Ken? — Dude snaps her picture, know I'm sane? He's seen her through the window, but she can't see *him* seeing *her*, know I'm sane? So he's gonna take the photo to the police, know I'm sane, except on the way, her boyfriend shoots him because he saw *him* seeing *her* — know I'm sane?"

He meant, "Do you know what I'm saying?" — But that's the way it sounded when he ran it all together in his sweaty desperation to sell his concept: "Know I'm sane? Know I'm sane?" This stocky twenty-five-year-old in baggy shorts and a backwards Dodgers cap had been pitching his made-for-TV movie script, rapid-fire, for a good half hour and I still couldn't tell what the hell he was talking about. *"Know I'm sane?"*

"No," I replied sadly. "No, I don't know you're sane. So far, I've seen no evidence at all that you're sane." I took off my glasses for a moment and massaged my bleary, grit-filled eyes with a forefinger and thumb. "Do you know *I'm* sane? Because if you do, kindly inform me of it. I've begun to have my doubts."

He just stared at me, jaw on the floor. "Man, you want to hear the end?"

"And what about my hair?" I carefully checked my own reflection in the lenses of my glasses before I turned them around and replaced them on my nose. Not exactly *the paragon of animals*, but no *quintessence of dust*, either, know I'm sane? "Tell me — do you think I need a better haircut, or is it just her? I mean, she? *The tongues of mocking wenches are as keen / As is the razor's edge invisible.* Was she mocking me, or do I need a razor?"

Now the poor schmuck was so confused he actually turned his baseball cap around the right way. He stood up, clutching his script, shifting his weight uncomfortably between black high-top sneakers, separated from the shorts by a pale, doughy, hairy expanse of calf-meat. "Maybe I should just leave my pages on your desk, man."

I nodded. "Right there, on top of the others. Thank you. Prithee, take your leave, sir. My assistant will call you if we're interested, and no one will call if we're not. By the way, your shorts are very long, for shorts — but one can't say long shorts, now, can one?"

That wasn't kind. But ever since last night, my last night with Ophelia, I'd become painfully sensitive to words misused, mispronounced, misplaced, and disrespected. Names spelled Hollywood-funny, like *Jazzminn*.

After ten years in network TV, I'm no English professor — but today, each violation of the language was irksome music, and the halls of the Hacienda Building rang with it. With endless creative-executive questions both rhetorical and nonsensical, full of sound, fury, and misplaced italics. Could you *get* any stupider? Could he *write* any slower? Could I *be* any more stressed? How funny is *that*? I *know*, right? *Know I'm sane?*

I think what gave words such staggering power today was that, last night, I said one powerful word I never should have said, never. God — I never should have let her make me say it.

I poured myself a glass of ice water and swallowed a couple of the pills I'd brought to the office with me. They were pink and white. In the brief period of time since leaving Ophelia's house, I'd developed a sort of Alice-in-Wonderland curiosity about my collection of untouched pharmaceuticals. While I knew these pills had not been prescribed to relieve a sudden hypersensitivity to bad grammar, I was pretty sure they couldn't make things any worse.

Unfortunately this pill didn't do a damn thing, at least, nothing I could feel — so I was stuck there in the Hacienda Building, alone with my thoughts. "Alas," I sighed aloud. I'd never said "alas" before; I think I liked it. My mistake was to think that someone else could see inside me. Especially her — the beautiful, happy, healthy Ophelia, a woman who seemed to come with her own laugh track, a sweet Midwestern girl with an observable allergy to sarcasm, profanity, and bad attitude — all, sadly, part of my character arc. I should never have inflicted myself upon her.

Right now, my life seemed as twisted as the front bumper of my Mercedes, caught in a permanent sneer since I slammed into that mailbox coming home from Ophelia's house, rounding the curve from Laurel Canyon onto Sunset Boulevard. It was going to cost a fortune.

That evening, after work, I walked into a salon on Melrose and gave a stylist named Juvencio fifty bucks and total creative control of my hair. I'm not sure whether I still looked terminally ill when I walked out of there, but at least I was terminally hip.

CHAPTER SIXTEEN

You didn't think. You shoulda thought.

— Nettie Mae Easley

Good Lord, *suicide*. It's not something I ever thought about before. People don't talk about it so much in the Midwest. It's one of those easy solutions to bad news that my grandma on my mother's side just couldn't tolerate, particularly in the case of young white men. Don't come up here telling me *you* got a reason, she'd say, when her big, floppy, eighty-nine year old brown ears would catch something about the suicide of a privileged young Caucasian male on the news. In fact, she was so offended by the idea, she often said that rich white boys who commit suicide ought to be shot dead.

But now, I think about suicide all the time. Not my own — as a good-looking person, it's my responsibility to stay alive, to fight to find contentment in this world, no matter what. I can't be despondent. It's just not fair to people with real problems. I may be a minority woman in a white man's world, but I'm *hot*. I must soldier on.

No, I'm not afraid for myself. I'm afraid for *him*. Why didn't I think of suicide before I let Ken Harrison stumble out of my house wearing my third ex-husband's sweatshirt? That's the dumbest thing I've ever done. I quit biting my nails in fourth grade, but now I'm at it again. I only hope Amaretto Peach enamel isn't poisonous.

It didn't occur to me that night that Ken might consider suicide. But now, I can't stop thinking about it. Not only is he dying, now he's angry and he's hurt, thanks to me — and a reckless driver besides. Right now he's the kind of guy that just might forget that he's dying just long enough to kill himself.

And he's a Hollywood executive. I know from experience they don't handle disappointment well. They're fragile, like hothouse flowers. Rejection makes them wilt.

I don't think he'll drive himself off a cliff — that's a vintage Mercedes he's got there. But there are other ways to do it. A gun? One deft, crimson slice to each wrist? He enjoys cooking, so I imagine his kitchen knives are kept in excellent condition. But somehow I just don't see Ken Harrison as the violent type. He used to work in comedy. Maybe I should just relax, I thought. And I did, for a while. That is, until I remembered the drugs.

I imagine Ken has all sorts of pills in his cabinet — you have to try them all before you know that none of them is going to save you, don't you? Well, they'd work for this. He wouldn't have to go to the trouble of swallowing a bottle of aspirin or sleeping pills from a shelf at Rite-Aid drugstore, like an ordinary person would. I'm sure a man like Ken Harrison, a creative executive, has had the best medical treatment money can buy at Cedars-Sinai. Everything in his medicine cabinet must be as powerful as Wade's latest set of sub-woofers. Just a few of whatever he's got stashed away at home would do the job in a hurry.

Would it have killed me to tell him I'd be his Dark Lady of the Sonnets, his Dark Lady of Hollywood? I'm a terrible actress, but I could have at least said the lines and left the rest up to Fate. After all, I wouldn't be the first actor in Hollywood to do . . . temp work. That's *awful*. There goes my mind again, thinking awful things. It's this *place*. Even though it was a lie, it wouldn't have killed me to take the part. It's no worse than being Woman with Cat #2. And my not taking the part, I'm afraid, might just kill *him*.

In a way, it's too bad that Ken Harrison is no Stone Jones. I have discovered that, thanks to Wade, I have the entire Stone Jones *oeuvre*, 1985 to the present, on DVD. Late at night, I have come to appreciate his signature acting style, his consistent willingness to act without thinking too hard about the consequences. Stone Jones, he's a killing machine, and right now, a good murder might be just the thing to take both of our minds off suicide, until it's *o-vah*.

CHAPTER SEVENTEEN

Blow, winds, and crack your cheeks! rage! blow!

— King Lear, *King Lear*

"Kenny — are you awake?"

It was 2 a.m., of course I was awake. Lying on the couch with my Shakespeare, sipping tea – not Earl Grey, this was some anti-oxidant shit with green tea and açai juice — wrapped in a plaid wool blanket against the late fall chill, lulled by light rain against my window. For someone who had spent his entire career in network TV, it amazed me how much my own life had come to look like Public Broadcasting.

Yes, I was awake. And this call would have gotten my attention even if I'd been sleeping. It was about two weeks later, and it was Ophelia. The mocking wench herself.

"Ophelia?"

"Yes, it's me." The voice that usually bubbled with laughter sounded dangerously near a sob. "I'm sorry to call you so late. And you probably don't want to talk to me, no matter what time it is . . ."

"It's okay. I'm up. I'm always up. And I don't know whether I want to talk to you or not, so go for it while I'm still deciding." I sat up on the couch, ran my hand through my spiky new hair cut and rubbed my eyes, trying to focus. "Is . . . something wrong?"

"I've changed my mind," she said, breathlessly.

"Excuse me?"

"I've changed my mind. I'll be your Dark Lady. The Dark Lady of the Sonnets. Your inspiration."

"Wait a second — calm down. What?"

"You heard me. I want to be her. I mean, I want to be she. No, it's her. What I'm trying to say is — I'll do it, Ken."

"Huh?" I'd like to have said something more poignant here, but — huh???

"Yes. I will. On one condition."

"A . . . condition?"

"Yes. I'd like you to kill someone for me. That is, if you're not too busy."

What kind of weird shit was this? Maybe I was sleeping, after all. "Who?" I demanded. "Who do you want me to kill, Ophelia?"

"Her. I want you to kill . . . *her.*"

"*Who?*"

"Her." Now she was sobbing. Her breath came in sharp stabs. "*Her.* Jazzminn Jenks."

I fell off the sofa. It hurt like hell. "Stay where you are, Ophelia. Just stay there." I clutched the receiver with one hand and, with the other, fumbled on the floor for my glasses, and my pants. "I'll be right over."

CHAPTER EIGHTEEN

An honorable murderer, if you will

— Othello, *Othello*

Things that love night / love not such nights as these.

As I raced up Laurel Canyon, water raced down. The light rain that had tapped against my apartment window was now a solid sheet, and L.A.'s narrow canyon roads could flood in seconds. Miniature mudslides of rock and dirt dribbled into the road, the tangled web of roots that usually anchored the dry hillside unable to hold on. There was lightning — not jagged bolts and thunder, but an occasional paparazzi flash that lit the whole sky. Luckily, there was no one up here at this time of night but me and my bent Mercedes.

What was this that had come to me in *the dead waste and middle of the night?* Just as sure as I'd lost Ophelia, she'd returned — as abruptly as she had arrived in the first place, as suddenly as she'd gone. I had surely come to believe in Fate but damn, I wished it would make up its mind.

It was raining so hard I could barely see. I'd like to offer another observation about Shakespearean tragedy: when something bad is about to happen, the weather always sucks.

I drove fast, but my mind moved faster. The Dark Lady was back. But was one's Muse, one's inspiration, supposed to call in the middle of the night and start making demands and setting conditions? Calling the shots — no pun intended? Inviting me, however politely, to commit murder one?

Somehow, whenever I envisioned Shakespeare alone with his Dark Lady, I never saw her saying much. He was writing, and she was just sort of . . . there, mooning around in a red velvet dress with a plate of cakes and ale or maybe bent over her needlepoint by amber candlelight. Okay, so my hallucinations are sexist, sue me. I just never pictured her yanking the script out of Shakespeare's hands to give story notes.

And I was having a problem with another thing: Ophelia wanted to kill a woman. Little, size zero, bottle-blond Jazzminn Jenks — dead, a toe tag on her pink bunny slipper.

By the time I reached Ophelia's house — in record time, despite the rain — I was still confused, but at least the storm had abated. Ophelia looked small, standing outside in front of the huge carved wooden doors in a white terry bathrobe, sheltered from the foul weather by the overhang above the expansive porch. Her eyes were red from crying but even lovelier than I had remembered. I refused to be distracted by them. I stepped out of the Mercedes, slamming the door so hard the car shook.

"Hi, Ken. How . . . how are you?"

How *was* I. "Well, it's 2:30 in the morning, I almost ran into Noah's Ark coming up through the canyon, and I've got chemotherapy in four and a half hours. I'm swell, Ophelia. Now, you want to tell me why you dragged me up here in the rain in the middle of the night?"

"I didn't drag you anywhere. You just said you were coming, then hung up the phone."

She was right, but I wasn't about to give that to her. "Hey, you called me up and said you wanted me to commit murder. You didn't expect me to roll over and go back to sleep, did you?"

Ophelia glanced around nervously, swung open the doors and motioned me into the dimly lit foyer. "Shhh. Let's talk about this inside . . . Gosh, what happened to your car?"

"Gosh, never mind what happened to my car. What happened to *you?*"

"I'm going to tell you, but let's go sit down. Please. In the kitchen. I . . . I like the haircut, Ken."

"Really?" I was pleased in spite of the situation. "Doesn't make me look too much like Brian Grazer?"

"No, not . . . *too* much."

I followed Ophelia through the living room, then through the den, where half a dozen Wade Starks stared down from the walls in collective disbelief. Hey, don't look at me, bald man. She's the one who called.

The little glass breakfast table in the kitchen bore a crystal bud vase, holding the crooked stem of a single pale yellow orchid. Next to this exotic bloom stood a family-sized box of Kellogg's Apple Jacks — a big, bright apple-green box — and a half-gallon jug of two-percent milk. In front of this jumbo box lay a dainty lace napkin, a silver spoon, and a fine porcelain bowl filled with soggy cereal O's, the milk stained pink by imitation apple bits bleeding red dye. God help me, the milk was the same color as the bunny slippers. Apparently I had interrupted Ophelia in the middle of this appalling snack.

"You eat *Apple Jacks?*"

"Only when I'm upset. Would . . . would you like some, Ken?"

If Ophelia had offered me any other food as an alternative, any other food in the world, *eye of newt and tongue of frog,* Apple

Jacks or? — believe me, I'd have gone for the other thing. But she did not, and I was feeling lightheaded. "Yes, thanks," I said reluctantly. "I think I would like some Apple Jacks, if it's not too much trouble."

Ophelia fetched another porcelain bowl, lace napkin, and silver spoon. Silently, she filled the bowl to the rim, way too much, and poured milk. Much to my surprise, the cereal was light, sweet, and went down easy. I immediately felt stronger. I waited until the sugar rush fully kicked in. Then, "Talk to me, Ophelia," I said. The occasional tear that splashed into her soggy Apple Jacks caused me to speak more gently than I had planned.

"I thought you might like to know that my *Bite Me* episode films in early December. But I won't be on it."

I lowered my spoon. "What?"

"I am no longer Woman with Cat #2. I got fired."

Fired — from a one-line part? No actress is *that* bad. "When? And what for?"

"Today. I was sitting in the commissary, having lunch with Bert DeMarco, discussing my character arc. We had just started to get into the second layer of motivation, what it is she really wants, when suddenly, Jazzminn Jenks appeared in the doorway. She never goes to the commissary, but I guess she must have asked where I was, and somebody told her.

"She walked over to the table, and introduced herself to Bert, sweet as pie. He was obviously impressed. In fact, everybody in the commissary was impressed, including the president of the network, who was in town from New York — and who, if I'm not mistaken, had been staring at my legs since noon. Anyway, after she blows a kiss to the president, Jazzminn pretends to be surprised to see me, and asks Bert what's going on. Bert tells her that I'm on *Bite Me* — and not only that, I'm the most talented newcomer he's seen since the debut of the show."

I was wrong. Maybe Bert *can* act.

"I guess Bert thought Jazzminn would be pleased by this — but instead her face turns green, and believe me, I've seen it that color before. She tells him that she can't spare me for even a second these days, and that she's so very sorry, but she thinks having me work on another show on the same network constitutes a conflict of interest. Otherwise, she'd fully support me in my acting career.

"Bert says that it's a one-line part so there's only one rehearsal session during my lunch hour and the show films on Friday nights, so he doesn't see any problem time-wise. And he frowns and says he doesn't understand how there's a conflict of interest if it's the same network.

"Then Jazzminn offers to have the president of the network come over to explain the conflict to Bert, right here, right now, in detail. Well, that does it. Suddenly, Bert understands perfectly. Lunch is over, and my 'character arc' is a flatline. Bert is terribly sorry; I'm a wonderful young actress; he wishes me the best of luck; here's the private number to his trailer if I want to talk about it later, wasn't that generous of him? But I'm off the show."

Well, there it was — and there was nothing I could do about it. I knew I'd pulled my last string when I got Ophelia the part, but now I was finding out there was nothing on the other end of it. Even though I'd stormed out of her house in that giant goddamned sweatshirt, cursing her, cursing *Bite Me*, cursing this whole damn town — there was a tiny, withered, water-starved flower somewhere inside my left ventricle that still hoped that her gratitude over getting the role on *Bite Me* might bring her back.

Now, I felt like one of those characters in a Disney cartoon who finds a genie in a bottle and then uses his last wish by saying something dumb like: "Gee, I wish I knew what to wish for." Even before cancer erased my laugh track, I always found that last, wasted wish more sad than funny, even if it was only Donald Duck.

"I'm . . . sorry, Ophelia. I'm truly sorry."

"Don't be sorry. Just kill her."

Ophelia's phone call had given me hope; *The miserable have no other medicine.* As I sped the through the storm, somehow through all my doubts I trusted that she'd give me a good reason to kill Jazzminn Jenks when I got there, that I would understand everything when I got there, that Fate was finally sealed. Why else, as I stepped out of the car, would the tormented skies become so miraculously clear?

But I'm sorry — weird, spooky omen or not, I was not going to murder anyone over a one-line part on *Bite Me.* I just had to figure out the best way to break it to her without her throwing me out of the house. "Let me think about this for a second, Ophelia," I pleaded. "Let me think."

"Don't think. Just *do.*"

"Don't think? Don't *think?*" That did it. I hate to talk about this stuff, but I'd had a few bad nights recently — to sleep, perchance to wake up bleeding profusely from the nose. I was informed that at this stage there was the chance of an occasional nosebleed — like I needed to be on hold for twenty minutes to find *that* out. I couldn't sleep, dead tired but I couldn't sleep — and right now I was staring into the beautiful, tear-stained face of the woman who took away my island of Sadilla. "Don't think? Jesus Christ, Ophelia, I'm dying," I shouted. "What else have I got to do but think?"

"Well . . . knock it off." Ophelia folded her arms and glared. "It's not going to help to think. You're — Hamlet-ing, Ken. That's what you're doing."

"Hamlet-ing?"

"That's right, spinning things around and around in your head until they don't make sense anymore. Hamlet-ing. I hate to be the one to point it out, but in your case 'To be or not to be' is not exactly a question. Stop sleeping on an invisible island. Time to give up your teddy bear, big guy. You're the Prince of fucking Denmark!"

Did Ophelia just say fuck — without even a sneeze? This had to be some sort of aural hallucination, brought on by another recent, recreational handful of those pink-and-white pills. But what she said hit home; at least for a moment, I had to stop and think about . . . not thinking. No, wait, I have to stop thinking about it, or else I'm thinking about it. Damn, look what she's done to me.

"Dying doesn't work in this town, Ken," Ophelia said calmly. "Murder does."

What kind of crap was that? "Dying doesn't work in this town, murder does." It sounded like a line from a Stone Jones movie — maybe that one that flopped because some misguided studio executive had the bright idea to set this one in the Old West instead of Los Angeles in the year 2075.

But, because I couldn't stop thinking, I thought about that. She was right — dying sure didn't work in this town. Witness my crash from comedy executive to piteous ghost of the Hacienda Building because word got out about the sorry state of my lymphatic system. *Oh what a falling-off was there.* I was out of the executive office building before I could say "terminal cancer."

I hate comedy, but Christ, I spent ten years in sitcoms — I know spit takes, not murder weapons. "Let's talk about this for a second, Ophelia," I began cautiously. "I know your feelings are hurt. I'm sorry I couldn't help you. But you can afford to lose this stupid role. Quit your job with Jazzminn Jenks. Go back to the Lana Bishop Theatre and do

Shakespeare — however poorly. That's what all those TV actors wish they could do, anyway. Don't blow this out of proportion."

"No, Ken, I can't afford to lose this role," she sobbed, laying the back of her hand across her forehead with theatrical distress. "I'm thirty-two years old — I mean, twenty-seven — and this is the last chance for me. I can't help it if my role of a lifetime is tiny and pathetic. That's still what it is. I mean, what it was."

"But I thought we agreed — you can't act, Ophelia," I was pleading for sanity, even though I wasn't sure I had any left myself. "What difference does it make now?"

"That's what makes it so important!" she exclaimed. "It's the only role I was ever going to have! It's not fair. I worked for this for ten years. Someone's got to pay."

Okay, that did it. I jumped out of my chair. "Goddammit, Ophelia — and don't even think about telling me to watch my language after that f-bomb of yours. Every cell in my body is going haywire and you're going to sit here and tell me I should feel sorry for *you*? That I should kill for *you*? Tell you what — I'm going home to see if I can get an hour or two of sleep before the next round of palliative chemotherapy. In the meantime, pour yourself another bowl of Apple Jacks, put yourself to bed, and be glad that when you wake up you don't have to wring the blood out of your pillow!"

There was a very, very long pause. Then, "it's possible to drown in shallow water," Ophelia said quietly.

"What's that supposed to mean?"

"If you don't kill Jazzminn Jenks . . . I'll kill myself."

"What?"

"You heard me. I'll kill myself right now. Either I die, or Jazzminn does. Take your pick."

"No way."

Scowling, arms stiff at her sides, Ophelia strode to her granite counter, to the wooden block of Henckels knives, and yanked one out. A paring knife. Obviously this woman did not know her way around her own kitchen. Hastily, she shoved the demure little blade back into its rectangular slot and pulled out another. Was this a twelve-inch ham slicer I saw before me, the handle in her hand? I've wanted that one ever since I saw it on the Henckels web site. She brandished it in the air.

"Try me," she hissed.

"Ophelia, put that down unless you're planning to make a sandwich."

"No." This time she laid the shining blade flat against her throat.

Damn. Fate had brought me back into the charmed vicinity of my Dark Lady, only to find her threatening to turn herself into cold cuts. Right now the only thing that kept me from laughing out loud was the new but already-nagging suspicion that she might actually do it. Not with that stupid knife, of course — but there are a lot of ways to get rid of yourself these days, most of them available in non-prescription strength at your local drugstore. Actresses will do a thing just because it's theatrical, and what's more theatrical than suicide, particularly when it involves a well-scripted farewell note?

Plus, she was right. It was possible to drown in shallow water. In fact, recently I've come to think it's *only* possible to drown in shallow water. When you're in deep water, baby, you learn how to swim. She was a deep woman in shallow water; I was a shallow guy in over his head. But I'm taking bets that I'm the one with the best chance to survive in Hollywood.

I would never kill myself, even though right now I could present a hell of a good case for it. It's just not in my software — anyway, in my case, what's the point? But she might. She didn't have blood on her pillow, or chemotherapy in the morning. Maybe if she did, she wouldn't worry so damn much about a bit part on *Bite Me*. But now she had me worried.

A few scholars suggest that Hamlet's Ophelia drowned for a sweet reason, reaching out over the brook to pick a luscious bloom from a hanging vine, but most of them think she flung herself into the water in a fit of passionate despair. Either way, academics agree, the chick was fucking nuts — and so, apparently, was my Ophelia. And I was the nut who had driven her off the cliff.

There I go, Hamlet-ing again. I sternly stopped myself and tried to concentrate on what Ophelia was saying. "Besides, Ken, you're the only person who could kill Jazzminn Jenks with no repercussions. See, by the time they find out you did it, you'll be . . ."

"Yeah." I felt a sudden surge of wounded anger as I stopped her from finishing the sentence. I swallowed it. I wasn't going to get anywhere by yelling at her because soon I'd be dead and she wouldn't, because her midnight pillow was white instead of red. I couldn't blame her for her clean, white pillow. For the moment, my goal was not to launch into some Hamlet-headed discussion of what was foul and what was fair, but to figure out how best to keep her well-manicured hands off the cutlery.

For the moment, it seemed, the best way to play this game was just to play along.

"You're right about that, Ophelia," I said, nodding. "It's a great concept, to have a dying man commit a murder. I like it."

"Yeah, that is pretty good, isn't it?" She sounded surprised at her own cleverness.

"Outstanding. You should pitch that to the network. It could be a reality show. The audience could vote on who we off before I die." Casually, I sat back down, crossed my legs, and munched a handful of dry Apple Jacks out of the box.

"Now, put down the ham slicer so you can tell me more."

"Well . . . that's sort of it." She lowered the knife, but kept it clutched in her delicate hand. "I've provided you with a victim, a motive, and even a weapon, if you'd like to borrow something from my kitchen — it's okay, I almost never cook. Plus, you won't have to go to jail. Doesn't that cover it?"

"Not quite."

"Oh . . . I forgot. And . . . yes, I'll be your Dark Lady. Your inspiration."

"Hmmm. I don't know. My part sounds like a hell of a lot more work."

"True," Ophelia said. I let my breath out slowly as I watched her replace the knife in its slot. "But you wanted me to give you a reason to live — well, here's one: Murder. Come on, Ken. Murder is worth living for. Every single one of those tragedies you love has a murder in it. If you're not going to do anything except mope around about dying, my being your Dark Lady is an utter waste of time. Now, do we have a deal?"

Do we have a deal, quoth my Dark Lady, my inspiration. The same words I said to Bert DeMarco last spring, when we offered him the highest per-episode salary of any star on the network. But what kind of deal was this?

She was right, I wouldn't go to prison for murder if I died just after the act. But I'd still be a murderer, and I'm . . . shit, I'm *not*. I can't commit suicide, and I can't commit murder. I almost wish I could, one or the other, but I'm just stuck in the middle. With Hamlet. The Prince of fucking Denmark.

But . . . what if I could play along with her for long enough that I'd die before the murder ever happened? Clearly she hadn't thought of that.

I closed my eyes for a second. Frankly, I didn't want to think of that, either, but really, what better way to ensure that she'd stay with me forever, at least, for my forever? If we were plotting a murder, she wouldn't leave me until the end, no matter how . . . no matter how much she might start to want to. And she would begin to want to, I knew it. She didn't know how dark it would get. I wasn't sure either, but I knew it would be darker than either of us could possibly imagine. Black water.

She was still standing there, close to the knives, her *catua* eyes flashing fire. God, she's beautiful.

But now I understood. Until I died, I'd play the part of murderer, play it to the hilt. What difference would it make to anyone but us? We were the only two characters in the cast. If that's what she wanted, she'd get a tragedy as big as *Hamlet* or *Macbeth* on an IMAX screen in RealD 3D. I only hoped I could be a better actor than she was.

It was Fate — finally, a sign, and about time. But if I may take the liberty of addressing Fate directly for a moment: From here on in, please, please, you have *got* to be clearer with me. I'm really not feeling well at all.

I held out my hand.

"Deal," I said.

CHAPTER NINETEEN

**Good thing you can run faster than
I can get up out this chair.**

— Nettie Mae Easley

Abe Heber was a kind and generous man — kind enough, when old age brought winter to his body and his heart, to give his castle, and his kingdom, to his daughters. Not to all three of them — his wealth would be divided between the two eldest, the ones he believed loved him the most. He banished his third daughter, the loveliest, from his home, furious because he thought her love for him was weak and insincere.

By the time he discovered that his two eldest daughters would only fight over his beautiful kingdom, it was too late. Abe Heber very quickly died of what his loving youngest daughter knew was a broken heart, although the official diagnosis was cirrhosis of the liver.

King Lear, except the castle was a mobile home and the kingdom was a trailer park somewhere in northern Montana. But as the tearful youngest daughter told her story on *Really, Girlfriend?* — the two homely older sisters pelting her wavy raven locks with pink sofa cushions, no motion at all in their own matching helmets of big blond hair — it only confirmed my strong belief that truth is stranger on *Really, Girlfriend?*

Though I imagine for my grandma on my mother's side, the story of the Heber family of Montana and the pink pillow fight that followed would not seem Shakespearean at all, and might only have confirmed her strong belief that white folks is . . . well, I just won't say it, that's all. She's an awful, awful woman, and I love her very much.

Given her strong and deeply embarrassing beliefs about heredity, Grandma never much cared for my dating white men — or marrying one, as in the case of Arnie, my first husband. Her point of view remains somewhat illogical, given that she adores my father — but logic means nothing when you're eighty-nine years old and mean as a wolverine. She says anything that comes into her mind. Now, my grandmother on my father's side was discreet enough never to say anything at all about my parent's interracial union. She just died.

As I recall, Grandma was more upset with Arnie for being white than by his latent homosexuality. She couldn't hardly hate the boy for something she figured he could change if he just put his mind to it, now, could she? But she would often call Arnie over to her rocking chair, motion to him to lean in close as if she had a secret, then tell him once again — followed by a long pause that seemed to demand an apology, or at least an explanation — that he was a white man.

Gosh, she'd be mad if she knew I was planning to commit murder with one.

"I thought we'd never get those fucking rednecks out of here," Jazzminn exclaimed after the taping, heaving a huge sigh as she pulled off her pink bunny slippers one by one and tossed them to the floor of the stage. They landed wrong side up, leaving each bunny face down, little paws outstretched on the new white maple floorboards like crime suspects yanked from their cars and spread-eagled on the pavement by the LAPD. Our local peace officers have a long history of getting this city into big trouble with that approach.

"It's a tragedy, really," I mused aloud as I rescued the bunnies, gathering them in my arms so I could stow them safely backstage in Jazzminn's dressing room closet. "He found out who really loved him, but it was too late to save his castle."

Jazzminn squinted her small, bright blue eyes at me, her tiny face blank and uncomprehending. "It's a *trailer*," she said as she padded barefoot down the narrow hallway to her enormous pink dressing room, me following with the discarded bunnies in my arms. "Look. Forget about the . . . Weavers, or whoever the hell they are. Ophelia, I have to ask you something. Is this business about *Bite Me* — you know, my totally destroying your one chance of landing a role on a network sitcom, even a stupid one — going to interfere with our working relationship?"

"Well, I do feel . . ."

"Don't tell me how you *feel*. Feel any way you want to. This is a practical question. Is it business as usual, or not?"

Yes, business as usual except that I just asked a dying man to kill you, I thought. I suddenly envisioned myself and Ken, face down on the pavement like those little pink bunnies on the dressing room floor, surrounded by black-and-white police cars with revolving red lights, the hot breath of two very large German shepherds in our ears and the cold barrels of two 38-caliber pistols pressed at the napes of our necks. He is wearing the Armani suit, and I look fetching even from the back in a cream-colored cashmere turtleneck and powder blue jeans. I wonder briefly if I'll get any sympathy from the jury because one of the officers seizes this opportunity to pinch my butt.

"Business as usual, Jazzminn," I said hoarsely, fear drying my throat. "It doesn't matter. I understand that this job takes precedence over my acting career."

"You don't have an acting career. Hey, you threw up this morning. I heard you. You trying to lose some weight?"

"No. I'm . . . just a little nervous about something that happened last night."

"Oh. Well, don't tell me about it. I don't care what it is. I just don't want you to be thinner than me. Promise you'll never be thinner than me, okay?"

"I promise."

"Good. Guess what, I hate that painting you bought for me." One of the things I do for Jazzminn is to buy art for her collection. Right now she only wants work by gay male contemporary abstract painters from Southern California. An art dealer she slept with recently told her that, statistically, those works are winning the highest prices at auction in New York these days. This particular painter isn't really gay, but when he found out what Jazzminn was willing to pay, he decided to come out of the closet anyway. Very generous of him, I thought.

"I have it on good authority that his work will be worth a lot of money in a decade, maybe less," I told her, putting the bunnies on one of the shelves that lined her closet, where a jury of twelve more pairs of black button eyes stared back at me accusingly.

"Oh. Except that ten years is a long time to wait for the money." Jazzminn's brow would have furrowed, if that were still physically possible. "God, do you know how old I'll be in ten years?"

"Yes, Jazzminn, I do know how old you'll be in ten years."

"Tell a soul and I'll kill you." For the past few minutes, Jazzminn had been busily yanking off the clothes she wore on today's show and throwing them on the floor. Eventually she'd get around to putting something else on, but for the moment she seemed entirely oblivious to her own nakedness. "Ten years. Art sucks. Oh well, I've already got money. Know what? I'm going to fuck Bert DeMarco. What do you think?"

"I think it's none of my business."

"Yeah, so do I." The barefoot Jazzminn stepped on top of her crumpled pale pink suit as if it were a bath mat. "But tell me anyway. You had lunch with him. What do you think of him?"

"I found him to be a very intelligent, thoughtful young man who enjoys serious conversation. Pants?" I suggested hopefully, plucking one of the multiple pairs of size zero pants from Barneys out of her closet and holding them out to her, averting my eyes from the blue-white hollows inside her protruding hipbones, as well as her alarmingly bouncy breasts.

Jazzminn took the pants but used them as a sort of flag to punctuate her thoughts instead of immediately putting them on. "Yeah? Shit. Well, I guess I'll fuck him anyway." She waved her gold Capris. "Hey, Ophelia, there's something I want to talk to you about."

"I'm more than happy to have a conversation with you, Jazzminn."

Last night I asked Ken Harrison to kill Jazzminn Jenks, and he said . . . yes. Now what was I going to do?

It's true that when Jazzminn walked over to Bert DeMarco in the commissary — just as he was praising my undiscovered talent as an actress — and yanked away my only chance of ever acting on TV, one last chance before my ten-year career ends forever, well, at that moment, I really wanted Jazzminn dead. But I couldn't imagine doing it myself. So I phoned the only person I know who knows anything much about death — Ken Harrison.

I called in a fit of passion. I have those. I'm very emotional. I'm not a good actress, but I'm an actress. It seemed like a smart idea last night. But now I was wondering how much I'd have to pay the Heber sisters to let me hitch a ride back to Montana with them in the trailer.

"I didn't say I wanted to have a conversation. That would involve me saying things and you answering," Jazzminn said. "I don't want you to answer. I just want to talk and for you to listen. Okay?"

"Sure. Chilly in here, isn't it?" Ken Harrison had agreed to kill Jazzminn Jenks, with a sudden light in his sad gray eyes and a rush of blood to his ashen face that made him look almost well. Even that awful Melrose haircut seemed to bristle with newfound energy. For a moment he didn't look like a dying man, he looked like a man with something to live for. It wasn't something I'd planned for, but I'd watched it happen with my own eyes. I caused it; therefore I was responsible. That was the logical conclusion. There was no going back now, was there?

Jazzminn finally stepped into the pants, not bothering to pave the way with panties. Thrilled by even minimal progress, I grabbed a stretchy lace top from one of her drawers, and, hoping to increase my odds of her actually wearing it, helpfully slipped it part way over her head instead of handing it to her. She'd have to pull the thing down or she wouldn't be able to see.

"All right." Her words were muffled. With the sheer black lace stretched over her face, flattening her surgically-altered features, Jazzminn looked ready to hold up a 7-Eleven until her little blond head popped out through the neck hole — or perhaps I was overly preoccupied with crime imagery these days. Impatiently, Jazzminn shoved her arms into the tight, elbow-length sleeves. "Here's the thing. I want to write a book about myself, go on a book tour, and sell a million copies." She placed her hands on her pointy hips. "Do you think I can write a book about myself, go on a book tour, and sell a million copies?"

I thought it over. "No, Jazzminn, I don't," I replied truthfully. "I don't think you can write it, and I don't think you could sit still and sign more than ten copies before you start using the f-word in public. I really don't."

"Okay, never mind. Books suck. They've got, like, all these *pages*." Jazzminn began to clap her hands with excitement. "Then I have another thing I want to do instead. Guess what? I want to start a movie company. Made-for-TV movies, you know? Starring me. I want to act before I get old. I'm already too old for features. They're for pre-pubescent idiot boys. Old broads do TV. The network already said they'd pay for it, and they've even given me my own production building over on the other side of the lot."

He said he'd kill her. For me. My hand wandered up to my neck. The ham slicer had nicked my soft, wrinkle-free skin. I'm younger than Jazzminn, but even if we were the same age my skin is less prone to wrinkling than hers due to a higher content of melanin. It's not vanity on my part, just a biological fact. White people wrinkle faster. At eighty-nine, my grandma on my mother's side has the complexion of a sixty-five-year-old. But flawless skin doesn't matter now. They take away all the mirrors on Death Row.

Ken wouldn't have to worry about mirrors, he was already on Death Row. But — wait a second. Ken was on Death Row, with a definite date set for the execution. A tasteless metaphor, one I'd never say aloud — but true all the same. I didn't know when it was, exactly, but I knew the date was soon.

What if I just played along with this murder plot until he . . . well . . . died? That way I wouldn't have to take away what, apparently, had given a dying man the will to live. I wouldn't have to call it off. It wouldn't happen. Not that I was in any hurry to have him die, but . . . why not take advantage of Fate?

You can't save the life of a dying man. You can only save what's left of it.

Maybe I'd done a good deed after all by asking Ken to murder Jazzminn Jenks. In a strange way, I was helping him. Just like he thought he was helping me until Jazzminn spoiled everything. Things always work out for the best, even in Hollywood. It's true. They really do.

"TV movies? That sounds like a great idea, Jazzminn," I said brightly. "And I think I know someone who can help you out. It's the same man who helped me get my audition for the role on *Bite Me*. He's a creative executive at the network. He used to work in comedy, but now he's in tragedy — I mean, he develops TV movies. Maybe he could help you. Oops, I'm sorry. I forgot I wasn't supposed to answer."

"Never mind, it's okay if you talk about *me*." Jazzminn was now busily checking her roots in the mirror. She had them done once every two weeks. Frequent bleaching had almost fried her sparse locks out of existence, thank goodness for hair extensions. She found one dark root and yanked it from the platinum forest. "Ouch — *God*. That sounds really cool. See? If you had that stupid part on TV you wouldn't be around to tell me stuff like this."

"It was one line, Jazzminn."

"Whatever. When can I meet him?"

"Soon." I whispered, because right then that's as loud as I could coax my voice to go. "I think you should do it very, very soon. He's . . . under some time pressure. I think you'd better talk to him while you can."

Jazzminn clapped her tiny hands again. "Yay! You rock, Ophelia. Arrange it."

"All right. I'll see what I can do."

"Don't see what you can do – do it. Hey, why are you whispering? It's annoying as fuck."

"My . . . throat is a little sore."

"No shit, try puking *every day*. Listen, I want you throw away all those bunny slippers in my closet and get new ones. I'm tired of them. And I don't think I want to wear this suit I'm standing on anymore, either. It's had my feet on it, eeewww. Throw it out."

"Sure." Jazzminn never wore the same suit twice, and she requested new bunny slippers approximately once a week. Unbeknownst to her, I was sending all the old ones to a Presbyterian orphanage in Glasgow, in honor of my proud if fictitious Scottish heritage. The orphans all looked like sad-eyed rabbits now in the pictures they sent to me, but at least they were warm. I was somewhat of a role model for them, an orphan from a remote yet beautiful tropical island who had made something of herself in Hollywood. Jazzminn's suits went to Goodwill, for needy size zero women.

"Wow, movies. How great is this?" Jazzminn looked so happy that I almost sobbed out loud. "Hey, I want lunch now. Could you cut my hard-boiled egg in half? Then cut the half I'm going to eat into fourteen pieces?"

"Don't I always, Jazzminn?" I said, relief washing over me. I had a plan now. I was fine. "In fact, I think today, just this once, I'll have the other half."

CHAPTER TWENTY

I have drunk, and seen the spider.

— Leontes, *The Winter's Tale*

There are two places where I cannot help but think of poor Juliet. One is when I pass by Chinese restaurants, it always pops into my mind now: "Parting is such sweet-and-sour." The other is at chemotherapy.

Before chemo, I always stand outside in the hallway instead of sitting in the waiting room with everybody else — Christ, those people have *cancer*. But that's not the hard part. The hardest part is after it's over, when the oncology nurses ask who's picking me up to drive me home. You're not supposed to drive after chemotherapy. The anti-nausea medications make you too drowsy. It is reckless, irresponsible and inadvisable. So I always tell them that my girlfriend Alice is waiting downstairs before I walk down the block, get into my Mercedes and drive myself. I know — I could kill someone.

During chemo, they put you in a very comfortable chair, it's a sort of Barcalounger where you can lean back and put your feet up. This creates the illusion that you have just dropped by to watch the Lakers game. It really is like being in somebody's den — no beer, but you can watch TV or read a magazine if you want to. It's not like I'd ever actually buy Cosmo, but being the competitive type, I like to see how well I do on those tests. You know: "Are you a PMK: Pulsing Mattress Kitten?" "What is Your Sex-Q?" These tests are targeted at women, but I'm confident that I score way higher than they do.

Yet and still it's not the magazines that make me think of Juliet. It's the drips — big syringes suspended on IV poles, the first one full of clear saline, the other a chemical solution of an eerie orange that probably glows in the dark. This orange liquid would burn your skin if you touched it, yet they do not hesitate to funnel it directly into my blood. It is refrigerated before it goes into the IV line so I won't feel the burn. *Presently through all my veins shall run a cold and drowsy humor.*

I feel as Juliet does that night in the nursery, sitting alone on her bed in the dark, holding the vial in her hand. The potion will render her corpse-like, stiff and cold, sans breath or pulse, for just long enough for the duplicitous mourners to bury her. Later, the friar promises, she will miraculously come back to life again, to be secretly reunited with her Romeo in the tomb.

So, I'm asking myself the same questions that she does. *What if this mixture do not work at all?* Or, instead of a cure, *what if it be poison . . . subtly ministered to have me dead,* the act of an impatient universe? Each week, I'm asked to defy both fear and logic and say, sure, go ahead, pump me full of toxic waste. All on the off chance that by taking one step toward death, I might get permission to take two steps back again.

It must have been even harder for Juliet. She was just a kid. On the other hand, she had blissful ignorance on her side. I know how it all turns out. And for me, with each dose the risk gets higher, the odds get lower, the difference between cause and cure blurs a little more. The only thing scarier to me than chemo is the rapidly approaching day when they will just turn, shake their heads, and wheel the big orange syringe away.

Today, however, as I stared at the needle inserted into the back of my hand, I wasn't thinking about Juliet, I was thinking about Jazzminn Jenks.

I had let Ophelia talk me into murder. I'd even allowed her to choose the victim. I mean, I knew I wasn't really going to kill Jazzminn Jenks for her, but even so . . . well, frankly, I was beginning to feel a little manipulated.

I knew this was a crime destined never to happen, but as I sat there in the chemo chair, going from hot to cold, taking it again, one more week, one more time not ripping out the tubes and running down the hallway telling all the nurses to go to hell, taking it — I found myself wanting to decide how Jazzminn Jenks would die.

I've worked in Hollywood for more than ten years. *I'm* the one with experience in story structure. I needed a Dark Lady in my life, not another damned writer. So here's the plot: No blood — ugh, no dyed blond hair with black roots matted red with blood, no hideous police photos, no Henckels kitchen knives, no gloves, no masks, no damn DNA evidence to get botched or mislaid by the LAPD. No. It would be clean, neat and simple. It would be poison.

I mean, it wouldn't be. . . but it would be.

I have quite a stockpile of pills in my medicine chest, all the ones I never took, choose your weapon. The death of Jazzminn Jenks would be caused by my supposed cure. There was some justice in that. Fate, you are such a pain in the ass — but you can also be fiendishly clever.

They started the drip, like ice under my skin. I closed my eyes and felt the taste of poison in my mouth. Ophelia, *this do I drink to thee.*

CHAPTER TWENTY-ONE

**Quit staring at your own self in the mirror
and come to supper.**

— Nettie Mae Easley

There was much to be done. Besides plotting a murder that would never happen, the time had come to officially disband the Ophelia Lomond Fan Club.

I may not have landed any major roles during my ten year career in Hollywood — no, I have to be honest, outside of student workshop performances at Lana Bishop Academy, I have landed *no* roles during my ten year career in Hollywood. But so far, the fact that I have never acted professionally has had no negative impact on my Internet fan base.

The Official Ophelia Lomond Fan Club started innocently enough — by chance, much like my maternal love affair with the Presbyterian orphans of Glasgow. Like many actors, I created my own website — *www.OhOphelia.com* — as a helpful adjunct to my resume. After an audition, I reasoned, I could simply tell the very interested director or casting agent to refer to the website for more information on my career and credits. Unfortunately none of them were quite interested enough to follow through, although they frequently left suggestive messages on my voice mail.

It's too bad, too. It's a great website. Because I didn't have . . . well, a career or credits in the traditional sense, I filled the blank page with an array of striking photos of myself, reflecting twelve of my different moods, including "reflective."

The shots were taken by a unit photographer I'd met on the studio lot shortly after my very amicable divorce from Wade Stark. Now there was an interesting man, not a suit at all — a former photographer for a foreign news service who had shot practically every world conflict since the Gulf War. Finally, overcome by anxiety attacks and landmine nightmares, he had decided to move to Hollywood to shoot publicity photos for studio press kits.

He simply approached me one day as I was walking to the commissary to pick up Jazzminn's lunch and begged me to allow him to take my picture because I was so lovely and his tired eyes "ached with war." It moved me to tears, especially with his accent. I had to agree to a request like that, particularly since I needed photos for the website.

During our series of photo sessions at his downtown loft on San Pedro Street, he told me that when he first came to Los Angeles he'd taken a portfolio of his shocking combat photographs to a group of young film executives, just to show them what he could do with a camera. He explained that the photos were from Sarajevo. The young executives frowned and said they were unfamiliar with the film.

While my web page received no hits at all from members of either the Producers or Directors Guild, due to the combination of my looks and Zlatan's equally astonishing photography, I began receiving e-mails from all over the world from people — all men, except for a very nice lesbian dentist in Prague — wanting to know more about actress Ophelia

Lomond.

Because it soon became impossible to answer all the requests individually, I removed the "disappointed Ophelia" photo and put in its place a biographical sketch, detailing my sunny childhood on the tiny Caribbean island of Sadilla. It never occurred to me until I met Ken Harrison how many insomniacs worldwide have perhaps found sleep on Sadilla's enchanted shores.

I also deleted the "confused Ophelia" in order to begin inserting a bi-weekly blog of my random thoughts on a variety of subjects, surrounded by a lovely border of hibiscus blooms. Not advice — I don't think you have the right to tell someone else what to do or not to do, what to be or not to be, if I may take Shakespeare out of context for a moment. Instead, I believe that my thoughts simply illustrated positive, alternative ways of looking at common problems.

Take promiscuity, for example — which television and movies would have you believe is a healthy, normal, and enjoyable state of being among the single, attractive, and affluent. That's not true. I can't for the life of me understand why someone would hop into bed with a person they don't love, maybe don't even really know. To me, that doesn't make any more sense than boarding a train to Fresno when you're trying to get to San Francisco just because it's a train — or calling to say "Happy Mother's Day" to someone else's Mom because yours is out grocery shopping at the moment you feel like saying it.

I didn't tell my fan club that the only men I've ever slept with are my three husbands. I didn't want to appear holier-than-thou, or overly reliant on vows and licenses. I don't need documents to tell me how I feel. I didn't sleep exclusively with my three husbands because it was legal or considered moral. I married them because I loved them, and everything else followed from there.

What I did tell my loyal fans, there in the little window surrounded by hibiscus blooms, was to wait for the right train, to wait and call when Mom comes home. I don't know if they listened when I begged them not to go to Fresno, when I told them to believe in exalted love, even in today's Hollywood. It's not something than can only happen on exotic islands, or in plays written in the 1600s, on castle balconies or in enchanted forests, or . . . in sonnets. It could happen in the 7-Eleven or a dentist's office in Prague if that's where your heart is.

I don't know if they listened. I don't know if Dr. Anna Svoboda, thirty-eight, ever stopped worrying about her thick ankles and waited for the right girl. Maybe I just should have told my fan club what my Grandma on my mother's side would have said — "Sleep around, you a whore" — but that's not what I meant, not at all. I don't judge such behavior. I'm simply baffled by it, disappointed by it. It's not really any of my business, but I don't want anyone, anywhere in the world to miss the train.

I suppose my three marriages might raise some question as to whether I am the right person to comment on this matter. But I have no regrets about Arnie, Carlos, or Wade. Though he was with me for only a short time, Arnie came out of the closet, discovering himself as both an artist and a homosexual. I like to think I played a small part in that — although in this case not saving myself for marriage might have identified the problem more quickly and saved my parents some wedding expenses. Carlos — such an astonishing actor, he can play anything, and then translate it all into Spanish over the phone for his adoring family in Guatemala. It was only right that his bright off-Broadway stage career should take precedence over our plans to have three extraordinarily attractive children in Los Angeles. I mean, our plan to have children — we didn't care what they looked like. We were just aware, looking at ourselves, that attractiveness was a burden our children would have to bear. Things happened for the best, like they always do. I only hope that, someday, Carlos wins a Tony on Broadway or gets a starring role in a major motion picture playing something other than a good-looking Central American cocaine dealer.

And Wade, wonderful Wade. He had a heart as big as his shoes. But he is basketball, and I'm . . . not. I couldn't be a basketball player's wife. I didn't want go to the games, to sit by the sidelines and watch. Not only did I have nothing to talk about with the other players' wives — I don't need cosmetic surgery, so I fully understand why they resented my attempts to join in — I just can't make myself care who has the ball. I don't understand the ball. When I see an object hurtling through the air toward me, my instinct is not to try to catch it or put it through a hoop, but to simply step out of the way. I don't enjoy arbitrary competition. I think life is about one's personal best, and encouraging the same in others. I hope that, someday soon, Wade Stark finds a woman who cares about the ball.

I did not make three mistakes. I made three choices, out of love. At the same time as I encourage my fans to wait for the right train, I must also encourage them not to be so afraid of finding a love and losing it that they never get on a train at all.

But what good are my positive alternatives now? Before, they were the thoughts of a Hollywood actress and that means something in this world, particularly when accompanied by such stunning photos. And, because they were invented to enhance the career of a Hollywood actress, the fictitious details of my sun-swept childhood on the tiny island of Sadilla served an urgent purpose that seemed to me to fully justify their lack of veracity.

But now, my observations are just the random thoughts of Karen Watts from Indianapolis, Indiana, fired from a one-line part, whose first and last acting job in Hollywood is to delay long enough to make sure Ken Harrison dies before he kills someone. Then, I'm selling Wade's house and going home.

Should I say goodbye, send one last positive thought out into the world inside a border of hibiscus blooms, before I delete my website account forever? I decided against it. I didn't want the world pining away for the beautiful Ophelia. The Ophelia Lomond Fan Club website, with all of my different moods, would simply disappear as if it had never been. As I should have done with Ken Harrison, I would quietly remove myself from their lives before they ever stopped believing in Sadilla.

CHAPTER TWENTY-TWO

Give me the glass, and therein will I read.

— King Richard, *King Richard the Second*

I could have sworn I did not sleep at all on Friday night, seized as I was at around eleven by a severe case of hiccups. I know that sounds ridiculous — hiccups — but man, tell me it's ridiculous after you've been through a whole night of it. But I must have dozed off eventually, just in time for the loud knock on my door to scare the crap out of me.

"I'm coming, but you've gotta give me a minute," I shouted as I slowly untangled my exhausted body from twisted sheets. I sincerely hope there are no big earthquakes before I die, because there's no way I could get myself out of bed and under a sturdy table or into a doorway before the building falls down. What's it to *him*, you may be asking.

I wrapped my naked self in my ragged plaid bathrobe — these days, it almost went around twice — and dragged myself to the door. "Who the hell is it?"

"Hi, Ken! Stop swearing at me. It's Ophelia."

"Oh, *God.*" Yes, today was Saturday — the day we'd agreed to sit down together and plan the murder of Jazzminn

Jenks. But, to the best of my foggy recollection, we had not at any point specifically designated 8 a.m. "I . . . thought you'd be coming later. And I sort of thought you'd call first . . ."

"I was planning to! But you said you're always up, and I was in the neighborhood so I thought I'd stop by." She was still speaking through the door. "I hope it's okay. And guess what? I brought a friend."

I suppose that, once upon a time, I felt as cheerful as that voice. Now, hearing it almost hurt, the way average decibels pound in the head of a person with a hangover. And she brought a friend — just what I needed to hear, in that bathrobe. But at that point I really couldn't think of anything else to do but open the door. I took a deep breath, clutched the robe around me, stretched my lips into my best imitation of a smile, and opened it.

I beheld Ophelia on the other side, dressed in a lovely rose-colored wool jacket, her curly hair pulled back into a pony tail, bearing in her arms the ugliest cat I'd ever seen.

"Good morning, Kenny!"

"Good morning, Ophelia," I replied. "Do you know that your friend is a giant rat?"

"It's not a rat: it's a kitty." Ophelia caressed the creature's thin, slightly greasy gray fur with a tenderness that made me ache with . . . well, something. Jealousy, maybe. Or perhaps this ache heralded the unwelcome return of my hiccups. Whatever the feeling was, it would not win out this morning.

"And I'm sorry I woke you up," she continued. "This cat was going to be my cat on *Bite Me*. I picked him up from an animal shelter in Beverly Hills so I could start rehearsing, but then I got fired. They said that if I didn't need him anymore, they would take him back. I can't keep a cat up in the hills. Last time I had one a coyote tore her to shreds. I cried for days. I was on my way to the shelter — they open at 8:30, I wanted to get it over with — when it suddenly occurred to me that . . . you might want him. You know, just for company. I know . . . you don't get out that much."

Startled, I shook my head. "Thanks, but I'm not going to live long enough to have a cat."

"But this isn't a healthy cat, Ken! This is a really old, sick cat. In fact, I got the oldest, sickest cat I could find — you know, for authenticity. He's perfect for you. I'm sorry. I shouldn't have said that, but you know what I mean."

Actually, one of the things I liked best about Ophelia was that she said things like that. Still, this plan was not going to work. "Ophelia, honey, I'm not even going to live as long as *this* cat."

"Well, I have to put him down for a second. His claws are stuck in my jacket. Do you mind if we come in?" Ophelia stepped inside without waiting for my response. She tried to lower the pathetic pet to the floor, but it kept scrambling back into her arms, apparently horrified by the idea of being dumped here, with me. Its greasy gray coat was a perfect match for the shag carpet.

Finally, Ophelia managed to disengage the animal without losing more than a few threads of rose-colored wool. It hunkered down flat, staring up at me with baleful yellow eyes, flinching as though raindrops were falling on its head. It had short black whiskers and was missing one fang.

"Nice place," observed Ophelia, her stunning eyes taking in my sparsely furnished home. I was suddenly too aware of the crumpled blanket on the couch, the empty prescription container on the floor, the thermometer on the coffee table next to *The Complete Works of William Shakespeare*, the melted ice pack that hung over the black leather arm of the room's only comfortable chair. I'd planned to clean up before she arrived, to remove all evidence that . . . that someone like me lived here. No — not someone like me. Me. Might as well say it.

"No, it's not a nice place at all. And thanks for thinking of me, Ophelia, but please — no cat."

"Okay, got it. Bad idea." Ophelia knelt and kissed the cat on top of its head. "Sorry, I was only trying to help. Well, can he at least stay where he is until we're done talking? I'd put him back in the Jag, but his cute little claws leave pinholes in the leather."

"It won't pee on the carpet, will it?" Not that it mattered much, here.

"Of course not. He's a very good boy."

"Then, sure. But, Ophelia, you've gotta give me a minute to shower and throw on some clothes. Make yourself at home, or at whatever-the-hell-you'd-call-this-place. I'd offer you coffee, but there isn't any. I've got plenty of tea though — and a coupla cases of ginger ale. And . . . soup. I think that's about it. Just help yourself."

"I'm fine. I had a latte and a very delicious apricot scone on the way over — and Starbucks gave me a special little cup of plain warm milk for Puddy, wasn't that nice? Take your time. I'll just stay out here and play with him."

This could be that cat's first time playing ever, I thought. "Okay, knock yourselves out. I'll be right back."

I'd had my superintendent adjust the hot water faucet in my shower so it would only go about three-quarters of the way around and then stop. I was so cold always, I'd lost my ability to tell how hot the water was getting. If I tried to judge the temperature by how it felt, I'd have burned off half my skin by now. Even though I could see the steam rising, to me the water remained defiantly lukewarm.

And because there is no joy in the lukewarm, my shower was, as usual, short. I shaved, combed my wet hair, and brushed my teeth very carefully to avoid making my gums bleed. Murderers don't have bleeding gums. Then, I put on a clean pair of jeans and two layers of sweaters, and rejoined Ophelia and her friend, who were by now playing a rousing game with my thermometer.

"Hey — I use that."

"I know. Sorry. He just jumped up on the coffee table and decided to push it off. I promise I'll wash it for you later, with lots of hot water and soap. Just let him keep it for now — it won't break on the carpet. And I don't want to rush you, but we need to get down to business. I'm getting my hair trimmed at eleven."

I watched her play with the cat for a moment. I was still picturing him sitting outside a Starbucks on Ventura Boulevard, his little gray butt ensconced in the soft leather seat of Ophelia's glossy red Jaguar, lapping warm milk from a coffee cup.

"Are you still sure you want to do this, Ophelia?" I asked.

"Do what?"

Did she really just ask that? "Murder. We're going to off Jazzminn Jenks, remember?"

"Oh! Yes. Of course, Ken, that's why I'm here." She nodded, but seemed distracted somehow.

The "that's why I'm here" part hurt a little. But what did I expect: "I came because, without your calling me, I knew that you were miserable last night, thirty-six years old and sleepless as a child. I came to comfort you because you've never been to Disneyland, I came because I knew?" I shook it off. "Murder," I repeated patiently. "Homicide, assassination, termination. We're talking about death. Think about it. Think about it real hard, Ophelia."

Ophelia got up from the floor, dusting errant gray carpet shags from the knees of her black skinny jeans. "What if I said no, Ken, I don't want to do it?" she asked. "What would happen then?"

What would happen then, indeed? After all, that's why she was here — the only reason. She just said so. That's why I'm here. Not because I needed her. Not because I was sick and alone and I needed her. I knew what would happen if she said she didn't want to murder Jazzminn Jenks. She'd say it, and then she'd go.

"Never mind. I was just kidding," I said hastily. "Ha. Ha. Besides . . . it wouldn't matter if you said you didn't want to help me now. I'd kill her anyway. How dare that little bitch ruin your career?" See, Ophelia? No point in having any second thoughts now, I'd kill her anyway, I repeated, desperately, in my mind. No need for you to leave me now.

"Now, Ken, I think you can kill the woman without calling her names," Ophelia chided.

"Sorry." I suppose I could infer from this that Ophelia still wanted to see Jazzminn dead, but I needed to be sure she was with me. If Fate was going to fuck me again — despite my repeated and, I think, perfectly reasonable requests not to be fucked — I might as well hear it while I was still feeling disappointed by my lukewarm shower.

"Suppose I told you that, if we don't kill Jazzminn Jenks, I've decided not to kill anybody? That if you change your mind about this now, no one will die at all — except, of course, yours truly? Then what?" I asked carefully.

"Oh, Ken — please don't say you're dying."

"Why the hell not? You said it first."

"I know. But I've changed my mind."

"I don't want to burst your bubble, sweetheart, but I don't think this one's up to you."

"I didn't mean that. I just . . . don't think we need to talk about it anymore, that's all."

"All right. Let's not talk about it. What should we talk about? The weather, maybe? How 'bout those Lakers? Who's up for an Emmy this year?"

"No," she whispered. "Murder. Homicide, assassination, termination. That's what I want to talk about . . . even though I don't really want to talk about it."

Well, you'd have to be pretty sick to accept that kind of logic, but, lucky for me, I am. "Okay, fine," I said curtly. "Just checking. We'll get down to business, then. The first thing I want to tell you is that I've selected a murder weapon. In fact, I have it right here in the apartment."

"Ugh — don't show it to me!"

"Now, now, Ophelia, we're in this together. The Dark Lady of the Sonnets was probably a dog, but there's nothing in the literature to suggest that she was a chicken. I really think you need to see. Follow me."

Reluctantly, Ophelia followed, seeming a little surprised when I turned a sharp corner into my tiny, steamy bathroom. "Open it," I invited proudly, pointing at the medicine cabinet with its cracked mirror on the door.

She didn't open it. "What happened to the mirror?" she asked instead.

I stood in this bathroom, staring into this mirror, on the day Dr. Hugh Goldberg of Cedars Sinai Hospital quietly suggested that I "put my affairs in order." I tried to wipe the tears away with both hands — but from the mirror, not from my face, like an asshole. I was trying to wipe tears off glass. I obviously was no good with mirrors, so I took my fist and I broke it. Then I took my other fist and broke it some more.

"Earthquake," I replied. "Come on, Ophelia. Open it." Ophelia covered her eyes, wincing as she pulled the handle. After a moment, she slowly lowered her hand.

"I don't see any weapons in here, Ken."

I was disappointed that the Dark Lady failed to immediately appreciate my carefully stocked arsenal. "Ophelia, there are enough pharmaceuticals in here to kill every talk show host on network *and* cable."

"Oooh. Now I understand." Ophelia reached up and ran her fingertips slowly over the rows of glass bottles and plastic containers. I was surprised, and annoyed, to see her eyes begin to fill with tears.

"What?" I groaned. An accomplice to murder can't afford to be so emotional. "Don't tell me — you've decided you just can't possibly let me kill Jazzminn Jenks. Fine. I always figured as much. Just . . . get out of here, Ophelia, and take that damn cat with you. You don't belong here."

"I'm not crying about Jazzminn Jenks," Ophelia whispered. "I'm crying because — your name is on all of these, Ken. They're all for you. Does it really take all of this, all these pills, just to keep you alive?"

I looked at the neat rows of containers labeled Kenneth Harrison. Two with a full glass of water, three with each meal. Caution: never take tablet No. 1 in combination with capsule No. 2. Yeah, I guess there were a lot of them. "Well, obviously not, because I didn't take them," I said coldly. "Believe me, I've got enough other noxious substances floating around in my bloodstream right now. Just be glad I'm willing to share. Please — don't do that."

"Sorry." She quickly wiped her eyes.

"Good." Satisfied, I continued my tour of the Kenneth Charles Harrison Not-Quite-Memorial Drug Museum. "My best stuff — that is, the most toxic — is over on the right. You've just got to help me think of some way to get her to take them."

"That's easy. I'll just grind 'em up and put them in her chipotle mayonnaise. Uh oh, I really have to sit down right now." Abruptly Ophelia pushed my worn toilet seat down with one finger, then closed the lid and sat on it, knock-kneed, both hands pressed over her mouth.

"You all right?" I asked, startled.

"I'll be fine in a minute," she said from between her fingers, curling her toes toward the ceiling. "I . . . just remembered that chipotle mayonnaise doesn't agree with me. I'm an actress, you know. We're trained in sense memory. We feel *everything*."

"Well, don't hurl. You're not putting any pills in any chipotle mayonnaise," I said. "That's not part of the Dark Lady's job description, thank you. You aren't the murderer, remember? You are my inspiration — and as far as I'm concerned, no one ever needs to know that but me. I've got to do it myself, somehow."

Ophelia uncovered her mouth and rose shakily to her feet. "All better," she said, with no conviction. "Well, I'm sure you'll come up with something. Take your time!"

"Easy for you to say."

"I'm sorry, Ken. I always say the wrong thing, don't I?" Ophelia reached out and touched my cheek with the side of her soft hand for a moment that didn't last nearly long enough. "But I want you to know, I've been thinking about this. Jazzminn wants to start her own production company. The network already gave her a building. She wants to start making TV movies next season — starring her, of course. That's your

department now, isn't it? If I tell her you're the executive who
recommended me for *Bite Me*, she'll climb right into your lap.
Besides, she's very single, and you're still . . . surprisingly good
looking."

I chuckled. "Yeah, 'good looking' that's been through the
wash cycle a few too many times. Nice try, Ophelia."

"You should learn to accept a compliment. Besides, you
are male. You are breathing. Trust me, that's enough for
Jazzminn." Ophelia laughed with delight. "This is perfect! I'll
talk to her on Monday. Now, you should have some breakfast,
and I guess I'd better take the cat back to the shelter."

We walked back into the living room, where the cat was
still trying to escape by sinking through the floor. "We're
leaving now. Come on, kitty." Ophelia knelt to pick up the cat,
which was now just as determined to stay glued to the floor as
he'd been before to avoid it. As she lifted his front half, he dug
his back claws into the carpet, his lanky gray body stretching
out like chewed gum after you finally notice you've stepped in
it and lift up your shoe in disgust. Finally, when the beast could
stretch no more, his reluctant back feet left the ground, one by
one, and dangled uneven in the air.

"Don't worry. I'm sure the shelter will find a new home
for you very, very soon," Ophelia cooed, playing with his
tattered ears.

Of course they won't, of course they won't — Jesus, *look*
at him, I thought. Nobody would ever, ever take this cat. He
was still just hanging there, long, gray and ugly, his back toes
splayed out, claws extended, trying vainly to reach the ground.
There would be no home for this cat.

I reached out to take the cat from Ophelia, cupping his
rabbit-like back feet in one hand as I grasped his body firmly
with the other. I had no idea how to hold one of these things,
but this seemed to work. "It's all right. I'll keep him," I heard

myself saying. At the same moment, the cat hissed at me.

"Really? You want him?" Ophelia was overjoyed.

"Want is a strong word, Ophelia. I just said the rat could stay — that's all." Awkwardly, I stroked his bony spine, eliciting another hiss.

"Kenny, that's great! I have cat litter and food and everything he needs out in my car." Ophelia was so excited that she embraced both me and the cat together. This made for quite an interesting sandwich. "Thank you so much. Now I won't have to worry about him. He'll have you." Embarrassed, she un-embraced us. "So . . . what are you going to call him?"

I thought it over. "Nothing."

"What do you mean, nothing?"

"I mean nothing. Look, he can stay, but I'm not naming him."

"Oh, come on, Kenny. You have to call him something."

"No name for the cat." I made my voice purposefully harsh to avoid a sudden urge to weep. I am not sure which is worse, hiccups or uncontrollable bursts of emotion, but by now I'd pretty much had it with both.

"Sure. Whatever you want, Ken. He's your cat." Ophelia backed away a few steps. "I'll just go out to the car and get his things. I also got him a new catnip mouse — you two will have lots of fun together with that!"

My cat. What do you know, I had my first pet. As the door closed behind Ophelia, the cat and I glared at each other. This was definitely a scene from *Bite Me.* A latent hiccup rocked us both. And then I did weep — because, as I may have mentioned, I am no good at all with mirrors. And here I was, staring directly into one.

CHAPTER TWENTY-THREE

**First time I see water in a bottle,
well, I just laugh.**

— Nettie Mae Easley

Mulholland Drive is named after Irish immigrant William
Mulholland, a self-taught engineer who built the two hundred
and thirty-eight mile Los Angeles Aqueduct in 1913 to supply
the growing San Fernando Valley with water from the cold
streams and clear lakes of the high Sierras. I don't mean he
built it himself, he had other people do it for him — about
four thousand workers, not all of whom lived to tell the tale.

I researched the life of William Mulholland after Wade
gave me the house on Vista de la Vida as a divorce present. I
thought if I was going to own a house off Mulholland Drive, I
should know more about this expensive winding road than the
way it looks in acrylics in the iconic David Hockney painting in
the Los Angeles County Museum of Art.

L.A. would be a desert if we didn't borrow our water from
somewhere else. While I appreciate the option of re-filling my
swimming pool whenever I choose, I also have to wonder
what, exactly, possessed Mulholland to spend his whole life

forcing water to flow in a direction it had no original intention of going. My grandma on my mother's side would probably attribute this obsession with controlling a force of nature to his . . . Caucasian heritage, but because I was born into a slightly more forgiving period in history when it comes to racial matters, I'm just thinking: *Men.*

I miss the Great Lakes. Frankly, I've been thirsty ever since I moved here. I know, we never drank out of the Great Lakes directly, and there's probably more bottled water in Los Angeles than anywhere else in the world. It just feels like there's never enough water here, despite William Mulholland's best efforts.

Today, driving home from the studio along Mulholland Drive, a twelve-ounce bottle of Evian from Jazzminn's refrigerator in my drink tray, I was thinking about William Mulholland and his contribution to Los Angeles— partly to take my mind off murder. But then the car in front of me, one of those big Escalades, vehicle of choice for the hip hop nation, big square hulks that make it look as if L.A. has declared war on itself, suddenly slammed on the brakes — so abruptly that I couldn't stop. I had to swerve my red Jaguar off the road to avoid rear-ending him.

There was no damage to either automobile, but I can't say there was no harm done because after my car stopped I rolled down my window and yelled out: "Hey, watch it, asshole!" The teenager at the wheel of the Escalade ignored me, cranked up his sound system until the car bumped and rocked, and sped on.

My hands flew to my mouth. I'd never called another person that before, ever. Think how awful that is, to actually call another person an asshole. I don't think when people use that word they're really considering the unattractive puckered skin surrounding the anal sphincter. They probably just want to say something loud and harsh to express annoyance. The word has lost all meaning and just become a sound, like a barking dog. But I don't use that word because I am envisioning an actual asshole. I know, I tend to be too literal at times.

But I do think profanity should be reserved for major catastrophes — famine, the AIDS crisis in Africa, nuclear war, the end of the world, several of our U.S. presidents — not for common annoyances such as losing cell phone reception in the canyon. And definitely not for Escalade drivers who brake too fast.

Save it for aggressive, large cell non-Hodgkin's lymphoma.

But I'm learning that cancer comes with its own kind of expletives, its own vocabulary of medical obscenities. Mysterious, terrifying sequences of letters and numbers. I see the words, letters, numbers, right in front of me, right in my face. They come after their names, attached to the people's names who are members of this website, *NHLfriends.com* — people you meet entirely by mistake when you skip your acting class to sit alone in your bedroom, the only light coming from one violet-scented candle and the computer screen, Googling "aggressive large cell non-Hodgkin's lymphoma." NHL — Non-Hodgkin's Lymphoma.

Billy G.: DX with CLL B cell. 6x Fludarabine. Transformed to prolymphocytoid CLL. Surgery to remove tumor c1/c2 vertebrae, radiation, 4 cycles of chemo suspended when I couldn't walk. Steroids have me walking. Jane, DX w/intermediate large B cell, Stage IIE, TX-CHOP x6. Sometimes this string of medical expletives ended with the word "remission," or "cure." Just as often, it didn't. Randy, age 17. I couldn't force myself to read what came after Randy's name.

I stared at the letters and numbers the same way I always

stare at the letters and numbers on the vanity license plates in front of me on the freeway, many of them inside references to the entertainment industry: GAGS4TV, SAGMMBR, 6FGRDEL, SCRPTDR. Sometimes I can crack the code, get the joke; sometimes I can't. Unlike Ken Harrison, I have never been a comedy executive. I'm not good at jokes. Sometimes I'm pretty sure I'm sitting there in rush hour traffic trying to de-code license plates that don't say anything at all — just random letters and numbers generated by computer and assigned by the Department of Motor Vehicles. And here I am trying to read them, trying to figure out the minds of people inside cars, people I will never meet, when I really should be keeping my eyes on the road, on the brake lights in front of me.

"I'm so very sorry," I whispered to the driver of the Escalade, but by then he and his excessively large vehicle were gone.

Thinking about it later, I'm sure almost smashed into that big, ugly Escalade because I kept seeing on the road before me, on the Mulholland Drive in my mind, not the shiny rear bumper of the Escalade, but a ghostly silver '78 Mercedes 450 SL convertible bearing the vanity plate: NOT2B.

CHAPTER TWENTY-FOUR

**What fates impose, that men must needs abide;
It boots not to resist both wind and tide.**

— King Edward, *King Henry the Sixth, Part Three*

Even though the sun was bright, it was cold as hell at
Venice Beach as the caravan of production trucks began to line
up in the sand. Crew members zipped their network logo
jackets up to their chins as they began snaking cable and
rigging lights along a short section of the concrete bike path
that ran all the way north to Malibu and all the way south to
Redondo Beach. Temperature doesn't matter in television.
Lights, camera, summer.

I didn't usually come to the set if I could avoid it, but this
time the director called me, a madman at 5 a.m., because, with
a forty-degree wind whipping in off the Pacific, getting Tyne
Daly into roller blades for the final scene was going to take my
own special brand of persuasion.

I nodded my thanks as a young, chubby red-haired woman
from craft services handed me steaming black coffee in a paper
cup. I couldn't drink it, but it kept my hands warm. Tyne
wasn't here yet. Still clutching my coffee, I carefully stepped

over the thick bundles of cable and walked alone down to the water's edge.

I started making patterns in the sand with the toe of my right Nike to keep myself occupied while not drinking my coffee. I love coffee, I used to drink it by the quart; now, it's like battery acid in my gut. So instead of drinking coffee, I drew with my toe. Not exactly a precision instrument, but I had a wide canvas — sand as far as I could see, pure and white except for the occasional half-smoked cigarettes jutting out of the sand at odd angles, some kissed with lipstick. All the world's an ashtray, and there are people in it who don't get cancer even though they kiss butts.

At first I just drew swirls: abstract, random. Almost as soon as I'd draw them, they'd fill with water and erase themselves, grain by grain, melting back into a smooth, wet flatness. Nothing you could write in the sand with your toe would last very long. That's bad if you have something you want the world to remember, but good if you just want to try something out, without committing to it, just to see how it looks written in cold, wet sand.

I wrote my name, K-E-N, and watched it melt. Then I went a little higher up the beach, further from the tide. I wrote it again. This time, my name lasted a little bit longer, but after a minute or two it melted, too. You could count on the words melting, no matter where you wrote them.

So I figured, maybe I'd go ahead and write M-U-R-D-E-R.

You know, just to see what it looked like before it melted away. I'd write it small, so in case some rich guy in a private plane was buzzing the beach, he wouldn't be able to see it and report me to whoever's in charge of the war on terrorism in the Venice Beach area.

Murder I wrote, hah, hah. Then, since I had some time to kill — that's also kind of funny, time to kill — I added a couple more letters: V.P., MURDER. Now that I'd gotten myself involved in concocting this story, that's what it should say on my business card instead of Vice President, Comedy Development. Vice President, Murder Development. I needed new business cards. And a gold name plate. Vice President of Murder.

Well, I had the whole beach, and time to kill. Nobody on the production staff could see me down here, I was too far away. So I added another word: *EXECUTIVE* V.P., MURDER. If I was going to plot a murder, I might as well be in charge, right? For once in my life, I might as well get total creative control. It felt . . . a lot better than it should.

For murder, though it have no tongue, will speak / With most miraculous organ. Right now, I could sure use a miraculous organ or two.

Of course I'm kidding, I told myself as I watched my name, my title, and my murder melt into the sand. I joke around. After more than ten years in sitcom, no one should take anything I say seriously, including me. It was time to stop joking around, writing nonsense in the sand. Time to stop enjoying it way, way too much. The words made me feel . . . strong. Too weak to drink a cup of watery java from Craft Services, but strong enough to kill. I liked writing it.

I saw the white limo pulling up beside the line of production trucks. I dumped my coffee into the surf and walked back up the beach to help Tyne Daly on with her roller blades. Hell, it wasn't time to kill: it was time to shoot.

CHAPTER TWENTY-FIVE

The lights burn blue. It is now dead midnight.
Cold fearful drops stand on my trembling flesh.
What do I fear? Myself? There's none else by.

— King Richard, *King Richard the Third*

The next day I learned that I would henceforth be free on Fridays because further chemotherapy was "contraindicated in my case." My body just couldn't take any more. They were nice enough about it. A lot of hands on my shoulder. "Son," Dr. Goldberg called me. I thanked them, and I left. I'm okay with this. I knew it was coming: it said so right there in the introduction to Shakespeare. "Comedy ends in marriage. Tragedy ends in death." Guess which demographic is mine.

I was glad I had my Oakley sunglasses, to hide my face outside. Funny how I used to think sunglasses were to keep the sun out of your eyes.

I wasn't going to have to play the part of murderer for nearly as long as I'd hoped — I mean, thought. Terminal cancer can apparently get more terminal, an absolute more absolute. I never looked up "palliative," but now I know it means "providing false hope," making you feel better so you won't know you are getting worse, so you won't even *know*. I didn't know that not having all those tubes stuck in me on a weekly basis would feel like someone had cut my connection to the mothership and now I was floating out in space. I should have known.

I went home to my rented condo, my *sterile promontory* adjacent to Beverly Hills. I considered vomiting, but that's such a cliché — the character vomits when he hears bad news. It's like the writer can't think of anything else that could indicate such overwhelming grief and sadness; anything else that could illustrate how it feels to sink into mourning for yourself; something that could possibly say, without words, how much you will miss you. It's just lazy writing, in my opinion. So I wouldn't vomit. I was going to get up now. Nothing to be gained, really, from staring into the water in a toilet. I wouldn't be a Hollywood cliché.

I couldn't break my mirror, it was already broken. Crash the car? The front end of the Mercedes already looked like I'd gone the wrong way on a one-way street. Put a fist through a wall? Another cliché, besides being expensive — and, I'm guessing, painful. Plus I wasn't even sure if I could do it. Nobody in a movie or a TV show ever has to hit a wall more than once to make a nice, neat hole. I'll bet real walls don't behave so well. I'd probably just keep on punching until my knuckles were a bloody pulp and the neighbors called to complain.

There also would be no cliché scene where I tell her, and we hold each other and cry. She already knows. Hell, she told me. She . . . *knows*, Kenny. How could I ask anyone to cry, expect anyone to cry for me, when nothing at all had changed except in my own mind?

I used the edge of the sink to pull myself up. The sink was another place where I would not vomit. Instead, I looked at my own face in the cracked mirror. I looked terrible. Sure, a rose *by any other name would smell as sweet*, but what if the thing *looked* like hell? What was it Tyne Daly's husband says in the movie, his voice a hushed and sexy whisper: "She just hasn't been herself since the cancer." That's why I look like this. Since the cancer, I am not myself. I don't look like myself. I am not myself. I can't be myself, because if I were myself, I'd cry myself to sleep tonight.

So who am I? Maybe I'm the guy who pulls open the cracked door of the medicine cabinet, takes out all the little bottles and containers and pours everything in them down his throat. Yeah, I'd die, but at least I'd have some . . . creative control.

Before, I'd told myself it was Fate — I'd stockpiled all this poison because, unbeknownst to me, one day I'd be able to pull open this door and show it to a beauty named Ophelia and tell her that this was how I planned to kill Jazzminn Jenks. Maybe that's not true. Nothing that stupid could be true. Maybe I was saving it all for myself, for today. Maybe that was Fate.

Or maybe not. I don't have to let Fate have total creative control over me if I don't want to.

Men at some time are masters of their fates. That's Cassius, in Julius Caesar.

I will be master of my own fate. That's Kenny Harrison, in Beverly Hills-adjacent. The time is now.

You know, it always cracks me up that suicide is illegal. That's like telling a driver that if he gets himself killed in an auto accident, his punishment will be thirty hours in traffic school. Suicide is a crime that anyone can get away with. But I'm the only who can get away with murder. Ophelia was right — because I'm dying, I could get away with murder. Vice president of murder. *Executive* vice president of murder. I could write it in the sand, or I could write it in blood.

I am not myself: I can see that in the mirror. I am a murderer. And I'm liking it. No cliché puking scenes, no fists through walls, no hugging and crying. *For murder, though it have no tongue, will speak,* you bet your ass it will. Doesn't matter who I kill, because I am not myself. It might as well be Jazzminn Jenks. I'll delegate that to Fate. Frankly, I don't have much time to shop around for the right victim. When I wasn't really going to do it, I had all the time in the world.

No more Hamlet-ing. We have a deal. I want to kill someone, and she wants someone killed. It's time for a tragedy, as big as *Hamlet* or *Macbeth*.

CHAPTER TWENTY-SIX

I sure did like that big mouse. The nose on him.

— Nettie Mae Easley

I cried all night, enough tears to fill William Mulholland's historic Los Angeles Aqueduct. But I finally dozed off, exhaustion getting the better of misery. Even in the face of tragedy, I am one of those women who need the recommended two thousand calories a day, a good moisturizer, and eight hours sleep.

And into my troubled dreams drifted the most lovely rainbow of an idea — an idea that would not only delay Ken's plan to murder Jazzminn Jenks, but might, just maybe, make him happy, if only for a day. We were going on a trip, somewhere he'd never, ever been before.

It felt like Christmas morning as I jumped out of bed bright and early, threw on a yellow silk robe the color of the center of a daisy, and rushed to the phone.

"Kenny? Hello! It's Ophelia."

"Yeah." The flat, one-word answer did not invite further conversation.

"Well. Hello. Sorry, I already said that." I was beginning to feel nervous, so I ran my fingers over the soft surface of the yellow silk robe to calm myself down. It worked; I love silk. "How . . . how are you?"

"Hanging in there. Didn't catch a hell of a lot of z's last night, but what else is new. What can I do for you?"

I was thrown by "What can I do for you" — expressionless, like I was speaking to those faceless men at tech support about my continual computer problems, or had dialed the 800 number to cancel my newspaper service during a vacation and was talking to a machine. I know, it was early — but frankly, this was no proper way to address the Dark Lady of the Sonnets.

Maybe something was wrong. "Are you . . . all right?" I quavered.

"You already asked me that. Aside from terminal cancer, I'm fine."

The sarcasm didn't make me angry, only a little more anxious and confused than before. I tried again. "Did you meet with Jazzminn Jenks? How did it go?" I sounded absurdly cheerful even to myself, and I have an unusually high threshold for cheer.

"Yeah. Met her. I'll tell you all about it later. Listen, Ophelia, I just got up. I gotta pee like a racehorse."

"Well, can you hold it for just a minute? I have a surprise for you."

I heard him heave a sigh and clear his throat. "Okay. Talk fast."

This wasn't going at all as I'd planned. I felt my lower lip begin to quiver. I cry much too easily. I must make a point of working on that in Advanced Script Analysis Workshop II at Lana Bishop Academy. My acting career may be over, but I still have two classes left in the series. Might as well apply them to real life.

And I wasn't giving up yet, either. I bit my lip as hard as I could to keep it still and grabbed another soothing handful of yellow silk. "Guess where we're going, Ken?"

"Not the best time to make me guess, Ophelia."

"I didn't mean guess as in really guess. I meant guess in the sense of the thing . . . one says before one goes ahead and tells. Guess as an introduction."

"Then don't play games — tell me." His words were clipped and cold.

Now the tears came. He'd completely ruined my surprise. "It's not a game. We're . . . well, we're going to Disneyland." I sobbed out the last word, I couldn't help it.

"Disneyland? Why the hell are we going to *Disneyland*?"

"Because you said you've never been."

There was a long pause. Then the hard edge on his voice softened. "Oh, God. Did I tell you that? About Disneyland? I don't remember. I'm sorry. My memory's shot, Ophelia. If I did tell you that, I shouldn't have. In fact, do yourself a big favor and don't listen to anything that I say from now on."

"Well, I did listen," I squeaked out. "You said you grew up right here in Los Angeles, in the San Fernando Valley, and your father worked for Disney Studios his whole life but never even took you to Disneyland, not once. You told me that. So . . . I thought you might like to go. With me. I've got the passes, and I'll buy the popcorn and cotton candy and anything you'd like. Kenny, we're going to Disneyland!"

"Oh. Ophelia, honey." Now he sounded like he could barely talk. Either he really hated me, or he was genuinely about to wet his pajamas. "Are you crying? You are. Oh. God. Please, don't cry. Listen . . . that's really nice of you. But . . . I can't. I can't do Disneyland. Not now. I don't . . . deserve it."

"You don't . . . deserve it?" This was awful. Now I was weeping as if I was that little boy in the San Fernando Valley and my Dad was refusing to take me to The Happiest Place on Earth. My parents took me to Disneyland even though we had to drive all the way from Indiana, with Grandma handing out biased opinions and homemade Rice Krispy Treats the whole way. I remember the sound of her knitting needles clacking next to me in the back seat for twenty-five hundred miles. And I also remember that it was worth it.

"Kenny, why can't we go to Disneyland?" Grandma would have rapped my knuckles with those knitting needles if I whined the way I was whining now.

"You really want to know, Ophelia?" Ken's voice turned hard again. "Because it's too big, that's why. I'll bet I can't even walk from the Goofy parking level to the tram, much less all over a two-hundred-and-forty acre theme park."

"We could get a wheelchair. I could push you." I was begging now. I didn't care.

"*Don't* say wheelchair. Plus it's November, too cold for me to wait in line to ride the Matterhorn, although it doesn't matter what season it is because in summer it would be too fucking hot. The Matterhorn — it's the only ride I ever cared about. I already know 'It's a Small World, After All,' and it just keeps on getting smaller. I didn't want to see pirate ships or cowboys, or spin around in a stupid teacup with Dumbo. I only cared about the big mountain with the frozen caverns and the snow beast inside. I always wanted to beat the snow beast. It's right in the middle, between Fantasyland and Tomorrowland, the Matterhorn — did you know that? Hey, guess what, for me, Tomorrowland *is* Fantasyland — hah, that's a joke. Besides, now I probably couldn't go on a big, beautiful ride like the Matterhorn without having a nosebleed, maybe even a stroke. So you'll just have to find some other poor screwed up guy with terminal cancer, whose mother is sleeping with his uncle and whose father had a heart attack at the corner of Mickey Avenue and Dopey Drive, and take him to the goddamned Magic Kingdom. Now, can I go, please?"

"OK," I whispered, stunned by this lengthy, scary, and factually detailed outburst. How did this guy know so much about a place he'd never been? "I'm sorry. I'm sorry for suggesting that we go somewhere like Disneyland together. Ken . . . excuse me, but did you just say your mother is sleeping with your uncle?"

"Stepfather, now. It's sick and twisted, but legal. Look, forget it — we don't keep in touch." He didn't sound angry anymore, just bone-weary. "Last e-mail I told them the stem cell transplant worked like a charm and I'm running five miles a day. Forget it. And, Ophelia, please, forget Disneyland."

"All right. I'll try." I did try; I couldn't. I could never forget Disneyland. "And . . . Ken?"

"Yeah." Same flat, impatient tone — canceling the newspaper, including Sunday delivery. Getting all the news he needs on the Internet." I know we're not going to Disneyland but are we . . . still going to kill her?" I said it because it was the only thing I could say that I was sure would keep him from hanging up on me.

"Who? Oh — yeah. Sure. Of course. But right now. . ."

"I know. Please — urinate. And right now I'm sorry there even is a Disneyland."

"Ophelia, don't say that. I'll call you. Soon. The murder's still on, okay? And hey — maybe we can catch a movie sometime." He hung up the phone very quickly as I sadly wiped my eyes on soft silk the color of the center of a daisy.

CHAPTER TWENTY-SEVEN

**Lord, we know what we are, but know not
what we may be.**

— Ophelia, *Hamlet*

I suppose I could have stopped to wonder why the offices of Jazzminn Jenks's Pink Productions are blue, but life is too short.

Whatever the color, the place was spectacular. Instead of the garish fluorescent light common to office buildings, a soothing natural sunlight from a series of rectangular skylights bathed the slate-blue walls of the entrance hall. The floors were made of a pale beige travertine marble, tons of it. It looked like Jazzminn had built her own studio version of the billion-dollar Getty Center in Brentwood.

And, instead of the obnoxiously bright production posters that hung on most studio walls — the dazed grins of the entire cast and crew, the shorter ones in front — this hallway displayed an exquisite retrospective of black-and-white fashion photos from 1920 to the present. A long, long row of thin, thin women with *a lean and hungry look*. Everything here still smelled new, and expensive.

Jazzminn's office was at the end of the hall, behind two wide, opaque glass doors, also vaguely bluish. Fully prepared to give them a push, I almost fell inside, flat on my face, when the doors slid open silently by themselves.

"You are Ken Harrison," said a voice, as I managed, awkwardly, to regain my footing. It was a stern voice, a voice that suggested I did not know I was Ken Harrison without being told, a voice that believed I could not be Ken Harrison without its permission. No, not a voice — *the* voice. High, nasal, and very, very famous.

I looked up from my recently disentangled feet at the wide expanse of glass desk in front of me — where, traditionally, the receptionist should be. Instead, behind all that glass, her size four, pale blue pumps resting on a sumptuous, silky, blue and cream Oriental rug, sat miniature talk show host Jazzminn Jenks.

"Yes, I'm Ken Harrison — through no fault of my own," I replied, stepping forward and affecting a grin. I felt great today. Fate, my new cat, who's to say, really? I hoped this feeling of internal well being had made its way to my face, rendering my complexion a little less Goth than usual. I extended my hand to Jazzminn. "I was expecting to have to make my way through a few layers of assistants before I got to you. This is a welcome — and may I say, lovely — surprise."

Jazzminn just stared at my hand for a while, her own small hands folded in her lap. Then, she reached out and snatched mine in both of hers. Her grip was tighter than I expected. "There are no assistants at Pink Productions," she said. "I have fifty-one staffers at *Really, Girlfriend?* but none here. This is my company, and I am the only one in it. I am in complete control of everything. Do you hear me? Everything."

"Very wise," I offered cautiously.

"I didn't ask for your opinion. I'm just telling you how

things are." Jazzminn dropped my hand abruptly. "Ophelia tells me you can show me how to make TV movies with me starring in them and have them all be hits. Can you?"

That sounded like something Ophelia would say. "I can certainly try."

"If all you can do is try, then get out of here. I've got to do this in a hurry — I'm a little bit older than I look."

"So is everyone in this town," I answered. "And, actually, I was just being modest. I'm the one who created *Bite Me*. The one who made a star out of Bert DeMarco. If I can do it for him, I can surely do the same for you and Pink Productions."

Jazzminn wrinkled her nose as I said Pink Productions. "I hate that name. The network said if I wanted them to bankroll the company and build me a building, I had to call it Pink Productions to promote Girlfriend. They just call it Pink. Ugh. I hate pink. Hey — don't ever tell anybody I said that."

"Your secret is safe with me." The idea of murdering Jazzminn Jenks just kept getting easier to get used to. I decided to make myself comfortable. This was going to be a long afternoon. I sat down in the chair in front of Jazzminn's desk, then slid in close. I gave her a long, admiring look, beginning at her diminutive feet and moving upward. I allowed my eyes to rest longest on her breasts — figuring she must be proud of such expensive additions, the way people always show you when they've just added a new home office or a Jacuzzi tub. "Frankly, I'm not crazy about pink, either. I imagine, with those eyes, blue's your color."

"Oh, shut up!" she exclaimed. "You're going to stand here in an office with blue walls, a blue door, blue rugs, and pretend to guess that I like blue because of my *eyes*? How stupid are you, exactly?"

I was startled. I suppose I had envisioned this meeting as an exercise in chaste seduction — me flattering an insecure, neurotic, would-be MOW star into hanging on my every word, she rewarding my efforts by laying on the insincere sweetness the way she did with the live studio audience. This was the natural order of things in Hollywood. But, obviously, I was going to have to try a different tack. And since I was feeling energetic today, I relished the challenge.

"Hmmm, let's see," I mused aloud. "How stupid *am* I. Well, how stupid would I have to be to volunteer my time to try to jump-start the acting career of an aging talk show host with no professional performing experience beyond reading psychobabble off a teleprompter? A daytime phenomenon who doesn't seem to grasp that MOWs are almost extinct, a long shot against sitcoms, reality programming and HBO, even if she takes this unique opportunity to keep her mouth shut for five minutes and listen to some advice from someone who knows what he's talking about? You want to know how stupid I am? You know, I just figured it out — not *that* stupid. If — strike that, when — I walk out that door, the only chance anybody will ever see you in prime time is if you land the starring role in the commercial for L'Oreal's newest color: Preternatural Blond. Good luck, Ms. Jenks."

With that, I stood up, turned, and left Jazzminn's office.

I was counting on two things. One, that Jazzminn did not know enough about prime time politics to realize that the network would jump at the chance to air any movie she decided to be in, no matter how wretched the script, regardless of me or anyone else. And, two, the hallway at Pink Productions is very, very long. I was only about halfway to the exit when I heard the pitter-patter of little feet.

"Hey. Stop."

"No."

"Please." I swear there must have been someone standing behind Jazzminn performing the Heimlich maneuver to get that word out of her.

I stopped but did not turn around.

"I don't understand why you walked out. I'm sure Ophelia told you I wasn't a nice person. Why act so surprised?"

"She did not tell me any such thing." Whatever else was going on here, I was not about to finger Ophelia for gossiping about the boss.

"Of course she did. Hell, I would. And I don't care because I know you won't tell anybody because you don't want to get her into trouble. Besides, I'm adored by millions, Harry Rosenstiel said so in the Los Angeles Times." Jazzminn laughed her Tinkerbell laugh and clapped her hands. "Nobody would believe you, anyway."

"Okay, you're right." I turned to face her. "Ophelia did, in fact, inform me that you are a card-carrying, broomstick-riding, bile-spewing, ball-breaking bitch — though not in so many words. Otherwise I would not have guessed."

"Told you so! Hey, are you sleeping with her?"

"No."

"Lying."

"No."

"Good." Jazzminn watched my face closely. She was a good foot shorter than I am so had to tilt her head upwards like a baby sparrow in the nest waiting to be fed. Her bright blue eyes were quite small, appearing average-sized only because of the thick layer of black mascara. They were actually quite pretty, though. "So, I'm not nice," she continued, with a shrug. "I don't like pink, either. So what? It just means you won't have to waste time on stupid compliments — and that comment about blue was stupid, Ken. I know you can do better. But save it. That kind of crap only works on women like Ophelia."

"Yeah, it was stupid," I acknowledged. "And you're right, I

can do better. I guess I underestimated you." I felt we were establishing a bizarre sort of rapport here. "And what exactly do you mean by 'women like Ophelia?'"

"And here I thought the comment about blue was stupid." Jazzminn shook her head in sympathy. "Please. The only person in Hollywood who wouldn't understand what I mean when I say 'women like Ophelia' is . . . Ophelia. It's only because of her that you're willing to put up with me, right?"

"Not at all."

"Lying!"

"Okay — *yes*." Jeez, this woman was exhausting.

"See? Told you. You don't have to worry about hurting my feelings, Ken. I *know*. That's why hired her. By the time people actually get to me, they've already melted like hot candle wax. We both know it. Men would die for her. Men would kill for her."

Or both, I thought.

"And what's weird is women like her, too," Jazzminn continued thoughtfully. "In fact, I like her, and I don't like anybody. That's why I couldn't let Ophelia go to work on *Bite Me* — she'd have the same effect on the folks over there as she has on everybody else, and I'd lose the only personal assistant that I've ever had who is actually a . . . person." Now, her frosted rosebud lips offered me a surprisingly genuine smile. "Look, I don't have to be loveable when I can hire loveable, just like I don't really have to have big boobs and blond hair when I can buy them. Why be Jane when I can be Jazzminn? I hope there are no hard feelings. Ophelia told me you're the one who got her that part on *Bite Me*. I'm just more powerful than you, that's all."

I shrugged. "No hard feelings. But, Jazzminn . . . doesn't it make you a little jealous to be around Ophelia, all day long? A woman like Ophelia? To watch people melt like candle wax?"

"No," Jazzminn replied — so quickly that I actually believed her. "It's just the luck of the draw. Ophelia can only be a woman like Ophelia because she's so beautiful. She doesn't know what it's like to have to bleach her hair every two weeks to keep it from being the color of a dead mouse, to pick her breasts out of a catalogue at a surgeon's office in Beverly Hills, to stick her finger down her throat on a regular schedule because she's got no metabolism whatsoever and the entire nation is focused on the size of her ass. We don't know what kind of a person she'd be if she weren't so naturally, effortlessly lovely. For all we know, she'd be just like me."

"Never."

"I knew you'd say that!" There came another burst of self-congratulatory applause from Jazzminn's elfin hands. "Well, think it over again while you're driving home. By the way — what do you think?"

"About what?"

"The breasts, Ken. I saw you looking. Everybody looks. What do you think?"

If there exists an etiquette book dealing with this situation, I would like to buy it. "Uh . . . very life-like," I offered.

"Want to know how much they cost?"

"No."

"Lying! Everybody wants to know."

"Okay. How much?"

"Seven thousand."

"Is that for the set?" Well, I had to say something.

"Really, Ken? *Per.* Wanna feel 'em?"

"What?"

"I asked you if you wanted to feel them. Don't worry — I won't feel it. I know, they say saline is safer, but silicone has better bounce."

Because Jazzminn Jenks had been kind enough to inform

me that I was Ken Harrison, I now considered extending the courtesy of telling her that she was a fucking lunatic. I decided against it. "What kind of a man do you think I am?" I exploded instead. "I'm not going to stand here in this hallway and paw your chest just because I'm sort of . . . curious."

"But you are curious! Knew it." She gazed down at them like the proud new mother of twins. "Amazing how these things seem to bring out the 'holier than thou' in everyone — including you. They were worth every penny, for the entertainment value alone." Carelessly, she reached down the front of her powder-blue jacket and adjusted her bra. "Well, if you change your mind, let me know. Some people like to feel 'em. Now, let's go back into my office and sit down. Nothing sucks like standing on hard marble in high heels."

I followed Jazzminn back into her office. She immediately sat down behind the glass desk and yanked off the pale blue pumps. Her fingernails were coral pink for the *Really, Girlfriend?* cameras, but the little toenails under her creamy hose were defiantly painted pale blue, the same color as the shoes. I decided to remain standing.

"Okay. How do I make hit movies?" she snapped her fingers. As far as I could see, there was no dog in the room. "Come on, Ken. I haven't got all day."

"Wait a second — slow down." I spent the next sixty seconds not killing her, then I spoke. "Yes, I have to say I thought, for one very inappropriate second, about . . . feeling them." I shook my head sternly as she pushed her chest forward to let me know the offer was still open. "Put those away, would you please? And I admit it, I know exactly what you mean when you say 'women like Ophelia.' But — forget about her right now. If I'm going to help you, find the perfect vehicle for you, I need to know what kind of woman you are."

Now, I sat down in front of the desk. I slid down in the

chair, crossed my ankles, slipped off the Armani jacket, and folded my hands across my stomach. I was the picture of casual concern. "Go ahead. Tell me all about Jazzminn Jenks."

"I sure hope you hire someone else to write the dialogue for your movies, Ken," Jazzminn replied, shaking her head. "But — okay. What do you want to know?"

"Well, why are you such a bitch, anyway?"

She responded to this with a little scream of laughter. "Mostly it's recreational," she said. "Plus, I kinda think the world owes me one. I didn't grow up on some flowery tropical island wearing a butt-floss string bikini, and I didn't win a full scholarship to study drama at Yale like Ophelia did — actually, I got accepted at Harvard, but I didn't have the money, so I went to Cal State Northridge instead. I didn't even have a car. I lived at home with my parents and took the bus. I was short, I was fat, I was dateless, and I was broke. I was smart, though. Everything I have — the show, the production company, the tits — everything I've got, I created myself. I earned the title of bitch, and nobody's ever going to take it away from me. Anything else you want to know, Mr. Harrison?"

I don't think I'd ever heard a woman refer to her own tits as tits. Even with my limited supply of red blood cells, I could feel myself blush. "No, that just about covers it," I said hastily. "Well, Jazzminn, I think we'd both agree that, however . . . not nice you might be in real life, nice is your franchise. Sweet is your franchise. Pink is your franchise. We have to go with that. The network won't accept anything but."

"Absolutely." She nodded so hard that her blond hair bounced. "I wrote it all down before you came in. Sweet, fragile, vulnerable, girlish, like you say, pink — but spunky, right? Can I at least be spunky?"

I shrugged. "Yeah, I guess you can be spunky. But let me decide 'spunky,' all right? After spending a little time with you,

I'm afraid your definition of spunky is going to be somewhere between a pit bull and a T. Rex."

She frowned. "No. I want to decide everything."

"Trust me, you won't be sorry," I said. "Think of Ken Harrison the same way you think of Ophelia, or . . . those tits. You hired all four of us for a reason. I'm here to be something that you're not, and believe me, you are not the best judge of what kind of role is going to make TV movie watchers love you as much your daytime audience does." I stood up and paced the room to show how hard I was thinking. "I see a light, smart, sophisticated comedy with a sweet, girlish, vulnerable-but-spunky heroine. A Mary Tyler Moore for the Twitter generation is my thinking. There are some terrific comedy writers on the *Bite Me* staff. Even though I'm not with the show anymore, they'd jump at the chance to develop something for you. Maybe you could even work with Bert." I wanted her to know I was on a first-name basis with DeMarco.

Jazzminn frowned. "A comedy? I don't think so. I want to be someone who's nice and sweet and all that crap, but . . . couldn't the story be a tragedy?"

"A . . . tragedy?" I stopped pacing and sat back down, suddenly feeling woozy when she said the word. "Uh . . . maybe your second movie could be a tragedy, Jazzminn, but I really think it's a mistake the first time around. This is no time to push the envelope."

"But people love sad movies," Jazzminn protested. "I see them all the time in the movie theaters, bawling into their popcorn. Personally, I don't know what the hell they're crying about, but they seem to really enjoy it. I want to do that to them. *That's* power." She squinted her small blue eyes at me, which only made them seem brighter. "Hey — I could die! What do you think?"

I coughed: there was a dull pain in my chest. "Big

mistake," I said quickly. "TV is not the same as a feature film, Jazzminn. You're not just a character the audience will never see again. No matter what the movie is, you are Jazzminn Jenks, the Jazzminn Jenks America welcomes into its living room every day. That's why your movie is going to be major. And believe me, the American public does not want to see you dead."

"Hey — it could happen off camera!"

"It doesn't matter where it happens. If you die, so does your TV movie career. Simple as that."

Jazzminn returned to pouting for a moment, and then nodded. "I guess you're right. But promise you'll at least think about my getting injured or something, okay?"

"You got it. I most certainly will talk to the writers about some kind of serious but non-dismembering injury from which you fully recover." I dabbed my clammy brow with my handkerchief. "So, are we about done for the day? It's . . . really warm in here."

"Is it?" Why was I was not surprised that Jazzminn took no interest in my discomfort? "Well, there is one more thing, Ken. I want to read something for you — just so you'll have an idea of my range. I know Cal State Northridge ain't exactly Yale, but I did major in drama there, even though I was too fat then to ever be a leading lady."

"Sure — go ahead." I figured my best bet for the moment was to stay seated, anyway. I leaned my forehead into my hand, my elbow resting on the arm of the chair, in the Thinker position — ostensibly to concentrate on her performance, actually trying hard not to pass out.

There were a few moments of silence as I continued to stare at the floor. Then, I heard the words begin to swirl around me. *Wild and whirling words. His* words. Some spoken, some sung, some sobbed, in a voice as clear as a chapel bell and mournful as the wail of a wandering ghost-child. Ophelia's mad scene from *Hamlet* — played with horrifying beauty by Jazzminn Jenks.

I raised my head — no longer ill, merely stunned.

There's rosemary, that's for remembrance. Pray you,
love, remember. And there is pansies, that's for thoughts.
. . . There's a daisy. I would give you some
violets, but they wither'd all when my father died . . .

In her voice I could see the flowers in Ophelia's agitated hands; I could smell the fragrant herbs, watch in grief as the dark velvet petals of the violets dried up before my eyes. I could hear the shattering glass of a mind broken at the same time as a heart.

And will 'a not come again?
And will 'a not come again?
No, no, he is dead;
Go to thy deathbed;
He never will come again . . .

"Stop," I pleaded. I was now back in the Thinker position, but this time only to hide the tears. I'd only read it, never heard it. Never heard it spoken the way it should be. "Stop. Please. I beg of you."

"Hey, what's your problem?" the grating voice of Jazzminn suddenly returned, live from the offices of Pink Productions. "Either I sucked or you don't like Shakespeare. Hello? Which is it, Ken?"

"No, no, neither of those things." The high-pitched whine rocketed me back through the time tunnel from dark Danish castles to sunny Burbank. "Actually, you were . . . wonderful,

Jazzminn. Amazing. I don't know what to say. I really and truly don't."

"Yeah?" Jazzminn asked, with a smug smile. "So, do you still think I shouldn't play tragedy, Ken?"

Yes, Jazzminn Jenks should play tragedy forever and ever, always, and *Really, Girlfriend?* and Pink Productions — in fact, the entire network — should go immediately and directly to hell. In fact, unless Jazzminn Jenks played Shakespearean tragedy, she should not speak at all. But that is not what I said.

This is what I said. "There's no such thing as tragedy in television, Jazzminn. There are just scripts where somebody dies at the end." I stood up slowly, testing to make sure that my legs would hold me. "I've gotta go now. I'm just *crazed* back at the office. I'll call you in a couple of days. But take it from me — stick with comedy. I've been in network television a long time, and I know what I'm talking about."

"Well, shit. Okay, then." Jazzminn grumbled. "I still think it'd be cool to die, though."

"Be patient, Jazzminn," I said.

CHAPTER TWENTY-EIGHT

**Feed him with apricocks and dewberries,
With purple grapes, green figs, and mulberries**

— Titania, *A Midsummer Night's Dream*

On the lips of the radiant Ophelia, so intimate with real laughter and tears, Shakespeare's words meant nothing. Yet when spoken by Jazzminn Jenks, dwarf-queen of bleach and silicone, troll who could only scowl and wonder what made other people cry at sad movies, they were such sweet music!

If this were seventeenth century Denmark, perhaps I'd have wandered the moors, hoisted a tankard of ale, blurted my confusion to poor Yorick's skull. Instead, I stumbled down the long, blue hallway of Pink Productions, back to the parking lot in front of the Hacienda Building, climbed into my Mercedes — its front bumper still a snarl of twisted metal — and drove as fast as I could to the gay Ralphs.

I suppose some among this casually dressed crowd of grocery shoppers may have stared at the gaunt, Armani-clad specter haunting the aisles, the only one here without a shopping cart, head bowed, pale, thin hands shoved into designer pockets, walking, walking. *Rest, rest, perturbèd spirit!* I did not care what they thought. I needed to be here among the familiar brands, the logical rows of fourteen -ounce soup cans, the vacuum-sealed packages of pre-cooked poultry, the neat bags of dried spaghetti and rigatoni and cannelloni. My sanctuary.

But as I wandered, I found myself in unfamiliar territory, even here. Instead of dried pasta and microwave soup, I was now surrounded by bright orange carrots with wild green tops; fat red tomatoes; bananas of pale new green and dark ripe yellow; purple grapes with taut skin, seeds and juicy flesh; rough brown potatoes. Lettuce — all different sizes and shapes of lettuce, furled, intricate, delicate, unruly. All piled high without cans or labels or wrappers. From jets in the ceiling came a fine, cool mist of water.

I was in the produce section.

I might as well have been lost in a forest, it was so long since I'd been here. I'm kept away now by the beast, the beast who dozes at the edge of the forest with one eye open, who awakes in anger and punishes me from the inside if I try to eat a hard, crisp apple, or carrots or grapes or anything raw or real. The only things that don't wake the beast come dried, shrink-wrapped, flash-frozen, or encased in aluminum cans.

I used to buy fast food because it was easier. Now, I have no choice because of the beast. My blood is a chemical spill, and my stomach only knows how to process food that has already been processed before.

I should have just gone back where I belonged — but I couldn't do that either. Standing here in the produce section was to hear Jazzminn Jenks read Shakespeare. Going back to my usual aisles was an invitation to grope her phony breasts. There was nothing in any aisle for me. The only thing that could have helped me now, standing in the produce section, was never to have come here at all — and it was too late for that.

If some people thought it was weird to see a guy in an Armani suit with no shopping cart wandering alone in the gay Ralphs, I've got to wonder what they thought when they saw him, there before a congregation of lettuce, drop to his knees and pray.

CHAPTER TWENTY-NINE

People in Hollywood, they swim all winter.

— Nettie Mae Easley

I love flowers, but this had to be the weirdest bouquet I'd ever seen.

I recognized the bright daisies, violets, and purple pansies from my garden. You almost never see pansies in a bouquet these days. They wilt like crazy if you pick them. But then there was also an herb of some kind. I don't cook often enough to know one herb from another, but this one had a pungent odor that clung to my fingers. Thyme, maybe? Basil? Cilantro is also very popular in California restaurants these days, although I don't much like the stuff.

"It's rosemary," he said patiently, stopping me before I could guess my way through the entire spice rack. "Rosemary, *that's for remembrance.* And look at the violets — no withered ones at all." Ken pressed the little clutch of tender plants into my left hand, then raised the hand and kissed it. "I don't know what kind of plant means I'm sorry, or I'd have put that in, too. I'm sorry for the stupid things I said. I don't remember them, but I'm sorry for them. I'm so sorry, Ophelia."

Well, I suppose I should have flung those floppy little flowers back in his face — it had been two weeks since he hung up on me, two miserable weeks. But I was so happy — no, grateful I think is the word — to see him standing there on my porch that I forgot how angry I was. Learning to sustain anger: Something else to work on before my acting class series comes to an end. "I thought you were dead!" I exclaimed, realizing the usual two seconds too late that this was exactly the wrong thing to say. "And I could kick myself right now."

"People say that all the time when they haven't seen someone for awhile. Don't kick yourself," he said. "I'm the one apologizing today. Please — forgive me?"

"Nope! I will never speak to you again as long as I live, Kenny." He wasn't dead, not at all. I could barely keep from throwing my arms around him, just for not being dead. "Come on in, sweetie."

"I was hoping you'd let me cook you dinner," he said. "And afterwards we could talk about . . ."

"Shhh!" I cut him off, suddenly remembering that we weren't alone. I kissed him on the cheek, but only to get my mouth closer to his ear. "Don't say anything about *anything*," I whispered. "I've got guests here. It's my book group."

Given the circumstances, I was sure this news would evoke some stammered response about leaving and coming back later. Instead, to my surprise, Ken grinned and strode right in. "You have a book group? Cool." Uninvited, he walked into my living room, where the women sat in a circle, books, glass dessert plates, and tea cups balanced on their laps. In front of them on the coffee table sat the weekly assortment of homemade cookies, baked by all the group members except me, I don't bake. They looked up in surprise as he entered.

"Hello, ladies," Ken said, clearly both pleased and amused to suddenly find himself the center of attention.

Well, here he was, and there wasn't much I could do about it. I was still happy to see him but wondered exactly how a male aspiring murderer was going to fit into my women's book discussion. I took a deep breath and began my introductions. "Girls, this is Ken. He works at the network, in TV movie development. We met on the lot. We're . . . collaborating on a major project."

"Wow, movies," burbled Amber — friendly, russet-haired, twenty-seven, and not at all bright, really. It had taken her two weeks to read the first chapter of our book. Since she was so visibly impressed, I decided to start my round of introductions with her. "Ken, this is Amber. She gets study credit from the drama department at UC Irvine for working at the ticket office at the Lana Bishop Theater. You already know Liz. This lady is Susan, my hairdresser, she's from Cambodia. And that's Rachel from the animal shelter in Beverly Hills, cat division. She's new to our group."

Ken had the good sense not to bring up his cat, and merely nodded affably at Rachel. Encouraged, I moved on. "This wonderful woman is Beulah Stark, Wade Stark's mom, my ex-mother-in-law." The very plump Beulah Stark wore her usual uniform of a loose print dress with a narrow belt at her non-existent waist, and a large flowery hat topped with what appeared to be mosquito netting. It was the same kind of hat my grandma on my mother's side and all of her friends wear to church on Sunday in Indianapolis. I still don't know where they buy those hats. Beulah's sagging ankles were held firmly in check by laced-up black orthopedic shoes with sensible heels.

"You're still my daughter, baby," said Beulah, with one of her enveloping warm smiles. I knew she'd say that. She always does, and I love her for it.

"And that extremely large woman sitting next to her is her daughter Maxie. My ex-sister-in-law. In case you hadn't noticed, she is with child, eight and a half months." I gave my Maxie a large, proud grin. "Just think, I'm about to become a . . . an ex-aunt!" The entire group laughed delightedly at that except Susan from Cambodia. Of course I had to laugh at my own joke, I am so rarely amusing. "How are you doing, Maxie? Do you need more crackers?" I asked when I was done giggling.

"I'm fine, honey." For the fifth or sixth time this afternoon, Maxie plunged her puffy hand into the large box of saltines at her side, pulled out a handful and munched. "Nice to meet you, Ken," she said with her mouth full, offering him a smile as wide and warm as her mother's, keeping cracker crumbs from falling on the suede sofa with two swollen fingers pressed against her lips.

"Congratulations, Maxie," Ken said. "Here — have some rosemary." He reached over to the little bouquet still in my left hand, pulled out a fragrant sprig and presented it to Maxie. She seemed startled but pleased all the same. The rest of the women just kept staring at him.

Beulah patted the empty sofa cushion on the side of her that was not occupied by her substantial daughter. "You come right over here and sit next to me, baby," she said — a combination of invitation and command. Ken hesitated and glanced over at me, apparently waiting for me to bail him out of this. I did not. I am not a vindictive person, but *he's* the one who decided to march into my living room. Besides, he hadn't called for two whole weeks. "You heard Mom," I said sweetly, gesturing at the sofa. "Please — join us."

Reluctantly, Ken sat down next to Beulah. She smiled and patted his hand. After another uncomfortable glance at me, he shrugged, smiled, and patted hers back. Then his eyes wandered over to the table that held the cookies.

"Nobody offered him nothing to eat. You want something to eat?" asked Beulah, misinterpreting his glance. She picked up one of the little china dessert plates with one hand and went for the butter cookies with the other, obviously planning to fatten Ken up as much as she could in the next ten minutes.

"No, no, please," he said hastily. "No cookies for me — I was just looking, wondering which one of you made the Madeleines. It's not every kitchen that has a Madeleine pan. I don't eat cookies. I . . . can't."

Beulah smiled at him, even more warmly than before. "You don't feel good, do you, baby?" she asked, patting his hand again. "And Amber bought them Madeleines."

I expected him to deny his illness, as usual. "No, I don't feel good," he answered instead, looking directly into Beulah's eyes. Beulah did not press for details, just kept patting his hand as she put the cookies she'd collected back on their original plate, one by one.

I realized then that, until this moment, I'd always been alone with Ken — never with other people since I found him in the audience at *Really, Girlfriend?* I can't explain it, but with the other girls around us he seemed . . . well, I hate to say it, but he seemed more like he was dying than usual. When we were alone together, I could almost forget it sometimes, but not here, in my book group, sitting next to the pregnant Maxie, radiant with the new life inside her.

Yes, I should have bailed him out earlier when his eyes had pleaded for it, sent him off to the kitchen with his goofy bouquet by himself until everyone else went home. I shouldn't have made him stay somewhere he so obviously didn't belong. And . . . I'd like to say I was more concerned with his discomfort than my own, but I'm not so sure.

I'm an awful, awful woman.

Trying not to stare at Ken, we all sat hypnotized by the rhythm of Maxie's plump hand entering and exiting the big box of saltines, in and out, in and out. He broke the silence with one word. "Although . . ."

"Yes, baby?" prompted Beulah.

"Although, I think . . . I think . . . maybe I could eat some of those crackers."

"Well then, somebody fix this boy a plate of crackers!" Beulah commanded, staring pointedly at Maxie. Obediently, Maxie assembled saltines in a semi-circle on one of the plates. "Good thing for you Ophelia invited the fat pregnant lady," Maxie said to Ken, blasting away the tension in the room with the sheer force of her smile. "This one's my first, and I'm forty-five. Guess I beat the ol' biological clock, huh?"

Amber from the theater box office snorted with derisive laughter. "Why tell him? He's a guy: what would he know about a biological clock?"

"Try me," Ken murmured, barely loud enough to hear. Then he shook his head as if to clear his mind and gave Amber a strained smile. "I mean . . . I think I understand how you feel. I read a lot of women's magazines." He gave me another sideways glance. "I mean, at the office. Research for my job — women are our target audience in Movies and Minis."

Abruptly, Ken set aside his plate of crackers and reached for a copy of our book, sitting on the coffee table: "*Big Ole Circle of Women*," the latest novel from best-selling author Winnie Epps. He flipped it over to take in the familiar book jacket photo of Winnie, wearing a turban and big hoop earrings, on the back cover. "Hey, I know this book. Our movie department at the network just optioned it," he said. "So . . . you're reading this crap on purpose? Jesus, even Lifetime Channel turned this one down."

At that, I took Ken's plate of crackers and started eating

them myself.

"Well . . . yes," said Maxie. "Actually, Ophelia was just about to read aloud to us from Chapter 17 where Sophie Marceau discovers that her long-lost mother is actually a voodoo queen in the Louisiana bayou. Ophelia's an actress, you know."

"Yes, I'm keenly aware of that," he replied. "I've seen her in Shakespeare — *breathtaking*. Look, I'm sorry — never mind what I said. What do I know? Go ahead. Please. Read." He had the nerve to wink at me.

"Okay, maybe I just will." I scowled, opening my copy.

"Wait," said Susan. "I want to know why he hates the book."

"Uh . . . me, too," confessed Liz, with a guilty look at me.

"No, please — go on with your reading," Ken said. This kind of thing is so subjective . . ."

"Who woulda guessed that silver-haired harpy witch o' the swamp coulda been my mutha?" I began hastily, doing my best to follow my acting teacher's instructions and visualize my life as a Creole foundling from a spooky, moss-hung New Orleans bayou. Unfortunately I was only able to visualize the bright interior of Studio 7, with Jazzminn Jenks lying dead and naked on the stage floor and Ken standing over her body with a Henckels ham slicer, wearing an Armani suit.

"Tell us, Ken," Liz interrupted me.

I closed the book with a snap. "Okay, fine. Tell us, Ken. We're only women. We're totally incapable of appreciating this book by ourselves."

"It's not just because he's a man . . . it's because . . . he makes movies," Amber murmured apologetically.

"For TV," I couldn't help grumbling.

"Look, I'm no writer," Ken began, clearly savoring the moment. "It's just that here's the beautiful Sophie Marceau, now a successful Washington tax attorney with two sons, and all of a sudden she's skulking around in the Louisiana bayou in the middle of the night with her ex-cop boyfriend and a butcher knife because he's talked her into planning a murder. And where did she get that accent all of a sudden? Sorry, I'm not buying it — what's her motivation?"

"And thank you for sharing the *next chapter* with us, Ken," I observed.

"Oh, hadn't you gotten that far? Sorry."

"Wow. Does she actually do it?" Lizzie demanded. "And why?"

"I've said too much already." I raised my eyebrows to let him know how very true that was. "But when we do the movie, we're probably going to have to change the ending because right now the damn thing doesn't make any sense at all."

"Look at the time — we're going to have to stop for today," I said abruptly, not looking at the time. "Please, take these cookies home with you, or I'll eat them all I swear. I don't mean to kick you out, but Ken and I have a lot of work to do tonight. Don't we, Kenny?"

"Can you come to our next group, Ken?" Amber asked shyly. "By then we'll have finished the book. It's two weeks from Tuesday, at my apartment. I live on Laurel, just above Sunset near the Laugh Factory."

"You can take my place, Ken — I'm due next Sunday," Maxie said as she rolled her way to her feet. She handed Ken the entire box of saltines, which he gratefully accepted.

"Uh, I have to check my book. But we'll talk. Goodnight, ladies. Drive carefully."

"You take care, baby," Beulah Stark said on her way out, giving him a big, red lipsticky kiss on the cheek and a hug that left him gasping for air.

"Thanks, I will." He turned to me after the women and their plates of cookies had made their way out the door. "Hey, I think they like me." He had a red kiss on his cheek.

"Well, I don't," I replied, only half-joking. "I don't suppose it ever occurred to you to just sit there quietly and eat your crackers?"

"It occurred to me. I decided against it."

"What I said is true. They think you're right just because you're a man."

"Yeah, I'm a man — barely. Note the similarity of my diet to that of a forty-five-year-old pregnant woman." He set the saltines down on a table. "Look, I'm sorry I spoiled your party, all right? I just felt like having a little fun. I promise I won't join your book group, even though I have a personal invitation from my girlfriend Amber. And I swear to you I'm not a man on purpose — honest."

"Okay, then I guess I forgive you." I laughed. Everything seemed all right again, now that they were gone and we were alone. "And I'm glad you had a little fun just now — I really am."

"Thank you." He paused. "And I forgive you, too."

"Forgive me? For what?"

"For being beautiful."

I frowned. "You'd better explain that."

"I admit, maybe your lady friends were a little too quick to assume that I know what I'm talking about just because I was the only man in the room. But don't you think that, on an average day, the world is just a tiny bit nicer to you because you're such a beautiful woman?"

"I . . . don't know."

"Oh, I think you do, Ophelia," he said. "You don't think that's why people do things for you — why some people will do anything for you? Because you are so goddamned beautiful?"

I thought that over for a moment. "You mean, people like you?" I shot back.

He held up his hands in surrender. "Forget I brought it up."

"I already have. Anyway, let's not talk about beauty. I have nothing to say about it. Let's talk about . . . murder. I'm dying to know how it went with Jazzminn."

He shrugged. "Me, I'm just dying."

I suppose it is wrong to become exasperated with the terminally ill, but that doesn't keep it from happening. "Please stop talking like a sitcom," I scolded him. "You aren't the least bit funny."

"Yes, I am. But I'm sorry. Come on, I'll make dinner, if you're not too mad at me to eat my cooking."

"Why — because I'm beautiful?"

"No, because you can't cook."

"True. Okay, sure. Thank you very much." I scanned his face anxiously; it looked even paler than usual against the dark blue suit. "That is, if you're feeling up to it."

"I feel the way I feel. It's got nothing to do with whether I cook or not. So please — come."

I turned to follow him, then stopped abruptly when I spotted something unusual through the tall windows by the front door.

"What's that?"

"What's what?"

"That." I pointed at the aged, dusty white Honda Civic parked on the gravel outside.

"Oh. *That.* That is my new car."

"What happened to the Mercedes?"

"I finally took it to the dealer's to be fixed yesterday. There was so much damage to the front of it, they said it could be in the shop for a month. A month is . . . a very long time for me, Ophelia. So I swapped it for this. Don't you think it's hot?

"Yes, it's . . . very hot," I replied, my voice breaking between the words.

He raised one hand. "No, Ophelia, don't . . . cry over a car."

"I'm not. Believe me, I'm not." I closed my eyes tight before a single tear actually fell.

"I hate this moment; ergo, I am getting the fuck out of it," he said evenly. "Run along now, to the kitchen — have you ever been there before? I have to go out to my new fully appointed luxury vehicle to get a few ingredients out of the trunk. I figured you wouldn't have anything for me to work with besides Apple Jacks."

My eyes were completely dry again by the time he returned, carrying a brown paper grocery bag. I was feeling happy again, and hungry. Ken hummed cheerfully as he removed the contents: Spices, soy sauce, Chinese vegetables, and an oversized bag of uncooked shrimp.

"Shrimp?" I asked in a small voice.

"Yeah. Trader Joe's. Hope you like 'em. I figured if I left 'em in the car they'd be just about unfrozen by dinnertime." He held up the bag to examine. "I was right."

"No. Oh, no." I stared at the horrible, bulging bag. "I can't eat them. I'm allergic to them."

"Really?" He was just about to slice open the bag, but stopped to eye me quizzically. "What happens to you? Do they . . . make you sneeze or something?"

"No. No sneezing. It's just that if I eat them, I could . . . well, I could die."

"You could die from eating *shrimp*?"

"Yes, I could go into anaphylactic shock and die." I found myself snapping at him, even though I was trying not to. Next to my beauty, this allergy was really my un-favorite subject. I don't know how many times I've had to explain to some bemused creative executive that taking me out for seafood is playing Russian roulette. Plus I'd really rather not have anyone thinking too hard about how unappealing I might look under neon emergency-room lights, wheezing, retching, with a full-blown case of hives. The autoimmune system is so unfair.

"I would have told you before, but I didn't know you were planning to come over, ruin my book group meeting, then cook me Shrimp Surprise," I grumbled.

"No shit." Ken seemed quite fascinated by this unfortunate glitch in my biology. "I'm sorry, Ophelia, I didn't mean to make fun of you. It's just I've just been dying for so long now, it's amazing to think it could happen to you, just like that, because of a little shrimp." Finally, he stopped observing me like I was some kind of lab specimen and smiled. "Weird as hell. But — no problem. What else do you have in your refrigerator?"

"I think I have some chicken breasts."

"Good. Then hand me that bouquet and get ready for my famous rosemary chicken."

Only then did I notice I was still clutching the bouquet. "Oh. Here. And thank you for understanding," I said. "Now, are you ever going to tell me?"

"You mean, what happens at the end of *Big Ole Circle of Women*? Never."

"How it went with Jazzminn."

"Okay — jeez, don't bite my head off." Ken was now pounding the chicken breasts flat on a Lucite cutting board, with a little metal mallet that I didn't even know I had. "It went fine. We've bonded. And she's as good as dead."

"What exactly are you going to do?"

"I'm not going to tell you. Yet."

"Why not?"

"I just think it's better if you don't know all the details. Safer. Remember — Dark Lady, not murderer. You'll find out soon enough."

I watched Ken hammer away at the chicken for a while. Then, happily, I remembered something. "What's the date today?" I asked.

"Where did that come from?" He glanced at his watch. "It's Thursday, November fifteenth. Why?"

"We . . . can't murder Jazzminn Jenks until after Thanksgiving," I said, hardly able to contain my joy. I'd found an *unavoidable delay*. "I have to go home for Thanksgiving, I promised my parents I would. I go every year. I'm leaving on Saturday."

"Oh. About that, Ophelia . . ."

"What? Thanksgiving?"

"No. Murder."

"What about it?'

"Well . . . the whole idea . . . Look, I'm no director, I'd never question your motivation, but now it's all beginning to seem just a little over-the-top, don't you think? I mean, I know *Bite Me* is the highest-rated sitcom on network and everything, but — murder?"

My heart jumped. Did he really just say what I thought he said? I studied him the same way he studied me when he found out I could die from eating the wrong kind of seafood. It was true — he seemed changed, somehow, from the last time I saw him. Paler, but more calm. Maybe he wasn't so eager to be a murderer, after all. But I decided to proceed with caution. I remembered too well how his eyes had filled with tears when he told me he'd never been to Disneyland, then a few days later didn't remember telling me at all.

"What are you saying exactly, Ken?"

"I don't know — exactly. I've just been thinking about it a lot." He laughed a little; it ended in a dry cough. "Hamlet-ing, I guess. Let's talk about it after you get back from Thanksgiving, okay? Hey, I think you're really going to like this recipe. I got it off the web."

I loved the chicken, loved the rosemary, loved the tiny French string beans he served on the side. The only thing I didn't love was that I was the only one eating. He didn't even wait for the question when he saw my eyes on his untouched plate. "Can't right now," he said, shaking his head. "Sometimes I can, sometimes I can't. Don't worry about it: I made it for you. Hey . . . would you mind if I lie down somewhere for a minute?"

"Of course."

Now he was wincing, clenching and un-clenching his fists as if he were testing his fingers to see if they would still bend. "Can you give me a hand?" he asked quietly.

A few weeks ago that request would have sent me flying to the phone to call a doctor or racing to offer him everything in my medicine cabinet. Now I just walked around to the other side of the table and helped him up. "Here, come lie down on the couch in the living room," I said as we walked, Ken leaning heavily on my shoulder. "It's nice and soft. A lot of my actor friends have slept here."

"Ah, Hollywood's real casting couch. Thank you. I only need a minute or two." He smiled weakly. "Hello, Ophelia, welcome to my life."

"I'll get you a blanket." I ran off up the stairs before he could stop me. I returned with the comforter from my own bed, a third-wedding present specially designed for me by Arnie, my first husband. His usual medium was acrylic paint, but he'd been excited by this opportunity to work in fabric. I loved it — a wild patchwork of satins and velvets, golds, oranges, reds and purples; I always thought that's exactly what it must look like inside Arnie's imagination. Ken opened his eyes briefly as I laid the comforter over him. "Awesome. This looks like a Sadilla sunset," he murmured. "And it's just as warm. Thank you, Ophelia."

I went back and tidied the kitchen while he slept, carefully disposing of the shrimp in the trash can outside the kitchen door like so much toxic waste. Then, even though I have a dishwasher, I did the dishes by hand. Because there was nothing I could do for Ken at the moment, it was soothing, distracting to do something useful that involved suds and warm water. I put the pansies, daisies, violets, and what was left of the rosemary into water in a teacup. Their soft stems were too short for a regular vase.

When I returned to the living room, Ken was off the couch and standing, suit coat on, carefully folding the quilt over his arm. He offered me a crooked grin. "God, just shoot me and save us all a lot of trouble," he said. "Better. Thanks, Ophelia. I can drive now. I guess I'm outta here."

I waited until I was sure that he was being honest about feeling stronger. Then I spoke.

"I . . . have to ask you a question, Ken."

"Shoot."

"I won't be back until the Monday after Thanksgiving. That's almost two weeks from now. Will you . . ."

"I'll still be alive then, yes."

"Stop it! That wasn't what I was going to ask. I have another question."

"Okay."

"Is it because I'm beautiful?"

"Is what because you're beautiful?"

"Everything. Like you said before. Everything." I could feel my lower lip starting to tremble. It hurt when he said that.

"Oh . . . oh, no, Ophelia," he said, putting a hand on my shoulder. "No, honey, I was joking. I joke around way too much. I mean, sure, some stuff is because you're beautiful — that's just the way it is. But not *everything*. And . . . nothing at all that really matters." He lifted his hand from my shoulder. For a moment I thought he was going to stroke my hair, but instead just squeezed the hand in and out of a fist a couple of times, testing again, then let it fall to his side.

"I'm not sure I believe you," I said. "But never mind, there's a third question."

"Christ, I hope it's easier than the last one."

I waited for a moment, then blurted it out. "I know, this is worse than Disneyland, but — do you want to come home to Indiana with me for Thanksgiving, Kenny? It's just all of my crazy relatives, but they're really fun — even my boring parents are okay after they've had some eggnog. Don't listen to anything my grandmother says and you'll be just fine. Everybody makes a different dish except me. I can't cook, so I set the table and fold the napkins into little turkeys. The men have to cook, too. I already know you can cook. Would you like to come?"

There was a long, long pause. "You have no idea how hard this question is," he said softly. "And you're right: this is much, much worse than Disneyland. No, Ophelia, I can't go to Indiana, not now. But I can't begin to tell you how much I appreciate the invitation."

"Well, I'm not leaving until Saturday. Let me know if you change your mind." I was glad that I'd asked even though I already knew the answer. "Goodnight, Ken. I'll walk you out."

"No, it's late. I must have slept for two hours. Go to bed, Ophelia — I know my way out. I'll turn off the lights downstairs. Besides, there's something I have to do before I leave."

I thought it best not to ask exactly what it was he had to do. I've read all about how chemotherapy tears you up inside on *NHLFriends.com*. I never really know what's going on inside of him, even though I read all I can. I didn't know whether he needed to lie down again, or get water to swallow a medication, or lock himself in my powder room for some sort of unpleasant episode. Or maybe he just wanted a big old bowl of Apple Jacks, he seems to like them. Whatever it was, I knew that it didn't involve me.

"All right. Make yourself at home, stay as long as you like, take whatever you need," I said. "I'm exhausted. I washed dishes tonight, you know. G'night, Ken. Take care." I lifted dear, gay Arnie's Sadilla-sunset comforter from Ken's arms, hugged it around my shoulders like a shawl and walked, yawning, up the stairs.

I was already under the comforter, dozing between cool gold satin sheets, my teeth and hair brushed, alarm set and lights off, in my favorite warm winter nightgown — when I heard the creak of the sliding glass door that leads from the kitchen out to the pool. I wondered why Ken was leaving the house this way instead of through the front door. Leaving the lights off, I got out of bed and tiptoed to the window to watch him go.

He didn't go. For awhile, he just stood out there in the dark by the pool, barefoot, his shoes in one hand, listening to the low gurgle of the Jacuzzi, staring pensively into the water, the pool lights reflecting on his sober face like a heatless flame. Then, ignoring the November cold, he dropped the shoes, stripped off his clothes and dived naked into the pool, a clean, swift dive that barely broke the surface.

CHAPTER THIRTY

Out, damned spot! out, I say!

— Lady Macbeth, *Macbeth*

I guess this is the closest I'll ever get to being a poet in this lifetime.

It was Monday morning, and I had in my briefcase a neat pile of very spunky MOW treatments for Jazzminn Jenks. In my obsolete department, we still called them Movies-of-the-Week even thought DVRs had smashed the concept of anything resembling a "week" in television all to hell. I wrote all the scripts myself. They were the result of a weekend of feverish work, and I mean that literally. I think my temperature was averaging 101 — now I wish I hadn't gone swimming, I really wish that I hadn't. They weren't bad at all, in my opinion — and after more than a decade in network television, I've read a lot of treatments.

I must admit I enjoyed making up six pen names for myself. I figured Jazzminn would be too interested in hating my ideas to notice that the one at the bottom of the pile was written by Sir Francis Bacon.

I shivered and shook, but I kept on writing. All I needed

here was a ticket back into Jazzminn's office on this sunny Monday afternoon, an answer for her multiple phone calls wanting to know why I was so fucking slow in finding her the perfect vehicle. It didn't have to be Shakespeare.

This time, I knew enough to wait for the glass doors to slide open without pushing them. Jazzminn was, once again, seated behind her vast desk, with no assistants anywhere in sight, lonely queen of her own blue castle.

"Have you got them?" she demanded. "Let's see."

"I'm just fine, Jazzminn, thanks for asking." I sat down without being invited, then took my sweet time in opening up my briefcase. "Here's what my writers were able to come up with on such short notice. These are funny, funny concepts. You're going to be pleased, Jazzminn. A couple of these are just perfect for you — but I think I'll let you judge for yourself and then we can compare notes." I held the sheaf of papers in my hand.

She snapped her fingers. "Gimme."

I moved, very slowly, to lay the treatments on one corner of the glass desk for her to take. Then, just as her coral pink nails closed in on the sheets of paper, I yanked them away. Due to her top-heavy state, her little body practically tumbled across the desk. My face — I hope — took on an expression of deep anxiety and concern. "But, before you read these, Jazzminn . . . I feel I have a duty to tell you something."

"God, Ken, I've been waiting for days here," she exclaimed. "I'm just *dying*. You are even slower than Ophelia. Congratulations, I didn't know that was possible."

"Thank you. And, please — try to be patient. This won't take long. I'm just going to tell you what the writers told me. Promise me you won't take this the wrong way. Understand that this is not the way I personally feel. It's audience research talking."

"What? Say it!"

"Understand that . . . prime time is just a wee bit different than daytime," I began, drawing out the moment. "Different demographics. The audience is younger, more upscale, more sophisticated. They expect a slightly different . . . look."

Her eyebrows shot up under her wispy blond bangs. "What the hell is wrong with the way I look?"

"There's nothing wrong with the way you look," I said, wearing my best expression of pity as I spoke. "Speaking as a man, I'd have to say your look is perfect. But now, you're venturing into a new daypart, and that's dangerous. Speaking as a network executive — and, Jazzminn, I must — I can only tell you what I know from experience, and that is, for prime time . . . frankly, you're going to have to knock off a few pounds."

I knew I'd pulled the pin out of the grenade. I waited for the explosion. It was louder than I expected.

"Knock off a few pounds?" Jazzminn jumped up from the desk. "Knock off *a few pounds*? I'm a size zero, you turd! There is no smaller size. I've had liposuction on every inch of my body that can possibly be sucked. You can't get any more bulimic than I am — ask anybody on my staff. I'm *bone*. The only possible way I could lose any more weight is to have these implants removed, and I swear to God that will never happen, *never*."

At first, there was something absurdly comical to her outburst, her little clenched fists. Then, to my shock and horror, she suddenly stopped cursing at me and burst into tears. She sat down behind her enormous desk, put her head down on her arms like a child and sobbed. "I'm not the fat girl anymore. I'm *not* the fat girl. I'm not, I'm not, I'm not . . ."

Is there a worse man than I, anywhere on earth? At that moment, I did not think so. These weren't the thrilling, high-drama sobs of Jazzminn's brilliant mad scene from *Hamlet,* just big, messy, hiccupy, mascara-smearing tears, the tears of the poor little overweight girl sitting alone by the Kool-Aid at the junior high school dance. I only wish she had continued to scream at me instead.

Along with concocting my script treatments, I'd put a great deal of energy this past weekend into trying to hate Jazzminn Jenks. I know I'm not myself, but whoever I was needed a reason to murder her beyond my own particular pain. I don't have that much energy left, and it's really hard to hate when you are this goddamned tired — Shit, it's even harder than writing. But, despite my weariness, I knew I had to keep on hating Jazzminn Jenks if I was going to kill her. So, in my feverish state, here's what I'd decided to hate her for.

I knew I could get what I wanted from Jazzminn by calling her fat, but what I'd decided to hate her for was being thin — so ridiculously thin on purpose, deliberately, methodically doing to her own body what this disease was doing to me. Didn't she know what a gift it was, to be able to eat, to be able to go to any aisle in the supermarket, to be a size . . . anything, as long as it was something? *Such are the rich that have abundance and enjoy it not.*

And she didn't just avoid food: she purged it on purpose. What an ass-backwards act, what a crime against nature. It's not like I didn't know about women who do that. I'm in the industry. I just never thought about it much until I got invited to join the ladies' book group. It made me sad and furious.

Right then, however, I couldn't remember to hate Jazzminn Jenks. I forgot to. I don't think I can give myself credit at that stage for realizing that, just maybe, she really had no more choice than I did. I think I just plain forgot. I can't remember whether I've mentioned it, but my memory's pretty much shot. All I wanted was to go to her, to put my arm around her shoulders, to stroke her blond hair, black roots and all, and gently tell her that I never meant to hurt her — I only wanted to kill her.

"Don't cry, Jazzminn. Please don't cry." I didn't stroke her hair, but I did put my hand on her shoulder. "It'll be all right. I think I can help you."

"How, you miserable son of a bitch?"

I felt somewhat better now that Jazzminn had gone back to verbally abusing me. I tried hard to remember my lines, the plot I'd written for myself over the weekend, while I still had enough strength left to despise her. Be strong. Stick to the script. "Well, Jazzminn, how do you think I stay so thin?" I asked, oh-so-casually.

She raised her head. "H-h-how?" she demanded. "Hey — you *are* skinny. The first time I saw you, I wondered if there was something wrong with you."

"Nothing wrong with me, except that maybe I'm too smart for this town." I took a deep breath in preparation for my next lie. "Listen, I used to weigh three hundred and fifty pounds. And I don't have to go to all the trouble that you do to stay thin, Jazzminn. I've got it all in one bottle. A new diet drug."

"Hey! How can there be a new diet drug that I don't know about?" Jazzminn shrieked.

I shrugged. "Gotta keep current, Jazzy."

"Shut up and tell me where it is. Where is it? Give it to me!"

I held up a hand. "Whoa, girlfriend. I don't have it here. It's not the kind of thing you carry around with you."

"Why not?"

"Because you don't need to," I said, with a knowing smile. "That's the beauty of this stuff. You don't take it day after day after day, while you do all sorts of tedious crap like eating a healthy diet and working out. We're busy people. We don't have time for that. This drug is . . . very special. The only way to get the kind of effects you're looking for in a hurry is to . . . swallow the whole bottle, all at once. The whole bottle, Jazzminn. It's a mix of different kinds of pills that all look different, but work together."

"A whole bottle of pills at once? That sounds totally gross."

"It is. You want to do MOWs, or not?"

She thought for a moment. "Okay. Tell me what it's called. I'll get a prescription."

"Oh, no, they'll never give it to you." I shook my head wisely. "They only gave it to me because I weighed so much, a last-ditch effort to save my life before I had a heart attack. No doctor in his right mind would ever prescribe it for a petite thing like you. But luckily, the stuff worked so well for me that I just happen to have an extra bottle, stashed away at home."

"Great! Can I have it?"

"Yes, you can have it," I said. "I've seen the kind of acting talent you've got. We can't let a pound of flesh keep that talent out of prime time. You'll be perfect by the time the cameras roll. I was saving the bottle for myself, just in case — but I'll give it to you. It's yours."

"Goody. Bring it to me." Except for the raccoon rings of mascara, her tears had completely disappeared. Her little blue eyes shone greedily. Suddenly, I didn't feel so guilty anymore.

"I will. But — for your own safety — I'd rather bring it to you at your home, give it to you there, make sure you take it properly and get you right to bed without having to drive home. It's going to make you a little . . . drowsy. I wouldn't want anything bad to happen to the star of our movie."

"I hate having people over. I don't like people in my house unless they're cleaning it. But, okay. How soon can we do it?"

I placed the stack of script treatments in her hands. "Well, we don't want to do it too soon. We don't want to run the risk of your ballooning up again before shooting begins. I'm thinking . . . right after Thanksgiving. Let me get out my book." I reached into the briefcase. "How does Friday, December 1, look for you? Say, around two?"

"Yeah that's good. Friday's good. We're not filming that week." Jazzminn clapped her hands. "I'll have Ophelia give you a map to my house — It's way up in the hills inside the Bel Air gates, kind of hard to find."

"Fine." I picked up my briefcase. "In fact, you might want to have her there, since we'll also be going over the treatments — just to . . . take notes, that kind of thing. Tell you what, I'll give her a lift, and she can help me find the place. I'm terrible with maps. I've got no sense of direction at all." Man, that last sentence just seemed to get truer every day.

"Cool. Friday." There was a very long pause, then: "Thank you, Ken," she said. Alert the media; Jazzminn Jenks just said thank you. Once again, those awful tears sprang to her eyes. "Thank you very, very much."

I swallowed hard. "You're very welcome, Jazzminn."

"Hey — do you want anything for the pills? You know, money?" Jazzminn was asking. "How about a new car — I saw your car outside, Ken. It's a real piece of shit. Or do you want me to have sex with you, or something?" Jazzminn's tears had disappeared as quickly as they had come. She said all this like she was offering to validate my parking. "I'll give you anything you want."

"No, I don't want anything that you can give me, Jazzminn." I was suddenly overwhelmed with weariness. "I'll see you next Friday."

CHAPTER THIRTY-ONE

**You better choose before
somebody else come along and take both.**

— Nettie Mae Easley

No matter what the weather, no matter how many hours I get snowed in at O'Hare, I always go home for Thanksgiving. Given the unorthodox cultural makeup of my family, we don't have much in the way of longstanding tradition — but this one's for sure. Thanksgiving is my favorite holiday because it's for all Americans; no particular race or religion required for admission, no gifts to exchange or return. I've been making the trip ever since I moved to Los Angeles — ten years of ice on the wings, delayed connecting flights and joyful anticipation.

That's probably why it felt so strange and sad to spend this rainy Thanksgiving Eve in Los Angeles, having dinner all alone at a Korean barbecue in a strip mall on Pico Boulevard a few blocks west of Vermont, even when surrounded by the welcoming and sympathetic faces of the entire Kim family.

I've never been able to persuade an industry executive to come with me to Koreatown, and they never give a reason — too far from the studios, maybe. That's the problem with people in Los Angeles: so many communities, but people only visit the ones nearest their own freeway exit. Not me, I go everywhere. It has been my ten-year plan to visit every neighborhood in Los Angeles in my red Jaguar.

This Korean barbecue — one of ten within a two-block radius all called "Korean Barbecue" – is my secret. Some people say it's dangerous in this part of town after dark, gang turf, but that's just silly. Everyone here always treats me like a queen. The parking lot attendant screams in Korean at everybody else that pulls into the cramped parking lot, shared by the Kims' restaurant, a nail salon, and a small pet shop that sells exotic birds. But for me he always finds a space and makes sure no one lays a finger on the Jag.

Usually, I come to this restaurant in spite of the fact that no one here speaks English. On this night, I came here *because* no one speaks English. If I was going to be alone, I wanted to be *alone*. Eating in this part of Koreatown lends a literal quality to the feeling that no one in my world understands me anymore.

My grandma on my mother's side certainly didn't understand — why I wasn't coming home, I mean. This year, I told her I had to work over Thanksgiving if I wanted to have any time off at all at Christmas. Jazzminn's staffers were all trading off this year, I said. Well that's just wonderful, Grandma had replied calmly. I could hear knitting needles clacking through the phone. If I wanted to spend my Thanksgiving running errands for a rich white midget instead of with my only living grandparent, well, that was fine by her. But while I was enjoying my fat-free tofu nut loaf turkey dinner out there in Los Angeles, I just might want to think about the fact that she was eighty-nine years old, and nobody on neither side of the family ain't never lived past ninety.

That made me cry, of course. She's an awful, awful

woman, and I love her very much. But even wracked by guilt, I couldn't go back to Indianapolis, not this time. The moment I realized how foolish it was to invite Ken to go home to Indiana with me was the same moment I realized I couldn't go back without him.

Nor could I tell him I was staying, since he certainly hadn't suggested it. He hadn't said: "Please, stay with me, Ophelia, I need you." After all, we were only plotting a murder together, we weren't . . . in a relationship.

So here I was, about twenty minutes by car and a lifetime away from Ken's drab rented condo near the Beverly Center, eating kimchi and pretending to be in Indiana. None of my friends had invited me to Thanksgiving dinner because I always go home for Thanksgiving, and I wouldn't have gone if they had — small talk becomes impossible when life's events loom so overwhelmingly large. Ever since I asked Ken to kill Jazzminn Jenks, I've become pretty antisocial except for the book group, and we've nearly finished the book. I rarely do lunch with suits, *executives*, anymore. I just keep Jazzminn company while she eats her fourteen pieces of hard-boiled egg and talks hopefully about her new movie career.

You can read all the mystery novels in the world and the one thing they never tell you is how very, very lonely murder is.

I wondered if Ken would go out with friends for Thanksgiving, or stay home all alone. Maybe he was in his little condo kitchen preparing a feast fit for a king; maybe he couldn't eat at all. Sometimes he can't.

Still, he was looking pretty healthy when he skinny-dipped into my swimming pool — that clean, perfect dive. If he wasn't captain of the swim team at North Hollywood High, he should have been. It was working — this murder that would never happen was, indeed, infusing him with life. I was smiling through my tears, thinking about the dive, by the time sweet

Mrs. Kim arrived with the check on a little plastic tray. Instead of after-dinner mints, she always decorates the tray with two sticks of Juicy Fruit gum. It's a charming custom.

But then I remembered something that made me swallow my gum. I began to choke on the Juicy Fruit as I thought about it: The fact that Ken might live longer because of this murder plot might mean that . . . he'd live long enough to have time to do it for real. He seemed to be growing paler and getting stronger all at the same time. Maybe strong enough to actually do it.

I didn't want him to die, but on the other hand . . . I'd sort of been counting on it. Either I was going to have to think of some plot twist to keep him occupied longer, or he was just going to have to hurry up and die already. I didn't know if I was a good enough actress to string him along for as long as I hoped he'd live.

Mrs. Kim was waving her hands and yanking the fire extinguisher off the wall; I don't know how that was supposed to stop me from choking on Juicy Fruit, but apparently that's how she responds to any and all emergencies. Luckily, I stopped gagging in time to keep her from blasting me with a faceful of bicarbonate of soda.

I stopped choking because I remembered another thing: Before he decided to plunge naked into my swimming pool, Ken had hinted that he might not be feeling so enthusiastic about murder anymore. He didn't say why, he never says much about what he's thinking — but there just might be a chance. I fervently prayed that this was true, even though I'm not a religious person in the sense of relying on the Bible or other sacred text— frankly, I think a person should be able to tell right from wrong without a manual. But I was praying now. If I wasn't an accessory to murder, I'd still be able to go back to Indianapolis for Thanksgiving next year — that is, if I didn't have to go earlier, for Grandma's funeral.

After Thanksgiving, he would come to my house, sit down in my living room in front of the fire, and tell me that he had decided not to murder Jazzminn Jenks or anyone else — and that I was a silly goose for ever having asked him to. We'd laugh at the whole idea — ha ha — I would gratefully apologize, and then he'd quickly forgive me and cook something. He always looks so very happy when he's cooking. I'd laugh again and tell him that, after my big Thanksgiving at home in Indianapolis, I could barely eat a bite.

And after that, maybe, he'd go swimming again — in swim trunks this time, because I'd be there. Not that I'm the least bit embarrassed by nudity — the human body is beautiful, and after all, I was a biology major — but his knowing that I was watching would change the dynamic of the situation, I think.

Around this time of year I usually turn the heat off in the pool. It's only on for guests, I don't swim. But now, despite my environmental concerns, I think I'll leave the heat on for the rest of the winter, just in case.

CHAPTER THIRTY-TWO

Hence, horrible shadow!
Unreal mock'ry, hence!

— Macbeth, *Macbeth*

Anyone who believes you can read every tragedy ever written by William Shakespeare and still plot a murder without seeing a ghost hasn't, well, read every tragedy ever written by William Shakespeare.

I'd like to apologize in advance for this ghost. Like all apparitions, mine hails not from somewhere out in the ether but from the mind. It can be no more inspired than my own imagination — and my personal knowledge of ghosts is pretty much limited to reruns of the Mr. Magoo version of *A Christmas Carol*. But please believe me when I say that seeing a ghost, any ghost, shoots white-hot, molten terror into the very marrow of your bones, no matter how badly that ghost is written.

At least Shakespeare's ghosts had the decency to appear in the dead of night. Mine shows up at rush hour while I'm on the 101 on my way to work. Hitchhiking, no less — shit, I almost hit a truck. I would have just kept on driving, except the ghost was holding up a brown cardboard sign with the words "Stop, Kenny" written on it in red marker. By that point in my strained relationship with Fate, I'd learned never to ignore signs.

So I pull over and the ghost gets into the passenger seat of the Honda — big black hooded robe and all. I would have tried to strike up a conversation, but judging from what I could catch in the rear view mirror, the thing had no face.

We rode in silence, except for Diana Ross. I'd been listening to the traffic report, but almost immediately the ghost reached out a drooping black sleeve and, with one invisible finger, started punching buttons until it reached oldies station K-EARTH 101. Satisfied, it leaned back in the seat, swaying a little to "Stop! In the Name of Love."

The spirit got out of the car when I did — it even remembered to lock the passenger door — and followed me into the Hacienda Building. I tried to concentrate on my work as the ghost helped itself to some coffee from the reception area, sat down in the chair in front of my desk, and picked up a fresh copy of the Tyne Daly shooting script. You can't exactly say that a creature without thumbs *thumbed* through the pages, but I could see them turning, briskly.

Although the presence was still scaring me half out of my skin, I couldn't hide a smile when it tossed *A Matter of Months* into the wastebasket before getting through the first act.

Apparently no one else in the office could see this ghost, although I swear to God there was less coffee in the pot each time it poured itself another mug. Four, total. Great. Now it would be up all night.

The specter waited patiently, black sleeves crossed, as a writer came in to pitch a few movie ideas (it took all the effort I could muster not to suggest a ghost writer. You see, I worked in sitcom for a very, very long time). It watered the wilting bromeliad while I returned a few calls. It even did lunch in the commissary with me and the head of the department, Blair Smith, who wanted to know what plans I had for the holiday. Staring pointedly at the ghost, I told her I'd had a friend drop in unexpectedly, from out of town.

I ordered one plate for both me and it — partly because I didn't want to tip Blair off to its presence, and partly because I figured one was plenty. My appetite is practically gone, and as for my guest — no mouth. I got us a sandwich, to avoid the whole silverware issue.

It was the Wednesday before the holiday, so, like everyone else in the office, the ghost and I left early. Traffic was bumper to bumper, with everybody heading out of town, but I didn't have a problem because the ghost drove. No, I can't explain that. Though nobody at work could see the ghost, as we entered my apartment together — well, right then I'd have bet a million dollars that cat would never come out from behind the sofa.

For a long moment, we stood there just inside the door, the ghost and I. Then, out of habit, I said, "Let me take your coat." Christ, I'm an idiot. The thing *was* a coat.

But then, much to my terrified surprise, and oh so very slowly, off came the long, long black robe. First the hood flipped back. Then the shoulders came down. The rope around the waist untied itself and dangled in the air for just a moment before it fell. Finally the entire garment sagged into a crumpled pile on the floor and just lay there. It looked like somebody had melted a monk.

Then, the mound of black fabric began to heave and pitch alarmingly; the cat hissed from behind the couch. From somewhere under the empty robe came a cloud of vanilla smoke — the kind they use on the set, mostly for dream sequences. And then, as the scented mist cleared . . . there stood my ghost. It wasn't invisible anymore. And it was a woman.

Instead of the black robe, the ghost now stood resplendent in a silken gown of powder blue. Her back was to me; her long, curly hair cascaded to her waist. It was just like Ophelia's hair, only . . . blond, bright blond. I saw that the roots were blond, too. I knew then that this creature could not be from Hollywood.

"Kill me, Kenny," the ghost whispered softly. "Kill me."

"You're a ghost," I whispered back — logic, for the moment, getting the better of panic. "Aren't you . . . already dead?"

"Stop asking so many fucking questions and do it!" the ghost shrieked.

"Jazzminn?" I gasped. "Jazzminn? Is that . . . you?"

"No, it's me, Kenny," the ghost replied, the voice suddenly full of good-natured laughter, a voice so comfortingly familiar I wished I could take the sound and hold it in both my hands.

"Ophelia?"

"No, asshole. Me." Much to my annoyance, the first voice had returned.

"*Who?*"

"Me." Now I didn't recognize the voice at all. It was sweet and sickening all at once. The creature turned around. She was short, like Jazzminn Jenks; her hair excessively blond, like Jazzminn's own very unnatural color. She wore Jazzminn's favorite shade, powder blue. But this was Ophelia's unruly hair; Ophelia's lovely face; Ophelia's tiny waist; Ophelia's sparkling *catua* eyes. Had there been no chair nearby, I'd have collapsed right there on the floor.

"Who the hell are you?" I sobbed out, clutching both arms of the chair. "Put your black robe back on and get your ass out of here."

"You watch your language," the ghost scolded. "You know who I am. I'm the woman you will poison; the woman you will kill. Kill me, Kenny . . ."

"I can't."

"Why, because I'm beautiful?" The ghost gave a ringing laugh.

"No — because I don't know who you are. Please, just go away," I begged.

"You have to kill me," the ghost said. "You promised. You have to kill me, no matter what I look like. Otherwise I'll know that everything is just because I'm beautiful, and that you are — lying!" Gracefully, the barefoot ghost walked toward me, holding out her lovely arms. "Besides, we have a deal."

"Nooo," I pleaded. "Please. I'm not ready for this yet. It's not even Thanksgiving."

"You wouldn't want me to start crying, would you?" She caressed my face with one finger. "You hate it when I cry."

"How can I hate it when you cry? *I don't know who you are.*"

The ghost took my hand; it was soft, soft as Ophelia's honey skin — but even colder than my own. "Come on, Ken. Show me where it is."

"What?"

"The poison, dickhead. What kind of a murderer *are* you?"

I suddenly felt hope. I'd already shown Ophelia where I kept my prescriptions. Surely, then, this specter was someone else. Maybe I could kill her after all. In fact, it might be good practice.

"It's in the bathroom. Check out the medicine cabinet. All the pills you could possibly want." I gave the ghost a defiant stare. "Go ahead, knock yourself out."

"Not that — I know where that stuff is," the ghost scoffed. Impatiently, she scouted out the room. "Ahhh. There it is." She crouched down in her silken dress and, from underneath the very chair in which I sat, dragged out a thick, writhing, hissing snake. The thing had to be three feet long. Triumphantly, she held the twisting reptile aloft in one hand. "This is what I'm talking about."

"What is it?" I asked, cowering in my chair.

"This, Ken, is an asp," explained the ghost, formal as a museum guide. "A deadly asp, like the one that killed Cleopatra in the play. Now this is what I call poison. All you have to do is take this asp, place it on my breast and I will become — like Cleopatra — ancient history."

"Uh . . . as I recall, Cleopatra placed the asp on her own breast before it bit her." I was desperately looking for an out. "Why do I have to do it? It's your snake."

"It's your murder. Aaaw, don't be afraid, Kenny. It's just an asp." I watched in rapt horror as she allowed the snake to nuzzle her neck, then kissed its thin, scaly mouth in return. "Besides, you may not have a thing to be afraid of."

"I have a ghost in my living room. I'm *concerned.*"

"Yes, but what ghost?" she demanded. "My hair is Ophelia's, but its color belongs to Jazzminn Jenks. I'm the same height as Jazzminn, but I've got Ophelia's eyes and face." The ghost and the snake did a jerky little waltz together across the room. "Sometimes my voice sounds like Ophelia's, and sometimes it sounds like Jazzminn's. Sometimes, I sound like both — or neither. So, I'd say you've got about a fifty-fifty chance."

"Of what?"

"The breasts, Ken," she snapped. "If they are real like Ophelia's, I die instantly when the snake bites. However, if the tits are Jazzminn's, the asp ends up with a mouthful of silicone, I feel nothing, and I disappear forever because you've held up your end of the deal. Like I said, fifty-fifty."

I squirmed in my chair. "Any chance you'll go away if I

make no choice at all?"

"Not a chance. Hey, did you get us a turkey and stuffing for tomorrow?"

I wanted her to leave more than anything. Surely this weird sister had to be more Jazzminn than Ophelia. Ophelia would never talk this way, never insist on impossible choices, never waltz with an asp.

But then, unlike Ophelia, Jazzminn Jenks had never asked me to murder anyone.

Well, I would have run, but there was no place to go. I drew in a painful breath. Then, I squared my shoulders — such as they were. "All right. I'll do as you say. Give me the fucking snake," I growled. Startled, the ghost handed me the animal. My skin crawling, I allowed the asp to loop its scaly length around my neck, trying not to gag as I felt the loop tighten.

Both the ghost and I watched, frozen, as the stupid, beady eyes and flickering tongue made their way slowly, slowly down my chest. Then, just as the hideous diamond-shaped head reached my heart, I grabbed its jaws in one hand and held them firm; with the other hand, I ripped open the front of my shirt. The snake's mouth gaped, a ghastly milk-white inside. I could see slow drops of poison beginning to form at the tips of its fangs.

"Now look — if you don't get out of here right now, I'm going to let this thing bite my breast, and you're going to have to choose what to do with the body," I hissed. "Now go. Trust me, this is one episode of *Bite Me* you don't want to see."

She hesitated. "Hey! No fair. That is not one of the choices. Besides, you'd never do it."

"Oh, I'd give it about fifty-fifty. I don't have a whole lot to lose." Holy crap, look at those fangs. Sweat poured off me. I felt my lungs would burst from sucking in so much vanilla smoke. "And I'm only going to count to three . . ."

The ghost thought it over, for what seemed like an eternity. "All right. Fine. Get your hands off my asp," she snapped. I handed her the snake, only too happy to oblige. "You win, I'm leaving. But you know what? I'll bet you don't even have a turkey for tomorrow. Hey — I'll bet you can't even cook."

"Go."

"I said I was going. But now you'll never know, will you?" The ghost laughed a hollow laugh. Very convincing — this ghost was a good actress. "Now you'll never know who I am. Never!" She slung the thick snake around her shoulders like a stole, slipped the black robe on over her silky powder blue dress, awkwardly adjusted her panties under the skirt and disappeared in another puff of vanilla smoke. Gone. Somehow, I'd managed to frighten off my very first ghost. I wondered why I was still terrified.

As I sat there, shaking, staring down at the torn handful of white cotton that was once my favorite shirt, the phone rang.

"Kenny? Hi! It's me."

This time, I knew who it was. This fact did not make me feel any more comfortable, however. "Hi," I choked out.

"What's wrong? You sound like you've seen a ghost." She said it, I didn't.

"Bad connection," I replied, my voice a little less wobbly now. "I'm . . . fine. How was the flight? Did you get snowed in at O'Hare? Midwest looked pretty bad on the news."

"Uh . . . no. It probably won't snow in Chicago until I'm trying to get back to LA, as usual." Ophelia laughed a little, then yawned audibly. She must be curled up in the corner of a piece of overstuffed furniture, a very big, soft, warm sofa or chair somewhere in Indianapolis, Indiana. "It's late here. Everybody else is asleep except me and the dog, so I'm going to get off the phone and go to bed. I just wanted to say . . .

happy Thanksgiving to you, Kenny. I hope you have a happy Thanksgiving tomorrow. I really do. That's why I'm calling you from far, far away in Indianapolis, Indiana."

"I will," I promised. I wondered then why I hadn't just let the asp go ahead and sink its fangs into my heart. "And a very happy Thanksgiving to you, too."

CHAPTER THIRTY-THREE

Uh-oh.

— Nettie Mae Easley

Somewhere between Ken's astonishing moonlight skinny dip and this moment, the thunderstorm in his gray eyes had turned into a tornado. He said he wasn't upset at all, but his stormy glare said otherwise.

"I waited for every flight from O'Hare to Los Angeles International Airport on Sunday from 6 a.m. to midnight, and you weren't on any of them," he said calmly — but jingling his keys in his pocket with such agitation that it made me want to clap my hands over my ears. "Luckily by that hour of the night the worst part of the holiday traffic was over. It only took me an hour and a half to get home on the 405 instead of the three it had taken me to get to the airport in the morning, what a break for me. Not that it matters now, but just as a point of information — did Wade Stark or one of your other loving ex-husbands perhaps provide you with a fucking private plane home from Chicago?"

"You're angry," I said.

"No, I'm not," he said angrily.

"I . . . flew into Burbank instead of LAX," I lied. His keys were still rattling like a jailer's, rattling my nerves at the same time. "I'm so sorry, I would have told you, but I had no idea you'd try to pick me up at the airport. No human being should have to pick up another person at LAX on the Sunday after Thanksgiving. That was so sweet of you to come, Kenny."

"Yeah. I'm sweet as hell," he grumbled. "Traffic was no picnic on the way over here tonight either, let me tell you. Everybody's back from Thanksgiving, and every car in Los Angeles was on La Cienega Boulevard trying to make a left turn into the Beverly Center."

"I know. It was like that on the way home from the studio, too."

Ken scowled at me. "Well, welcome back. So, how was your Thanksgiving?"

"It was lovely, as always." Actually, I had food poisoning on Thanksgiving, I'm pretty sure it was the kimchi — I've never been that sick in all my life. But I certainly wasn't going to tell a dying man about it, especially not one who seemed ready to kill me. "Uh, how about you?"

He didn't answer the question. "Friday," he said instead. "Today is Monday. Tomorrow is Tuesday. It happens Friday."

"Oh." That was not what I wanted to hear. Unwelcome tears started in my eyes. "On Friday. Hmmm. Maybe I should check my schedule, but my iPad is upstairs," I babbled. "I'll go get it, although I think the battery has run down. It'll take a few hours to charge up. But first . . . I have such good news! Maxie had a girl on Saturday. Only five pounds, seven ounces, but she's fine. A girl — it was a surprise, she didn't have an amnio even though she's forty-five. I must be going nuts — before Maxie had the baby I kept thinking, I wonder if I'm going to be an aunt, or an uncle?"

Ken did not laugh.

"Well, I thought it was funny."

"Maybe. But I hate comedy. Besides, we're talking about murder here."

"You know, Ken, since we've already waited until after Thanksgiving, maybe we should just wait until after Christmas — maybe even New Year's," I suggested — casually, I hoped. "What do you think, Kenny? You know, the holidays are always so busy, even without homicide . . . "

"Hello, this is me not laughing again. Fuck — *no*," he snapped. "I'm sure you can understand why I'm not wasting a lot of my time planning my New Year's Eve party, Ophelia. I want a tragedy as big as *Hamlet* or *Macbeth,* and damn it, I'm going to get it. Friday at 2 p.m. At her house. I'll pick you up at one. Don't worry: I'll take care of everything. I'll tell you exactly what to do. You just be here."

I shuddered — then frowned. "I thought you had chemo on Fridays."

"I did, but now I don't. There's been a change in my treatment."

"Oh." I studied his pale face hopefully, but his expression provided no message except a general dissatisfaction — with me, I guessed. "That's . . . good, isn't it?" I asked. "No more chemo. It must mean you're feeling better."

"Yeah, that's exactly what it means, Ophelia," he said coldly. "Yeah. I feel much better. I'm fucking fine. I'm so glad you had a wonderful, wonderful Thanksgiving in Indianapolis, Indiana or Indianapolis, Ohio or Michigan or wherever the hell it is. And right now, I gotta go."

CHAPTER THIRTY-FOUR

We have scorch'd the snake, not kill'd it

— Macbeth, *Macbeth*

On Tuesday, I went to lunch with Danny Gordon in the commissary. He invited me — dropped by my office, just like that. I was so damn shocked, I forgot to say no.

It was awkward. First, Danny apologized for what happened with Ophelia and *Bite Me* — not his fault, outside his jurisdiction. "She really was beautiful, Ken," he mused, as morose as always. I've known Dan for five years, but I can't remember ever hearing him laugh. Executive vice president of comedy development — Jesus, that's like hiring Hamlet to do stand-up.

"*Is* beautiful, Dan. She's still living. Actors don't always die when they don't get the part."

"Exactly my point. You know, women aren't exactly topping my priority list these days, Ken," Danny continued, not listening to me. "I mean, I *prefer* women. That's not what I'm trying to say here, you know that." He paused to wipe his hands on one of the little antiseptic towelettes he always carried. "But I've been so *crazed* lately, between the mid-season

replacements and getting the Palisades house finished —
Never try to talk to an architect: they're all, like, spatial
relations, and I'm strictly verbal — The whole *sex i*ssue hasn't
been key for me this year if you get what I'm saying. I'd kind of
. . . *shut it down*, maybe that's the best way to put it. Like
farmers say about cornfields, it was *lying dormant*. Or, what's
that thing comedians always say when they're not getting a
laugh so they tap on the microphone: 'Hey, is this thing on? Is
this thing *on*? I've got to tell you, I was starting to wonder if it
was. You know, *on*." Dan was still wiping his hands. "But she .
. . that girl, Ophelia . . . God, Kenny, when I saw her — for the
first time all year, I think I felt *movement*."

"Don't tell me anything else about your penis, Danny," I
suggested. "Ever."

"I know, I'm just saying, I was so *relieved* . . . Anyway,
here's the thing, Kenny."

"The thing?"

"It's *Bite Me*, Ken."

"What about it?"

"It's not funny anymore."

"It never was, Dan."

"I know that. What I mean is, people aren't watching it
anymore. Something's changed. It's not funny in a different
way than it . . . wasn't funny before. The ratings have been
dropping since Halloween. I don't know what it is." Dan
wrung his antiseptic hands. He's the only person I know who
actually wrings his hands. "The demographics are all wrong
now, Kenny. Men, 18 to 49 — I don't know where they've
gone."

"I think you'd be surprised by the intensity with which I
don't care, Dan."

"I'm not asking you to care, I'm just asking you to help."
Dan was perspiring visibly. "Maybe Bert DeMarco's character

should get married and have a baby, what do you think?"

"A baby? Diapers and pre-school? Kiss of death for a nine o'clock romantic comedy."

"Okay, lose the baby. Don't like 'em anyway: they're too small. Come on, Ken. You created this show. You . . . you *are Bite Me*. Can you do something for us?"

I tried to answer this question as accurately as I could. "Can. Won't."

"I know, I said some things at the beginning of all this that weren't thoughtful, Ken," said Dan, still wringing his hands. "Selfish, even. I'm sorry. I'm not a bad person, I know I'm not — I polled the staff before I asked you to lunch. But I don't expect you to accept my apology. I just hope you'll accept my money. The network's money, I mean. How much would it take to get you to come back?"

"You mean you'd pay for Aspen next winter? Skis, too?" I gasped. "Done! Oh, wait, sorry. I forgot. I'll be dead."

"See, Ken? That's funny," Dan almost sobbed. "*You're* funny. That's why we need you. Come on, how much? I understand your point, but . . . you could leave the money to your wife."

"I don't have a wife."

"Really? Then who was that red-head I always used to see you with at the wrap parties?"

"That was my girlfriend, Alice. We don't live together anymore."

"Oh, I get it. She probably couldn't live with . . . well, never mind. She always sort of scared me, anyway — *way* too intense. How about this? You could donate the money to cancer. That would be very humanitarian of you, Ken."

"Why would I donate money to cancer? I'm against it."

"See? There you go again," Dan said sadly. "You're a very funny man, Ken Harrison. And I've got a blank check here that says I take that very seriously."

"Dan, I have to go," I said gently. "I have to go because you're here, and I don't want to be with you. I don't want to be with you at all."

CHAPTER THIRTY-FIVE

**O Time! thou must untangle this, not I;
It is too hard a knot for me t' untie.**

— Viola, *Twelfth Night*

I read somewhere once that the intersection of Wilshire and Westwood Boulevards, just south of UCLA, is the busiest one in the country, maybe even the world. I got more than a few traffic tickets here myself during college, trying to make a left behind two other cars without waiting for the next green. Late for class, as usual. During rush hour, cops camp out here like vultures with doughnuts. Not the safest place to drive. And definitely not the safest place to stand, paralyzed, in the middle of the street.

The sign had stopped flashing. The letters in front of me glowed bright, red, and warning: "DON'T WALK." Well, I *wasn't*, was I?

Horns blared. Cars whizzed by me in the evening dusk, swerving crazily to avoid slamming me to the pavement. I just stood there in the intersection, dazed by headlights, the only human being in a sea of hurtling metal. "Hey, get out of the road!" yelled a man in a BMW as he raced by, tearing himself away from his cell phone conversation just long enough to offer me the finger. "Man, what drug are you on?"

This may not be the best place to discuss it, but I have a problem. It's a tomorrow problem. What I mean by that is, there are way too many of them between me and murder. *Tomorrow and tomorrow and tomorrow / Creeps in this petty pace from day to day.*

I was okay on Tuesday afternoon when I had lunch with Danny, but not on Tuesday night — that is, now. I did not feel better anymore. Damn, there are a lot of cars in Los Angeles.

This morning, I called in sick. I told Blair Smith I was coming down with a cold — always my story of choice when I'm faking it. Like somehow that's a more acceptable excuse for staying home than terminal cancer. But that's what I said.

"It's nice to hear from you again, Ken, but — I don't understand," Blair replied, ever so politely. "I'm sorry about your cold, but you really don't have to call in sick anymore. You quit yesterday. Right after lunch. We all did that little goodbye thing with the bagels, in the conference room, like we always do. Don't you remember?"

"Oh, yeah." I remembered now. *Think* before you pick up the goddamned phone. I could feel myself blush, even though I was alone. I tried a laugh. "Okay, so I don't have a cold."

"Are you all right, Ken?" Blair sounded genuinely concerned. "Anything I can do for you?"

"No, no, nothing — I'm fine. I'm just . . . not coming in to work today, so I called. That's all. Sorry. Old habits die hard. Goodbye, Blair." I hung up quickly.

Read Shakespeare: that is my advice. Just don't read it *again*. If I hadn't, I wouldn't be standing here in the cold and dark in the middle of Wilshire Boulevard with my arms wrapped around *The Complete Works of William Shakespeare* and a Prius up my ass.

I should have watched TV instead. I could have watched *Bite Me*. Instead, last night, I began flipping through my Shakespeare again, for the first time in weeks. And that night, words that had endured for four hundred years started flying out of control, like sleeping bats startled from their cave.

I remembered murder; I remembered death — *O, proud Death*. I remembered knives and swords, poison and revenge. I remembered storms, such sheets of fire, such bursts of horrid thunder, the foul womb of the night. The fire-eyed maid of smoky war, all hot and bleeding. Great danger — *the greater therefore should our courage be. I will die a hundred thousand deaths / Ere I break the smallest parcel of this vow*. This was the best of Shakespeare, the most powerful, the clearest — when too, too solid flesh *did* melt, and blood flowed from the stage.

But now, all I could see in front of me was doubt. I turned the pages, faster and faster, looking for something that would defuse my mounting fear. Instead, I got this kind of stuff: *"There is no sure foundation set on blood; / No certain life achieved by others' death"* . . . *"What to ourselves in passion we propose, / The passion ending, doth the purpose lose"* . . . *"The rarer action is in virtue than in vengeance."*

"How all occasions do inform against me, / And spur my dull revenge!" said Hamlet. I loved that line. But now revenge was dull — even revenge, revenge with an exclamation point, my favorite part of every tragedy, seemed to have lost its edge. Now, it sounded like an old ham slicer that could no longer cut, clumsy and useless.

Well, Hamlet always was high-maintenance, I reassured myself. Anxiously, I turned to *Macbeth*. If only for sheer body count, I could always rely on the story of Macbeth to keep me in a murderous mood. And if he failed me, I only had to think about that wife of his. But what was he saying here? *And nothing is / But what is not.* "And nothing is / But what is not"

— Jesus, if you're going to leave me in that intersection, you might as well just push me in front of a bus.

Now, the only words that seemed clear, that seemed to signify anything at all, were those that spoke the poetry of mercy, forgiveness, kindness — kindness, nobler even than revenge. And love — shit, the word was everywhere. The voice of all the gods made heaven drowsy with the harmony. Stony limits cannot hold love out. And the sonnets — don't get me started. *This thou perceiv'st, which makes thy love more strong, / To love that well which thou must leave ere long.*

I could not fall in love with that which I must leave. Please, God, not now.

Never mind murder. I was going to die right here in the fast lane if I didn't get moving soon. Flinching, I held up my hand to halt the cars careening toward me. I forced my legs to carry me the rest of the way across Wilshire Boulevard, then for ten more cold and endless blocks uphill to the campus bookstore, underneath the Student Union. I should have parked closer, but there's never anyplace to park in Westwood.

When I got there, exhausted, I pushed my way to the front of the line and slammed the big, pea-green book down on the counter. No one stopped me — people just moved away. "Can I sell this back? It's a used book," I gasped out, clutching the counter in front of me for support. "I bought it here. I want to sell it back."

"We usually only buy 'em back at the end of the term." The kid behind the counter picked up the book and examined it, his squinting face all pimples and suspicion under blond dreadlocks. "When did you buy this, anyway?"

I thought hard. "Eighteen years ago."

"Really? Then guess what?"

"What?"

"You can return this book — *not*. Dude, you bought it the

same year I was born."

I imagined this guy playing Hamlet: "To be — *not*!" "Well, can I donate it or something? Take it. Please."

"Maybe to some library, man. We don't want it. It's too old."

"Of course it's old, you little snot. It's Shakespeare."

He sighed, bored by my existence. "What part of no don't you understand? I'm going to have to ask you to either leave, or buy a book. I've got people in line here."

"Fine." I didn't need some freshman with pepperoni pizza acne to get rid of this book for me. I walked out of the bookstore — and, with a thud, dropped *The Complete Works of William Shakespeare* onto the sidewalk just outside Ackerman Hall.

The book landed on its worn spine, open to this page of The Merchant of Venice: "The quality of mercy is not strained / it droppeth as the gentle rain from heaven / Upon the place beneath: it is twice bless'd." And, I'm not making this up: At the same time as I read the words, it started raining, ever so gently.

CHAPTER THIRTY-SIX

You ain't never listen except when you shouldn't.

— Nettie Mae Easley

Glinda is a lovely, lovely human being. She is the model of old-fashioned womanhood, a '50s retro glamour girl; so dainty and feminine I can hardly believe she's only been a transsexual for four years.

"Here, doll, don't cry anymore," she said soothingly, handing me not an ordinary tissue, but a red satin hanky embroidered with a beehive, the state seal of Utah — that's where she's from, Salt Lake City. "Let me make you some tea, unless of course you'd rather have coffee, or cocaine. I have all three."

"Tea would be fine, thank you so much." I was loath to actually blow my nose on such a patriotic handkerchief, but also so stuffed up I could barely breathe. I let out an unattractive but unavoidable honk — then, embarrassed, balled the soggy red silk up in one hand. "And, Glinda, thank you for rescuing me before I did something I'd regret."

Glinda nodded wisely, running her hands through her strawberry blond fall and crossing hard, muscular legs, sheathed in thick, beige hose with seams running down the back. She wore a pink satin dress with a flared skirt and a matching pink headband. It looked as though the strawberry fall might be attached to the band. Her long narrow feet were encased in beige kidskin flats that bulged in spots over knobby toe joints.

"I don't know exactly what's going on with you, doll, but when I see a gorgeous woman sobbing outside a man's apartment door like her heart's just snapped in half, I figure whatever she's about to do, she damn well better stop and think about it." Her voice was rough, smoky. "Besides, I don't think he's home right now." Glinda then surprised me by looking down at my feet. "Also, I dragged you in here because I wanted to ask you where you bought those pumps. I've been looking for pumps exactly like those. Where did you get them? And I wonder if they come in a size eleven?"

"I'll bet they do. Nordstrom's has the best size selection in Los Angeles." I dabbed at my nose with the soggy red ball. "I'll check next time I'm there. I'd like to buy them for you, for being so kind."

"No way, I couldn't possibly let you do that, no way! I'm an eleven double A, narrow in the heel."

"I'll remember."

"No, I won't let you to do it! Do they come in plum? I look real good in plum." The six-foot Glinda stood up on her long, hard legs, strode to the kitchen and returned several minutes later with a mug of tea in one hand, with the bag still in it, the Lipton tag hanging over the side. She had a mug for herself in the other hand — no tea bag. "Microwave okay?" she asked, handing me the one with the tea bag. It was lukewarm, but I appreciated the effort. Besides, anything would be warmer than my cold hands. "So tell me what's going on with you and my skinny neighbor with the closet full of

Armani suits." Gilda leaned in confidentially. "You two an item?"

"No. Not at all. I guess you'd call him a friend."

"He's good looking. He never once looked at me, though, not the way I like to be looked at." Glinda fluffed her strawberry fall. "I think it's because I'm so tall, I'm taller than him in heels, but after all I've been through there's no way I'm giving up heels. Men are intimidated by my height: that's the problem."

"Yes, I'm sure that's the reason, Glinda."

"He's real sick, doll."

"I know."

"The walls are awful thin here, sometimes I hear him up late at night, sometimes he . . ."

"Don't tell me, please don't tell me," I begged. "I understand. God help him." Glinda sat down next to me, pensively twirling an ankle that bore a thin gold chain with a little charm poking through the hose. "He's nice. He lets me borrow his *Hollywood Reporter* whenever I want. He just leaves it outside the door. I don't think he reads it anymore. I'm not in the industry, but I love to know who's screwing who, you know? I'll hate it when they go all the way digital. So . . . it's AIDS, right?"

"No, not AIDS. He has cancer."

"That's real sad. And don't worry: I wasn't going to tell you I hear him throwing up, although God knows I hear that too. I wasn't going to tell you about him coughing like a chain smoker, or moaning late at night or any of that. I know people get creeped out by clinical details, even though I don't, seeing as my dick is probably in some medical lab in a jar of formaldehyde. I wish there was a donation center or something. No, none of that — I was just going to say that, sometimes, I hear him reading some kind of poetry. He reads out loud, even though there's no one there."

"Shakespeare. It's Shakespeare."

"How about that. Is he an actor? He's got a nice voice."

"No. He's a network television executive. Movies and miniseries."

"Miniseries." Glinda sighed. "I still love those. They hardly ever make 'em anymore. I'm the only person left in Los Angeles who doesn't get cable, I think. I bought *The Thorn Birds* on DVD. Are you an actress? I'll bet you're an actress. You're so pretty."

I paused before answering. "No, I'm not an actress. I can't act at all."

"Too bad — you're so pretty."

"Yeah, it's too bad I'm so pretty," I sobbed.

"That's not what I meant. You don't listen too good. I hope you heard what I said about my narrow heel." Glinda took a sip from her own mug, which did not smell like tea at all, something more along the lines of bourbon. "How can it be bad to be pretty? I wanted it all my life, even when I still had five o'clock shadow. And now I am. I'm real pretty now. Don't cry anymore, doll. It'll make you nauseous. Why did you come here today, anyway?"

I would have blown my nose again, but by now the red handkerchief was so soggy it would have done no good at all. "He's about to do something that's terribly, terribly wrong, and it's all my fault," I choked out. "I wanted to talk to him. I wanted to try to stop him."

"Really? What's he going to do?"

"Actually, it's something we were going to do together. *Are* going to do together, unless I can talk him out of it."

"Fair enough. What?"

"I can't tell you."

"Okay, don't tell me. He's real sick, doll."

"I know."

"He had a rough night last night. I'm not going into detail, but he didn't sleep at all — not that I'm spying on him, although God knows I'd make a great spy, I've got the legs to go with the trench coat. But I can hear. He wanders around all night, like a ghost."

"He can't sleep."

"I don't listen on purpose. I'm just home a lot. Some of my old friends don't really . . . understand. We don't see each other that much anymore. So I'm home. Doesn't bother me to hear it — I just feel sorry for him. So, here's my two cents . . . what's your name?"

"Ophelia."

"Pretty, like you." Glinda reached a muscular hand toward my face. "Are these curls natural, do you mind if I touch? I'm in the beauty field professionally." I nodded tearfully and allowed Glinda to examine my hair. "Ophelia . . . I've heard that name somewhere." She wrapped a golden-brown curl around one large finger. "Oh, yeah — it's in some of the things he reads, the poems. Well, here's my two cents, Ophelia: Maybe you should just let Mr. Kenneth Charles Harrison do what he wants to do. That's his name, right? It's on the address labels on the *Reporter*. Just let him do what he wants to do. And you know what else? You should help him."

"I should help him do something . . . awful? A really awful thing?"

"Look, people have to do what they have to do." Glinda let go of my hair and took another big swig of her "tea." "I did what I had to do, even though no one back home is speaking to me anymore, there ain't no such thing as a Mormon transsexual, doll. It's not up to you to decide for him. Come on, the man is as weak as a kitten. Whatever he plans to do, how bad could it be?"

I couldn't tell her how bad it could be.

"Okay, you're not talking because you're real unhappy about him being so sick. I understand," Glinda said reassuringly. "There's a lot of things I don't want to talk about either, like how my daughter used to come visit me in the hospital after the operation, and we'd talk about the weather and stuff. Then later I'd hear her bawling her eyes out in the hall, just like you were today. That's her picture on the shelf over there. She's twenty-two. I haven't seen her in four years. She doesn't visit me because she doesn't like Los Angeles, she says. Anyways, I don't think you should worry so much. Whatever it is, I don't think he's going to do it. I don't think he can. I hear a lot through the walls. I don't think he has much time. Just humor him, doll. Humor him till it's over."

I sipped my tea and cried silently for a while, tears running into the mug, dripping into my lap. "Is that what you really think, Glinda?" I finally asked. "That I should just wait it out?"

"Yes, I do. And I don't know Mr. Kenneth Charles Harrison all that well, but I know him well enough to know he's not going to do anything this messed up world ain't seen before. He's nice. You should have seen the Thanksgiving dinner he cooked for me."

"He . . . cooked Thanksgiving dinner for you?"

"Well . . . he didn't cook it for *me*. He spent all day cooking dinner, a big-ass turkey and all the fixin's. He was banging pots and pans around in there like the drum section of the USC marching band, with the Macy's parade on TV. Then he came by and asked me if I wanted it. Said he didn't feel much like eating. Said everything tasted like sawdust in his mouth. Said the weirdest thing next — said he made the whole dinner to prove to a ghost that he could cook. I didn't argue with him, just went on over there and got myself a golden brown roast turkey — it was beautiful, Ophelia. I was going to go out with some friends who are at different stages with their hormone treatments, over to Pink's on La Brea for some Thanksgiving chili dogs, but this smelled way better. So I just stayed in my condo here by myself and had a feast. I've still got leftovers frozen, if you want."

Then Glinda smiled sadly. "I also stayed home because I kind of wanted to be around, you know, just in case he needed some help or something. He . . . didn't look so good. I knocked later to say thank you and sorta check up on him, but he didn't answer."

Glinda had set her tea mug down on a side table, next to mine. She said nothing when I reached for hers instead of my own and chugged whatever was in it, holding the mug to my mouth with both hands. It was strong enough to make me cough. "I wonder where he is now," I gasped when I could talk again.

"Don't wonder. Just give it a rest for a while, doll. Leave him alone and he'll come around. That's what I'm doing with my daughter. One day, she'll come to Los Angeles to see me. I know she will. After all, it's only been four years."

"Okay." I sighed and drained Glinda's mug. My head swam. "Glinda, I know we just met, but I like you." I was having more trouble than usual coaxing my lips to form words. "You've been so sweet to me, and from what I'm hearing, you've been wonderful to Ken, too. You're right, I should just stop for a while, just leave it alone. Things always work out for the best, I really believe that . . . Glinda?"

"Yes, doll?"

"I still plan to get you the pumps — size 11, double A, narrow heel, plum if they're in stock — but also . . . I wonder if you might like to go to Disneyland with me. Right now. I have two passes that I haven't used, right here in my purse. I need something to do tonight. Have you ever been to

Disneyland? We could go out the back way: I'd just as soon not run into him tonight."

"Of course I've been to Disneyland. Everyone's been to Disneyland!" Glinda exclaimed. "I love Disneyland." Her big brown eyes grew misty. "My God, it's been such a long time since I've been to Disneyland that last time I was there, I was a man."

"Good. And don't tell him I was here, okay? Please."

"My cherry lips are sealed." Glinda jumped to her substantial feet and grabbed her black patent leather pocketbook and a little pillbox hat that looked like something Ethel or Lucy might wear downtown shopping, with little white gloves. "If we hurry we can be there in time for the Electrical Parade. What kind of car have you got? A sporty kind of car, I hope. Come on, let's go." She glanced down at my right hand, still clutching the wet state seal of Utah printed on red satin.

"And — you can keep the hanky, doll."

CHAPTER THIRTY-SEVEN

**You do what you want.
I'm gonna take my pill and watch my stories.**

— Nettie Mae Easley

Trying to do the right thing has led me to this: Sitting in the studio audience — front row — at the Wednesday night filming of *Bite Me*, watching a tall blonde with no hips carrying a sleek Siamese with slanted eyes as blue as her own, and speaking the one line that was to have been mine: "Doctor, what's wrong with my cat?"

My date for the evening was also blond, but about a foot shorter than the new Woman with Cat #2. I attended the filming with Jazzminn Jenks. Really, girlfriend.

This was a big night for the audience; not only had they gained entry to the glamorous behind-the-scenes world of their favorite situation comedy starring Bert DeMarco, they were also sitting within camera-phone range of superstar Jazzminn Jenks. True to her pink TV image, Jazzminn smiled and waved at the fans, then laughed and clapped her tiny hands at all of Bert's antics and blatant double entendres. You can get away with a lot after nine o'clock, even on network TV. Somehow

Jazzminn managed to keep on smiling and waving as she leaned over to me and said, sotto voce: "Bert DeMarco ain't good enough in bed to justify *this*. I could kill you for talking me into coming."

"Channel 5 has their entertainment guy here. I'm sure he'll want to get your comment on the way out," I whispered reassuringly. "It'll be good for our ratings."

"Oh. Ratings. Ratings are cool. I like great big numbers. Goody." Jazzminn was beaming again. Her ability to instantly segue from rage to pleasure when dangled the right bait ranks as her most endearing quality. My grandmother on my mother's side can do that, too. That's probably what's kept her alive for eighty-nine years. I realized for the first time that if she were a tiny, forty-five-year-old white woman with enormous breast implants, my grandma would be very much like Jazzminn Jenks.

"If it would help, I could fuck Bert again, too," Jazzminn was offering. "For the ratings."

"Very generous, Jazzminn, but no need. I'm sure the audience will draw their own conclusions."

I did not choose to torture myself by accepting Bert DeMarco's groveling invitation to the filming of my former big-break episode without a reason. I had a plan.

I had one more acting class left, tomorrow. That meant that, technically, today was my final day as Hollywood actress. I planned to make the most of it. I was pleased with myself for having figured it all out in my bubble bath last night.

It rained at Disneyland. Glinda and I had a lot of fun anyway, but I was so chilled by the time we got home that the only thing standing between me and a winter cold was a long soak in my deep Jacuzzi tub, contoured to Wade Stark's outsized proportions. I like to be cold enough to need a hot bath. It reminds me of being home in Indianapolis, where people don't need their name above the title to be happy, where it's enough just to wake up in the morning and discover that your car door isn't frozen shut. I like to take a loofah sponge, fill it with suds, then squeeze the loofah at the tip of my toe and let the bubbles run all the way down my leg. The bubbles pop and tickle when they hit the water. It's one of my favorite sensations — petite, but complete.

In my bathtub, I concluded that even though I was the one to suggest that we murder Jazzminn Jenks, I couldn't be the one to suggest that we *not* murder her. Ken Harrison was different from any suit I'd ever known, but still, he was a suit. He couldn't help it. It was in his DNA, and I trust the laws of biology. He was a creative executive, and I knew enough about Hollywood to know that the only way to get a creative executive to greenlight a script change is to make him believe it's his idea.

And, while I know that I will never be asked to name the designer of my gown on the red carpet at the Academy Awards — because I can't act, not because I don't know how to dress — I did learn at least one thing from devoting myself to the technique of the late, great Lana Bishop: The only way to get your audience to believe what you're doing is to believe in it yourself.

If I wanted Ken to talk himself out of murder, I had to convince him that I was still so angry at losing the role on *Bite Me* that I was ready to plunge a dagger into Jazzminn's heart myself. Then I'd let him talk *me* out of it. In short — pardon my language — I had to scare the shit out of him. Since with my luck he probably wasn't going to die tomorrow, I only had two days left to turn myself from sweet Ophelia into a raging Lady Macbeth.

To that end, while soaking in the Jacuzzi tub, I tried to re-read *Macbeth* — just to get myself in the mood. But each time I tried, I'd find myself flipping ahead to the comedies. In my Shakespeare anthology that I've had since Yale, the tragedies are in the front, comedies in back. Despite borrowing my stage name from the bloodiest tragedy of all, I don't much care for that kind of negativity. I just liked the name, Ophelia, because of the way it's pronounced. It doesn't have quite four syllables, yet it has more than three. Three and half, really. Things for me are never quite one thing or the other. I'm used to it by now.

I don't know how Ken can say he hates comedy. I really think that today's sitcoms should borrow some of the magical mayhem of *A Midsummer Night's Dream* or *The Tempest*. Think how much more delightful Bert DeMarco would be frolicking through the woods to find true love than he'll ever be groping around in the broom closet with an unemployed bathing suit model in "The Heavy Petting Zoo."

But, oh no — another blow. Here I'd forced myself to become part of the live studio audience of *Bite Me*, intent on the goal of wringing from myself one last ounce of rage at watching this tall, blond, hipless actress perform the role that was rightfully mine, but darn it, she was *good* — even in that one line, so sincere, sweet and smart. The line sounded so much better coming from her than during any one of the hundreds of times I'd practiced for my mirror at home, each time with the emphasis on a different word: "What's *wrong* with my cat?" "What's wrong with *my* cat?" What's wrong with my *cat?*" Listening to her, for the first time I really did want to know what was wrong with the cat. I was less inclined to wring her neck than to go backstage to congratulate her on her performance.

Jazzminn leaned over to me. "Hey, she's great, I'll bet she gets her own spin-off — and look at those hooters, wonder who did those!" she whispered loudly, a comment clearly intended to upset me. I wish it had, but it didn't — both because I have nice breasts, and because she was right about the performance. I fervently hoped that the nameless actress portraying Woman with Cat #2 might, someday, be promoted to Woman with Cat #1. And due to the emotions aroused in me by her character's concern for her pet, I vowed to make yet another generous donation to the cat division of the pet shelter in Beverly Hills.

My plan had backfired. Here I sat, not angry at all but, once again, hopelessly, tragically happy. Helpless, I decided to go ahead and enjoy the show. I don't know why stuff that's not funny at all when you are watching at home seems hysterical in the studio. Even Bert's antics in the closet with the model were funny in a way, despite her unnecessarily revealing outfit. I've never understood why the censors do not allow nudity, yet it's perfectly all right to show the female body shoved and twisted into a medieval torture chamber of push-ups, garters, and thongs.

I was laughing tonight. But tomorrow, I would devote my final acting class to becoming the ice queen of tragedy. To paraphrase the wicked Lady Macbeth: screw it – I'd glue my courage to the sticking place and not fail.

Of course, if you know anything at all about psychology, you've got to figure Lady Macbeth must have had a very, very unhappy childhood. The play doesn't tell you a thing about her early family life or how she must have felt about living with the heartbreak of obsessive-compulsive disorder. Maybe she never really wanted to be the wife of the Thane of Cawdor any more than I was cut out to be married to the NBA. And, if I'm going to get through this, I've *got* to stop caring.

CHAPTER THIRTY-EIGHT

**I pray you do not fall in love with me,
For I am falser than vows made in wine.
Besides, I like you not.**

— Rosalind, *As You Like It*

I was on my knees in the produce section at Ralphs; now, I'm on my knees in dirt. These days, I'm trying as hard as I can to stay standing, but I just keep ending up in this position. There's dirt on my clothes, dirt on my hands, on my face — no, mud, because that's what you get when you wipe tears off your face with dirt on your hands.

Above me is bright pink bougainvillea, a most excellent canopy; down here, there's dirt. I am in the hidden world beneath the flowers with ants, snails, lizards, and the rats that live in the ivy. Beside my right hand is a neat pile of small round objects I'm pretty sure are skunk shit.

I can take a lot, I have, I've taken it, I've taken all of it, but there's a limit, and I'm at it. This is the limit. It has to stop now. No — it has to stop . . . before now. I can't have seen what I just saw. I can't.

Had I but died an hour before this chance! Actually, right now

I'd settle for five minutes. Come on, I need five minutes. I'm pressing as hard as I can on my temples to keep my head from exploding, which explains why now there's also dirt in my hair.

I thought I hated mirrors, but now I hate windows even more. Because there is no light through yonder window, no light at all, only darkness, and all I want to do is break the glass.

The thing is — I knew this. I should have remembered; I should have known. *What a piece of work is man* after a stem cell transplant, what a fucking piece of work — I read thousands of pages, but didn't remember the most important thing. I remember it now.

It was right there in the Introduction to *The Complete Works of Shakespeare*: She would inspire me, she would bewitch me. She would betray me.

"The tortured tone of these sonnets also suggests the Lady may have betrayed him by entering into a love affair with another."

For I have sworn thee fair, and thought thee bright, / Who art dark as hell, and black as night.

I wasn't supposed to come here on Thursday. I was supposed to come here on *Friday*. I'll wonder until my dying day (which could be, like, next Tuesday) why I came to her house today, why I thought I needed to see her, to talk to her just one more time before we murdered Jazzminn Jenks. That idea was about as bright as re-reading the tragedies. I don't even know what I planned to say. I should have waited until Friday. It wasn't very long. I should have stuck to the script.

What do you do when you ring a doorbell and nobody answers? If you've got any kind of sense, you leave and come back tomorrow. But no — not Ken Harrison. When Ophelia didn't come to her door, I figured she didn't hear the bell. After all, it's a big house.

So I walked around to the back, thinking maybe I'd see her

in the kitchen, or in the living room, through those big windows that look out across the pool. If I saw her, I'd tap on the window — lightly, so as not to frighten her. It wasn't that dark. She'd see right away that it was me. Besides, she wasn't the type to scare that easy.

I was right. She was home. I saw her, there in the living room. Then, I saw *him*.

I stood staring for a moment — then dropped to my knees so they wouldn't be able to see me, there under the window. They were sitting on the sofa together, side by side. The light was low, golden. They were talking — just talking — earnest, intimate, looking deep into one another's eyes. I don't why, but it bothered me more to see them talking this way than if they'd had their arms around one another and their tongues halfway down each other's throats. Maybe it's because it looked so much like each one understood what the other was trying to say.

Then, they stopped talking. She reached out and took his hand in her own very soft one. She took his hand. This hurt me more than if it had happened the other way around. Not only doth the lady not protest too much — she makes the first goddamned move. Now, they appeared to be laughing. They were getting up. She was leading him somewhere by the hand, still laughing. They were walking away. Where were they going? They were headed for the stairs — going upstairs, together.

I couldn't see them anymore. It was getting too dark. But I saw in my mind her wide, wide bed before a glowing fireplace, with a comforter in all the colors of a Sadilla sunset.

In that instant, I changed my mind about who to kill. Twice. But just as quickly, my revenge went dull. I stopped myself, because . . . what was here, in this window, was not betrayal. That's the truth. If this were betrayal, I'd still have anger on my side.

Instead, all I have is shame, *murd'rous shame.*

What was I thinking — what did I think, to believe that I still was enough of a man to be betrayed. To betray me is to betray nothing. You can't be the mistress of nothing, nor can you betray it. I'm a man with no demographic at all.

It's not like I didn't know there's nothing left of me. But now I can see before my eyes that she knows it, too, has known it all along, probably knew it even before I did. She doesn't . . . she is only kind to me, the way she is kind to love-struck waiters and neurotic talk show hosts and old, sick cats. It's what comes naturally to her. She doesn't even have to think about it, she has so much to give. I can't remember if I ever thanked her for her kindness.

Five minutes, that's all.

So, you see, I can't call this a betrayal. There's not enough left of me to betray. I don't need to know who he is. I don't need to know his name. Whoever he is, he is my friend, for showing me the truth that Ophelia was too kind to tell — the kindest cut of all. I should have known all along that this tale was no *Romeo and Juliet.* First clue: they *both* die.

For me, there was no Dark Lady, any more than there was an island of Sadilla. Maybe there was no such lady for William Shakespeare. Now that I think about it, what kind of fool scholar would keep searching for her for years and years, just because the Bard seems hot for her in twenty or so sonnets? Hello, the man was a writer. They get paid to make shit up.

Pardon my language. I mean, fuck you.

But right now, I have to get up, off my knees, out of the

dirt. I have to care less about what I've seen than about being seen. I can't let her see me. I've got get out of here.

CHAPTER THIRTY-NINE

My dismal scene I needs must act alone.

— Juliet, *Romeo and Juliet*

The upside to living out your worst nightmare is it doesn't keep you awake anymore. That night, I slept soundly. In fact, I slept late. This is even more remarkable when you consider that I slept in my car, parked in the middle of the vast hilltop parking lot of Griffith Observatory in Los Feliz.

This is my favorite spot in L.A. It's where they shot *Rebel Without a Cause.* I call it the star sandwich. There's the stars above, the ones you can see faintly with the naked eye, more clearly through the observatory's mammoth telescope — and the stars below, the pulsing arteries of headlights, the endless, edge-less glitter of potential that is Los Angeles at night. Old stars, and new ones. I like being between them both, in a star sandwich.

I probably would have slept even later, but at about 10 a.m., a bright square of sun through the windshield hit me directly in the face. Friday, December 1, was another relentlessly beautiful Southern California day.

There's a pain factor to waking up after a night with your

head wedged between the steering wheel and the dashboard of a 1987 Honda Civic. I took my head in both hands and performed a minor chiropractic adjustment. It didn't work, but I had no time left to worry about this, my most recent failure. I had to go home; there was much to do.

I left the observatory, made my way home via the curves of Sunset Boulevard, showered, changed into my dark blue Armani suit just back from the dry cleaners, and fed the cat — now in hysterics because it was after 10:30 and his dish was still empty. Any break in his morning routine and he's sure he will never eat again. I can understand this.

"Look, I'm *sorry*." I must have said it fourteen times, but it made no difference. He just kept looking at me that way.

I ate nothing myself. This morning, I was more concerned with cooking than eating. I set about preparing the most important recipe of my amateur culinary career: The bottle of pills that would kill Jazzminn Jenks.

A few of these, a few of those, plop, plop, plop. All different sizes and colors. I had to be realistic here — how many pills could the little bitch actually take? I'd downed enough of this stuff myself to know what it was like. Revenge would not be sweet, but bitter and hard to swallow.

Double, double toil and trouble, fire burn, cauldron bubble, yadda yadda yadda, plop, plop, plop. With each plop, I could feel the sensation of the pill going down my throat, the fleeting fear I always have when I take one that it will get stuck on the way down and I won't be able to tell anyone, because I have a pill stuck in my throat. I dumped some back out, substituted others, poured some back in. Finally, I was satisfied.

Before I extinguish the brightest star in daytime television, I'd like to share an observation I've made after many years of reading television scripts. There's a line someone always says somewhere around the middle of the story as a lame excuse to re-cap the plot: "Let me get this straight." I've never heard anyone say it in actual conversation, but on screen, you hear it all the time. Just like in movie trailers, there's always somebody in a public place, spinning around and around with their arms flung wide open like Julie Andrews does in *The Sound of Music* to show reckless abandon, or love, or joy, or that you've got big plans to ditch the convent or whatever the hell. Try that in real life and you'll get yourself hauled off to rehab.

"Let me get this straight." It goes something like this:

"Let me get this straight: do you mean to tell me you plan to kill America's favorite talk show host for a bright angel from an island that does not exist — a most amazing woman who could never, ever love you and whom, perhaps due to your recreational experimentation with your own chemotherapy medications, you persist in believing is Shakespeare's Dark Lady — all because you made the mistake of reading sonnets instead of sitcom scripts on one dark and lonely night?"

"Let me get this straight" is to Hollywood what Fate is to Shakespeare: Whatever follows these words is true — foul or fair, black or white, no matter how ridiculous or futile or utterly, utterly hopeless. I stashed the bottle in my briefcase, straightened my tie, and left the apartment.

Yeah, I'm going to do it. Today. I've been coming to terms with a lot of things recently, and guess what? I don't like it. I'm signing off. I'm through understanding things, dealing with things, realizing that nothing in this world is ever black or white — over and over, in a hundred different ways, each more humiliating than the one before. No more. *And nothing is / But what is not*, said Macbeth. Well, bite me, Macbeth.

The reason I'm in such an up mood today, despite the fact that my night in the Honda has left me a permanent hunchback, is that I, Kenneth Charles Harrison, am announcing my return to the world of black and white, where I was before I got cancer and met this girl who refuses to be either one. I don't owe anybody an apology. It's just *easier*, and I'm so tired I want to cry. Murder is most definitely, clearly, indisputably bad, and today that feels damn good.

The fatal vision I saw last night, on my knees in the dirt, doesn't change my mind about murder. It only tells me that if I'd done it sooner, I could have avoided looking through the fucking window in the first place. That's why Fate kicked my legs out from under me outside her house last night. Fate did not send me to Ophelia the night before my murder so I could tell her that I loved her. Fate sent me because I needed to see with my own eyes, through clear glass, how foolish I have been. And to think, I'd begun to feel that murder was madness. No. Love is. For me, love is.

At one o'clock, as scheduled, I knocked on Ophelia's door. She opened it, very slowly. She looked like she had not slept at all. She was dressed in worn black slacks, a ragged black sweatshirt and a homely pair of horn-rimmed glasses. Her hair hung in a lank tangle down her back. I've got to say Ophelia looked worse than I'd ever seen her look — which was still *so* hot. She did not greet me, just stood there, looking at the ground.

"You okay?" I asked her, not sure whether I cared or not.

She nodded.

"Afraid?"

"No, not all. I think murder is a beautiful thing." She sounded absolutely terrified. "I may have neglected to tell you this before, Ken, but I actually love blood. I adore violence. In fact, I own every film ever made by Stone Jones. On DVD."

I raised my eyebrows. "Really? Interesting. Well, I guess I'm glad, seeing as we're on our way to a murder. *Not* on DVD."

"I'm glad, too." Her voice shook. "You see, that's why I

asked you to murder Jazzminn Jenks in cold blood while brandishing a very sharp knife. I am actually a very bad person, even though you might not believe it from looking at me. I have a heart of stone. I'm bad to the bone. Anyway, come on. Let's do it."

"Okay, Ophelia."

"Then . . . here we go."

"You got it."

"Yes, I would so very much like to kill. I love murder. I must revenge the injustice that has been done to me, to us, by Jazzminn Jenks. I'm ready to go with you, Ken."

I paused and stared at her. "No, you're not."

"Yes, I am."

"No, you're not." I shook my head emphatically. I knew what I'd come here to tell her, but I found myself saying something entirely different. Actually, shouting it is more accurate.

"You are definitely not ready," I yelled at her. "You're not ready at all. If you're going anywhere with me, Ophelia, you're going to . . . to change out of those clothes, and . . . do something with your hair. I'm wearing a fucking Armani suit — I may look like hell in it, but at least I'm wearing it. This is my tragedy, as big as *Hamlet* or *Macbeth*, and my Dark Lady is not going to look like she's headed for a Dodgers game!" I hadn't planned on saying any of this, so was surprised to find myself so furious that I was shaking. I was making a fool of myself, a mortal fool, I but couldn't seem to stop. "You can look ten times better than I ever will again without trying half as hard. You can be beautiful, and damn it, you will. Be an actress, Ophelia. Dress the part."

Shocked, she looked up from the floor. Then, the *catua* eyes flashed anger. "All right. If that's what you want, that's what you'll get. Give me ten minutes, you . . . jerk!" she cried out. Tough talk — from Ophelia, anyway. Then she turned and ran away from me, up the stairs.

She was true to her word. It took her only eight minutes to trade the black rags and the clunky glasses for an elegant eggshell pantsuit, high-heeled sandals and a choker with three strands of lustrous pearls. Her hair, a ratted mess at last viewing, was now a shining river of brown curls, tied back with a cream satin ribbon. I gasped when I saw her, poised at the top of the stairs. More beautiful than ever.

"My God. You are exquisite, Ophelia." It came out as a long sigh.

"I know." Her words were two ice cubes. Graceful as a model — even though she's shorter, those women are giraffes — she made her way down the stairs, one hand lightly sweeping the oak banister, her eyes focused deliberately away from me on some faraway spot on the opposite wall.

"Too bad," I added when she reached the bottom, "that you're all dressed up with no place to go."

That's what I came to tell her.

Her *catua* eyes weren't on the opposite wall anymore. They were on me.

"What did you say?"

"Sorry. I guess I should have mentioned this before you changed your clothes and put in your contact lenses and fixed your hair and everything. You're not going anywhere."

"What??"

"But look on the bright side," I added cheerfully. "You're going to look great while you watch the story on the six o'clock news."

"Kenny, stop this." She took a few steps toward me. I wanted her to be angry, but what was this disgusting thing in her voice that I heard instead — pity? Add that to the list of things that are off my list, as of today. I backed away, clutching my briefcase — full of bad script treatments and lethal narcotics — like a shield against my bony chest. *I must from this enchanting queen break off,* right now.

"No. Ophelia, you chose murder. You chose the victim. You chose . . . well, all I'm trying to say is, you're all out of choices. I have creative control." My voice trembled. "Do not even think about following me, do you hear? Don't even think about it. It doesn't matter anymore whether you're the Dark Lady. It doesn't matter who the hell you are. None of it matters. I'm going alone. I *am* alone. Goodbye, Ophelia."

Then, I turned my back and walked out the front door of the big white house on Vista de la Vida for the last time. I slammed it hard behind me. And I never even looked back to see the expression on her face.

It wasn't until I got into the Honda and put the key in the ignition that it started — the sensation that every cell in my body was exploding all at once. It felt like they were running in all directions to get away from the pain, like people trapped in a burning building with their clothes on fire. My joints were like narrow doorways where bunches of them got wedged, shoulder to shoulder, in their frantic haste to get out. I groaned, clinging with all my might to the steering wheel to keep myself from sinking onto the floor. I would not end up on my knees, not this time. "Stop it," I commanded out loud, through clenched teeth. "Just stop it . . . stop . . . stop running. Don't you get it, you little assholes? *There's no place else to go.*"

And, after awhile, they stopped. I don't know how long it took, but they stopped running. Cautiously, I opened my eyes and lifted my head from the steering wheel. I felt weak, sweaty, dizzy, there were flashbulbs popping behind my eyes — but the fire was out. I wanted the sun to stop doing that, I wanted it to stop getting bigger and smaller like that, and I don't think the windshield of a Honda is supposed to keep melting over and over into a rippling pool of water. But I kept hanging onto the steering wheel, and eventually that stopped, too.

At this point, I knew I had no choice. Slowly and carefully, I got out of the car and, with the neatly tended gravel crunching under my feet, walked back up the driveway to Ophelia's house. I rang the doorbell. She opened the door, still a vision in eggshell and cream even with tears slipping down her face. She looked shocked to see me again, even more shocked when I held out the car keys to her.

"This murder is mine," I said, steadying myself with one hand against one of the tall, white pillars of the porch. The sun was getting bigger and smaller again. "But, Ophelia — would you mind very much if I asked you to drive?"

CHAPTER FORTY

I told you not to get into a car with that boy!

— Nettie Mae Easley

I don't know whether we weren't speaking to each other or we didn't have anything to say. Either way, the ride to Jazzminn Jenks's Bel Air estate was dead silent.

My hands shook on the steering wheel of Ken's ancient white Honda Civic. I was still in shock. I'd worked so hard in my last acting class: why didn't he back down, call the whole thing off, sickened by my cold-blooded, murderous fury? I had snarled, paced the floor, gestured in the air like a madwoman — at least, I'm pretty sure I did. I was so *good*.

I should have refused to drive the car. But then he would have driven — head on into an SUV, probably, killing innocent people instead of Jazzminn Jenks, and there was no logic in that. I had no right to let that happen, especially since I'm the one who hatched this ridiculous plot in the first place. So I took the keys out of his shaking, sweaty hand and I drove — surprised, really, by how well a beat-up 1987 Honda Civic handles the Bel Air hills.

I was so scared by now that I forgot the way. I had no idea

where I was going — both literally and the figuratively. "Right or left?" I demanded.

"Huh?" Ken's eyes had been closed, but now they flew open to see that we had come to a fork in a cool, leafy road. His knuckles tightened protectively on the handle of the briefcase in his lap. "I thought you knew where Jazzminn's house was."

"It's been a long time. Look at the directions, please. Right or left?"

Ken fumbled for the printout from Google Maps lying next to him on the console. This car was much too old to have a nav system. This printed page was all we had to guide our folly. "Uh, left."

"Thank you."

"Ophelia?"

"Yes?"

"Thank you for driving."

"Shut up, Ken."

He fumbled with the latch on the briefcase. "No, I can't shut up right now, I have to explain to you what we're — what *I'm* — going to do. I'm sorry, I didn't want it to happen this way, Ophelia, but this is the way it's happening. I've got the stuff in here. I told Jazzminn they were diet pills and that if she wants them to work, she's got the swallow the whole bottle."

"Diet pills?"

"That's right." He took a heavy glass bottle of pills out of the briefcase. "I told her she was too fat for prime time. She bought it."

"Diet pills?"

I'm not sure what I expected Ken to say at that point, but that sure wasn't it. I was equally surprised by my own reaction. Because suddenly, instead of sobbing hysterically, slapping him in the face or throwing up — the three options I'd been most seriously considering — I found myself laughing. *Laughing.* This was the worst. Laughing so hard that tears came to my eyes. My dainty pearl earrings swung back and forth like tiny pendulums. I didn't just laugh, I roared with laughter. Guffaws, titters, peals, gales — I ran through the whole Thesaurus of laughs. I laughed until I couldn't breathe. I snorted with laughter, like a pig. I laughed so hard I had to pull the Honda over to the side of the road to keep from running it into a ravine. I may have no flair for comedy myself, but I know what's funny.

"Ophelia?" The blank look on Ken's face made me laugh even harder. He looked like Wile E. Coyote after being shot out of a cannon by Bugs Bunny. "Do you mind telling me what exactly it is you're laughing at?"

"I'm sorry, Ken," I gasped. "I know, this is a murder. I'm scared out of my wits. And right now, I'm pretty sure I hate you. But — you told her they were diet pills? A big, giant bottle of diet pills? That's just so *funny.*" I wiped my eyes, envisioning the scene. "Oh, Lord. I love it. I can just see the expression on Jazzminn's pinched little size zero face when you told her she was fat."

"As I recall, that moment wasn't funny at all. It was, in my opinion, one of the very worst moments of my life," Ken scolded. "Stop laughing, damn it. Poor Jazzminn is going to be dead before prime time."

This sent me into another embarrassing but thoroughly enjoyable round of guffaws. "Oh, Ken, I'm so sorry," I moaned. "I just can't help it. I can't. I can't stop laughing."

"Murder is no laughing matter," Ken said primly. "And in case I didn't mention it, I happen to have cancer."

At the word cancer, I just exploded. To my own horror, I laughed until the button popped off the waist of my cream colored slacks and rolled under the seat. I couldn't even pull myself together long enough to apologize for my outlandishly inappropriate reaction to the mention of aggressive, non-Hodgkin's lymphoma. But then, another surprise: He was laughing too, or rather, trying not to — staring at the floor, biting his lower lip, but unable to control himself.

"Please, please don't make me laugh, Ophelia. It hurts," he begged, vainly trying to turn the first burst of merriment into a cough.

"That's because you have cancer," I giggled.

"Oh, did I tell you I have cancer? I guess I forgot, because I have cancer — ha!" he roared. "Oh God, I think I just broke two ribs."

We both laughed and laughed, non-stop, for at least ten minutes. We howled. We groaned. Tears ran down our cheeks. Finally, spent and exhausted, we both leaned back against the seats, still hiccupping and wheezing. "I haven't laughed like that in eight months," Ken finally said, wiping his eyes. "I may never recover. Oh, man. Thanks, Ophelia. I needed that."

"You're welcome." Welcome, welcome, welcome. I smiled as relief flowed over me. It was over, all over. Everything was fine. Things had worked out for the best, just like they always do. I straightened the cream satin ribbon in my curly hair, started the car, and pulled back onto the road, chuckling and shaking my head.

Then I felt Ken's hand on my shoulder, much too strong for a dying man. He dug his fingers into the bone until I gasped in pain. Something was going wrong here, all wrong.

"Hey, you turned right. I thought I told you it was a left," he barked.

I slowed the car and regarded him with surprise, trying unsuccessfully to wrest my shoulder from his grasp. "Yes, I know. But we're not . . . going back home now?"

"Why would we be going home, Ophelia?" He wasn't

laughing anymore.

"Well, Kenny, it's not like I meant to laugh, but it's just, after that . . . you know, I just thought . . ."

"Don't think, Ophelia. Do not fucking *think*."

"But Kenny, both of us laughed . . ."

"Yeah, but only one of us laughed 'til it hurt. *God*, it hurts." He released my shoulder, but it still felt like his fingers were digging into me. "Joke's over, Ophelia. Turn this car around right now, or I'll do it for you. I mean it. Do it. Turn left. Oh, *Jesus*." He doubled over in the passenger seat, sucking his breath in through his teeth in little gasps, like a student in some kind of hideous Lamaze class for dying men. He clutched the bottle of pills with such force that I thought the glass would break in his hand. "*And nothing is / But what is not, And nothing is / But what is not* — you can't get that straight, not ever. It's been tangled up for centuries," he moaned. "*And nothing is / But what is not*. It's a tragedy as big as *Hamlet*, or *Macbeth*, a tragedy . . ."

"What are you trying to say, Ken? I can't hear you. I don't understand you. Please, tell me, what are you trying to say?" He was writhing in agony, mumbling the words, over and over, terrifying nonsense. I thought he was going to die right there, I really did. And for a moment I hoped that he would die because it would solve everything. Everything except that if he died . . . he'd be dead.

Instead, after a long, long minute, he raised his head. "Comedy is not in my demographic anymore. Murder is," he said, his voice hoarse but eerily calm. "Now are you going to turn left or not?"

He was still alive. He hadn't died laughing after all. There was no choice here, really. The old brakes squealed as I reversed directions and turned left.

CHAPTER FORTY-ONE

**There is no shuffling; there the action lies
in his true nature**

— King Claudius, *Hamlet*

And I thought Ophelia's house was big. The estate of Jazzminn Jenks has its own moat. I kid you not, once you get inside two sets of electronic gates, the whole place is surrounded by a fucking moat with a drawbridge over it — a bridge you can't get across without another deeply personal conversation with a disembodied voice in an electronic box.

Ophelia was on the driver's side so she answered the questions, in a very shaky voice. Yes, it was Kenneth Harrison and Ophelia Lomond; yes, we had a two o'clock appointment with Ms. Jenks.

"And the purpose of your visit?"

Ophelia didn't answer that one — just looked over at me, doubt clouding her perfect face. I swear next time I commit a murder, I'm driving.

"Tell him we're going to kill her, but the good news is you can take the rest of the day off," I said under my breath, thoroughly disgusted with Ophelia. I was sitting up successfully now so I leaned over her and talked to the man in the box myself.

"Hello there, this is Ken Harrison. Movies and Minis. We've got a pitch meeting, some new ideas for Ms. Jenks's production company."

"Oh, yes. *Pink*." Here in Beverly Hills, even an invisible man drawing minimum wage behind an electronic box got off on letting us know that he knew the in-house nickname for Jazzminn's company.

"Pink," I agreed. "Very."

"You're in, baby," said the voice, as the drawbridge slowly lowered.

Once over the bridge, we still had to drive almost a quarter of a mile, past tennis courts, gym, spa, and guesthouse, before we saw anything resembling a front door. Apparently you could be a houseguest of Jazzminn Jenks for weeks without ever seeing either Jazzminn Jenks or her house.

Finally, we approached a building that Ophelia indicated was the main residence. It was one of those contemporary pieces of architecture with a capital A — kind of a big origami, folded out of sheets of glass and brushed stainless steel. In today's brilliant sunshine, the metal panels glowed almost white. Ophelia drove up the wide, circular driveway and stopped the car in front of the porch.

I opened the car door and stepped out. I was still wincing a bit from that laughing fit but was now pretty sure I hadn't broken any bones I'd need this afternoon. With the bottle of pills still in one hand, I walked around behind the car to the driver's side to open the door for Ophelia.

"Shall we?" I invited.

Ophelia did not answer this question but did get out of the car. Slowly — my only option at that point — we walked up to the door. She pushed the little black button on yet another electronic box.

We waited for a voice, but none came. Ophelia frowned and pushed the button again. Still, silence. We raised our eyebrows at each other. "Okay, let's do it the old-fashioned way — knock," I suggested. "Would you, please? I'd do it, but my hands are full."

Ophelia nodded, then gave a polite rap on the metal door. Nothing.

"Harder."

This time, she pounded on the door with both fists. There was no answer — but, to our surprise, the door swung open, slowly, slowly, as though manipulated from the other side by an invisible hand. Apparently it was not locked, not even shut very tight. We stepped into the spectacular three-story entrance, our footsteps hollow on the white marble floor. We didn't see a soul.

"This is very weird, Ken," Ophelia whispered. "Usually she's got the maid, the butler, the gardener, the nutritionist, her personal trainer — when he comes to Studio 7, we call him the 'impersonal trainer' because he's this big mean German guy who won't talk to anybody. There are always all kinds of support staff, sort of wandering around trying to look busy. There is something seriously wrong here."

"Other than the fact she's about to be poisoned, you mean?" I hissed back. "Look, every time I went to see Jazzminn at Pink Productions, she was always alone — she said she wanted complete control. Of course, she's alone. That's why she left the door open for us. Besides, I told her the diet pills might make her a little drowsy, but the two of us would make sure she got to bed before it happened."

"Make her . . . *a little drowsy?*"

"Ophelia, start laughing again and I swear I'll kill you."

"Look — I think she left us a note." Ignoring my threat,

Ophelia reached out the perfectly French-manicured nails of her right hand to pick up the small square of fine notepaper that lay between two tall vases of bright sunflowers on a marble-topped table in the entryway. I read it over her shoulder:

HELLO, O. AND K. I SENT THE HELP HOME EARLY TODAY BECAUSE THEY'RE A BUNCH OF FUCKING IDIOTS. I'M OUT BY THE SWIMMING POOL. HURRY UP: I CAN'T WAIT TO BE THIN! – J.J.

The note was quite friendly, by Pink standards. I shrugged. "See? I told you she'd be alone. Let's go . . . O."

"Okay, K." Ophelia said, then cleared her throat sharply, I'm sure to avoid pissing off a dangerous lunatic like myself by starting to laugh again at this bizarre bit of dialogue. They say the ability to enjoy bad puns is one of the last things to go.

"The pool is in the back, just behind the solarium. Wait'll you see this pool, Kenny, you'll die. Okay, I guess from here on in I should always just say I'm sorry before I start talking. Come on. Follow me."

It's impossible to walk through Jazzminn's house without making a lot of noise, because of the marble floors. Ophelia's little heels clicked along in perfect rhythm. My steps were louder, and less regular, because lately my left leg has been dragging a little. I don't know why, and I'd rather not think about it just now. You can't tell the difference at all on carpet, but here I had a definite Quasimodo thing happening. Ophelia didn't notice, or else kindly ignored my new sound effect.

I really didn't want to see another swimming pool in my life, ever — but Ophelia was right. If death wasn't already written into my contract, this was a pool to die for.

It was Olympic-sized, banked with long strips of perfect

green lawn, and a host of skinny cypress trees lined up on either side like members of a very tall wedding party. This pool had a diving board, also of competition dimensions, soaring high into the blinding blue December sky. A thousand little crescent moons of sunshine rippled playfully over the clear aqua surface of the water. Moons of sun — what a concept. Giddy with pleasure, I watched the sun-moons dance in perfect rows across the pool. For a moment, I forgot about the Dark Lady, the Blond Bitch, and the intended purpose of this meeting. All those little moons dancing in the sun made me feel much, much too good for a man about to take out his hostess.

We were standing in the grass, that kind of short, expensive grass that looks like velvet, near the shallow end of the pool. So it took awhile for me to see that the pattern of sun-moons wasn't rippling in unison at the other end of the water, down at the deep end. The moons were dancing the wrong way. Not in straight lines, but outward, in a series of slow concentric circles.

Also strange: At the other end of the pool, in the grass, stood a white wrought iron table, bearing drinking glasses, a frosty pitcher of something, lemonade maybe, and few plates of some kind of hors d'oeuvres. Hard to tell from a distance, but I think they were the low-carb celery and carrot variety that everybody eats but nobody likes. There was no one sitting at this table.

"Ken!" I pulled my eyes away from The Mystery of the Empty Table just in time to see Ophelia begin to run down the endless lawn toward the deep end of the pool. "My God — Kenny, look, she's in the pool!"

Dumbly, I re-focused my eyes on the water. In the middle of the concentric circles of dancing moons at the deep end of the pool floated a gleaming octopus of bright blond hair.

I can't run, Christ, I can barely walk — but despite the fact that it was impossible, I found myself running after Ophelia. Even with my rakish new limp, I soon caught up with her. Now we were standing together at the deep end, close up, staring down, where we could tell for sure that the blond octopus was Jazzminn Jenks.

We could see one shoe, one spike-heeled, powder blue Jimmy Choo pump, hanging on the very edge of the pool. Its expensive toe seemed to be testing the water. We could also see an additional tray of spilled carrots and celery lying upside down in the velvety grass.

It didn't take an LAPD detective to figure this one out. Jazzminn Jenks — alone without servants, perhaps for the first time in her life bringing food to a table to serve to someone else — had apparently been undone by this generous and unfamiliar act, tripped on her spike heel, and tumbled headlong into the sparkling water where she now floated face-down — dying, maybe already dead.

I don't know what I was thinking as I dropped my briefcase and the heavy bottle of pills, which rolled off crazily down the lawn and came to rest at the foot of a tall cypress tree. I can't remember what was going through my mind as I kicked off my shoes, tore off the dark blue Armani suit coat, and dived into the deep end of the pool. Dived — hell, I practically fell in on my head, smacking the water hard, swallowing a lot more than I wanted to. Maybe I wasn't thinking at all.

Because if I was thinking, I would have been thinking, now, let me get this straight: I'm going to risk what's left of my life to save her life . . . so I can . . . kill her?

But I wasn't thinking, I was swimming. I really haven't got the strength to do both at the same time anymore. My head was below the surface. My glasses somehow stayed fixed to my face like swim goggles as I plowed through the water toward Jazzminn, eyes open, tiny aqua bubbles streaming past me on either side. I came up beneath Jazzminn, heaved her body over so her face would be above water, and, with one arm across her chest, began dragging her toward the shallow end. A sobbing Ophelia ran along beside us on the lawn.

I don't know if Ophelia knew that we had reached the five-foot mark when she jumped into the pool beside me. I have no idea whether she knew before she jumped in that she was in the shallow end, where she would be safe from drowning. I have no idea what she may have been thinking when, with plenty of the dramatic flailing characteristic of the non-swimmer, she helped me lift Jazzminn out of the water. But I do know this: I could not have done it without her.

Jazzminn wasn't breathing as we laid her little body out by the edge of the pool. I wasn't sure I was breathing, either. "Dial 911, or the guard at the gate or something," I gasped, dropping to my knees beside Jazzminn — Ken Harrison, assuming his standard position. "*Go*. I think I remember how to do CPR. It doesn't look good, but I'll see if I can bring her around." Wide-eyed, the dripping Ophelia ripped off her own high-heeled shoes so she could run faster, then fled barefoot into the house.

At this point, I had no confidence at all in my ability to breathe life into anyone; this was siphoning gas out of an empty tank. But I just kept going through the motions, like a robot. Air in, my lips against hers — air out, my mouth to one side. Both of my hands gently pumping her absurd silicone chest, lending new meaning to the term "artificial resuscitation." Well, she said I could feel 'em.

Between pumps, I grabbed her left wrist and searched for a pulse. I don't know if the feeble sensation underneath my fingers was her pulse, or just me, shivering like a dog at the beach in my wet clothes. I didn't know, but I didn't stop. There's a rhythm to it, in and out, up and down. After awhile, you don't have to think.

I just kept on doing it — and she kept on not breathing. Her eyes stayed closed. Her little face was blue. Blue, her favorite color. "Come on, Jazzminn," I pleaded, my eyes stinging with chlorine and tears. "You said you'd do anything for me, anything I wanted. You owe me one. Please, please, girlfriend, just this once, for me . . . try hard as hell to think pink."

I don't know how long this went on. Didn't matter — she was dead. I was just doing what lifeguards do, we keep on performing CPR on dead people until somebody with a siren and better credentials arrives at the beach to tell us what we already know. It's been a long time, but I remember the drill. The kid and I were both seventeen.

In the continuing, hideous silence that was Jazzminn not breathing, I could hear sirens screaming. I would have screamed too, but I didn't have the time. Inside the house I could hear feet, lots of them, running on hard marble. I kept the rhythm going, air in, air out, as I heard the sliding door open, heard the hard marble footsteps turn into the dull thud of shoes running on velvet grass. Now, there were people all around me.

I looked up. From down here, people are huge and strangely out of proportion, like the faces in a house of mirrors. Cops, tall men in armed guard uniforms, people in assorted medical garb clutching oxygen bags and other lifesaving gadgets — and, already, an army of local newscasters and their guys with cameras, lenses trained on Jazzminn's lifeless body. I couldn't see Ophelia anywhere among the faces in the house of mirrors.

"She's dead," I told them — just as a geyser of pool water

spurted out of Jazzminn's blue rosebud lips directly into my face.

"Let me get back to you on that," I added, as I bent over and resumed CPR. My own heart slammed against my ribs, but I forced myself to stay calm in order to continue working on hers. A couple more breaths, in and out, a few more pumps of the chest, and then her little blue eyes flew open. I could hear the hiss of air flowing into her lungs.

Now her face was turning pink — pink like a bougainvillea bloom, like soft bunny slippers, like the set of *Really, Girlfriend?* like the milk in a bowl of Apple Jacks — an astonishing, living pink. She must have started breathing on her own a little while ago, when I thought she was dead but kept on performing CPR anyway, like a lifeguard should. I just didn't feel it.

Just think — I'd missed a miracle happening under my own hands, all because of a couple of size-D breast implants. I started to laugh hysterically, although I'm pretty sure it sounded more like I'd swallowed my tongue.

As I laughed, more water gushed out of Jazzminn's mouth, then a streak of profanity as blue as her face had been only a few minutes before. Her face wasn't pink any more either, it was red, bright red.

"Get the fuck off me!" Jazzminn screamed hoarsely, shoving me to the side, face down into the grass. The grass does not *taste* like velvet. Moaning and clutching my ribs — now they *were* broken — I rolled over on my back, spitting blades of grass from between my teeth. With one hand I pulled off my glasses, in two separate pieces. The busted wire rims from Oliver Peoples had cut me just above the nose. Jazzminn was still screaming. "Who are you? And what the hell are you trying to do, kill me?"

She obviously had not yet figured out who I was or what had happened. Cameras hungrily recording her every move,

Jazzminn shook her wet, stringy blond locks and sat up, cussing and spluttering, mascara running down her cheeks in little black streams. All the newscasters looked disgusted — the best celebrity story of the year and they were going to have to bleep every word the woman said. A medical technician shoved an oxygen mask over her mouth — I'm not sure whether to help her breathe or shut her up.

"She's alive!" somebody cried out, a few beats too late to read as genuine surprise. I can't see too well without my glasses, but I think it was that irritating woman from KTLA, the prissy one with the red pixie haircut — as usual, stating the obvious for her cameras. I think she'd even managed to bring tears to her own eyes. "Thank God, Jazzminn Jenks is alive. This young man saved her life!"

"Who is he?" someone else demanded.

"Yes, who are you?" asked the teary-eyed KTLA anchorwoman, crouching down low to shove a microphone into my bleeding, grass-stained face.

I know this was not the most opportune time to wax philosophical. But even as I dragged myself up to my hands and knees, retching chlorinated water into the grass, I couldn't help but marvel at the reality of the moment: Had Ophelia and I not come here today to kill Jazzminn Jenks, she'd be dead now.

I plotted a murder and ended up saving a life. Not the life any sane person would have chosen to save, perhaps, but still a life. What do you know, this was a happy ending. Shit — a happy ending. Did this mean that, no matter how desperately I'd tried all these weeks to prevent it, my tragedy had turned into a comedy? Had foul turned fair while I was busy trying to remember how to perform CPR?

No, that wasn't right either. Comedy ends in marriage, tragedy ends in death. Nobody was getting married today, and unless there was something somebody wasn't telling me, I was still dying, fast.

In TV episodes, there's usually the A story and the B story — the A story being the main plot, the B story a less important and usually amusing bit of side business. Like, Dr. Bradley Sykes saves the life of an injured horse and makes a little boy's day (the A story) but also accidentally flushes the cuff links his girlfriend gave him down the toilet, so has to go crawling through the New York City sewer system late at night wearing his zany roommate's leaky scuba gear to find them (the B story).

I don't want to sound paranoid, but right then I began to wonder if I was the B story in a script about someone else. Maybe this was really Jazzminn's story. Maybe Fate gave me aggressive, non-Hodgkin's lymphoma, dragged me through a stem cell transplant, made me read *The Complete Works of William Shakespeare* — including 154, count 'em, 154 sonnets — put me through a meat grinder, basically, only to make sure I'd be on hand at the right time to keep Jazzminn Jenks from drowning.

Or maybe my role in this universe was even less significant. Maybe Fate engineered this whole goddamned murder scenario just to teach the lovely Ophelia Lomond the importance of knowing how to swim.

Now, I don't have to be the star of the show. I'm no actor, I do my work behind the scenes. But if Fate gave me terminal cancer as a fucking *B story* — well, I'd have a problem with that, I really would.

And yet I felt so extraordinarily happy, euphoric even. I was still shivering, puking, bleeding — but the sun was warm against my face. Thoughtfully, I knocked pool water out of my ears with the heel of my hand. This had to be my story, my happy ending, because I was . . . happy. I don't know how anyone else felt right then, but I was happy. And — hah — ending. I know, that's not funny.

If you want to play by the strict rules of Shakespeare, I guess my story wasn't a tragedy or a comedy. But after more than ten years in network television, it seemed fitting that my life made sense by the rules of TV, not the rules of the Bard. I have an announcement to make: The tale of Ken Harrison is . . . a *dramedy*. Well, at least that explains why I'm going off the air.

Weakly, I raised my head and reached for the microphone. Startled, the red-haired KTLA newscaster let me take it from her hand. I figured since I had the mic, I'd introduce myself, politely explain what had just happened here today, then ask whether any one present could possibly explain to me how to get *that* straight.

"Ophelia . . . wherefore art thou?" I whispered instead. All eyes turned toward me as my amplified voice rang out to the very tops of the tall cypress trees. Then, darkness. *Their candles are all out.*

CHAPTER FORTY-TWO

No more of drowning, do you hear?

— Iago, *Othello*

DYING MAN SAVES TALK HOST'S LIFE

Normally I don't read the newspaper because journalists really are a bunch of assholes. But you can understand why this headline caught my attention, even though, from my point of view, it was upside down.

I cleared my throat — tried to, anyway. "Hey, uh, good morning," I croaked out; no clue what time of day it actually was. "Would you mind if I take a look at that paper for a second?"

The heavyset male nurse standing next to my bed had today's Los Angeles Times jammed under his arm. The front page peeked out from under the back flap of his mint green jacket as he stood with his back to me, his very large ass in my face, adjusting the plastic tubes snaking out of my wrist.

"You're awake. Hey, man, you're awake!" Startled, the nurse turned and stopped fiddling with the tubes. The newspaper fell to the bed just out of reach of my hand. "Uh, stay right there — I mean, where are *you* gonna go — what I'm saying is stay conscious, okay, buddy? I'll get the doctor."

"No, no, please, don't call anybody yet." Agitated, I plucked at the sleeve of his mint green uniform with my tube-infested arm. With the other, I thrashed my way out of my tight cocoon of white sheets. "Let me just read this first, okay? Give me five minutes. Please."

He ran a hand through his thick, straight black hair, shaved around the bottom and long on top. "Dunno, man, they told me to call the second you . . ."

"I'm still unconscious, for a little while longer. Come on, help me out here. What's your name?"

"Alejandro." The nurse glanced around furtively, as though a hidden video camera might catch him in the act of disobeying orders. He had to be just out of nursing school, no more than twenty-two. He'd be dead by forty if he didn't lay off the doughnuts. "Well . . . okay. Here," he said, picking up the newspaper and placing it in my hands.

I pushed the tubes to one side so I could hold the newspaper up close to my eyes. I had no idea where my broken glasses had ended up. I squinted at the small print. Saturday, December 2. Tomorrow already.

"Thank you, Alejandro."

"You need me to read it for you?"

"No. I just gotta hold it close. Lost my glasses."

"We better stop talking. Somebody'll hear us and be in here in two seconds." Alejandro lowered his voice as he settled down next to me on the bed. I was a little surprised, but there was no place else to sit since my small room had no chair. And, I hate to admit it, right then I was glad to have his big ass there, making a dent in the white sheets, close to me.

"Thanks. I owe you one." I didn't have to lower my voice. My throat was so raw I could barely hear myself talk. Alejandro pushed the plastic container of water on my tray a little closer, so I could reach the straw. I tried to arrange the newspaper so he could read over my shoulder, but he shook his head. "You go on. Saw it all last night on the news. But I'll take that puzzle, you know, the one by the comics where you circle the words, if it's okay with you."

I wanted to keep the puzzle. After all, now that I wasn't plotting a homicide, I really didn't have a hell of a lot to do. But it seemed like fair trade for access to the front page, so I gave it to him. "You saw it on TV? Please tell me I didn't throw up on camera."

He nodded sympathetically. "They cut away real quick, though."

"Wonderful. And I must have sounded like a fool — you know, that thing I said before I passed out."

He frowned, trying to remember.

"You must have heard it. I said it right into the microphone. 'Wherefore art thou, Ophelia.' Jesus. I can't believe I said that on the news."

"You didn't say nothing like that. You just said: 'Help me.' That's all you said: 'Help me.' I heard it." Alejandro nodded for emphasis and returned to circling words with a stubby yellow pencil. "Who's Ophelia?"

Okay, I was losing my mind, along with everything else. I was hearing myself say things I never said. But maybe this at least explained why she didn't answer me, why she never came.

I didn't tell Alejandro who Ophelia was, and he seemed to lose interest almost immediately. As he worked his puzzle, I read my story.

DYING MAN — well, it doesn't get much clearer than that. Sorry, Mom, I should have e-mailed. There was even a picture, right there above the fold, on page A1. Jazzminn Jenks looked like hell, I looked worse — but at least *I* was smiling.

Jazzminn Jenks, queen of daytime talk, was rescued from drowning in the swimming pool at her Bel Air home Friday when a network entertainment executive and Jenks's personal assistant found her unconscious in the water and pulled her to safety.

The executive, Kenneth Harrison, 36, performed artificial resuscitation and CPR while the talk host's assistant, Ophelia Lomond, phoned for aid. Shortly after he revived the petite, blond Jenks, Harrison became incoherent and lost consciousness. He was taken to Cedars-Sinai Hospital, where doctors confirmed that he was under treatment for terminal cancer and had only a month left to live.

Harrison remained unconscious but in stable condition at press time. Jenks, also treated at Cedars, suffered no injury and was released after two hours of observation.

In an exclusive interview with the Times, Jenks said Lomond and Harrison had come to her home to discuss new film projects for Jenks's fledgling entertainment company, Pink Productions, when they found that Jenks had tripped on her shoe and fallen face down into the water.

Jenks said Harrison never mentioned his health problems during several prior meetings, adding: "Get me the [expletive deleted] out of this [expletive deleted] hospital and away from these [expletives deleted] doctors before I [expletive deleted]."

Later in the afternoon, Jenks's publicist issued this statement from Jenks: "My thoughts are with Ken Harrison and all people who have known the heartbreak of cancer. And I'd like to thank the wonderful emergency medical team at Cedars for helping to save my life."

At the scene of Jenks near-fatal accident, LAPD officers collected Harrison's briefcase, his broken glasses and a large bottle of various prescription drugs that Cedars physicians confirmed were chemotherapy medications, as well as others used to relieve its debilitating side effects.

Harrison's oncologist, Hugh Goldberg, said the medications were prescribed to Harrison over time during his eight-month battle with aggressive non-Hodgkin's lymphoma but was at a loss to explain why Harrison would be carrying such large doses of the medications, all potentially lethal, mixed in the same container.

Lomond, 27, said tearfully that Harrison had been despondent over his illness and had talked of ending his own life.

In a sad and ironic twist, KTLA anchorwoman Erica Elfman was killed on impact when her news van crashed into an MTA bus on the way back to KTLA's Hollywood headquarters after covering the rescue at Jenks's estate.

For more stories on Jazzminn Jenks's harrowing ordeal, see 2-3A. An appreciation of Erica Elfman by Harry Rosenstiel, 34F.

Alas, poor Erica. She interviewed me, Alejandro. Now she was buried in Section F. Fate has a very warped sense of humor.

But even in the midst of my guilt about Erica Elfman, I couldn't help but laugh to myself about the Dark Lady of the Sonnets — she was an actress, after all, and not a bad scriptwriter, either. I had tears in my own eyes as I read of my heroic efforts to save a life even as I bleakly contemplated suicide. It was nothing short of brilliant. No one would have reason to question this explanation — except of course Jazzminn Jenks.

And I knew Jazzminn well enough to know this: She wouldn't trade the drama of being saved by a dying man for the unsympathetic act of charging that same dying man with attempted murder — a story that also would involve confessing herself to be a weight-crazed psycho. She was, if nothing else, a pragmatist. Besides, I'd be dead before my own murder trial, what would be the point, really?

"You done reading yet, guy? Cuz now I really got to tell someone, before I get into trouble."

"I'm done. Did you . . . finish your word puzzle?"

Alejandro smiled as he rose from the bed, then opened my door just wide enough to slide his big body out. "No, I never can finish them, but I always like to try. Listen . . . I'm sorry you're going to die and everything."

"Thanks, Alejandro."

"That was a real nice thing you did for that skinny white lady with the big tits."

I nodded and closed my eyes. It hurt too much to speak.

"Step back — please, everyone, step *back*." It was only a matter of seconds before I heard the stern voice of Dr. Hugh Goldberg on the other side of the closed door. I guess I had a lot of visitors waiting outside.

"I hear you're back with us. How are you feeling, Kenny?" He slammed the door quickly behind him.

"I'm . . . fine."

He put his hand on my forehead. My eyes watered as he pulled down my lower lids and peered in, no idea what he thought he'd find in there — fish, maybe. "You have some bruises, your temp's up a little, but no water in your lungs — you'll be okay, with some rest." His smile was warm beneath his white hair. "You did a brave thing yesterday, Ken. But from here on in, son — no swimming."

I nodded. Most times when oncologists think they're funny, they're not.

"There are a lot of news people here, Ken. Do you feel up to making any comment?"

"No."

He nodded. "I'll tell them maybe later."

"Tell them I'm dead."

"We'll see. For now, I'll just go out and make a little statement. That okay?"

"Sure." He was probably going to use the "no swimming" line again.

"Thanks. You need anything?"

"Glasses."

"Sorry, can't help you there. Hungry yet?"

I shook my head and waited for him to say okay then, get some rest, I'll see you later.

"Okay then. Get some rest. I'll see you later." Dr. Hugh put his hand on the doorknob. "And drink a lot of water: you're dehydrated. Oh, Ken, besides the reporters, that woman who was with you in the ambulance wants to see you. Ophelia . . . Lopez, isn't it? Should I let her in?"

I inhaled sharply. "She was there? In the ambulance with me?"

"Yes, Ken. The whole time."

"She can come in," I said.

"She's been here all night. We told her to go home, change her clothes, come back in the morning, but she wouldn't. She's . . . I hope you don't mind me saying so, but she's a knockout, Ken." His face took on a dreamy look I'd never seen there before. I visualized breaking his jaw.

"She told me you drove to Jazzminn's house," he continued. I was touched that Ophelia knew how much this little white lie would cheer me up, but Dr. Goldberg was clearly not amused. "Christ, Ken, you didn't tell me you were still working, still taking meetings, still running around town like . . . like you did before. *Driving.* That's insane. You don't need me to tell you it's time to slow down here before you kill somebody."

Before I kill somebody. "Sorry," I replied coolly. "I figured I could keep on driving and taking meetings because I had not yet read on the front page of the *Los Angeles* fucking *Times* that I only have one month to live." My voice cracked against my will. "I thought you said *months*, Hugh."

"I said that in October, Ken. It's December." Dr. Hugh Goldberg was apparently unfazed by my reported suicidal tendencies. "Anyway, I've got to get out there and talk to these yahoos. Goodbye, son. Take it easy. Remember, plenty of water."

Dr. Goldberg stepped out, and, a moment later, the door opened a crack. I heard Ophelia's voice say sharply to someone: "Please, just leave him alone, would you?" Then, she was inside.

The eggshell pantsuit was somewhat the worse for wear after her unplanned dip in Jazzminn's pool, and her long hair had dried in limp snakes. Her high-heeled sandals must still have been somewhere on Jazzminn's lawn, because on her feet she wore only a pair of those sterile paper booties doctors wear over their shoes in the operating room. I could just see some smitten surgeon, gloved hands lifted in the air, barking out the orders: "Cancel the kidney transplant, man, this woman needs footwear!"

Ophelia padded over in her mint green paper shoes, put her hand on my shoulder, and kissed my cheek. Her clothes and hair still smelled of chlorine, such a fragrant perfume. "Kenny. I'm so glad to see you," she said. She smiled, her tired face filling my hospital room with light.

I was so busy looking at her, drinking her in through my myopic haze, I'd forgotten how I probably looked. I remembered now. I turned my face away from her toward the wall, twisting up my tubes in the process. "I'm glad to see you, too," I said. "But I'm not sure I'm glad to have you see me."

"Oh, stop it, Ken. You look great. How are you feeling?"

I tried to say: "I'm fine." And, just like everything else in the past forty-eight hours, it didn't quite come out as I'd planned.

"I feel awful. I feel horrible. It's absolutely terrifying to feel the way I do right now, I hope to God you never have to." It was agony to talk, unbearable, like swallowing power tools, but I kept on talking. "I'm sick, I'm scared, I'm cold, I'm lonely, and most of all I'm . . . so very, very sad. I don't want to die. I can't begin tell you how much I don't want to die."

I don't know if my words shocked her as much as they did me. Hot tears began to roll down my cheeks. "This is what I didn't want to know," I sobbed. "This is why I wanted to be a murderer, not a fucking lifeguard. When I was a murderer, I deserved to die. Don't you see what a horror it is, for me to have something to live for when I've only got a month to live? I'm drowning, Karen. I'm drowning."

I never called her Ophelia again, after that. And she never said anything about it.

Karen sat down on my bed and put her arms around me. She was sitting in Alejandro's Dent—I'd named it after him, like a Mars crater after the scientist who discovers it. I clung to her and wept. I cried until my chest ached and my guts cramped and her delicate eggshell shoulder was all stringy with snot. It was like our laughing in the car, except crying. I cried until . . . well, until I was done crying, I guess. Then, I cried some more.

After the storm cleared, she handed me a neat stack of white, scented Kleenex from her purse, took out another handful to wipe her shoulder — then, discreetly, her own eyes. "No, you're not drowning," she said, very softly. "You're not drowning at all. It's just what you wanted, a tragedy as big as

Hamlet or *Macbeth*. You didn't have to kill anybody to get a tragedy. It's right here, with us, in this bed. You discovered you have something to live for, but too late."

She didn't seem surprised at all that this observation reduced me once again into a heaving mess of tears, snot, and power tools. I hope she didn't take this to mean I wasn't desperately grateful for her words.

"I've got my spare pair of glasses in my bag — want to try 'em and see if the prescription's near enough?" she asked in a few minutes, cleaning me up again with a fresh pile of Kleenex. "They're those rimless ones, pretty unisex. At least you'll be able to see."

"No. Keep your glasses." Suddenly, I wasn't grateful anymore. I pushed away from her like an angry child. "Where the hell were you?" To my surprise, my voice sounded close to normal. It seemed that the last crying jag had miraculously cleared my throat.

"Excuse me?"

"Oh, give me the fucking glasses." I snatched them and put them on — crooked. Because they were her glasses, I sort of expected the world to turn instantly rose-colored, but the only change in my vision was the weird warp from her prescription, a couple of shades stronger than my own. "I was there all alone, trying to get her to breathe, I couldn't get her to breathe, and you didn't come back," I scolded. "Last time I tried CPR it was nineteen years ago, and the kid died right there on the beach. What kind of an idiot would trust me to save a life? *Where were you?*"

"Gosh, I'm sorry, Ken." Calmly, Karen reached out and straightened the glasses for me. "I just thought it might be to our advantage if one of us took the time to run over to those two LAPD officers who were just about to confiscate as evidence a bottle filled with enough narcotics to kill a rhinoceros to tell the sad story of how you were considering suicide. Correct me if I'm wrong."

"Oh." Now did I feel stupid or what? "Uh. Thanks."

"Don't mention it. Besides, I did trust in you, Kenny. I knew you could do it. I knew you'd save her."

"Yeah, right. And I suppose you're also going to tell me you knew all along that I was never going to kill her."

"No. I mean I hoped you'd change your mind, up until the very last minute — but I never knew for sure. I always knew you were strong enough."

I wondered whether this called for a thank you. Instead, I blinked in consternation. "Well, if you thought I was really going to kill her and you didn't want me to go through with it, why didn't you call the damn thing off a long time ago?"

"Weeell," she began slowly. "At first I asked you to kill Jazzminn Jenks because I wanted her dead, I really did. But later on, I didn't do anything to stop you because . . . this murder seemed to be the only thing that was keeping you alive, Kenny. I should never have asked you to kill her, but after I did, it seemed like I'd given you something to live for." She began to cry quietly into her own handful of perfumed Kleenex. "And I didn't want you to die."

"Why?" I demanded. "Because you didn't want to live with the guilt?"

"No, asshole. Because I just didn't want you to die."

I think I called her Karen for the first time that day because it was the truth and I was so damn tired of lies. I figure she must have called me "asshole" for the first time for the same reason.

"So you were trying to save my life," I murmured.

"Yes. Not forever, but for as long as I could."

I thought she was done, but from the agitated way she was twisting the end of one of her chlorinated curls, it soon became clear that she had something else to say. And, after a pause, she blurted out: "There's one other thing. I wasn't going to tell you this, Kenny, but . . . I also had a backup plan. I hoped you'd change your mind, but I figured that, if I could keep you plotting this murder with me long enough, keep you interested long enough, you'd . . ."

"What?"

She shifted uncomfortably in Alejandro's Dent. "You know . . ."

"Oh. You mean *die* before I actually did it?"

"Well, if you must put it that way."

"How the hell else should I put it? You wanted to keep me alive, but you hoped I'd die?"

"I didn't hope you'd die. I *knew* you'd die. I was just trying to . . . take advantage of the timing. But then I was so happy that you didn't die that . . . well, never mind. I'm sorry. Do you hate me?"

I shrugged. "No, I don't hate you. I don't hate you because, well . . . that's what I was planning too — that is, until I started liking the idea of murder, really liking it. And, I hate to say this, but it's funny."

And then, there it was — the size-ten laugh. I have no idea what I'm going to do without that laugh. "It is, sort of, isn't it?" she asked, doing a one-eighty from being apologetic to being real damn tickled with herself. "I was *funny*."

"Hey — not that funny." I scowled to keep myself from laughing again, too. "Okay — we both wanted me to die before I killed someone. I'm slow, but at least I've got that part. But tell me this: Did you know that you weren't going to drown in Jazzminn's pool? That you were jumping into the shallow end?"

She seemed surprised by the question, and thought for a moment before answering. "No. That I didn't know. I just jumped in."

"Thank you for that," I said. "Thank you from the bottom of my heart, Karen."

"You're welcome, from the bottom of mine. But remember, you jumped in first. You saved her life, Kenny."

"We could debate this point all night, but I'm short on time — so I'll just reiterate, thank you," I said. "And, since we're doing truth here, there's one more thing I should say. It was never murder that was keeping me alive." I reached out and took her honey-colored hand with my pale, bruised one. "It was . . . you. Not murder. Not the tiny island of Sadilla and its dazzling sunsets. Not the Dark Lady of the Sonnets. Not Ophelia Lomond. Not chemotherapy. Just you. Karen Watts of Cincinnati."

"Indianapolis."

"Yeah, whatever. Wherever. It was you."

She smiled and squeezed my hand. "Thank you, Ken. That's a very nice thing to say."

Had I said enough? Probably. But when it came to saying more than I should, I was definitely on a roll today. "Nice — for you. Not for me."

"What do you mean?"

"Because I was so wrong."

"About what?"

"About everything . . . who is he, Karen?"

"Who?"

"The guy you were with the night before we went to Jazzminn's. Thursday night. I was outside your window. I saw him."

"You were looking in my window on Thursday night? You mean, you're a murderer *and* a stalker?" She started to rise from the bed.

"No, no." I grasped her hand tightly and pulled her back

down. I started playing with her soft fingers then, running the ends of my fingertips over the smooth, polished edges of her nails. "I came to your house that night because I wanted to tell you that I love you. I love you, Karen, I do — I have to say it, even though I know you don't want to hear it. But as soon as I saw you with him, someone . . . healthy, someone normal, someone full of life, I knew I'd imagined something that was never there. That's what love is supposed to look like. You couldn't love a man like me. You shouldn't love a man like me. I'd made a terrible mistake. So I left before you ever knew I was there."

Karen picked up the plastic container of ice water from my tray, extricating her hand from mine in the process. "Can I have some of this? I'm thirsty." Nothing this woman said surprised me anymore. I nodded permission — although I couldn't imagine anyone wanting to drink after me, out of my glass full of death and ice water. Apparently unconcerned, she took a couple of sips. "Not that it's any of your business, but that man you've decided I'm in love with is my acting partner from the Lana Bishop Theater. We trade off with a different actor for script analysis class every month. We were rehearsing a scene from *Macbeth*. Thursday night was my last class, and we went to my house afterward to work on what we'd learned."

"Your acting partner?"

"You catch on so very quickly, Ken. Yes, that's what I just said. I was trying to be Lady Macbeth so I'd be able to scare you out of murdering Jazzminn the next day — but I was so bad at it we decided to give up, go upstairs and get the Scrabble game out of the closet to play a round instead. Scrabble I'm good at."

Well, son of a bitch — a case of mistaken identity. See, that's my problem with Shakespeare's comedies: he always pulls this kind of crap. But for once, I was pleased to be the one mistaken. "That means you didn't sleep with him?"

"Once again, *so* not your business, Ken." She shot her Kleenex into the wastebasket with an aim that would have made Wade Stark proud. "But I think you can gather from context that I did not."

"I've got no business feeling happy about that either, but I do." I grinned widely. "Thank you for telling me that, Karen, even though it's none of my business."

"I didn't tell you. You guessed," she replied. "And don't flatter yourself — I don't sleep with every man I play Scrabble with, Kenny, whether you're alive or dead or in between. I just don't. The only men I've ever slept with were the ones I married. I mean, I slept with Carlos and Wade before we got married, too. I'd already saved myself for marriage once, for Arnie, and I think we all know that ending. But before or after marriage, they were the only ones."

"That statement would mean a lot more to me if you hadn't been married to half the men in Los Angeles," I observed — to cover my elation. "And what the hell were you doing running lines and playing Scrabble the night before a murder?"

"Like I said, I was working on my Lady Macbeth, trying to screw my courage to the sticking place even though I was scared out of my mind. And the point I was trying to make here is that I've only slept with men that I've truly loved. I know that's a strange concept to grasp in Hollywood, maybe I was born into the wrong century or something — but that's the way it is for me and always will be."

I was surprised by this, and even more surprised to find myself feeling envious. Another thing I'd missed out on, I guess — what it feels like *not* to sleep with someone. "It hasn't been that way for me, Karen. I've made mistakes. Not that many, but enough," I confessed.

"It doesn't matter, Kenny," she said. "I wasn't trying to tell you that I'm right — I only told you because I want you to know . . . who I am. It's just something about me, like I'm near-sighted and beautiful and thirty-two years old and allergic to shrimp and I don't know how to swim. I've made plenty of other kinds of mistakes, believe me. Like asking you to murder Jazzminn Jenks and ruining what was left of your life. Can you ever forgive me for that?"

"Sure, don't worry about it. And by the way, I'm going to teach you to swim if it's the last thing I do. It probably will be." You know what, this was the strangest conversation I'd ever had. None of the parts fit together, but somehow it flowed like water. "And it's me who was born in the wrong century." I looked straight into her multicolored eyes through her crooked glasses as I said it. "Because in this century, I can't be one of those men, the ones that you loved. There's no pain worse than knowing that I never could be."

"Why couldn't you?"

"Karen — *look at me.*"

"I am looking at you. And I'm asking: Why couldn't you?"

I had just closed my eyes so that, in case she did look, she wouldn't see all that pain I was talking about a little while ago. Now I felt a wild little thrill of hope that made them pop open wide again. "What are you trying to tell me . . . that you do love me?"

"No, Ken. I don't love you."

"I see. Thank you for telling me that."

"But I'm telling you that I could. Do you understand?"

"You mean, do I understand why you would fish my heart out of my chest with your bare hand and then throw it into the middle of Ventura Boulevard? No, not really."

"Ken, listen to me. I don't know if I can figure out how to say this — but I'll try. The reason I don't love you is not because of what cancer has done to you, because of the man . . . you think you aren't any more. Yes — I've read them, too. *Love is not love that alters when it alteration finds.* Sonnet 116."

"Yeah? Tell that to my ex-girlfriend Alice."

Karen ignored me, rushing right on. "But that isn't it. The reason I don't love you is . . . I haven't had time. Love takes time, there wasn't enough time, and there won't be enough time. So we won't ever know if I'd fall in love with you. You won't know and neither will I. In some ways you are luckier than I am, because time speeded up for you, so you already know. For me, things are still just going along at regular speed. So I'll never get to know whether or not I'd love you, whether or not there would ever have been a marriage of true minds. It's . . ."

"A tragedy?" I asked gently.

"Yes. For me, it is. Because I think I can guess the answer."

"Don't tell me," I said, holding up my hand. "Because I can't cry anymore today, I really can't."

"I won't. But I must tell you that, at the same time cancer has altered your body, love has altered . . . you. It's true, Kenny. I like the alteration that I find. I'm happy if I played some small role in that."

I smiled. "I'm pretty sure I'm still an asshole, but thank you. And you didn't play a small role my tragedy: you were the star. And you were good — which means, my love, that you couldn't possibly have been acting."

"I sense that I am being insulted here. But I'm going to ignore it, because I have a proposition for you."

"Oh, God. I don't have to kill anybody, do I? Because I'm really tired."

"No. I would just like for you to sleep with me."

"What?"

"You heard me."

"I thought you said you don't love me."

"I don't."

"Then what about never sleeping with a man you don't love, the way it is and always will be? What was all that crap about being born into the wrong century?"

"I meant every word of it. But for you, I'll make an exception."

"Why? Because I'm dying?"

"*Yes*, because you're dying. I thought we'd already established that this is part of the package, Ken. Some things are because you're dying, just like some things are because I'm beautiful. But not everything. And . . . nothing at all that really matters."

I suppose I could have offered some high-minded excuse about not sleeping with her because she didn't love me, but, hey — not in *this* century. Instead, I told her the truth, even though it just about killed me. "I'd like that very much. But . . . I don't know if I can."

She thought that over. "You can get into my bed, can't you?"

"Yes."

"You can sleep, can't you?"

"Yes. I'm not sure I could have said that a week ago, but yes — I'm pretty sure that now I can sleep."

"Then you can sleep with me. That's all I asked you to do. Anything else is purely optional."

I laughed heartily at that. I guess love *had* altered me because never before could I have imagined finding humor in the possibility of not being able to get it up, in any century. "You're right, I guess I can do that."

"Then do we have a deal?"

"Deal." I shook her hand. God — *I shook her hand.* "That is, if you promise never to breathe another word that refers even indirectly to the comparative functionality of my dick. I would love to sleep with you, and I gratefully accept your offer. That is, if . . . I ever get out of here."

"I talked to Hughie about it. He said I can take you home tomorrow."

"Hughie?"

"Dr. Goldberg. He asked me to call him 'Hughie.' That was sweet, don't you think?"

I decided not to share with her my thoughts about "Hughie." "What do you mean . . . take me home?" I asked instead, cautiously. "You want to give me a ride to my condo? Thanks, but it's just a mile or so. I can grab a cab."

"First of all, you're not going to 'grab a cab' anywhere. You know you can never get a cab in Los Angeles. And no, I don't mean to your condo. That's an awful condo. I want you to come to my house. I want you to stay there until   . . ."

"Until I die?" I thought nothing she could possibly say would surprise me anymore, but that sure did. "You want me to die at your house?"

"I don't want you to die at all. But yes, I'm asking you to come die — I mean live — with me." I was already holding one of her hands, and now she took the other. "I've got an extra bedroom on the first floor, so you wouldn't have to worry about the stairs. I'll be away at work during the day unless Jazzminn fires me, but Beulah Stark — you know, Wade's mom? — says she wants to take care of you while I'm gone. She really misses Wade since he moved to Detroit. She'd love to be someone's mother again. She's all mother, that woman. I called Wade while I was waiting for you to wake up, and he likes the idea, too. What do you think?"

Beulah Stark. Wade Stark's mom. I'd only spent a few

minutes of my life with her, but I could still hear her buttery voice saying: "You don't feel good, do you, baby?" God, I wanted to hear it again. And Wade thinks it's a good idea. But I shook my head.

"I don't need somebody who wants to bake me cookies, Karen," I said harshly. "I'm not going to be dying the way I was before, you know, when I could still . . . consider homicide. For this last month I'm really going to be dying. There'll probably be . . . equipment. Wheelchairs, tubes, IVs, that kind of stuff. I don't know how much it's going to hurt, or what I'm going to do about it when it does. I've got no idea what body fluids are going to come out of me, or where the hell they're going to end up. I've never died before, but from what I've heard I'm guessing I'll be swearing like a sailor. You want all that to happen right there in your beautiful white house, up there in the hills? You sure that's what Beulah wants? What *you* want?"

"Yes. I want you to stay with me. Please, Ken, stay with me."

I took a long, long drink of ice water. "Then, yes. I will. Thank you. " I said it very slowly and carefully to keep my voice from going all high and quavery at the end of the sentence, like helium leaking from a balloon.

"I'm glad," Karen said.

"Me too. So. Are you going to let that guy come over to play Scrabble with you again while I'm there?"

She thought it over. "Probably."

"Well, if he does . . . can I play too? I like Scrabble."

"Are you good?"

"Yeah."

"Then sure, if you want to."

"What about John?"

"Who's John?"

"The cat. John is the cat."

"I thought you said you weren't going to name the cat."

"I didn't *name* him. I just started calling him John. You got a problem with that?" I said, annoyed. "I know, you've got coyotes and skunks up there in your neighborhood, but it won't matter. He's afraid to go outdoors. And most of the time he just sleeps at the end of my bed, anyway. I think I've even got enough cat food to last him until he dies. Okay if he comes with me?"

"Of course." She glanced downward and bit her lip to hide a smile. "By all means, bring John."

"Quit laughing at my cat. You're . . . sure, Karen?"

"Yes. Like I said, bring the cat."

"Not about the cat." I turned my face away from her again. "About me."

"Trust me, Ken." She turned my face away from the wall with her hand, then kissed my lips. "I'm sure."

I tried hard to trust her. I came very close. "So I guess we're set, then," I said. Once again, my voice threatened to wander off somewhere I could not let it go. "Let's pin down the details tomorrow, because right now I really need for you to leave."

"I know. You must be very tired," Karen said, much too brightly. "And anyway, it's time for me to get out of these clothes, I think my bra is still wet, and go find some shoes that aren't made of paper. You keep the glasses, Ken. They look good on you. I'll see you tomorrow."

Karen was just standing up to leave when Dr. Goldberg — pardon me, Hughie — knocked, and, without waiting for permission, popped his head in the door. "Ken, I know you probably feel like shit right now — pardon my language, Ophelia — but can you handle one more visitor today?" he asked.

"Jazzminn Jenks is here, and she says she'd like to thank you for saving her life, in person."

CHAPTER FORTY-THREE

I know. I know, child.

— Nettie Mae Easley

My grandmother on my mother's side never hesitates to tell me what she thinks, but what would she think of *this*? For once in her eighty-nine years, I truly believe she would be speechless.

But I also believe that, somewhere deep down inside her raggedy old heart, she would approve. I'd rather not speculate on exactly how she'd phrase it — but she'd approve. This is so big that it cancels out all the things she usually fusses about, all her judgments and opinions. This is big. Bigger than *Hamlet*, *Macbeth*, and Nettie Mae Easley.

"Are you sure?" I asked him, carefully. "You just got out of the hospital this morning. Maybe we should wait a day or two."

Ken shook his head. "I don't . . . wait, Karen."

I said a few things very fast so I wouldn't have to think too hard about that. I asked all the obligatory houseguest questions. "How's the bed in the guestroom — did you get some rest? Got enough blankets? Can I get you something to eat? Is there extra toilet paper in the guest bath? I always forget to check, and nobody likes to ask. Was the shower hot enough? This house is so big that sometimes it takes the water longer than it should to heat up in the guest bath. I hope you didn't unpack, the housekeeper can do it for you tomorrow. She comes on Mondays . . ."

"The bed is great, the shower was hot, and I helped myself

to some Apple Jacks while you were outside trying to get John to come out from under your car." Ken's hair was still damp from the shower. He was barefoot, dressed in a simple plaid shirt and worn jeans. Did I miss the Armani suit? If I did, it was only because if he were still wearing it, that would mean it was still a few months ago. He looked like he'd already lived here a long time. "Chill, okay? Go sit by the pool and read the paper," he told me. With visible effort, he hefted today's untouched newspapers from the coffee table. The Sunday papers are always huge, especially in December. He placed the awkward, recyclable load into my arms, glossy holiday advertising supplements shooting out from every side. "Here — Los Angeles Times, New York Times, and the LA Daily News. Maybe at least one of them got our story straight."

I tried vainly to gain control of the slippery stack. "All right — as long as you're sure."

"Christ, stop asking me if I'm sure. I don't have time to be sure," Ken exploded. Then, embarrassed, he tried to make amends by retrieving Parade magazine and the comics from the floor. "I'm sorry. I'm a rude son-of-a-bitch houseguest. If I were you I'd tell me to move out right now. Uh . . . what's the underwear situation?"

"The underwear situation?"

"Karen, I have terminal cancer. If I'm going to get through this, I need serious underwear."

I must confess I have beautiful lingerie, drawers full of it. Not that awful wired-up stuff that pinches and pokes. Mine is all comfortable, elegant – real cotton and silk, no synthetics. Being a Midwestern girl, I'm usually pretty practical, but this is one area where I spare no expense. Sometimes I just spread all the pieces out on the bed to look at, then put it away again. It's fun to fold. I haven't slept with anyone since my divorce from Wade, but that doesn't stop me from loving lace, silk, and satin against my body, even tiny seed pearls on the outside if they're not someplace that they'll catch on my clothes. I particularly like to wear dark honey lace, the same color as my skin; it's like being naked, but all dressed up at the same time.

I've always worn lingerie for myself, not for my husbands. They just take it off in the dark without ever seeing it and it ends up on the floor. Arnie is the only one of my husbands who truly appreciated my underwear, and I think that's only because he was imagining how he'd look in it. I gave him some very nice items when we split up. Lingerie is for us, even though men think it's for them.

I was wearing honey lace today. I didn't think this would happen so soon, but I was glad I'd dressed for it. It's a terrible thing to think, but I couldn't help wondering if Ken's condition might slow him down enough to actually enjoy honey lace as much as I do. I'd like that. "I don't know exactly what you have in mind, but I believe the underwear situation will meet your needs," I answered shyly.

"Excellent." A smile broke across his worried face. It made his gray eyes crinkle at the corners. He's not old enough to have crow's feet, but I think the lines show because his face is so thin. "Excellent. Now, go away."

"For how long?"

"An hour, tops. Until the sun goes down. The intercom rings to the pool house, right? I'll call you. By the way, speaking of phones, some guy from TV Guide called while you were out chasing the cat, wanted to interview us both. I told him to go fuck himself."

"Charming."

"Sorry, but what could I do? He was an asshole. You know what, I'm beginning to wish I'd just let the little bitch drown. Okay, off you go. I'll see ya later."

Ken always curses more when he's nervous. I'm learning

to ignore it. I slipped a finger into my jeans and down the front of my blouse to confirm that I was, indeed, wearing the underwear that I had promised – even though I love lingerie, I also tend to forget what I put on in the morning. I'm that way with earrings, too. I have to reach up and touch them when someone pays me a compliment to know what they're talking about. Reassured, I took my three slippery newspapers, grabbed a sweater, and headed for the pool house.

Steam rose from the surface of the aqua-blue water, already going gray and moody as the sun began to slip behind the San Gabriel Mountains. The heat is still on in the pool, even though it's December. These days, I have this nightmare where I watch ice form all over Los Angeles — on the houses, street signs, palm trees, starting from where I'm standing and radiating outward, a thin glaze creeping over everything until it's all ice as far as I can see. It starts when I turn the heat off in the pool. I'm not sure nightmare is the right word for my dream, though. It's fantastic the way everything glitters when it's coated in ice. I'll turn it off soon, I will — just not today.

I stretched myself out on one of the lounge chairs and tried to read the Sunday papers, but instead I ended up just staring into the moody water, not doing anything at all. I hugged the cable-knit sweater my grandmother made me tight around my body as the sun went down.

I jumped when the phone rang just behind me, in the pool house. Telephones scare me now. There have been calls all day long ever since he moved in, from doctors, pharmacists, suppliers of medical equipment. I hand him the phone. He gives terse, tight-lipped answers to questions I can't hear. "Yeah? When? Right. A little. Sometimes. Not yet. Well, what can I expect? No, I can't. All right. Thanks." It takes him at least five minutes to smile again after each one of those calls.

Cautiously, I picked up the receiver. "Hello, is this Ken?"

There was a pause. "No, it's not me. It's someone else."

"I know, that was stupid. It's just that so many people have been calling, I wasn't absolutely sure it was going to be you . . ."

"It's after five on Sunday. The medical dimwit patrol is off duty for today," Ken said. "It's me, Karen. I mean, 'tis I. And I would be very pleased if you would join me in your bedroom now."

"You climbed the stairs? You didn't have to climb the stairs. The guest room would have been fine."

"I'm already up here. Please, just come. And — knock before you come in."

I opened the sliding glass door into the kitchen. The house was dark. Ken must have gone up to the bedroom before the sun went down, without turning on any lights downstairs. I sniffed: the air in the kitchen smelled like toast. And another one of those herbs I can't identify, something Italian. My goodness, he must have . . . cooked. I laughed out loud right there in the kitchen. The fact that he'd cooked kept me from being quite so scared. I ran up the stairs. Standing in the dark hallway, I knocked loudly.

"What the hell are you knocking for? It's your bedroom," said Ken's voice from behind the door.

"You told me to knock."

"Oh, yeah. Right. I forgot. Sorry. Please — come in."

There's something very special about being formally invited into your own room. But when I pushed open the door, it wasn't my room at all. It was a glowing chamber of candles, yellow candles everywhere, on the floor, on the furniture, on windowsills high and low — tiny hypnotic flames dancing with their own shadows, too many to count. A big flame burned in the fireplace. So lovely.

Ken was sitting on the edge of the bed, still in the plaid

shirt and jeans. The clothes hung loosely on his frame, but with candlelight on his face he appeared to have acquired a Malibu tan while at Cedars-Sinai. John the cat was stretched out in front of the fire, eyes rolled back in his head. John looks like he's been run over by a motorcycle when he sleeps.

"Be honest, Karen, is this over the top? You know — too 'Phantom'?"

"No. It's breathtaking, really," I said, meaning it. "How many candles are there in here?"

"One hundred, exactly. I had Ralphs deliver 'em to the side door while you were out by the pool. I was sure the delivery guy would either show up early or late and fuck the whole thing up."

"It's a fairyland. Arnie's quilted comforter really does look like a Sadilla sunset now."

"Yeah, it does," Ken said, pleased. "What's with this bed, though?"

"What do you mean?"

"I mean I've never seen such a big bed for such a small person."

"Wade."

Ken groaned. "Sorry I asked."

"Sorry I answered." I sat down on the bed next to Ken, took his hand, and squeezed it. "Would it help if I told you that, because of Wade, all of the Detroit Pistons pray for you in the locker room before the games?"

"No. I mean, yes. Oh, God – no!"

Suddenly, Ken jerked his hand out of mine and slid off the bed onto his knees. I watched in shocked dismay as he began scrambling across the floor on all fours towards the window. What was he doing on the floor, why couldn't he walk? This could have nothing to do with the size of my bed, the size of Wade, or the Pistons praying while snapping their towels. "No, no, no," he repeated as he crawled. "No, no, please, no, not yet, they can't, they can't go out, not now . . ."

Then I saw it — in the middle of a row of six candles on the floor in front of the window, two candles had gone out. Still on his knees, Ken was shaking, gulping back sobs as he grabbed a candle from the end of the row and tried to relight the ones in the middle with its flame, but their short, blackened wicks would not hold onto the fire. "No, no, no . . ."

"Stop, Ken, please — I'll fix it. Let me fix it." I couldn't watch this. I jumped up and ran to where he knelt, crouched down beside him, and grabbed the burning candle out of his hand, wincing a little as a dollop of hot wax hit the side of my thumb and hardened there. "The part of the wick that's not burned yet is stuck flat in the wax. All I have to do is take my fingernail and pull the wicks up straight so I can light them, see?" I concentrated on the task of lifting wicks out of wax, glad in a way to witness the wreck of my French manicure instead of listening to the strangled sound of his sobs.

Carefully, I lit the middle candles with the end candle, and then put the first candle back in place. "There. All set. That wasn't so hard, was it?" I closed my eyes, swaying on my heels — was afraid I was going to faint. My burned hand stung.

When I opened my eyes, Ken was leaning on the wall, hands over his face. Slowly, he removed his hands, revealing tear-streaked cheeks. He gazed at the row of candles, all burning again. He didn't say thank you or anything like that. "You hungry?" he asked weakly, gesturing toward the bureau where a large plate stood covered with aluminum foil. "I made hors d'oeuvres. Ingredients also courtesy of Ralphs."

"I . . . could eat."

"Okay, I'll get the tray. *Don't* tell me you'll get it. I'll get it."

The warm fire dried Ken's cheeks as we sat on the floor, eating buffalo mozzarella on toast with sliced tomatoes with fresh basil leaves, John snoring between us. The vet says he has a deviated septum. Ken ate more than I did, which pleased me. When the plate was empty, he pushed it aside and stood up.

"I forgot all about the champagne. There's champagne too," he said. "For you, that is. If I drink it, I'll fall asleep. I'll grab the bottle. It's on ice in the bathroom sink."

"I don't want champagne, thank you."

"Damn. I wanted to get you drunk before I get naked." He was joking, but his face took on the same sober look it had had earlier, after the phone calls. "I don't want you to see me naked. I don't want you to see me naked almost as much as I want to see you naked."

"I never get drunk. And I'm not taking my clothes off unless you do," I said calmly. "Besides, I've already seen you naked, that night when you went swimming in my pool. You looked fine. Skinny, but fine. And contrary to what men would like to believe, in the non-erect state, a penis is a penis."

"What do you know about penises? You've only seen three of them: that's not a statistically significant sample," he smiled for a second, but then the sober look returned. "Besides, I'm not worried about that: that's pretty much the only part of me they've left alone. I'm worried about you seeing at all the bruises where they've stuck needles and shunts and tubes in my arms, in my legs, in my chest. I don't want you to see how my bones stick out. I don't want you to be disgusted or scared. It would kill me if I made you feel that way about me, Karen."

I knew that I wouldn't be scared, or disgusted. If anything, it would be comforting to know, instead of imagining. I also knew that there was no point in trying to explain that to him. "Well, I'm nearsighted. I could take out my contacts, if you want," I offered.

"Oh, Karen — would you?"

"Of course." I smiled, grateful for such an easy solution.

"I'm so nearsighted you'll look like Michelangelo's David. Besides, if I take out my contacts I'll see two hundred candles in here instead of only one hundred."

Ken took off his glasses and surveyed the room, gray eyes wide. "Hey, you're right. That is very cool. Better than champagne."

"When I was a kid I used to take off my glasses when I came downstairs on Christmas morning so I could see the Christmas tree that way. Then I'd put them on again and make it clear," I said. "I used to think I was lucky to be nearsighted because it meant that we had two Christmas trees, not just one. I was the only girl on the block with two Christmas trees."

"Yes, you were the luckiest girl on the block," Ken said. "But I'm not sure you still are, not tonight."

I'd like to have said, yes, of course I am, lucky — but I couldn't. Ken put his glasses back on, not waiting for it. "If I take off my glasses I can see two hundred candles, but I can't see you," he said. "It's a no-brainer. The glasses stay on. Go take out your contacts."

"All right, but I'm going to take off my clothes first," I said, promising myself to say nothing further about candles, or Christmas trees, ever. "I'd like to be able to see your reaction to the . . . underwear situation." I slipped off my clogs, hopped out of my T-shirt, sweater, and jeans and tossed them to the floor. I spun around on my toes in the candlelight, in honey lace, enjoying being me even more than usual, at least while the moment lasted. "What do you think?"

"*O, she doth teach the torches to burn bright!*" Ken whispered, drawing in his breath. He stepped toward me and grasped my forearms, one in each hand, looking me up and down with such pure joy that I blushed — not just my cheeks, my whole body, I think. That expression on his face gave me at least one good reason not to cry for a few minutes longer.

"No, not what does Romeo think," I scolded. "What does Kenny Harrison think?"

"Me? Oh." He shrugged. "Well, Kenny Harrison is no Shakespeare, but he suggests you go deal with those contact lenses before he loses his last hard-on before Forest Lawn."

"You have such a way with words, Ken. May I?" He nodded permission and tried to hide his proud smile as I ran my hand over the modest bulge in his jeans. Men break my heart, they really do. They think it matters. "All right, I'm going," I said. "Please be fully naked upon my return. I won't be able to see a thing."

I considered leaving the lenses in my eyes. How would he ever know? But I'd promised. Plus I knew if I wasn't careful I'd cry them right out of my eyes. It would be easier not to see. I wasn't disgusted or scared or any of the things he was worried about — just sad. Things always work out for the best, except when they don't. I took out the lenses, stripped off the pretty honey-colored bra and panties with lace and seed pearls and walked naked into a room filled with two hundred candle flames.

I really can't see without my glasses, so I was startled when I felt Ken's arms wrap around me and his body, all jagged bones and cold skin, press itself against my back. I couldn't see him. But I could feel how he looked, an exact imprint of him in my own flesh. Taking out my contacts made a difference to him, I suppose, but it didn't change things much for me. I still knew what I knew.

We stood there silently, his arms around me from behind. Gradually, his cold body grew warmer. Or maybe it was just the heat from mine, warming his. I couldn't tell.

"I won't say I love you, Karen," Ken said softly. "I won't say that I love you. I won't do that to you tonight."

"Thank you, Ken."

"Besides, I'm glad you don't love me. It makes it easier to leave you, knowing that I'm not hurting you the way I would . . . if you did. We can just enjoy this night."

Don't cry, don't cry, don't cry. I turned around to face him. "I'd like you to know how very glad I am to be here right now," I said.

"Me too. That's why I don't want to mess things up by saying that I love you — even though I do, very much," Ken said. "But I do have something else I'd like to say on the occasion of sleeping for the first time with the Dark Lady of Hollywood."

"What's that?" I asked.

"Thanks for re-lighting those candles for me."

"That's it?"

"No." He grinned widely, no tears in his eyes. "What I really want to say is: Fuck Disneyland."

Ordinarily I don't care for that kind of language, but I'm sorry, Grandma — it *was* funny.

CHAPTER FORTY-FOUR

Neither rhyme nor reason can express how much.

— Orlando, *As You Like It*

All this has been the long way of explaining how I came to be the first-ever male guest on television's most popular daytime talk show, *Really, Girlfriend?*

The show usually airs a few weeks after it tapes — but this time, for the first time, *Really, Girlfriend?* was going live. The network rushed my appearance onto the air on Tuesday, December 5 — only two days after I got out of the hospital. Nothing worse for ratings than a live talk show with a dead guest. I can say in all modesty that my exclusive TV appearance was an event, what the networks call "appointment television." Gets the viewers to tune in even without a strong lead-in program. Nobody was DVR-ing *me*.

I fidgeted under the hot stage lights. I've got so many odd sensations in every corner of my body now, it's impossible for me to sit still for any length of time. Today it felt like there was something crawling around under my skin. Karen grasped my right hand to stop my fingers from their staccato drumming on the arm of my chair. "Take it easy," she whispered. I nodded, scowling at the studio audience even though they'd waited for hours outside Studio 7 for the chance to see the man who saved Jazzminn Jenks from drowning.

I'd spent way too much time working in TV to ever want to be on it. But you spend a couple of months plotting to murder a person, what are you going to say — no, I won't go on your talk show? So I agreed to be America's first boy girlfriend, on two conditions. One, that nobody put any goddamn makeup on me — this is the way I look, get used to it — and two, there was no fucking way I was wearing the bunny slippers. I may have conspired to commit a felony, but I have my standards.

And there was one more thing: I told Jazzminn I would not go on the air at all without Karen by my side. I got her on network television after all — though I'll always regret that I couldn't do it in prime time.

And as much as I objected to it at first, the more I thought it over, the more it felt right to me to be sitting here, between Jazzminn and Karen. It was a formal end to things, a closing — the couplet at the end of a Shakespearean sonnet. One foul, one fair — which isn't fair — that's why one of them is foul. Nobody's fault, just Fate. Besides, Jazzminn's new tits did turn out nice.

Of course, there was another couplet for me, a private one, one with no studio audience. I'm going to come right out and say it: I was a lousy lay. I barely made it through, and even so, she did most of the work. She even laughed at me a couple of times, and there was this one embarrassing moment where she had to shake my shoulder to wake me up. But I'm proud, awed, humbled to talk about it, because I had such a good time, the best, and I'm pretty sure she did, too. The last time was sweet, no sorrow. And it was the last time; I don't kid myself about that. That's it. From here on in, we're talking

Scrabble only. But I don't care, as long as I'm playing it with Karen.

"I need to clip on your mic, Mr. Harrison. Is right here comfortable for you?"

"Yeah, that's fine." I let young, skinny crewman in blue jeans clip the device to the lapel of my suit coat. Not Armani, just a regular gray suit from the back of my closet, I can't even remember where I bought it. On the way home — can I call Karen's house home? It feels weird — we'd stopped off at my condo to pick up the cat, some clothes, my geeky spare glasses, and a few other things to take with me to my new residence high above the city lights on Vista de la Vida. Glinda the transsexual cried when we knocked on her door to say goodbye.

"How long 'til we go on the air?" I asked the technician. He didn't have to answer. I heard the cheery pink *Girlfriend* theme music swell as the producer intoned: "In five . . ."

There were balloons, flowers, and a gospel choir from some Baptist church in South Central Los Angeles — even a surprise visit from the mayor, who gave me a heavy wooden plaque and declared it Kenneth Charles Harrison Week in the greater metropolitan area. At that point, I'd have traded the whole shebang for a glass of water. All I had sitting next to me was a network logo mug full of bad coffee.

I also got a standing ovation from the studio audience, although that didn't impress me much. I haven't watched a lot of these talk shows, but from what little I've seen you get a standing ovation for having any kind of disease, even if it isn't terminal — just cough a couple times and these people are jumping out of their seats.

People just kept on saying thank you to me, and of course I thanked them for saying it, which means I actually said thank you more times than anyone else, not that I'm complaining.

No real surprises, but it was good TV. I only wish KTLA's Erica Elfman were still alive to tell the viewers all about it tonight on News at 10.

"Before our time is up, I have an announcement to make," Jazzminn was saying. I was surprised to see her clasp her tiny hands in front of her chest, tears glinting in her small blue eyes. "This show is special not just because the brave Ken Harrison has made the effort to be here with us despite his devastating illness. I wanted him to be here with us, with me, because . . . he may not know it, but his decision to dive into deep water to save my life helped me to make a big decision of my own."

Okay — I was listening. "It's something I haven't even told the network — but the only way I could do this is to say it on live television, where no one can talk me out of it," Jazzminn continued breathlessly. "Today isn't just a very special installment of *Really, Girlfriend?* It's the last show. Ever."

A gasp went up from the studio audience. The crew started buzzing even as they tried to concentrate on keeping their camera equipment rolling. Karen looked stunned, too. And I couldn't help it: "What?" I spluttered into my tiny microphone.

"That's right. I've decided to leave the show to pursue my acting career, full time," Jazzminn said, still clutching her hands together in front of her as if in prayer. "Many of you know about my new company, Pink Productions. I founded it in order to develop made-for-TV movie projects for myself. But I've changed my mind about that. I'm going to turn Pink Productions into a non-profit repertory theater company, performing the plays of William Shakespeare. We'll devote our first several seasons to the tragedies. Sometimes I'll act — but the truth is, I really want to direct."

Well, I just sat there with my mouth hanging open. I sure hope I didn't drool. But Jazzminn didn't stop there. "And, in order to thank her for her role in my rescue, I'd like to invite my beautiful personal assistant, Ophelia Lomond, the woman who helped Ken Harrison save my life, to be the first member of my new repertory theater company. Ophelia is a poor orphan from a tiny Caribbean island who has grown up to be a fine aspiring actress. I hope I can help her, in my own small way." At that, the studio audience burst into applause without even waiting for the prompter.

I didn't know it was possible for Karen to look even more stunned than she did when she heard the news that *Really, Girlfriend?* was over for good — but I saw it happen with my own eyes. There was a long, long silence. Then she spoke.

"No," she said.

"No?" Jazzminn's eyebrows shot skyward.

"I mean, no thank you."

"Let me get this straight." Another milestone — the first time I'd ever heard a person say "let me get this straight" outside of a Hollywood script. Jazzminn unfolded her praying hands. She rose from her chair and put those hands on her hips, elbows out, and one pink bunny tapping the floor. I watched as her blue eyes narrowed into little pissed-off slits. "Let me get this straight. You, my overpaid, incompetent personal assistant, are turning me down, on live television — on my show?"

"It's a wonderful offer, Jazzminn," Karen said, sounding genuinely distressed to be hurting Jazzminn's feelings, even after that little speech. "I can't tell you how grateful I am, really. But I have an announcement to make, too. I wasn't planning to say it on the air because . . . well, because nobody cares. But I was going to tell Ken about it after the show. You're a wonderful actress, Jazzminn, Ken told me you were — but I'm not, and I'm quitting the business." Tears began to spill down Ophelia's cheeks but behind them was her rainbow smile. "Ophelia Lomond is my stage name, and I'm giving it up, as of now. And I'm not from any tropical island — I'm from Indianapolis, Indiana. My real name is Karen Watts, and I've decided to quit acting, quit my job with *Really, Girlfriend?* and go to medical school. I want to become a cardiologist."

On live TV there's always a delay of several seconds in case anything needs to be bleeped out. But anyone who can read lips got the gist of what Jazzminn said in response to that.

I was wrong before. *This* was good television.

And, given the murderous expression on Jazzminn's little face, it now looked like I'd better step in as moderator if I wanted Ophelia to still be breathing by the end of the show. I adjusted my mic. "I think the audience would like to hear what you have to say, Karen," I invited pleasantly. "I know I would. And Jazzminn, for once in your life, please shut the fuck up." Yeah, they probably bleeped me, too.

"I was a biology major at Yale, and I was good at it," Karen continued, with an anxious glance at Jazzminn. "I love everything about the human body, and how it works. Especially the heart — it's so mysterious. I also discovered that I'd like to be able to save lives, Jazzminn — yes, even yours." Her trembling voice was gaining strength as she went on. "Watching Ken breathe life back into you out there on the grass, I knew that day what I wanted to do with my life — and I'm going to do it. In a way, he rescued me, too. Thank you, Ken. I mean it. Thank you."

My dry lips moved to form the words "You're welcome," although I'm pretty sure I did not make a sound.

"Ken's oncologist, Dr. Hugh Goldberg, has already agreed to write my recommendation to Yale Medical School, his alma mater," Karen added. "If you're watching, Hughie — thank you, too." She blew a kiss into the air.

The studio audience went nuts, God bless 'em — I guess I was going to have to hang around to sign some autographs after all, even though my hands ache. As they clapped, you could almost hear the little rat-maze wheels whirring inside Jazzminn's frowning forehead, trying to calculate the best way to react for the cameras. And, in a moment, she padded over to Karen in her pink bunny slippers, held out her arms, and gave my Dark Lady a big bear hug — as close as she could get, considering the size of her chest. "Congratulations, girlfriend," she said. "Congratulations, *Karen.*"

Take it from me, the last-ever male guest on *Really, Girlfriend?*: No matter how little time you've got left, there will always be surprises. *And nothing is / But what is not* — it's true. But really, it's not so bad once you get used to it.

I don't know if you'd call it pain, exactly — just pressure. A sensation. In my chest, in my abdomen, both places where the heaviest concentrations of lymph nodes are. That's where my cancer is, in my lymphatic system — on an internal freeway that takes it wherever it wants to go. If I were going to try to explain it to Karen, I'd tell her it's like I'm slowly being pushed out of my own body, like there's not enough room, like I've got to share my breath with some new and insistent set of lungs. All I can do is try to keep some space for myself. Still, in a weird way, I'm . . . comfortable. And, for the first time in months, when people ask me how I feel, I know the answer.

To quote *King Henry the Eighth:* "*I know myself now; and I feel within me / a peace above all earthly dignities, / a still and quiet conscience.*"

To quote my Honda: Objects in my rear view mirror are no longer closer than they appear.

I'm fine, thank you.

And right now, it's time for me to go home. I'll spend the rest of my days with my new family: Karen Watts from Indianapolis, Indiana; Beulah Stark; John the cat; and maybe an occasional visit from Karen's former acting partner, the

Scrabble guy. We'll play Scrabble and I'll whip his ass. Sweet.

Other than that, I don't really have any big plans for the rest of my life. I'll give Karen swimming lessons, try out a couple of new recipes on Beulah, make myself useful around the house while I can still get around. I don't know, maybe I could dust or something. And, if I can, I'll go to the next meeting of the book group, since they've finally finished reading *Big Ole Circle of Women*. I assume it still sucks, but I heard Maxie's going to bring the baby.

And, speaking of reading, I thought I'd give Shakespeare's comedies another shot. I have time to read them again, at least some of them. Maybe there's something I missed the first time around.

I've noticed in the past few days that my eyesight's getting worse, much worse. I haven't mentioned this to anybody, not even Karen, but I'm pretty sure I'm going blind — I'll be blind before it's over, I can tell. But Karen will read to me when I can't do it for myself anymore. I don't need to be able to see to hear the words. And I don't need my eyes to know how very beautiful she is.

Arts and entertainment journalist, Diane Haithman was a Los Angeles Times Staff Writer for more than two decades. She is a major contributor to Deadline Hollywood industry website and its print publication, Awardsline. She serves on the adjunct faculty of the University of Southern California's Annenberg School for Communications and Journalism. Before joining the LA. Times Diane was West Coast Bureau Chief, movie critic and Hollywood columnist for the Detroit Free Press. She is co-author of *The Elder Wisdom Circle Guide for a Meaningful Life* (Penguin/Plume 2007). Diane lives in Studio City, California with husband Alan Feldstein and Alley the dog.

Diane welcomes your comments at
dianehaithman@gmail.com

CPSIA information can be obtained at www.ICGtesting.com
Printed in the USA
BVOW01s0430230414

351428BV00002B/4/P